T0063496

REMNANT OF HELL

Men Without A Purpose

DON M. RUSSELL

Order this book online at www.trafford.com
or email orders@trafford.com

Most Trafford titles are also available at major online book retailers.

Printed in the United States of America.

ISBN: 978-1-4907-3280-0 (sc)
ISBN: 978-1-4907-3281-7 (hc)
ISBN: 978-1-4907-3282-4 (e)

Library of Congress Control Number: 2014906252

Trafford rev. 04/03/2014

www.trafford.com

North America & international
toll-free: 1 888 232 4444 (USA & Canada)
fax: 812 355 4082

CHAPTER ONE

The July Sun Bore Down on Marshal Carson, hot as the surface of a well tended pot-belly on a January morning. But the sweltering heat was a simple nuisance compared to the problem tucked away in that whiskey-wash forty yards up the street.

Apprehending Muley Tatum and his sidekicks wasn't going to be simple or easy, but Carson was damn sure he'd get 'em. He felt it in his bones . . . somebody else was going to die today. When that feeling came it'd always panned out, definite as the stink of burned hide on a fresh branded steer. He was confident too, it'd be one or more of the culprits in the saloon that was to be graveyard rubble, not him or the man at his side, Deputy Travis. They'd be the purveyors of death, not recipients.

"If you don't come outta there now, Muley, you'll not leave Spickard alive." Carson's warning shout was akin to blowing into the wind, toting no obliging effect to the hooligans inside the Yellow Moon where the earlier killing had taken place. Rad Carson tried talk for several minutes; even before he started, he knew his words would squirrel into empty ears, but it was his duty.

The position in which he'd placed himself was disgusting, belly down, and propped up with elbows on the smelly ground behind a water trough. He swallowed hard and clinched his teeth, the words pushed out of his mouth slow and pitiless, like a groundhog edging through a jagged hole in a board fence, "A hell of a way for lawmen to deal with derelicts, them firing at us like a tin target in a shooting gallery."

Again he shouted across the rut-marked street separating the rows of bleached board buildings, commanding Muley Tatum and his cohorts to give up their guns. "Thrown down and come out, Tatum." His voice raked with anger. But same as before, the response was a drunken, hideous laugh followed by a volley of gunfire. The three despoiled men holed up inside the saloon were decided, mind-fixed for a shootout.

Muley Tatum bellowed, from one step inside the louvered doors, "Go to hell, Carson! Me and my boys will paste your guts all over the street if you move from that hole you made for yourself." A deceitful grin, concocted with inner-bitterness, creased his face. He cut dark eyes around the corner, shifted to see though the acrid smoke and spun the cylinder of the Remington, checking new loads he'd thumbed into the revolver.

Intolerable heat owned the frontier Kansas town, shadows were thin and no breeze to push back the stale air. Perspiration spanked the lawmen's shirts and dotted their faces. Carson figured the scoundrels inside had time on their side, they were clear of the sun and able to move around, which he and Travis gave up when they took to the cover they did.

'Fortunately none of the townies were in jeopardy of catching a stray bullet'. Carson satisfied the thought with a deep breath. The street cleared of people when the first shots exploded inside the saloon and the terrified young wrangler leaped from the batwings, his wrinkled straw hat clinched in a fist, he ran, first from the brutal exploits, and secondly to employ the marshal.

It started as a calm morning in Spickard; quiet until the outlaw scum came riding into the settlement just after the bank clock struck ten. These were same men the marshal had run out of town just a week ago. A few random, disorderly shots were fired by the troublemakers back then but no real damage done. He'd threatened to throw 'em in jail, now he wished he had.

This was different, merciless. Muley Tatum, a larger than average man who'd always been a weasel, along with his cronies, have soaked up way too much whiskey. They shot up the drinking establishment, wounded the barkeep, and killed Miles Courtney, a much respected local rancher. The puncher who'd busted into the Big Biscuit Café ten minutes ago, a cowhand from Courtney's ranch that'd stood with him in the saloon, interrupted the lawmen's lunch with frantic word of the shooting.

It happened that this was also a morning the old bullet wound in Rad's shoulder had chosen to act up. The occasional throb and stiffness didn't bother much unless rain joined with a cool prairie breeze. But for whatever reason today, the void of foul weather made no difference, the shoulder was an annoyance.

"Guess I'll have to go in after that no-account skunk and trim that mop of long black hair from his noggin," Carson bleated quietly to himself. Flexing his bothersome shoulder as he rested on his elbows, he took occasional glances over the two foot high board tank.

Carson glumly turned his head and looked at his deputy lying along side, munched his lips in a show of mild frustration, and raised a gloved hand to wipe sweat from his brow. This wasn't the first time, and likely not the last, that he'd have to lay his life on the line to rid his town of outlaw trash.

He and Travis, the twenty-four year old deputy, who'd been on the job just two weeks, had dived behind the horse trough when a volley of lead whistled overhead as they loped up the dirty roadway anxiously making their way to arrest Muley and his two roughshod side-kicks.

The marshal flexed his lips, his eyes locked on Deputy Travis, "You'll have to throw lead their direction when I leave this slop hole and make for cover out front of Hampton's store." His glare questioned the deputy momentarily. He hoped he'd figured accurately about the new lawman he'd favored the town council to hire; this was going to be one hell of a test, his life being on the line.

Rad tapped the brass star that hung on his worn leather vest, hankering for luck, "Okay, Travis, on the count of three, make the lever on that Winchester jump. You'll have to keep their heads down a spell till I can make the boards and those barrels." He flipped a thumb toward the other side of the street forty yards down and on the opposite side, next door to the Yellow Moon Saloon.

Rad Carson was a thin waisted, stout muscled man, taller than average, wide shouldered and owned a quickness that nature hadn't fostered to many. He nodded to the deputy as he counted, "One," rising to one knee he pulled the tan Stetson down tight, "two," shoved his Peacemaker into the holster so both hands would be free to catch his weight upon reaching intended cover in spite of the hindrance of the agonizing shoulder. "Three." Carson leaped clear of the smelly trough following his deputy's first shot but a wedge of mud from seepage at the end of the water box spoiled his footing and sent him sprawling. He swiftly righted his sturdy six foot frame, regained momentum, and anxiously fingered the big Colt on his thigh to be sure it was in place.

Travis's Winchester rang out; four, five, six, seven slugs ripped into the doorframe and shattered the window where one of Muley's men had been firing. The pesky outlaw at the window withdrew as Travis peppered the saloon with lead. He stepped back in place when the rifle quieted and the deputy poked his head up. The skunk-drunk man abruptly lifted the hand gun to chest height and made it buck. Lightning and flame once again stabbed from the barrel toward the lawman.

Marshal Carson heaved his agile body the final ten feet and flopped onto the weathered boards behind the flour barrels with an eruption of stowed air. *'Thanks, Travis'*, he grimaced and mumbled to himself, knowing the deputy had fulfilled his obligation in the best way possible.

"Give 'em Wild-Billy-hell boys!" Muley Tatum, the outlaw leader, urged his men. He knew Rad Carson wouldn't back down, that'd been his reputation ever since he pinned on the badge three years ago. "Don't let that law-dog get any closer. Kill him before he steps a boot on this side of the . . . damn, he's comin' . . . kill 'em—kill 'em!" Muley threw three quick, wild rounds at Rad just as the marshal braced his backside against the outside wall of the Yellow Moon.

Tatum's two sidekicks were dividing their shots, their targets several yards apart. And shooting at Carson was awkward; the marshal was on the like-side of the street they held.

"The first one of ya's that puts a bullet in him gets a hunert dollar bonus," Muley screamed. The big outlaw rubbed a dirty fist across his mouth and his ruddy dark eyes shuttered raucously as he took two steps backward. He flexed his lips and ducked back under the staircase, making his way catlike to the rear door of the Yellow Moon.

"I don't know, Patch," Lucas, the hooligan that'd been firing from a window shouted to his cohort, "I'm thinkin' neither of us is gonna collect on that bonus." His voice was pitched and scratchy. He looked around for Muley, hoping for workable instruction, or at least, more words of motivation.

Patch saw a mixture of fright and confusion in the reaction of his partner as his head jerked repeatedly in searching the shadows of the saloon for Tatum. He squinted, his eyes cut all corners of the room but came up empty, "Why, that dirty son of a sidewinder, he's gone," Patch shouted, "and left us to mop up the mess he made by killin' that old man." His glance reflected to the man on the floor, Miles Courtney, whose eyes were fixed and his head lying unnatural in a pool of blood.

"I ain't stayin' to save his sorry ass," Lucas turned. But before he could take a step, Rad Carson crashed through the large, multi-pane window and slammed to the floor; his hand filled with the Peacemaker, he rolled and fired from the cluster of shattered glass and splintered window casing. Pain seized his shoulder but was disregarded. The gun bucked twice and a slug crashed into the outlaw's left side. A shower of crimson droplets flew from the man's right underarm; the .45 caliber chunk of lead had passed through both lungs before existing. He yelped and convulsed to the sawdust floor, a flush of blackened blood spilling between his teeth. His eyes rolled, fluttered, and life leaked from his young body.

"I'm through . . . I'm through." Patch screamed when he saw his fellow gunman fall. He went to his knees in the center of the broad square of tainted light that fought through the dust, both hands flailed high toward the chandelier overhead. One fist clinched his crumpled, rust colored hat as a sign of submission. A man that removed his hat was a man ready to crawl, not ready to fight on.

Carson's deep coffee-colored eyes moved over every square yard of the dingy barroom, hedging briefly at the jumbled conglomeration of tables and chairs in the rear. The hammer of the Peacemaker was back and the barrel jerked in a steady but constant movement. He searched the ragged stairway. With his eyes and gun twitching upward, he shouted to Patch, "Up there?"

"No," Patch Gillis answered, his breath hot with liquor and irritation, but cloaked in fear for his life, "out the back door like a chicken running from a coyote." He tilted his ragged tassels of dingy blond hair toward the back of the room but remained rigid on his knees, arms extended upward.

Rad slid the Colt into leather as he held focus on the kneeling outlaw and a spit of silence found its way into the room.

As if responding to a behind-the-curtain-whispered-cue, the batwing door creaked softly; Deputy Travis stood in the doorway, his feet braced wide and the rifle held at the ready, bright sunlight silhouetted around him, "You okay, Marshal?"

"Yea, I'm fine. You did a job out there, likely saved my bacon." He nodded in appreciation. "Good way to start earning your thirty-four dollars this month," the marshal added dryly. A slight grin followed his remark before his eyes swung away. He slowly made his way over the few steps to where Patch remained kneeling, the outlaw's hands held high. A trace of panic set in as he followed Rad's progress toward him, sensing the lawman's anger.

"Guess you're gonna lock me up in that pig sty you call a jail, are ya, Marshal?" His voice was shaky and eyes blinked with a liquored-up laziness.

"That's right." Rad stood over the roughshod gunman whose mouth had cocked into a sassy grin. "I'm locking you up!"

A mock, snide-ridden smile came to Patch's lips, followed by a deep breath extolling a partial release of apprehension. But his thought betrayed him.

The toe of the marshal's boot smashed into the man's stomach with the force of a mule kick, "After I teach you a thing or two."

Patch yelled and rolled onto his side just in time for the heel of Rad Carson's boot to land with a jolt, flush on the bridge of his nose. "That's for shooting at me and my deputy."

Patch Gillis, his face bloodied and the breath still absent from his lungs, rolled over onto his back, arms thrust full away from his sides in semi-consciousness. "And this," the marshal drew and cocked back the hammer of the .45, "is for shooting Otis . . . and killing a man in my town." The Colt spit fire and the slug tore through the palm of Patch's gun hand. Splinters and a spray of blood, clogged with sawdust, flew from beneath the smoking hand.

The wounded outlaw bellowed and writhed like a chicken with his head freshly missing. He exploded in a frenzy, clutching at his wrist and his body surging from the waist with a pumping action, he screamed, "Damn you, Carson, I didn't kill nobody, Muley did the killin'."

"Yea, and you was just standing by . . . drinking a beer," Rad said to the screaming man, in a nonchalant tone. He slowly holstered the Colt and turned toward the bar, knowing Otis, the bartender, would be there on the floor behind the polished-top structure, according to the cowhand's fluster of rapid shouting in the restaurant.

Marshal Carson found his way to where the injured bar-keep was lying sprawled awkwardly on his back. He bent and pulled the apron strings from the expansive midsection of the hefty bald headed man, straddled the man, placed his hands under the man's arms and lifted the woozy barkeep from the broken bottles of sour mash. Rad helped him to a wooden crate; quickly inspected the wound and wrapped the man's upper arm with the white cloth. "The bullet went clean through, Otis, you're a lucky man. I'd say the doc will have you patched up and back serving this rot-gut stuff in no time." The two of them hesitated at the end of the bar and looked down longingly at the body of Miles Courtney.

"Miles saved my life," Otis said, his face drawn, "Muley was coming 'round the bar to shoot me again when Miles took in after him with that there broom stick." He indicated the broom lying on the floor with a nod of his head.

"Why'd he shoot you in the first place?"

"When I told him he owed a dollar and six-bits, he said he'd already paid for the bottle." Otis sniffed and rubbed at his nose, "I told him he was mistaken; he said I was callin' him a liar—pulled his gun and shot me . . . shot me like I was a scoundrel dog beggin' for a bone."

In the center of the room Travis had up-righted the wounded, stoop-shouldered and blubbering outlaw, had him by the shirt collar and guiding him toward the door. He lifted his chin and asserted, "When I get this chunk of pasture-dung locked up, I'll get both Doc Hankins and Cyrus, the undertaker, headed up this way."

Rad looked at his up-start deputy with a glow of satisfaction, "Like I said before, good job, deputy . . . you're earning your keep." He followed quickly with another remark, more for the ears of the used-up prisoner than for Travis, "If he gives you even a smart-ass remark, go ahead and shoot him, save the county some money on a judge and trial."

The young wrangler that summoned the lawmen stepped inside the door just after the deputy jerked Patch outside. He glared back over his shoulder, "I'll be on hand to see that sumbitch hang." He slowly picked his way through the chards of glass to stand by his boss's twisted body. "This shouldn't have happened." The youngster's hand went to his forehead and rubbed grudgingly as tears welled up, one sliding down a sun-browned cheek. "This is gonna bear hard on his wife, and Jenny, his daughter. The two of them thought more of this man than of life itself." The youngster turned red-rimmed eyes to Rad, "Likely some of the men back at the ranch will come after that man." His head flicked toward the door.

"What's your name, son?" the marshal asked.

"Name's Spencer, Spencer Cline, friends call me Spence."

"Okay." Rad raised his eyes from the rancher lying on the floor, "I Hope you're wrong about that statement Spence, he's my prisoner and ain't no body getting' past me to get to him." The boy's expression showed he comprehended the sincerity of Rad Carson's statement. "And," Rad continued, "according to Otis here, it was Muley that killed your boss, not my prisoner. The judge will have the final say on that."

Carson glared at the back door where Tatum had turned tail and run. The scowl on his face told his inner thought, *'I'll get that rotten no-account vermin if it's the last thing I ever do, he'll pay for this with his life.'*

The marshal put a firm grip on the boy's shoulder and started him toward the door, "What I want you to do is get back to the ranch and tell this man's family that he's been shot and killed; you tell the family, not the ranch hands." Rad gripped the younger's shoulder tighter, "And tell them not to allow the hired hands to try to take revenge," he hesitated, "because if they do, I won't allow it, and it's likely some of them will get hurt. I don't believe the family wants that to happen."

Spencer read the depth of truth in Marshal Carson's face. He stepped outside, turned and looked back longingly, understanding the marshal was counting on him to keep a big problem from getting bigger. What he was to do back at the ranch, and just how to do it could make a difference; it might be that more lives could be in jeopardy. He understood that now.

CHAPTER TWO

The following day broke in the usual manner; roosters on each side of the little prairie town of Spickard cautioned the sun about rising through the resilient, purple haze. A solitary freight wagon drawn by a team of four head-dropped draft horses slothfully made its way down the hard packed street. A bearded, middle aged man with sun-wrinkled lines at the corner of his eyes, his tired face protruding from under a rolled-front, used-up straw hat, held the traces in strong weathered fingers. He provided an occasional cheek-winching click and a flick of the slim leather linings over the broad backsides of the horses to keep them drudging forward.

At the jail, Marshal Carson lifted the hissing pot from the cast iron stove top, the first coffee of the day. It'd been a peaceful night, other than Patch Gillis cursing about his throbbing hand. Rad thought about young Spence and how he must have handled the news about Courtney's death at the ranch. *He must have done it right, nobody came after my prisoner,* Rad thought appreciatively as he poured the steaming black liquid into a tin cup for Travis and another for himself. His head turned as he shouted over a shoulder, "You want coffee, Patch, it'll give you something else to complain about, ya better have some!"

* * *

Up the road thirty miles was Dodge City, painstakingly rejuvenated within minutes of a bleak break of dawn, the scattered, youthful scarred wranglers, toughs of the previous night, stretched indolently as they slowly vacated the semi-comfort of doorways. Distant agonizing sounds of bawling cattle, along with shrill whistles and shouts from trail-frazzled cowboys, from the bottom of Railroad Street, filled the air as the wranglers pushed nearly eight hundred head of dirty, frizz-bodied, slobbering long-horned beeves into the rustic, splintered pens.

Muley Tatum leaned against an overhead support post in front of the Top Of The Trail Saloon. He stood with his legs crossed and munching on a thin cigar. One hand searched unceremoniously under a disheveled black leather vest. Soon a lucifer snapped into flame with a casual talent, touched off a marginal twirl of smoke from the tightly rolled leaf of Virginia tobacco. From his vantage point at the edge of Front Street he could twist his head and see the rail line's cattle cars lined up, readied to load. Through the dust he was able to make out the lariats and sombreros swinging over the heads of men on horseback, every one of them whistling or screaming half-word directives.

The saloon behind the dark-clothed outlaw held only remnants of the prior night's festival of energetic, drunken cowhands. Half of the kerosene lamps adorning the chandeliers had been snuffed and only six toned-down wranglers occupied the room. The barkeep mopped at the counter top and cut contentious glances at the few lingering customers as he dipped and drained beer mugs. Pungent odors of cheap whiskey and tobacco smoke remained undaunted, clinging to every square inch of the derisory, contemptuous chamber.

Upstairs, a meagerly clad, but well rounded woman with flesh-drooped arms and tousled dark hair, a cigarette hanging loosely between her pouty, rouged lips, stood with one arm braced against the doorframe. With the other arm she tugged at the open collar of a shaggy-faced, bleary eyed cowboy, edging him toward the stairway. His pockets were turned inside out. In his stupor condition, when he eventually came full awake, he'd not come to know whether he'd spent his cash or been robbed. In a matter of speaking, there was little to no difference.

A neatly dressed, riverboat-type gambler pushed back his chair and tucked a deck of rough edged playing cards into his coat pocket. He'd already poked a substantial amount of paper cash into a money belt that bulged under the shiny silver vest where a gold watch engraved with a wingspread, soaring eagle rested in a side pocket. He pushed through the batwings and left the saloon, walked up behind Muley on the boardwalk out front and shifted his eyes to the commotion that held the outlaw's attention in the distance. "Four-legged-cash," the gambler quipped as he slicked back the thick, black head of hair in order to fashionably place the off-white Stetson on his head.

Muley Tatum jerked his head around, one arm still propped up supporting the hand engaged in tethering the dark cigar. "Whatcha say?"

"Money on the hoof." The gambling man said as he raised his eyebrows, "Some men take a chance with God's filthy creatures, and others with cards. I happen to enjoy possibilities with the paperbacks myself." His smirk verified the remark. He squinted while taking a sustained look toward the cattle pens and continued, all the while scratching at a shoulder. "That's what I like; that and sleeping in a real bed, either alone," his brows rose, "or with a nice smelling female." He lowered his voice as he drawled, with a New Orleans inflection, "Better than bedding down with a stinking cow that poops on its own feet."

"Yea, I guess so," Muley spoke back as his eyes carefully examined the man's girth first, and then studied him sketchily from head to foot. He slowly rolled the cigar between his thumb and forefinger, his mind busy with a method to separate the gambling gent from his holdings he couldn't help but recognize. Muley blew a cup-sized puff of smoke out of the side of his mouth and offered, "You beddin' down in one of the local hotels are ya?"

"Yes, sir, I am." The saloon-slick pointed a finger the opposite direction from the cattle pens, "I'm booked at the Drover Palace right up there". His eyes fetched the distance.

"Ain't that a coincidence, so am I." The grin on Tatum's face was nearly as oversized as it was deceptive. "In fact I was just about to take leave of this place and head back to my room." He nodded as if reminding himself, "I'm in Dodge on a mission to purchase cattle. My next appointment isn't until this afternoon; figured I could get a couple hours of shut-eye before that." Muley's attempt at pretense was well fashioned. "We can walk there together," he waggled his head toward the hotel, "if you don't mind?" He focused on his prey in a jovial, buoyant, manner; coercing a confirmatory response.

It was easy to see the man was reluctant, but his resistance melted quickly. He pushed back the side of his coat in a way that suggested indifference in order to expose the underarm holster filled with a .41 caliber hand gun, figuring to dispel any dishonest intentions on behalf of the stranger he'd just met, if by chance there was such a thing.

Muley Tatum nodded twice and with a smile said, "Shall we?" And the first steps were taken toward the Drover's Palace.

The alleyway's location was perfect! Tatum quickly scrutinized the area close around. '*Nobody in sight*'. Slick as a snake's strike, he implacably struck the gentleman-card-shark across the nose with the barrel of his six-gun; it crunched and he crumbled. The only other sound was the flushing of the man's lungs before Muley stuck the six inch knife blade in the side of the poor soul's neck and pulled it downward. The outlaw was good at his trade. He smoothly ripped open the man's coat and shirt, sliced through to the money belt and jerked it away in a single motion, put the sole of his boot into the man's face, twisted and shoved. He'd be dead in seconds. '*That stupid bastard, he can sleep with cow poop now, and forever.*' Muley Tatum thought, recalling the man's earlier discourse.

Tatum walked from the alley with a toothy lip-stretching smile, already having jostled the loaded money belt down the inside leg of his trousers, it rested comfortably; the far end dropping into the top of his boot. Anyone who might be looking his direction would see him adjusting his belt and believe he'd just relieved himself in the alley, as cowpokes commonly did. He continued his trek along the boardwalk, not realizing he left bloody footprints behind, his right boot held tell-tale signs.

Soft music and a lovely harmonizing feminine voice flowed from the doors of the *Prairie Lady* saloon. Several patrons had their attention pasted to the curly haired lady dressed out in a frilly red dress that left very little to the imagination. "Rehearsal," a finely dressed man, complete with a diamond stick pin in his silk tie, said when he leaned toward Muley as the outlaw edged up to fold into the gathering.

"Oh!" Tatum smiled his easy-to-manufacture-smile, turned to the man behind the bar and inaudibly, slowly mouthed the word "Whiskey." The barkeep nodded and quietly served up a glass and a bottle. The devious, deceitful murderer moved to a far table, found a current issue of the local newspaper, sat and stretched his legs out full in the direction of the lovely young lady and her admirers. He reluctantly passed noncommittal judgment on the songstress and her aficionados as he lazily sipped whiskey and nested there reading the paper, intending to put some time between his killing of the gambler and the upcoming increase in morning activity on the streets of Dodge City.

It didn't take long. The melodious, gorgeously dressed songstress hadn't finished the second rendition of the fifth song following Muley's arrival when a lawman strode through the door, his eyes glued to the floor and a shiny Remington revolver filling his gloved hand.

Tatum looked up, his forehead wrinkled as he became absorbed by the actions of the man wearing a badge and carefully examining the floor. Then it hit him. He rolled his boots to view the soles. Slight traces of blood remained on the heel of one boot but the prints the lawman followed seemed to have disappeared in the crowd surrounding the singer. But it wouldn't take long for the law dog totin' a gun to look his way.

"What's going on, Franklin?" The barkeep halfheartedly inquired, gazing past the apathetic crowd of enthralled lady's admirers with a fixed, desolate expression.

"Who was the last man to come in here?" The lawman's abrasive voice was clear.

He'd no more than got the words out of his mouth until two explosive rounds from Tatum's Colt stung the saloon like thunder in a cave. Franklin, the deputy, spun around too late—his revolver spit flame at the floor and all hell broke loose. He'd been hit hard. He jerked and sprawled in the manner of a lightning-struck longhorn and barroom patrons spread in all directions. Muley, not knowing where a back door might be, holstered the six gun and crashed through the swinging entry doors riding the back of an elderly man and the piano player. Once outside he simply fell in behind the others, wearing a look of anxious innocence.

The first unclaimed horse at the hitch was snatched up; Muley was in the saddle and his boots slashed into the flanks of the roan mare all the way up Dickinson Street, past the livery and south across Railroad Street toward the old buffalo wallows. His principle thought was to put distance behind him and his freshly acquired mount. He rode feverously what he figured to be a safe, comfortable distance but then began to wonder where he'd point the wheezing nostrils of the used-up cowpony under him.

The grass south of town was depleted. The earth had been trampled with the holding of cattle that had come north up the Chisholm Trail, leaving barren hard-pack, a few ornery weeds and scattered stones, not much else. Ahead, Muley caught sight of a wrangler camp. They were pulling stakes, evidently heading back to Texas, or wherever they'd started the cattle drive likely two to three months ago. He kicked the fresh rested horse into a moderate gallop, setting his mind to come alongside the chuck wagon before the backdrop was closed and stored for travel.

Tatum yanked back on the reins, the roan half-skidded to a stalwart halt as the outlaw smiled a toothy, "Hello." He glanced at the three men, two of them drovers, the other one undoubtedly being the camp's cook, as he slid from the saddle. "Ya wouldn't happen to have an extra biscuit for a man who's as hungry as a bear climbin' outta a winter's sleep, would ya?"

"Just got everything locked away, mister." The scrawny, white bearded man scowled at the new arrival as he took in the large man dressed in black. He slapped the drop-down door shut, twisted the keeper-bar and grimaced, "You shoulda' been here five minutes sooner." He turned with a hardened look of disgust and walked away.

"I got some fresh food here, partner." One of the young cowhands cut his eyes from the cook and Muley to his saddlebag. He lifted the flap and poked his hand into the leather bag, pulled out a white cloth, unwrapped the contents and said, "Here, mister, I got a couple biscuits and some hogback what was left from breakfast. You're welcome to 'em."

"Much obliged, cowboy." Muley accepted the biscuits, looked at the cantankerous cook and grinned before he bit into one. The cowhand smiled and Muley chomped. The skinny, bearded cook with his shirt sleeves rolled up to the elbows, glared at the both of them with irritated blue eyes under a set of wild, off-white brows. He hesitated, and with a dubious glare, he set a boot on the riser, stepped up and hefted his light-weight frame onto the padded, spring-braced wooden seat. He spat and took up the leathers.

The two wranglers watched as the chuck wagon pulled away with the whistle and flip of the traces. The young man that provided the biscuits offered a slight offhand leer and said, "He's near always a little grumpy in the mornings." He watched, waited as Muley bit into a biscuit, began chewing, and asked, "I guess you musta' come from Dodge?"

Muley kept chewing and gauged the young man, waiting a few second before he swallowed, and said, "Yep, just got word this morning from Amarillo that my folks' ranch had been attacked by Comanche a few days back, I sold my whole outfit to a cattle company and lit a shuck." His eyes assessed the undertaking of his remarks by the cowhands.

The two wranglers looked questionably at one another. Smirks and twisted-lip smiles broke between them. "You're funnin' us ain't ya mister," one said, "them Comanche ain't raided down that way for nigh onta' seven-eight years and you got no trail gear with ya."

The outlaw rolled his eyes, surveying his surroundings, "Yep, ya got me," Muley laughed and hunched his shoulders in a sign of submission. "I figured the two of you to be smarter than to believe that . . . just wanted to test your metal." He extended a hand to what appeared to be the older of the two, "My name's Tatum, Muley Tatum."

"Muley?" The man bit at his lower lip to keep from breaking into a laugh. "That your real name?"

Muley's face was rigid and he shot beady eyes at the man. "Maybe, maybe not, but as far as you're concerned it's Muley." Their hands remained clasped in the introductory handshake. It was quiet, inquiring eyes kept busy, asking questions of another man wasn't proper. That point was as firm as granite, but also as awkward as a drunken preacher on a Sunday morning. The young man pumped Muley's hand once again, "Right, Muley it is." His eyes were near as deep as the outlaw's and his handshake a bit more firm. "I'm Pete." He twitched his head toward the other man, "And this here's Jesse, we're the Longley brothers from Pampa, Texas.

"Well, okay." Muley looked at the chuck wagon up the way and made note of the half dozen cowboys that drew along side of it as they looked back. "They's about to leave ya."

"We ain't in any big hurry-up," Jesse responded with his eyes squinted toward the wagon and the men on horseback. "Texas will be there when we get the urge." He scuffed a toe in the dust. "This is the first time we ever been away from the panhandle . . . I reckon the panhandle will wait a mite if we don't hurry."

Tatum took a long look at the youngsters. They both appeared to be in their twenties, slim build, and muscled enough to persuade their shirts beyond wrinkles. They both had rolled brim, well worn felt hats and wrangler trail clothes. The wily outlaw had seen their kind before—men that had yearnings to do something other than what they had experienced or seen so far in their lives. Questions were locked in deep-rooted eyes, provoking an emptiness that needed tending to with answers that lingered beyond any horizons they'd experienced.

"So, you Longley brothers ain't in no hurry to get back to Texas?"

"Not really," Jesse spoke up, "You got something else in mind?"

"Wouldn't be hard to pick something better than branding cows in Texas."

"You mean like stealing?" Pete glared at Tatum with confidence braced in his jaws, took a deep breath and said, "Why did you leave Dodge City so fast, now that we know it wasn't nothin' to do with your family and Amarillo?"

"You got a pretty good head on your shoulders, Pete." Muley rubbed his heavily whiskered chin, "Maybe you can tell me." His eyes latched onto the oldest Longley brother's deep-set brown eyes.

"I figure ya stole something and vamoosed afore the law could catch ya."

Tatum took a second before he responded, "You're close to the target, boy, but not near the bull's eye." Tatum reached under his belt and tugged the money band out from his pant leg. "This here is poker winnins' . . . not the kind of poker a man-of-the-cloth might play," he smiled his ingenuous smile, "but the kind that whittles away another man's stake a bit faster than church-bazaar poker." His statement held a lot of truth to it, he just chose to omit the part of the story as to how, and who, had actually won the money. He went on, "The no-account gamblers I took it from thought they knew the game, but I showed 'em a thing or two." He lifted his eyes, "They started cussin' . . . it was time for me to leave."

Tatum's hand slowly started to drop toward his six-gun, but before his mind was fully made up, Pete Longley cleared leather with his. They starred at one another in silence for a full five seconds before Muley plastered that egg-sucking grin on his face and said, "You boys have got the makin's. The three of us could team up and make some real money—lots more than what drivin' cattle and eatin' dust pays a man." He switched his glare from one of the Longleys to the other in rapid fashion. "That is," he hesitated and scratched at his cheek, "if you ain't afraid." The weasel part of the man bluffed to get back on top in the conversation.

CHAPTER THREE

Flames sputtered and chewed at the sticks of dry cottonwood Pete Longley punched into the blaze. The flickering of the fire, aided by trivial snaps and occasional hissing, gave off a tranquil, unperturbed sentiment that partnered with the lonesome passing of the day. Jesse lazily rolled a cigarette and stared indolently at Muley Tatum's concerted efforts to shave using a six inch knife blade in the nearly depleted sun, aided by the petulant light of the fire, using an amber whiskey bottle as an indisposed mirror.

The air began to cool as dull shadows grudgingly faded into total darkness. The fresh, new association of men mustered together on the south Kansas prairie lands, listlessly ripened in some measure and settled into place by the time stars blinked into a full pattern.

Jess Longley looked up, his head resting on saddle leather. He'd always held affection for calm prairie nights. It was a time to let his mind wander, to question what life might hold in other parts of the country. The moon, looking like a large worn scoop, glistened behind a drifting haze against the onyx sky halfway between the horizon and the uppermost point in the heavens. It occasionally separated from ghostly charred clouds and coated the barren hillside with stretched sheets of transparent ivory. A loathsome coyote yelped annoyingly a half mile away, in all probability, along the same dry creek bed the three men chose for the night. Jesse's last thoughts, before sleep overtook him, were of Colorado, a place he felt sure he'd find a life he'd love, if only he had the chance. Maybe tomorrow brother Pete would come to his senses and share the longing for the freshness of the Rocky Mountains, never seen before by either of them.

* * *

The sun struggled to push aside the dull gray light of morning as the strange mix of personalities aroused from their night's sleep within a few ticks of the clock of one another. Muley was the first to speak, "Well look at us, all on the same heartbeat, like our meetin' up was the will of the Gods!" He looked over at Pete, "You got any more of them biscuits?" He said it knowing he'd eaten the last of them himself.

"We ate all the food we had with us last night. Me and Jess had planned on bein' with the cow outfit, not feedin' out of our possibles; got more coffee though, a man can't go nowhere without his coffee." Pete Longley stretched, bent and lifted the rifle from beside his saddle, "I'll walk the creek bank," he indicated his intentions, "and see if I can jump up a cottontail—won't be as good as the breakfast 'ol Cookie made up on the trail, but it'd put a hush to the wolf in my stomach. Go ahead and stir them coals," he nodded at the wisp of smoke stemming up from the bed of ashes, "boil some coffee and I'll be back with something to eat even if it ain't rabbit."

Jesse nodded and rubbed his eyes. He and Muley both watched Pete as he disappeared from view behind a grouping of small willows. "He pretty good with that long gun?" Muley asked as he inched over to the sticks of wood and began to build on the fire.

"Likely the best you've ever seen." Jesse scratched at the back of his neck and went on, "Can also draw faster and shoot that six-gun empty quicker than a man's eye can follow. Our pappy taught us to shoot early on; he always said a man could live in Texas if he had a nose for water and a gun in his hand." Jesse turned his head to look straight on at Muley, "That's when the Comanche was still raidin' in the Panhandle." He grinned . . . as did the cunning, dark-witted outlaw.

Muley extended a gloved hand toward Dodge City as the three of them sat their horses on the hill overlooking the wild, frontier town alongside the Arkansas River. "Looks right peaceful in the morning, don't it?" The grin that was a constant part of the outlaw's face beamed in the brightness of the morning light. "You boys go on over to the mercantile and get us supplies. I'm gonna see if my horse is still in the alley back of the saloon. I've had that horse for three years, ever since I got out of that rotten jail up in Hays." He sensed he'd said something he didn't intend and added quickly, "Got all drunk up and started a fight with a damn lawman." His eyes hid the truth as he finished, "I don't want to lose 'er now, she's been good luck to me."

Jesse gave the roan under Muley the once-over, "Where'd ya get that one?"

"Borrowed 'er on a kinda hurry-up basis yesterday morning." Muley chuckled as he clicked the roan gently and headed down the incline dodging rocks and picking through the sage and bunch grass.

The Longleys fell in behind, several yards back. Jess looked over to his older brother, "This guy is full of surprises, ain't he?"

He thought Pete might be reconsidering their tying in with Tatum, but Pete responded with just a simple smirk when he said, "The man's got a lot of babble . . . and guts; I think we can learn a few things." Pete cut his eyes back to Jess, "That don't mean we're connected to this guy like barbwire is to a fencepost though." They moved on down the incline slowly, allowing Muley to get well ahead of them so's he could be seen first by any of the folks in town and they'd not associate the three men as being together.

The Longley brothers rode the street, reading signs and watching townies which outnumbered cow punchers at this early hour. Horses at the hitch rails kept their tails spanking flies and made occasional easy stomps. Shoulders at the base of their manes shook to void the flies to another cow pony alongside. Pete and Jesse drifted past a lawman who was pointing, giving directions to a pair of men dressed in business suits. Jesse eyed him uneasily for a few seconds, leaned, making his saddle squeak mercifully, and spoke softly, "I reckon if Charlie Bassett was still around he'd have Muley locked up or hung, don't you think, Pete?"

"Well, we don't know," Pete talked over his shoulder, "just what the ol' coot really done here in Dodge." He clicked a cheek and went on, "Says he played some trick poker," Pete twisted his head around, "and sounds like he's a horse thief; Bassett would have had his hide nailed to the wall somehow, I suppose."

The Longelys pulled rein at Farnsworth's Supply and Grocery and stepped down. Both of them lazily searched the street and walkways with squinted-down eyes, looking for their innovative associate. They flipped reins over the weathered pole, not rightly thinking they'd see him, but somehow feeling the obligation to look.

Once inside the wood-framed, admirably hand crafted two level structure, they gazed appreciatively. The place was chock full of trappings, beyond anything they'd witnessed back in Texas. In due time, they related their needs and made light conversation with the middle-aged gentleman behind the counter. He wore brass wire-framed spectacles, green garters at the elbows, a black ribbon bow tie and a short brown leather apron, he too was an elaboration not found in the skittish part of the panhandle they called home. But he shore enough looked the part of a store-keeper.

Once the store clerk had placed the supplies on the counter, Pete Longley opened the saddle bags, looked inside and squashed his lips together in thought as he began to pack the food supplies appreciatively, not knowing just what the trail ahead held from them. He tossed the tobacco and papers to Jess. "You be in charge of this stuff, you're the one what's the biggest user."

Jesse stuffed his assignment into his shirt without comment.

Having finished with his packing, Pete dug into the pocket of his Levi's, pulled out a small roll of currency and looked up at Mr. Farnsworth, "Better give me a couple boxes of .45's for the handguns and some .44's for the Henry." He raised his eyes to the ledge holding the ammunition.

The storekeeper turned back toward the shelf behind, stretched an arm up as high as he could reach, twisted his head around and asked, "One box or two of the 44's?"

"Better make it two, we'll be on the trail goin' west and ain't never been up there—don't know what to expect." He glanced over at Jess and lifted his brow a mite as if he was guessing what their new partner had in mind.

"Two it is." Farnsworth plunked the boxes on the counter and extended a glance to the bell that jingled over his entry door. A shallow smile grew on his face as he offered a welcome to the newcomer, "Howdy, Sheriff Hinkle, be right with ya, soon's I get these young fellers tab figured and collected."

"No big hurry, Elmer, I'm just making rounds and investigating about that fella that was killed yesterday morning, a man outta Kansas City they say." The lawman cut a short stare to the Longleys but made no gesture toward them.

"What makes you think I'd know anything about that?" Farnsworth answered without raising his head from the tablet where he was adding a column of figures.

"Well, I figure he was killed just about the time of morning you usually move those barrels out front and open them shutters over that far window; thought maybe you might have seen something—or somebody.

The man was clubbed and stabbed just inside that alley down there next to Mullin's place." He pointed and then cocked his eyes back to Farnsworth who looked up, "He was a low-life gambler, ya know!"

The store owner didn't comment on the sheriff's remark but looked over his glasses at Pete, who had changed his focus to his younger brother. "That'll be two dollars and twenty-two cents, mister." Farnsworth looked at Pete, and then back and forth between the two, seeing a flash of pensiveness between them. He repeated, "Two dollars . . ."

Before he could finish, Pete spun his head back, "Yea, got it right here," he opened the roll of bills he held in his left hand, handed the man two dollar bills, stretched a hand into another pocket and drew out coins. "Ten, twenty", he counted out two dimes and two shiny pennies. He handed the coins to Farnsworth, "Guess that takes care of us, and we thank you." He grasped the cartridges and saddlebags from the counter, handed the cartridges to Jesse, put the leather bags over his shoulder and they started toward the door, their eyes downcast and moving slowly toward the sheriff and back to the floor.

"Sheriff, you might ask these fellas if they'd seen anything about that killing you're investigating, you can't tell who might know something." Mr. Farnsworth had been around the problematic town of Dodge City a long time; he could tell the sheriff's remarks had struck a slight nerve with the two men in his store buying trail supplies and more than a little ammunition.

Sheriff Hinkle drew his hands to his hips and took a long pair of steps to his left, just enough to stand more readily in the path that would lead the Longleys to the door. He knew Elmer Farnsworth was as sly as a mustang stallion protecting his brood mares. Not much of any kind of trouble could slip past him; he could smell a nuisance before it was to come to his territory.

"Well," Hinkle drawled, placing both hands on his well-rounded stomach and an inquisitive sheen clinging to his face, "you boys know anything about the gambler's murder?"

Pete didn't hesitate. "Nope." His brow wrinkled slightly and his eyes held the lawman firmly, "I believe I heard you say that was yesterday morning?"

The sheriff bobbed his head and spoke, "That's right, around seven thirty, maybe quarter to eight. And at eight o'clock sharp, it was the same man, we're believin', that killed Deputy Franklin Montee over at the Prairie Lady Saloon."

"Wow!" The word fell out of Jesse Longley's mouth like a rotten apple dropping from a tree.

Pete hurriedly picked up the slack, "We wasn't even in town. We came in with our trail boss and our herd Sunday, train-loaded 'em on Tuesday and left town after noon on Thursday . . . we wasn't even here in Dodge yesterday. Sorry, we don't know nothin'." He took another step toward the door.

The sheriff blinked and reacted readily but in a mild manner, "If ya left town Thursday, what are you doing back here on Saturday?"

Jesse felt his face redden a bit, but Pete hardly hesitated, "We heard there was a new strike of gold up in . . . ," he hesitated, turned to his brother and nodded, "on Battle Mountain, near Cripple Creek, Colorado, while we was here in Dodge. Me and my brother," he flipped a thumb toward Jess, "got to talkin' about it Friday after we'd started on the trail back toward Texas and figured, what the hell, we ain't never gonna make any money rounding up cows, let's just give Colorado a try." He hunched his shoulders, "A couple of gold nuggets will pay a man more in one day than herding cattle for most onto three months."

In truth the Longley brothers had indeed heard about the gold strike and had a fairly lengthy conversation, maybe more like a daydream, while sitting and staring into the campfire Friday night. Pete had made a lighthearted remark about going there, buying a pick and shovel and putting Jesse to work while he consorted with the perfumed ladies in the dance halls.

The sheriff and Farnsworth looked at each other with raised brows. "Okay," the lawman stepped his wide body aside. He twisted the end of his mustache, munched his lips together and drawled, "If you don't mind, I'd like to take your names . . . not that I suspect anything other than what you say, but I want to add your names to my investigation record; looks better to the judge when I testify at the inquest Monday," he leaned forward a few degrees, winked and said, "if ya know what I mean."

Outside, at the hitch, Jess spoke to Pete softly through cautious lips, "Killed a gambler and a lawman?" You reckon it was Muley the sheriff was huntin'?"

The two of them had a notion the sheriff's reference was indeed about Muley, but more out of desire to think otherwise than give heavy consideration to it being their new found friend, they flashed glances all around and continued a leisurely packing of their gear to move on. Pete didn't answer Jesse's poignant question, other than with a brief inquisitive eye to eye stare. He flipped the bags behind the saddle, tied them in place, loosely gripped the horn and cantle and looked across the leather concave at Jesse. After a few seconds of silence, he said passively, "We're riding outta town that way." He indicated west with a nod.

They stepped up, settled in place, and clicked the horses into a walk toward the end of town. Jesse turned several times, looking over a shoulder before the road emptied into vacant lots. His mind filled with thoughts he didn't care to figure on.

Passing Boot Hill each of them took lengthy, twisting glares at the rock-strewn bone yard setting above the roadway before halting momentarily in an inquisitive gathering of thoughts. Boot Hill had a far reaching reputation throughout the West, and was readily acknowledged in the metropolitan areas of the East where it had been immortalized in newspapers well beyond St. Louis. Stories of the "*Well Planted Boot Hill Cemetery*" had appeared in populated cities like Cincinnati, Philadelphia,

Boston, New York, and the like; being written about by reporters and journalists that commonly expanded on the truth in order to sell more newspapers and periodicals. The reporters also knew it planted interest and intrigue in the *uncivilized frontier,* and that helped to make their jobs secure.

Pete was the first to speak, "Between Bassett, Masterson and the Earps, they made that quite a gathering place." He said it with a ceremonial shaking of his head before they booted their mounts. They continued stealing glances until they could no longer see either grave markings or weathered wrought iron configurations, but the images and imagination lingered as they rode in quiet depredation for the next few minutes.

At the crossroad signs two miles out of town the Longleys edged off the road, found shade under a giant elm, and waited, as was their agreement with Muley. The horses chomped long, green grass, but with any sound from the direction of town, they'd raise their heads, and with highly pitched ears, listen with indifferent anticipation for someone or something that might be coming their way, momentarily negating the lush grass.

Each of the Longleys had their own personal thoughts about the future as they waited. Pete sat on a flat rock, inanimately picking up pebbles and tossing them at a half rotten tree stump. His eyes weren't focused, submitting to the deeper intensity of his mind. And Jesse, sitting beside him, scooped hands full of scrabble dust and sifted it hand to hand until it dissipated, his thoughts drifting toward the home place and ma and pa. He knew Pete's mind was fixed. He didn't know why, or what drove Pete, it wasn't like him at all to fall in with a man of Tatum's makings, a man that appeared to be bad all the way through, not an honest, forthright bone in his body.

They were indeed at a crossroad.

CHAPTER FOUR

"For God's sake Pete, we've been here more than two hours waiting for that no-account." Jesse threw his arms out in visible disgust, "I'm thinkin' he's gone off somewhere else or maybe got thrown in jail back in Dodge." He vigorously pointed toward town, his mouth firm and eyes blinking, anger openly apparent.

"Maybe so." Pete casually scratched behind his ear and looked toward town. "We'll allow another ten minutes and then decide," his demeanor quite different from Jesse's.

"Decide what?" The younger brother was disconsolate.

"Decide on whether to go back to Dodge or head up that-a-way." Pete threw his head north, his expression totally blank.

"You mean to Colorado?" Jesse had started rolling a smoke; he dropped the fixins' and stared pie-eyed at Pete. "That gets my vote," he exulted. "I'll pack my butt onto that saddle real quick-like if you're serious."

"We'll see right soon." Pete hunched his shoulders and stared in the direction he'd indicated, "I ain't wanting to go back to Texas—not till maybe next spring . . . we've come this far, let's make our way out . . ." The sound of a galloping horse broke his thoughts.

"Did'ja think I wasn't coming?" Muley half-yelled as he yanked the reins and dropped from the saddle all in one motion. "Got'er!" He held the bridle strap high, raising the horse's head, a ring of confidence in his tone. Pride showing on his face like a school boy with a hand full of gumdrops, "Ain't she a pretty thing?"

The mare was shiny black with a white blaze from her eyes to the dark rust color of her muzzle, and her stocking front legs supplemented her definitive, quality lines very nicely. Muley's saddle was black also, trimmed in silver, but worn with untended nicks and smudges, no longer a worthy compliment suited to the horseflesh it sat upon.

Pete lifted his hat and extended the hand gripping it to his side, "Good looking animal, alright," he clicked a cheek, clearly impressed with the horse. "I can see why you took a risk."

Jesse was put off; he shrugged, pulled at the string of the bag of tobacco with his teeth and fingered the paper, not ready to join in the jubilation of Muley Tatum. The loud, vile man's appearance voided the appealing mental image he held for seeing the Rocky Mountains of Colorado. "Nice horse," was the best he could muster as he ran the cigarette paper over his tongue.

Tatum eyed Jesse uneasily; he could tell the young man's feelings about him were on the downside of inconsiderate. His plans, however, called for both of the Longleys to play support rolls for what he'd planned after hearing what he was able to extract from a pair of teamsters from the Prairie Lines Stagecoach Company. The span of time he spent wetting down a dry hic-up in a Dodge City saloon was worthwhile, money could be had!

"You boys got coffee boiled?" Tatum looked around. "I've got some news for ya, but I'd shore like to do it with a couple swigs of whiskey in a cup of strong coffee. Did ya's get any whiskey with them supplies?"

"We got plenty coffee." Pete offered back. "I suppose if you want whiskey, you'll need to do the supply buyin' next time." Pete had worked for a ranch foreman back in Texas that was a hard-case, it was there that he found a man had to push back, or a rascal like Tatum would run over a lesser man.

In a matter of minutes the three men were sitting on their heels, a slight haze of steam rising from tin cups. Tatum had described the drunken teamster's explanation of the new Cimmaron Bank's cash reserve account being funded by The First State Bank out of Dodge City. Once the Longleys had absorbed that, the crafty outlaw began making marks in the soil with a stick, further explaining his plan, "Jesse, you'll be the man lying at the side of the road here." He scratched an *X*. "I want ya to have one of your legs turned back and an arm pinned under ya, that'll make it look genuine like ya was really hurt." Muley cocked his head and looked from under his brow at Pete, "You'll ride up quick-like just as the stage comes into view where they can see ya good." He turned back to Jess, "He'll jump down beside you." Muley braced Jess with strict eyes, "You don't move . . . cause you're bad hurt." The stick drug through the soil, creating a line from the mark indicating the stagecoach to where the Longleys were to be. Tatum flipped a thumb toward Pete, "You'll wave for the stage to stop to help you . . . you're bent over your hurt friend. They'll stop and . . ."

"What if they don't stop?" Jesse interrupted, glaring at Muley.

"They'll stop." Muley rasped, and gave Jess an unyielding look. "They always do." His dark eyes flashed equal to the annoyed tone of his voice.

Jesse jerked his head and fixed a stare toward Pete. Pete simply nodded in response.

Tatum took up the stick and started again, "I'll be back here, in cover where they can't see me." He poked the stick in the ground and made another *X*. "When the stage stops, I'll climb up the backside of it and get the draw on both the shotgun and the rein man." Muley then drew back and displayed one of his weasel grins, "Easy as pickin' eggs from under a layin' hen . . . baak, baak, baak," he mimicked the sound of a hen and fell back on his rump with a gurgling laugh, getting himself all caught up in his antics.

Pete glared at the outlaw obtrusively, "Nobody gets shot! Right, Muley?" He spoke with somber authority, not appreciative of Muley Tatum's light-heartedness.

"No need." Muley glared back. He stood up, dropped the amusement from his expression, dusted off the seat of his pants with both hands, and without looking directly at either Pete or Jesse, he said, "If you two don't even want to carry them shootin' irons, its okay by me. I'll have mine, got to, can't be no holdup otherwise." A sneer came to his face, "They won't hand over the strong box if we just ask 'em polite like." He stuck the pointed stick in the ground and walked over to where the coffee pot sat on a rock beside the fire, poured fresh coffee into his cup and asked, "Either of ya's want more?"

It was quiet for a spell as the plan was absorbed by the Longleys. Muley stood alone, looking over the top of the cup as he drank, sizing up his newly acquired sidekicks. *'Pete was a tough sort, he'd do fine . . . Jesse, well, he'd have to be watched!'*

Breaking the disgruntled quiet, Jesse spoke with a sour tone, "So what's this holdup worth to us?" It was plain and clear that he didn't like the idea, not one bit.

Muley cast back one of his side-ways grins from the corner of his mouth, "How 'bout fifteen thousand . . . that's what them teamsters said—and I figure they'd know better than most; they's the ones we're gonna take it from."

"You mean they're the men that'll be drivin' the stage outfit?" Jesse smiled a smile of skepticism, he could hardly believe it.

Tatum just lipped another wide smile and nodded like a school boy, "Yep!"

A short minute passed before Pete spoke up, the reality of the amount of money sinking in before he indifferently said, "Fifteen thousand." Pete ran his hand across his mouth repeatedly having said it. After a brief hesitation, he asked, "Split three ways?"

"Now there's where we gotta have an understanding," Muley tossed the dregs from the tin cup to the ground and walked toward the brothers. He put his hands on his hips and slanted his eyes to Pete's, "Seein' as how I'm the one that squeezed the information outta them teamsters and it'll be me that mounts that stagecoach doing the gun-work, I figure I'm entitled to say," he rubbed his chin and pursed his lips, "sixty percent. That'll leave you boys," he rolled his eyes as if calculating, "six thousand between ya's—beats the hell outta nursemaidin' cows, wouldn't you say?"

Pete threw his glare over to Jesse and nodded twice. Jesse hunched his shoulders slightly in reply, leaving the decision to his older brother.

Muley watched their responses, "Okay!" Muley clapped his hands, seemingly in jubilation, rubbed them together having seen the acceptance. The elaborate baroque smile of his filled his cheeks. "Now, let's get this outfit over to the road toward Cimmaron where our plan is going to play out tomorrow."

* * *

Back in Spickard, the neatly dressed young Courtney woman stood before the marshal, "Yes, Marshal Carson, I'd like to see the man you've got locked up back there." The shadow of a smile found her lightly painted lips, her head tiled flippantly.

He eyed her precariously, giving thought to possibilities; *should he grant her the request?*

Carson stood, elbows out, hands resting snug against his gun-belt on either side. His demeanor firmly opposed to the lady's petition. "Miss Courtney, you do understand that the man we're holding in jail isn't the man who actually killed your father, don't you?" Rad Carson wanted to persuade Jenny Courtney away. His intuition urged that he not allow the daughter of the murdered man to see the foul-mouthed outlaw, Patch Gillis.

"I know that," she dropped her head, "I just think that perhaps seeing that man will somehow help me to be near my father." She then glanced up into the stern brown eyes of the marshal, "I'm doing this partly because of my mother, she asked me to look into his face and tell him the man he killed was the kindest and most benevolent man in the state of Kansas, if not in the entire United States of America. And I told her I'd do it. So if you please, Marshal?"

She was a soft, very feminine woman, neatly attired, her hair fluffed with gentle curls and tied with yellow ribbons, one on each side of her head. The dress she wore was of finely sewn off-white fabric, decorated with rows of dainty flowers in lines that pleasantly accentuated the form of her body. The handbag she clutched matched caringly and her soft blue eyes were the kind that would melt a man if the perfectly shaped nose and finely sculptured lips, with which she formed her words, didn't.

Rad Carson knew he wasn't going to be able to sustain his negative position much longer. He looked out of the corner of his eye at Travis Floyd, his deputy, as he sorted out the thoughts the nineteen year old Courtney girl explained. Travis offered a look of *why not,* and the marshal studied on it a few seconds more.

"Okay, miss, but you've got to understand, the man is wicked. He may yell things at you, or about your father that may be hard for you to bear . . . he'd say them just to hurt you." Marshal Carson was giving the young woman another chance to back out of seeing the prisoner.

"I can handle it, Marshal, the man can't hurt me anymore than I've already been hurt." She wiped the corner of an eye with a small white lace handkerchief. "But thank you."

Carson lifted the ring of keys from a peg and motioned for Jenny Courtney to follow. He opened the door separating the jail cells from the office, stood in the middle of the opening and spoke in a clear, orderly manner, "Patch, there's someone here to see you . . . I'm counting on you to be on your best gentlemanly behavior or be damn sorry for it later, okay?" His face firmed up, lips tightened, he turned to once again give the pretty lady a disapproving insinuation.

"Yea, sure," Patch grumbled back.

The few steps were taken slowly. "Well, that's him, Ma'am." Carson lifted a hand toward the outlaw who was sitting on the bunk in the subdued light at the rear of the cell.

Patch looked up, unconcerned at first, but quickly his eyes perked up and he started toward the bars separating him from the marshal and Jenny. "Well . . . ," he drew the word out. "What have we here?" He drawled and raised his good hand to grasp the steel shafts before him. "My, my, do let her in, Marshal, I'll let her put her cute little . . . ." His words faltered and he jerked back. Jenny's faced pinched. She held a chrome-plated four shot rim-fire Colt, cocked back the hammer and tried to bring it level. The marshal's hand caught her wrist as the gun discharged, the shot crashed into the ceiling where Patch had hunkered down, his hands pulled to his twisted face.

"He needs to die," she cried. Her face knotted, anger leaped from her mouth, her arms flailed in an attempt to break free of the marshal's grasp, but she couldn't do so. "Let me go—let me go!" She twisted and jerked; the hand gun fired again, but the bullet struck only the back wall of the cell.

"Jesus!" Patch shouted, "Stop the bitch!" He was half under the bunk.

"What the damnation you trying to do?" Marshal Carson barked and grabbed at her. She dug finger nails into his arm. He yelled out, "Travis . . . get back here!"

Suddenly she went limp. Her body melted like a wet rag and her head drooped. Carson, holding her from behind, had a strong arm around her waist, his other hand still locked onto the wrist of her hand that held the gun. Travis immediately reached out and took her from the marshal's grasp, lifted her into his arms and clumsily started back to the front office.

Patch spotted the short barreled Colt lying on the floor, near enough to the bars he figured he could reach and snag it. He went flat, crawled quickly, stretched an arm through the bars and had a finger inside the trigger guard. But a rough soled boot stomped his hand before he could retrieve the gun. "No you don't!" Carson's response was well timed; once again his boot was effective against the outlaw associate of Muley Tatum. "Get back, back in your cage." Rad Carson snapped. The outlaw's yelp and cursing gave satisfaction to the marshal. "Too bad she didn't have time to shoot you," Carson bellowed as he gave Patch an infuriated look, "Maybe I'll go get her—give her another chance." Carson pocketed the stubby gun and shuffled to the doorway separating the areas of the jail. "Damn," he roared. He tramped through the door and stood in rigid uneasiness, anger and frustration wired stiffly into his jaws.

Travis had the girl sitting in a chair, her face pale as whitewash, her eyes open with tears welled up and spilling over both cheeks. "I'm sorry," she cried, "I know I shouldn't have done it." She sniffed amid erratic sobs and shook her head side to side, curly strands of soft brown hair waving unsparingly, "He took my father from me, away from me and mother . . . I hate him so!"

"Damn!" Carson shouted once more. He glared at the stunning young lady, his head shaking in disbelief as to what had taken place. "Never would I have thought . . ."

The front door suddenly swung open. Carson's hand flew to the tied-down holster, filled it with his six-gun, hammer back, he froze! The young wrangler, the man that beckoned the two Spickard lawmen to the saloon where Miles Courtney was killed, pushed inside and looked about frantically. He'd heard the gunshots, but hadn't anticipated what he saw before him.

The marshal calmly flipped the Peacemaker back into the leather, an edgy smile of relief found his lips, "Glad to see you, Spence." Carson quipped sarcastically and continued, "You bring this young lady in to do the killing did you?" Fire leaped from Rad Carson's eyes as he read down the boy, but one could see the lawman felt more respite than anger.

"I had no idea." Spence scratched at his forehead and stepped forward. He looked to the back of the room, his expression registering dismay, "Did she . . . well, did she shoot him?"

"Tried damn hard." The marshal said, "But didn't get it done."

A brief spell of quiet was broken when Spence conceded, "I'm sorry, Marshal, real sorry. I had no idea she was going to do anything like this. I brought her to town for making funeral arrangements with the preacher and Cyrus, the undertaker." The young man was sincere; Carson could tell. He shook his head and went on, "She said she wanted to come by here and thank you, that's all, just to thank you."

CHAPTER FIVE

The burial of Miles Courtney was very emotional, not only for Jenny and Mrs. Courtney, but for the town in general. Miles had been one of the four original founders of the young Spickard community. And even though he'd relegated his life to the ranch in recent years and was no longer a member of the town-council, he continued to be held in high personal regard by everyone who'd ever known him.

Rad Carson held his brown Stetson in his hand as he approached Mrs. Courtney, "I'm very sorry, Ma'am, for your terrible loss." Mrs. Courtney was still shy of her forty-fifth year, but the lines in her face, deepened by ranch-work and the harsh Kansas sun, suggested an age greater in number.

"Thank you, Marshal," she responded with bleary eyes, her mouth partially covered with a small lace-edged kerchief. She lowered the kerchief and spoke timidly, "And I do want to thank you for overlooking the dreadful incident with my Jenny. She loved her father so very, very much, as did I, and she was overcome . . ."

"I understand." Rad Carson looked over to Jenny, but spoke to Mrs. Courtney as he did so, "She's a very strong willed person that I'm sure you're very proud of; I know I would be if she was a member of my family."

The two Courtney ladies bobbed their heads appreciably and allowed a slight smile to acknowledge Marshal Carson's compliment.

"Her courage reminded me of my grandfather, Kit Carson," Rad said, "he was a man that feared nothing, and he had an unapproachable sense of righteousness and fair-play . . . I believe he would have done just what Jenny did if he'd been in her shoes."

"Goodness! I had no idea you were related to Kit Carson, Marshal." Jenny voiced puzzlement, "I'd never associated the names . . . I suppose I should have, you being the very brave man that you are."

"Now you've got me embarrassed." Carson wet his lips and blinked. A couple of seconds passed as Carson rimmed his hat around his fingers, "None-the-less, I offer my condolences to the both of you, and I'll leave you good ladies be with this information, "It looks like my prisoner, Patch Gillis, will stand trial at the end of next week. Judge Wilkinson will be here in Spickard to handle the proceedings. Gillis is charged with being an accessory to murder, and also, felonious use of a firearm with intent to kill. He'll likely do ten to twelve years up in the state prison."

"Good!" Spencer Cline spoke up from a few feet away, "I want to be there. I suppose the judge will want my testimony."

Carson turned toward the young man to respond, "I'm glad you're here, Spence, it saves me a trip. The judge has subpoenaed you as a witness," Carson acknowledged with a dip of his chin and resettling of his Stetson onto his head, "and I would have had to ride out to deliver it, I hope you wouldn't mind stopping by my office before you leave town."

"I'll be there, Marshal, soon's I take these folks back over to the church." He indicated the Courtneys with a twist of the hat he held waist high.

They said their good-bys; the young wrangler escorting the ladies toward their carriage and Rad Carson initiating his trek toward the law office.

Travis was sitting in the marshal's chair uneasily, pouring over a letter from the governor when the marshal arrived. He looked up, a forlorn expression pasted on his face.

"You look like a boy caught with a hand full of peppermint sticks and no money to pay for it!" Carson quipped light-heartedly as he pushed the door shut behind him.

"I wish I'd left this one for you." Travis reached up, extending the paper with an embossed Kansas state emblem, which was readily identified by Rad Carson before he held it in his hands.

"Not bad news, I hope," Rad grinned."

"That'd have to be left to a man's personal opinion," Travis answered as Carson grasped the letter. The deputy stood, vacating the marshal's chair in anticipation of the marshal's response to the letter. He knew his boss was going to want to sit.

Carson's eyes narrowed as he slid behind the desk, his focus glued to the single page of paper. He gripped the brim of his hat, removed it slowly, placed it on the desk and concentrated on the letter's content. He soon turned and looked up at Travis, "Holy beJesus!" His faced was stolid and empty. "U. S. Marshal? Dodge City?"

"Now you know what was eatin' at me." Travis said broodingly.

"According to this, Judge Nathaniel Wilkinson nominated me to become a United States Marshal, and the governor, John P. St. John, with approval from President Grover Cleveland, has appointed me to the office, but instructs me to office out of Dodge City; that's thirty miles from here!"

"Starting on the first of next month," Travis exclaimed dryly. "That's only, let's see," he glanced at the wall calendar, head nodding the count, "eighteen days from now."

"I don't see how I could leave Spickard," he scratched at his cheek, "and not that soon if I was to do it." Carson glared disconsolately at his deputy.

"Judge Wilkinson sure enough held you in high esteem. He made some real strong statements about your handling of duties." Travis was forward and sincere, acknowledging the content of the correspondence. "And evidently the town council supports your appointment too." Travis Floyd's demeanor lapsed into deep thought momentarily, "I wonder if that's why the council worked me over like they did, thinking there was a good possibility that you'd be leaving Spickard, and they'd need a replacement marshal."

Rad Carson studied Travis for a short time and thought about the questioning statement he'd just made. "They sure didn't make it easy did they? At that final meeting we had, I thought they was going to starve us to death—they kept asking questions of the two of us well past supper hour. I suppose now we know why."

The deputy had doubts, "I don't know, Rad, I ain't been a lawman but a few days."

"I chose you to be my deputy, partner, 'cause I knew you could handle a tough job, and if you'll remember, that's what I kept pounding into the councils' heads." Carson's focus stayed on Travis for another moment, making sure his confidence in him was absorbed. Seeing it taking place, he turned back to the correspondence from Governor St John's office. A long minute of silence settled into the room before Carson leaned back in the chair, "I'm going to have to sleep on this," Carson retorted, "I like my job here, and the people, Spickard's my home!"

* * *

"This is the spot I had in mind." Muley sat loosely in the saddle, his body twisting as he surveyed the surroundings. "The stage will come from there," he pointed and at the same time bobbed his head. "Those trees will block the view of the road so when the driver and his gunny see ya, Jess, they'll be close enough to tell yer hurt, lying in the road up there." He indicated a location, "And they'll not be so far back to give 'em time to suspect anything, like a hold-up." The big Muley Tatum grin welled up, "And I'll be behind them rocks there," he pointed, "ready to mount that coach."

Jesse watched as Pete studied the setting quietly. He could soon tell Pete was passively satisfied. Jesse walked his horse to the side of the road where he figured he needed to be in order to play the role of being injured, lying in the road, the spot Muley had depicted when the plan was established at the crossroad the previous day.

"You boys are the key. If you play your parts right, this will be easier than breakin' sweat on a hot day. And all I'll have to do is say *'please'* to them teamsters." He placed the palms of his hands together under his chin, mocking a prayer image and chuckled impishly. "But, just in case, I'll keep my six-gun handy," Muley laughed. He then turned, heeled the black mare into a side-step to exhibit his insolence, and without further discourse or question he shouted, "I'm goin' to locate that stage and money-box." He spurred his horse, lipped a stinging whistle and bolted toward Dodge City

The Longleys were seated, ill at ease, on a log in the shade alongside the trail, thinking about the ordeal in which they'd agreed to take a part while Muley rode his black mare along the stage route toward Dodge. "That man can't sit still can he?" Jesse quipped, "He's a bundle of nerves and hogwash." Jesse drew deep on the cigarette and blew a cloud of smoke from the corner of his mouth, "You think he really wrung the information about the stagecoach money outta them teamster fellas like he said?" Jesse didn't wait for an answer, and continued, "I'd come more near thinkin' he made up the whole story; he ain't smart enough to trick 'em with his talk." He paused, waiting for Pete to say something. When he didn't, Jesse went on, "Dog gone it, Pete, I don't know if I'm cut out to be an outlaw—I don't feel too good about this."

"Muley's different alright." Pete spat out a spindle of dry grass he'd been chewing and spoke rather softly, "But remember, we ain't never been out of Texas and ain't never been around an outlaw before," he paused temporarily. "I suppose outlaws aren't like most people, they couldn't hardly be, and still be outlaws." Pete drew a deep breath and turned his gaze to the stage trail, "The man is clever, not stupid," Pete's eyebrows arched upward, "I still believe we can learn a few things from him, and the thought of havin' six thousand dollars is right appealing."

The younger Longley fixed his thoughts on Pete, drew again on his cigarette and blew the smoke out over an extended lower lip, recognizing his brother was beginning to take stock in having a considerable chunk of money.

"It'll work out fine, Jess, "don't let yourself get wound up." Pete locked his eyes on Jesse's, "I've worked the whole thing over in my mind several times. I figure Muley's got his neck hung out; you and me, well, we're okay so long as we don't draw down on them men perched up atop the coach." He reached over and slapped Jesse on the shoulder, "Doing what we're going to do don't make us outlaws." He paused and patted Jesse's shoulder once again, "I agree the man's a notch or two off plumb, but I keep thinking about what that money will do for us and our folks back in Pampa."

"There he comes! Too late to back out now, even if we was a'mind to." Pete stood and pulled their horses' reins loose, handed Jesse his, and said confidently, "Let's get to it, brother."

Muley had his black mare lathered. He skidded her to a stop, turned her a full turn and snapped out his words, "I rode damn near clear to Dodge lookin' for 'em. If I'd had to go any further I'da gone on into town and got us some whiskey. "He chuckled richly, matching his grin. Then, in a more somber manner, "They're about four or five miles back and coming at a pretty good clip, moving faster than I figured, but we still got plenty of time."

"I ain't in no big hurry to flop down in the dust," Jesse voiced reluctantly.

Muley gave him a callous look, turned to Pete and blubbered indifferently, "Well, everybody's got a job to do so's we can make this easy—if we don't do our jobs right, then we gotta do it the hard way."

"We're okay, Tatum, we know what to do." Pete retorted. He then bobbed his head at Jesse, "They can't be here in any less than ten to twelve minutes, don't travel mor'n six to seven miles in an hour. Take it easy. When we hear 'em come close we'll set to our positions." He motioned toward the brush at the road's edge, "I'll be over there, Jess, and ready when you are."

The three of them waited quietly, listening. Muley idled in his saddle easily, not a sign of nervousness. Pete stood with his arms folded, seemingly relaxed but concerned. Jesse's thoughts darted in different directions, thinking of his folks, mostly his mother, and back to the present as he felt his heart beat strong in his chest. He fretfully envisioned how he'd spread his body on the ground to appear injured and wondered if indeed the teamsters would fall for the charade. No one spoke. *'Somehow Pete always keeps his wits about him,'* Jesse thought to himself as he ambled to the spot in the road where he'd play his role.

CHAPTER SIX

They saw in the distance a blurred dust cloud raised by the team of six draft horses and the bulky, wheeled carriage. Several minutes passed before the vociferous whistle of the driver was heard, and not long thereafter, the rattle and squeaks of the coach.

Muley hunkered down behind a large rock secluded by a tangle of brush. A pair of big leaf cottonwood trees loomed overhead and threw shadows across the lair of the crafty outlaw, making it impossible for him to be seen by the oncoming teamsters.

Jesse lowered his body, laid his hat aside, twisted an arm under his back and threw a leg as perpendicular to his body as he could, creating a tinge of pain. He felt the warmth of the sun on his shoulder and the side of his face. He lazily squinted through one eye where he could see both his brother, Pete, and the turn where the coach would spring into the open as it rounded the crook in the roadway. It was about to happen!

Suddenly, there was Pete, his horse's front legs stiffened, the hooves stabbed into the hard ground, skidding, and shafts of dirt billowed. Pete flew from the saddle, his role playing out as an obliging, ready to lend a hand, companion to an injured man.

The stagecoach driver jerked back, stubbornly leaned away hard with his legs stiff and boot soles firm against the hardwood frame. A grimace locked into his wide-eyed face, he yanked the traces and yelled, "Whoa; whoa!"

Jesse's reflexes decreed that he repulse, reposition his body from danger, but he remained earnestly steadfast against his will as the team of big dark horses came closer.

"Help!" Pete cried out and threw an arm up toward the stagecoach, "He's hurt!"

The shotgun rider sprang to his feet as the stage ground to a restrictive halt. "I don't like this!" he screamed. With that he swung the scattergun toward Pete and thumbed back the hammers. But he hesitated, not definite of the circumstance.

Jesse, his eyes squinted and still, could see beneath the coach. Muley rushed toward the rear of cumbersome vehicle, rose and disappeared. The driver twisted his head toward the shot-gunner and then back to the exasperated, provoked horses under his command. Confusion ruled the moment; in seconds, however, Muley's head popped up over the top, his revolver held high, he rapidly clawed his way toward the front of the coach.

Jesse started to rise—too soon! The shotgun man waved the double barrel ten-gauge in Jesse's direction!

Muley's revolver roared and spit fire. The confused coach guard's body lurched forward and then flung backward instantaneously. He suffered two fatal wounds, one in the back from Muley's gun, the other to middle of his chest. The man's weapon discharged in reflex and the combined forces threw him from the stagecoach, sprawling to the ground with a sickening, gruesome *crunch.*

"Don't shoot . . . don't shoot me!" The driver screamed as he held the traces snug, hands high. Muley jumped into the seat beside the driver, reached down, and in a single motion dropped the metal box over the side.

"You!" The driver shouted, leaning back away from the enraged outlaw. The word hadn't much more than registered that the man recognized Muley Tatum than Tatum etched a horrifying laugh and pulled the trigger, his slug ripping into the man's face. Blood splattered, spotting Muley; his face dotted with a half dozen strikes that tauntingly edged downward in crimson trails. He apathetically back-handed them away with two wisps of a gloved hand, with virtually no thought or consideration.

Pete Longley stood at the road beside Jesse, a smoking six-gun in his hand, his face disconsolate and vacant as he watched Muley dump the driver's lifeless body from the coach. The horses whinnied and stomped in place, awaiting a command, growing ever more nervous and uneasy. Muley hurriedly stepped down, hesitantly inspected the money box as he passed and with gun in hand, threw open the passenger door. Two ladies were inside, one a Negro, likely a maid to the other woman whose face was covered with a dark mesh veil flowing from a hat decorated with colorful flowers and feathers. She was glamorously dressed in fashionable millinery store clothes. The two of them clutched one another and pressed against the door on the opposite side from the coach's door, fear pasted on their faces, but as quiet as a church mouse. "Well, what have we here," Muley screeched, as he animatedly examined the passengers with glowing eyes that dropped into an impassive emptiness. He took a short step back, abruptly clutched and removed his hat.

Pete Longely rushed to affront Muley, "Wait . . ."

"Awe, don't get yer bowels to boilin', Pete, I ain't no woman killer. I'm not what most would call a *gen-teel* person I reckon, but I sure ain't inta harmin' women." He slammed the door and the horses swiftly took the slack out of the harnesses, the metallic snap of the door's latch being their signal. Muley dropped an arm, flailed it across his midsection and waved his hat at the coach's rear as it jumped forward. A washed-out grin decorated his sun-darkened face before he resolutely tapped the black hat snug to the top of his head and turned back to face his cohorts.

Both Longleys were amazed, finding it hard to accept that this evil, heinous man who would kill a man and laugh about it, had a far different set of standards when it came to a woman. The despicable man had a surprising soft spot in him. Giving the women no added thought, he exclaimed with a smattering of pride, "We got the money, boys!" Muley put his boot sole against the lifeless body of the shotgun man, and with a buoyant grunt, pushed him away from the strong box.

Jesse Longley, in a dubious, impasse frame of mind, lazily stepped aside as the coach moved past. He watched despondently as feminine gloved hands gripped the base of the window from within; the top of a flowered hat and a bonnet brim emerged cautiously with a slender hand holding it secure. It all soon faded in the haze of dust.

Pete swung open the cylinder of his revolver and punched a cartridge into the opening, flipped the gun to lock it away and slid it into his holster without taking his eyes off of Jesse. Both of the Longleys realized they'd crossed a threshold, killing a man, even though Muley Tatum had shot also, was a big step, one they hadn't planned. It was still sinking in.

Tatum, however, was in a celebration mode. Gaiety besieged the man, putting his warped, bizarre values in a near frenzy. "Com'on," Muley coaxed the Longleys, waving them toward him, "let's get this present opened." The sickening chuckle and smile he possessed were in their most festive, repulsive form.

Tatum blew the lock off the strong box with a single shot and dug into it. His demeanor softened. Jesse watched him, realizing he could never really understand the man's behavior. It seemed to Jesse that Tatum gained his greatest pleasure from the deception and killing, more than gaining the prize that was the supposed reward.

"Just like they said, fifteen thousand, them boys was straight up honest wasn't they?" He tossed aside a few pieces of mail before he arranged the currency into stacks, rose up from his knees and hurried over to his black mare where he lifted black leather saddlebags and started back. "Ain't you boys gonna pack? We can't stay here long." He looked in the distance, toward Cimmaron, "When that stage rolls into town and that bank don't get their money, they'll send out a posse . . . it'd be a good idea for us not to be here, don'tch'ya think?" He was also tapping into the pleasure of seeing the two tenderfoot outlaws in the stupor they bore.

"Ain't we gonna bury them?" Jesse motioned toward the dead teamsters.

"Hell no! The posse will find 'em and take 'em back to Dodge City . . . that's what posses do best." Tatum's glare let Jesse know he thought of his comment was *simple minded*. He yelled an order to urge them into action, "Come on men, get yer money up and jump your backsides onto them ponies and follow me."

Pete, who was always confident and self-assured, was slow to react. Jesse affronted him, looked into his face questionably and called his name, "Pete, what's wrong?"

The minimal answer was a sluggish shaking of his head side to side. He blinked twice and told Jesse in a soft voice, "Muley's right, we gotta get outta here. Get your gear-bags and take up our share, mine's full of supplies."

Tatum squirmed in the saddle and kept his horse in motion; he yelled again, "Com'on, hurry it up, we ain't campin' here!" He heeled the mare and sprinted a short distance, yanked her to a stop and came back as quickly as he left, "Look boys," he shouted, "this ain't no cattle drive, we ain't got a couple months, mount them nags and let's git, I ain't telling ya again."

"You go on!" Pete screamed back, "We don't need you to tell us." Pete's hand went to the butt of his six-gun.

Muley's face slackened, "I know a place," his voice became normal, "it's about thirty miles south; I got friends there." The eccentric outlaw's attitude changed from domination to a near plea, "They'll put us up for a few days, by then the posse will give up and we can go on." The sultry grin reappeared; he said teasingly, "Hell, maybe we'll go back to Dodge, that's a busy town where people like us come and go same as a change in the weather."

"Okay," Pete's response was nominal. He put a glance to his younger brother; enough for Jesse to comprehend. They stepped up and put boots in their stirrups.

One long day later the three men sat a rise and viewed structures a half mile away and a bit off-center of the wide, shallow valley; one was a sod house built into the hillside with a crude pair of wood steps at the bulky framed doorway. A lean-to with half-walls and a twig-thatched roof supported by crooked posts stood nearby. Seven ragged cedar trees claimed an area near the front corner of the sod house.

There were other trees that noticeably stood out, a half dozen large ones, the kind that nature didn't normally put on the lands of this region. They orderly stood guard to another building, an enormous building by standards of the Kansas prairie. This one of finer quality, including sawmill boards, framed windows and a roof of wood shake shingles, set twenty yards downhill from the soddy, it too was showing age. There was a spacious garden, windmill, hog corral, a large barn and two small outbuildings. A creek, high banked on the other side, with an ample growth of willows dispensed alongside near a quarter mile in length, giving evidence of good water, was five hundred yards down-slope of the house at the foot of the rock-strewn valley floor.

"You call that a town?" Jesse sneered.

"Didn't say it was a town," Muley retorted, "said a place . . . if you was listening."

"How many people?" Pete asked.

"Over at that soddy," Muley nodded, "usually three; man and his woman, and a boy." Muley chuckled. "Well, the young one is a man in age but a boy in mind," he chuckled louder, "crazier'n a hog chewin' on snakeweed." He said nothing about people in the big building, just nudged his horse forward, but soon stopped again. A simple, improvised sign atop the large structure came into view. It declared, *Buffalo Lodge, Complete With Saloon.*

"Buffalo Lodge?" Jesse lamented.

"Shore was." Muley injected, "This here, where we're sittin', was once overrun with buffalo, thousands of 'em within fifty to sixty miles. See that there set of wagon ruts running along side of the creek and disappearing over the rise yonder? That's where the hides was carted outta here by the ton, wagon after wagonload they tell me."

"And the lodge, was where the hunters stayed, I suppose." Pete remarked.

"The ol' boy from England tried bringing one of their traditions of sport shooting to America . . . started out that way for a year or so they say. Didn't last long though. What started as hunters became more like shooters! Once they cut down on a herd, they'd sit and shoot, sometimes for hours, or 'til their rifle barrels got too hot to shoot anymore." Muley scooted his hat back on his head. He continued to survey the impressive landscape stretched out before him, and enjoy his dominance in the knowledge he was relating to his new associates, subordinates in his mind, and they lapped it up like a coyote taking water from a stream on a hot day. "They didn't take the meat, just hides, left the meat to rot or food for the varmints." He squinted, brows wrinkled, "It was a couple years later that the market for their bones come about," he moved his head side to side, taking in the full scope of the land, "then more senseless men come here, killed even more." Muley sat quiet for a short spell, his jaws flexing before he continued, "Yep, the shooters first, and later on, the bone pickers."

Pete responded drearily, “I’ve read about the buffalo hunters up this way. We had some in Texas, but not near the bunch that was here.” He gazed at the wide expanse of rolling prairie, halting at the bulky structure that stood out from the others, “Whoever put up that fancy mansion must have thought he was starting a town, like the buffalo was gonna last forever.” He looked at Muley with a tinge of sorted-out respect in his eyes, but Muley just sat trance-like, staring at the lodge building.

“We’ll be bunkin’ at the lodge, I’m guessin’,” Jesse opined.

Tatum lit up, he stretched his neck as he turned toward Jesse with his teeth exposed through wide lips and giggled, “Boy, that long ride done you some good, you said something with some brains behind it.” The black-attired outlaw wrenched the reins and started off, cackling at his deft humor, belittling the Longley youngster.

Jesse’s face tightened as he watched Muley ride away, “I may have to shoot that no count son-of-a-bitch someday.” The stalwart tone of discontent in his voice reminded the older brother that Jesse didn’t want to be here, or anywhere, with Muley Tatum.

CHAPTER SEVEN

The front door of the lodge building swung open exposing a drably dressed man in wrinkled gray trousers and an unbuttoned, faded blue shirt. The suspendered older man stepped out, an arm crooked to support the hand pressed against his lower back, he appeared either cautious or a mite feeble. He sported a face full of untidy, heavily streaked gray whiskers. Wire rim glasses pushed up on his forehead toward a scrappy hairline matched his facial hair. The dull shirt suited him rightly, hanging open, exposing muted underwear from his midsection to an uneven circle around his neck. After a moment he lifted the cane held in his right hand in salute to the oncoming rider and shouted, "Muley Tatum, that you boy?"

The black horse came to her normal skidding halt, Muley pulled his hat off and swung it back and forth in front of him, shouting laughingly, "Don't shoot me with that cane Uncle Pug, it's me alright, Muley."

The elderly gentleman twisted his upper body, leaned backward into the door opening, and shouted wryly, "Come on out here, Ma, we got kin folk come to see us."

Muley hopped up the double steps and grasped the man he'd called Uncle Pug by the shoulders, "You don't look a bit older than the last time I was here." The big Muley Tatum smile budded and blossomed like a sunflower in July. Without slowing his brusque antics or lessening his colossal smile he turned and threw a hand toward the Longleys who had reached the tie-rail, "And these boys are my associates, Pete and Jesse."

The two newcomers tipped their hats while drawing the reins around the slick rail. Pete snapped a quick knot and found a weak smile, "Happy to meet ya."

"Yiieee, Muley, it is you!" A squatty-figured, bronze-skinned woman in a long skirt bounced through the door and raced open-armed toward Muley. She stuck her face into his chest, threw her arms around him and clicked her cheek repeatedly as if coaxing chickens to feed. Her long black hair flowed with the wind as she tugged the fully seasoned man in circles, her feet virtually dancing in rhythmic joy. "Yiiee, yiieee," she twice again shrieked before she stopped and moved back arm's length, and with her head cocked, said slow and lovingly, "It is so good to see you . . . you make me so happy that'd you come to see papa and me." Her grin matched the warmth of a full, vanilla moon.

The bulky-sized house was neat and well kept. Four enormous buffalo heads hung high on the wall at the rear. The large area front and right of center offered six oversized chairs cushioned with well worn cow hides. Pete thought, *'perhaps buffalo hides would have been too cumbersome, harsh and too much stringy hair.'* An immense fireplace took command of the big room, its stone front showing signs of lapping winter-flames escaped from within the fire chamber. Four sturdy support timbers stood upright in the massive living area of the lodge. They were situated in equal positions to carry the burden of heavy cross-members and broad roof rafters. In the rear there was a kitchen area with another fireplace and a flat-topped cooking stove, ample storage cabinets, and a long cumbersome table cut from timber with similarly styled benches on either side. Three sets of two-tier beds were in the left corner, and behind them, a blanket folded over a rope providing privacy from a solid-built four-corner featherbed with lumps aplenty.

Pete and Jesse left the gathering to care for the horses. Muley had already taken his bulky saddlebags and bedroll inside and stuffed them under the bed he declared to be his.

"What do ya' make of this, Pete? Seems these folks claim Muley as one of their own." Jesse yanked his saddle clear and draped it over the side of a stall in the barn, "I don't suppose I ever considered that rascal to have family." Jesse's arms rested against the saddle, his face blunted in thought.

"I noticed they didn't ask why we'd come way out here," Pete remarked, "and I'm of a mind that they knew we wasn't along with him just to provide company." He lifted the black, silver trimmed saddle from Muley's horse and gazed at it momentarily, "This was a fine piece of work at some time. He must have paid a pretty price for it."

"Huuumm, you're jokin' ain't ya? I doubt he paid a dime; likely he stole it off somebody, didn't pay at all."

Pete cut a glance at Jesse and widened his eyes, seemingly in agreement. He went on, "That Uncle Pug ain't no spring chicken, I figure he knows Muley's on the hideout from the law. I wouldn't be surprised but what Muley has been here before for the same reason."

Pete and Jesse dropped the subject, smiling at one another, and made their way into the buffalo lodge. Though they'd been briefly inside a few minutes earlier, the ambiance was again overpowering. They found themselves gawking as they wandered over to where Uncle Pug and Muley idled comfortably on wooden rocking chairs topped with supple cowhides.

Jesse built a smoke. Uncle Pug watched, his eyes blinking in nippy intervals, sucked on his well worn pipe stem and commented, "Don't know why a man would fool with them papers when he can thumb tobacco into a pipe." Jesse and Muley eyed one another and grinned. Jesse made no reply, simply squinted friendly like at the old man from the corner of his eye and struck a lucifer to his cigarette.

Several feet away, Magdalena hummed joyfully as she prepared a dinner of cornmeal tortillas and heavy pork soup laced with onion, peppers and beans. "I have been saving a can of peaches and a can of pears for a special occasion, we'll have them both tonight with our supper." Happiness was a full halo surrounding her joyous, sagging frame. She clapped her hands, threw her bulky arms in the air and merrily cooed, "Oh, what a happy day!"

The day had drawn on toward dusk. The sun assembled the few stringy clouds above the horizon into a pale, translucent ribbon and beckoned the shadows to fade into darkness across the low rolling prairie. Everyone sat comfortably in the cowhide chairs with warm food in their bellies. Muley found a newspaper; Pug relaxed with his feet up, his spindly pipe adding to the hushed gratification of evening.

Once Magdalena had cleared the table, she blissfully gathered a bottle of rye whiskey and five ceramic cups from the cabinet. Her smile was delightful as she clunked the bottle neck on everyone's cup with congenial eyes and humming a light melody. The warm glow of the spirits, plus the contentment of the evening's stillness, slowly meshed the unusual mixture of personalities into a steadfast camaraderie. Whiskey, and a quiet setting beyond simple, unconstructive happenings, has a way of instilling simple depth and soft emotion into one's spirit.

The Longelys were willing listeners of Tatum family remembrances. The stories of old, back in Missouri, came to the front in a melancholy fashion, perhaps particularly affable, being associated with the dull glow of the kerosene lamps. Uncle Pug, his given name, Roland, was the brother of Muley's father. He and Magdalena, the excitedly happy woman of Mexican descent, wife of Pug for the past forty years, had at one time shared a farm with Muley's folks in southwest Missouri. It sat ten to twelve miles east of Joplin, where both sets of parents scratched a living from rocky soil, raising meager row crops, along with pigs, chickens and a pair of milk cows.

It came to light that Muley's grandpa, Pug's brother, left Missouri in the spring of 1860 and headed for the gold country of California. In route there, crossing the prairie lands, he became engrossed with the massive herds of buffalo in west Kansas. He and a wealthy English gentleman, a man by the name of Henry Willoughby, who came to America searching out opportunities for a group of wealthy investors from Berkshire, England, somehow partnered up in Dodge City. Willoughby was overly impressed with the gigantic beasts, both in the size of the animals and the colossal numbers. The two newly acquainted associates, at the decisive determination of Willoughby, decided to temporarily forego California and reap the prosperous rewards of the buffalo.

Pug related the story in such a manner that it fully engulfed the Longleys, it being far beyond anything they'd seen or even heard of in the Texas panhandle.

"Well," Pug drawled, "the Willoughby fellow didn't hardly live long enough to see the finish of this place being built. He was killed, trampled by a herd." Uncle Pug relit his pipe and blew smoke through his whiskers, slowly settled back and went on, "My brother tried to reach Willoughby's family back in England, tried several times. But no one ever answered back. He just eventually reckoned them rich fellas back there went on and found another man to do their investment work for them."

"There was many years that men hunted buffalo for sport; but a time came that somebody back east started making hats, coats, and the like outta them hides." Pug shook his head, "That was when the sport aspect ended and money took to rulin' the kill, the massacre, ya might say. The hunters realized they didn't have to chase the creatures on horseback. They found out if they'd sit and not move, the ignorant animals wouldn't run or shy away even if one was killed standing almost next to him. After that it was killing just for the almighty dollar, no longer a hunt."

The old Tatum gentleman told stories for over two hours, jumping from Joplin, through Indian Territory, Wichita, and then back to the

Missouri Ozarks. He liked telling them, and his fashion of storytelling had a way of making one's mind wander into it like seeing the events take place as you looked on, feeling you were there.

Following a brief pause to the recollections, Uncle Pug stared down, his gaze seemingly locked on the floor; he stroked his beard methodically, and then said wearily, "The fire!"

The words had little effect at first; but then both Magdalena and Muley casted deep, wondering eyes on the old man. He didn't look up, didn't see the sorrowful flush come to Magdalena's cheeks. He went on to remember the terrible wind and lightening; recalled the trees bending and creaking, the roof stress-growling, the windows whistling, the wind invading the little log house. "Even the flames in the rock fireplace felt the wind, bent and licked at the dark hollow up in the chimney," Pug related, his eyes fixed on the floor, his pipe providing recurring pause.

Magdalena cast bleak eyes on Uncle Pug in a gesture that could have been considered a plea, a trivial appeal to end the story, but yet she was caught up in the profound drawl of the words coming from the man. She said nothing.

Pete and Jesse felt as if they had intruded, become involved in a family secret that wasn't intended to fall on the ears of outsiders, but resistance was turned back. They waited for the ominous tone of the man's voice to go on.

He told of the lightning, "Two strikes, the likes I'd never seen as a matter of fact, it was as if God Himself chose to punish the Tatum family, puttin' the lot of us inta the throes of hell itself." He looked up, into the faces of the four people sitting close, "The wrath of The Lord struck us," head lowered, he whispered softly, "we didn't know why, don't know to this day."

He then sat up, becoming near rigid. His face darkened and came placid, "I was able to wrestle my family outside, grabbed all the bedclothes I could gather in my two arms, wrapped the two children in 'em." His eyes gazed cast-iron-hard to the bleak empty corner of the room in a pinch of silence. And then, with a stroke of his streaked, wintry whiskers, he drawled on, "Me and Magdalena, along with the kids, struggled against the wind and found shelter in the smokehouse shed down the path behind the burning cabin." He clicked the pipe stem gently on his lower teeth, as he thought through with another hesitation. "No one was able to escape the other cabin, my brother, his wife, and two boys, we thought that to be the case." He looked up and raised his brow, "The rock-stacked chimney was blasted by the monster lightning bolt and the big stones flew crazy-like, like they was mere pebbles, crashed down through the thatched roof and spread fire straight away everywhere in the cabin." Pug rolled his eyes under his white-brow, gruffed his throat and went on, "I ran around the burning cabin, tryin' to find somewhere void of fire, somewhere a body could get through, and maybe save someone." He quietly twisted his lips and rationalized how he found a place, and a boy. "The youngest of the family, came crawling out, it was Muley here." The old man grinned out of the side of his mouth and winked at Muley before he limply continued. "His hair was smokin', hands and arms blackened, and sparks of fire burned holes in his night clothes. It was like he was a remnant of hell." Another smile found the old man's face whiskers, "Stubborn as a mule he was . . . still is, it got him outta that hell-fired cabin that night it did."

Magdelena stood, and with a sheepish grin exposing modest gladness she said, "He always missed his mother after that, took a big piece of his heart away, losing his ma; it left him with a tenderness toward all women, it did." Magdalena grinned brightly and persuasively at Muley, swung her arms wide, the palms of her hands open, and in a frail, approaching sob said, "That's all, more stories tomorrow, it's late, way past bedtime."

Muley walked over to his uncle, bent and hugged him about the shoulders, "God bless you, Uncle Pug, you old jackass your own self; been a long time since I'd heard that story." He grinned, this time awkwardly,

“Thanks for all you’ve done for me.” He then turned, kissed Magdalena on the cheek and sighed, “Good night, we’ll see you in the morning.” He squeezed her hand, “I look forward to one of them big breakfasts you cook up so almighty good.”

CHAPTER EIGHT

Pete awoke drowsily, blinked in woozy reflex, wondering if he'd heard a commotion outside. *'Must be two or three o'clock,' h*e thought when he rolled over, knuckled his gritty eyes and looked through the window near his bed. A horse whinnied! It happened again. *'A posse?'* An uncomfortable sensation rose in his stomach.

He threw his legs over the side of the bed, felt for his pants and boots, quietly stepped into both as he buckled his gun belt and tip-toed cat-like to the window. Nothing came into view that would resemble the worst of his thoughts—a posse. The moon allowed dark shadows to fall from the big trees, changing value as they swayed, making it difficult to distinguish any movement. He could see nothing, no activity to indicate alarm.

Brother Jesse and Muley were in their beds; the sounds he recognized as Jesse's usual soft snoring assured that he was sleeping soundly. *'It wouldn't be proper to peek behind the blanket curtain where Pug and Magdalena slept, I'll not do that.'* Standing rocklike, careful not to make a move that could influence his judgment, he gazed longingly through the window and studied the shadowed areas, the barn and outbuildings, for a few seconds. Another whinny from the horses in the barn, two horses this time, made the decision for him, he'd step outside and maybe slip over to the barn.

The door pushed well back and a loud squeak announced its opening, a sound he didn't recall from the four times he'd walked through it earlier. He held the clasp and pulled easily to half shut it behind him . . . There! A man ran from the barn.

"You! Stop!" Pete shouted, drew the six-gun and cocked back the hammer, but held it, questioning, not sure if he should fire. The dark figure quickly moved to the steps affronting the soddy, stopped and stood there looking back at Pete. *'The man Muley had described as being a man in description but a boy in mind,'* Pete thought.

Noises erupted from the lodge. Muley hastened to the door, half hopping as he tugged at his pants, gun in hand. In the night air he leaned over Pete's shoulder and mumbled, "What the hell's goin' on?"

Pete pointed to the human shape and the sod house. "That man there, he ran from inside the barn when I stepped outside."

Just then the dark figure disappeared into the low-roofed prairie house and pulled the door shut behind him.

"Haha, ha," Muley laughed, "That's Fritz, the growed son of the man and woman that lives there. They work for Pug and Mag; he ain't no threat, just out doin' some of the crazy-ass things he does."

The thump of Uncle Pug's cane striking the floor intermittingly emerged. Muley turned toward the sound, stepped through the door and raucously proclaimed, "Just Fritz out runnin' in the middle of the night again, go back to bed, ain't nothing!"

Pete drew a deep breath, "Glad I didn't shoot." He dropped the gun into the leather and went back inside the lodge. He slid a consoled glimpse at Jesse and spoke in a whisper, "I thought maybe a posse had caught up with us."

* * *

"Rad, I'm going to wait until after the trial of this Patch Gillis fella tomorrow before I swear you in as a U. S. Marshal; that'd make sure your testimony comes from the marshal of Spickard, not a territorial lawman," Judge Wilkinson said light-heartedly as he pulled the mayor's door shut behind them.

"You know I'm disappointed that I have to move over to Dodge City, don't you?"

"Well, Rad, that was Governor St. John's doing. That town has settled some, but still has a lot of danger to be weeded out before it can be safe for the citizens. You're needed over there more than here in Spickard." The Judge rattled on, "The Earps and Mastersons, along with their sidekicks they deputized, weren't anything more than vigilantes, a crooked gang with badges. Getting rid of them took some doing by St. John, he planted the need for them boys to find another hell needin' a lid . . . told 'em if they didn't, he'd find a way to either lock 'em up or hang 'em." Wilkinson's eyes hardened and a quiver to his lip made the fluffy white mustache wiggle before he continued, "If they'd been in Dodge any longer the town would have been set back to a time before the cattle business grew it to a proper size. Their law work made 'em a lot of money—can't say anything good about what they did for the town except make it known to the common folks back east." He drew a shallow breath, "It'll take time to rectify the obliteration."

Carson let the judge's words hang in the air a time before he responded, "There'll still be town marshals in Dodge, not just me, right Judge?"

"Oh yes, marshals and George Hinkle, the Ford County Sheriff, will continue to hold office, you won't be alone in keeping order, not by a long shot. Your assignment is to take charge." The judge lifted his brow, "No easy chore, Rad, and you'll have to figure out for yourself just how."

"No help from you or Governor St. John?"

"The letter will go out. Both St. John and myself are sending official notice to Hinkle and the town marshals, but you know how that is," he took in long breath, "what's written, even official business doesn't make a mind-set in most men; the work you'll have to do is show them all in your own way, you're the lawman in charge."

Rad gave a slight *'humph'*, a notion of understanding, not necessarily a message of satisfaction. "I hope your letters have a better way of communicating my position to those lawmen than I can muster in my mind right now."

"Your job is a tough one, Carson. We looked a long time for the man to fill the position." He clinched his lips and slowly nodded several times before saying, "But I'm sure we found the right man." Wilkinson's eyes near sparkled as he invoked a contented grin.

Rad bobbed his chin in agreement. His sturdy disposition and strength of character came to the front, even though he did it with a hint of humility, "I suppose everything's in place. I'm set to be there in six days, and the council in Spickard has approved Travis to take over her . . . course I'll look in on him time to time."

The next time Judge Wilkinson and Carson met, six men entered the courtroom and orderly took the prearranged seats. One of them rose and handed the judge a neatly folded paper. The Judge unfolded and silently read it, lifted his eyes and looked about the surrogate courtroom, glared at Patch Gillis and pounded the gavel to the table top. "Vernon Patch Gillis, the jury has found you guilty of the charges brought against you. Therefore I hereby sentence you to the Kansas State Prison in Lansing, where you will spend the next seven years of your life." He twisted his mustached lip, blinked, and continued, "May God be with you in the aspiration that you will see the error or your ways and by the time you leave that institution, Mr. Gillis, you will have become a changed man," Wilkinson waved his gavel at the prisoner, "a man that will return to society to become a favorable citizen of the fine state of Kansas." He jerked his head in an affirmative nod and slammed the gavel to the table, "This court is adjourned."

The room buzzed with light commotion. The faces of the Courtney ranch hands were hard and braced with questionable frowns. They'd anticipated Gillis would get more jail time. Talk among them centered on ten to fifteen years. But it was done, leaving Mrs. Courtney and Jenny in sobbing remission; for them it wasn't the sentence of seven years, it was the ceaseless agony in the loss of Mr. Courtney.

Once Patch Gillis had been taken away, the judge pounded the gavel once more to gain attention. He moved from behind the table and boisterously started, "For you folks that may not know, your good marshal, Rad Carson, has been appointed a United States Marshal. He's been designated to serve the United States of America and the state of Kansas from Ford County. And I'll swear him in to serve in that capacity here and now. For any of you that would like to remain and view such honor on behalf of Marshal Carson, I ask that you please stand quiet as I do so."

The following morning U. S. Marshal Carson left Mrs. Pennington's boarding house, the pack horse and saddlebags packed with his belongings. He had pictures of a few of his relatives, two of his grandfather, Christopher Carson; one an illustration of him as a young trail guide, and the other when he was commissioned a U. S. Cavalry Brigadier General in 1865, three years before his death. He had also, a few changes of clothing, an extra saddle, ten guns he'd collected over the years and a couple dozen books, some of which were law books he'd purchased from the county. He considered them beneficial in his capacity as a lawman; they rounded out his personal worth.

It had rained lightly an hour before Rad rode into Dodge City. The town was quiet as the community remained subdued from the downcast weather. He walked the horses down Division Street, a street defined primarily by the saloons, the enterprises in town that boasted numerous customers. The boardwalks were thinly occupied. The street, sticky with mud, was sparingly being used other than barroom customers crossing irrationally. A scruffily attired man, outfitted in a soiled derby hat and a dull coat buttoned high on the chest and hanging open otherwise, stood smoking his pipe as he leaned against a façade post. He looked up at Carson and raised his pipe in friendly salute. *'Wonder if he knows of the Satterfield Boarding House?'* Rad reined in toward the man and asked.

"Yep, go right ahead as your goin' on this street until you come to Hickory, you'll see a sign at the corner; turn left there and you'll find the Satterfield's place a few doors up."

"Much obliged."

Judge Wilkinson had recommended Satterfield's, said it was extra clean, had good accommodations for horses, and most importantly, the best food in Dodge City. And, as if that wasn't enough, they gave lawmen a discount and was it in easy walking distance from the law office that had been arranged for him.

CHAPTER NINE

Uncle Pug was up at first light. He drew lightly on his pipe and squinted through the grainy light of the morning. He watched men in the distance; studied them as they stood down to allow their horses to drink from the creek. Their casual, unhurried movements exposed no effort toward secrecy, which lead the old man to believe them harmless, undoubtedly not lawmen. He went inside.

Pug stuck the tip of his cane in Muley's ribs, "Get up, son. There's four men down by the creek!"

The outlaw nephew rolled onto his back and drew a hand across his brow, dropped the hand and assessed Pug's face before he drawled, "You don't seem worried none."

"Seem friendly . . . just thought you'd like to know."

"Yea, thanks." The words spat from his mouth like he'd taken a bite from a tart apple. He rolled out of bed, stepped into his pants, shuffled to the open door and looked out. The strangers were still standing down, one between horses and watching as they muzzled the stream. The other three men drew into a knot and had their faces drawn toward the house. They wore a conglomerate of clothing, from range duds to most everything else; no uniformity, except that each of them appeared well armed, not the type of men anyone could mistake for cowpunchers.

The Longley brothers pulled on their shirts and inquisitively gathered behind Muley, waiting to hear anything he might say. Without cutting focus from outside, he put an arm back and calmly ordered, "Get me my boots and them magnifiers."

Pug lifted the long glasses from the cabinet and placed them in Pete's waiting hand. Pete handed the glasses to Muley over his shoulder, his attention hard fixed to the men at the creek.

Muley adjusted the glasses, studied for a few seconds and spoke softly, "That looks like Buzz Lathrop and Charlie Joe!" He lowered the magnifiers and turned to tell Pug, "You remember Buzz; he's the one that beat the hell outta Fritz a couple years ago!" He turned back to the lenses, "Don't think I know the other two, but if they're with Injun Charlie Joe, they's okay."

The four men mounted, left the creek and walked their horses up the slope. Lathrop hefted his hat and waved it, the same signal used by Muley when he and the Longelys had approached the lodge two days earlier. One of the men with him was a mustached Mexican. Hair curled from under his dirty dark sombrero; leather chaps with lengthy fringe jiggled with each step of his pinto. Another man, Muley didn't recognize, was taller than most, on the chunky side too. Muley thought he looked like a saloon piano player; he wore a dusty derby hat, a ragged deep gray coat buttoned at the middle and topped by a shabby short fur vest; he chewed a fat cigar.

Magdalena watched and listened from near the flat top stove. The coffee had been boiling four to five minutes. She took down tin cups and placed them on the stove top.

"Let's take the coffee outside, Ma," Uncle Pug said. "Them boys look like they should have been in the creek for a spell before they came up here." He sniffed for effect.

Muley stepped outside; Pete and Jess right behind, and Pug close after them. "Howdy." The man named Charlie Joe called out as they drew close and he placed his dusty hat back on his head atop a lengthy braid of hair. "Good to see y'all again." His smile sold the words.

Muley recalled some boys of the old group ribbed Charlie Joe, calling him half-breed, which he continued to brush aside, denying it, but he'd always touted a long, single braid of harsh, black hair at the back of his head, giving credence to the Indian tag.

"What the hell you doin', Charlie . . . you done spent all that money have ya?" Muley yelled back over a chuckle. "Or did ya take a squaw woman and she wooed ya out of it?"

"Been clear to Santa Fe by way of Pueblo, Colorado." He fingered a thin ebony mustache and laughed. "Them folks down there didn't take to us like the good people of Kansas," he laughed again. Charlie and Buzz swung down light-hearted-like but the other two waited in the saddle; seemed they were waiting for a sign of approval, or a welcome.

"Come and sit," said Muley, "we got hot coffee, if ya think ya can handle something that don't have no kick-ass in it." He chuckled slightly, turned and touched the Longley brothers on their shoulders, "This here's Pete and Jesse, friends of mine up from Texas." He hesitated, waiting, giving definitive attention to the others, strangers to him, waiting for Charlie Joe to give names to the two men he didn't know.

"Oh . . . Oh," He responded with his head bobbing, "Yea, this here cigar smoker is Bo Cantrell. And that there," he pointed, "ornery Mex is Miguel Avino. They're friends from . . . well, Bo from Colorado and Miguel from Santa Fe. Say hi, boys."

Muley spoke back, "You remember Uncle Pug and Magdalena don't ya', Charlie?" He turned to Buzz, "And you too, Buzz."

That renewed introduction of Buzz to Pug and Magdalena caught only a bitter frown from the old folks. The Longleys gave simple *howdy nods*, not sure what to do having observed the response for Buzz from Muley's aunt Magdelena and uncle Pug.

The usual cheery face Magdalena exhibited was absent as she crowded all of the cups on three fingers and with the apron covered other hand she moved among the men and poured steaming hot coffee. Her solemn expression was that of a priest. Her eyes flashed an upward, bitter blink when she came to Buzz, which he failed to notice.

"We'll leave you younger folks to your doins'." Uncle Pug reacted to Magdalena's irritation, pulled the door back and allowed that she step through in front of him. "We'll put more coffee on to boil."

Once inside and away from the door, Magdalena's lips thinned and her eyes grew taunt, "Why did *he* come back . . . that Buzz?"

"He ain't stayin'," Pug answered, "just passin through." He bent, leaned on his cane and looked through the window, "And if that ain't the case, I'll put a bug in Muley's ear to keep him outside—don't want him sleeping in the house, don't want no more of his money either."

When Charlie Joe and Buzz landed with Muley two years ago, each of them presented Magdalena with twenty dollar gold pieces. That was before the conflict.

Twenty minutes passed. The old folks kept a wary eye glancing through the window as the morning sun bloomed large over the horizon and short spells of quiet from outside were broken with laughter. "I guess maybe they got stories needin' told," Pug spoke to Magdelena, the white whiskers camouflaging his mouth moved lightly. She felt his words reflected an anxiety, perhaps a tinge of jealousy.

The seven men rose in a manner befitting a jury, sat their cups on the porch, brushed dust from their backsides and slowly strung out. Muley waved over a shoulder, "We're going to the creek."

"I guess they figure on scraping off some saucy smells." Pug turned to Magdalena as he said it. "They can shore use it, them four must'a come clear from Santa Fe staying clear of water." Pug waited, continuing to watch through the wavy glass, "Hope that Buzz fella don't think smelling better will get him a place at the table in here, cause it won't."

The sun was well positioned in a blue morning sky by the time the bizarre cluster of men made their way up the grassy slope. They made way toward the lodge with a slow walk, intermittent laughter punctuating their progress. Uncle Pug had a hand resting on the window sill as he glared out, "Looks like them boys from Santa Fe even washed shirts, they look as if they ain't yet fully dried."

Magdalena gathered a pan of biscuits and another of hog back and beans as she started toward the door, "Bring them plates and coffee, Pug, let's get these vittles out to the porch before them boys all get an idea to come inside."

A rifle shot blasted the stillness. The world halted!

Buzz Lathrop's feet kicked up, arms flailed, and his hat flew. He jerked to the ground as a horrid moan flushed from his lips. A deep red blemish blossomed on his shirt and rapidly grew in the center of his chest. A leg thrashed but twice and death quieted him. Horses tied out front of the lodge bolted, startled by the sudden eruption in the morning hush. One broke loose and pranced away impulsively, its head swaying in whimsical distortion.

"Up there," Pete Longley shouted, pointing to the figure of a man behind a haze of gray smoke well up amidst limbs of one of the large trees alongside the lodge building.

Bo Cantrell hastily stood over Buzz and inspected the wound in the center of his chest. Blood had stopped pumping and a miniature puff of smoke lifted through the hole in the shirt. His eyes were fixed, gapped wide. A gathering of dense blood escaped from the corner of his lips. Bo yelled, "You rotten, lame-brained" . . . drew his revolver, twisted, located his target, and fired at the shadowed object in the tree.

Muley threw his hands in the air toward Bo and screamed, "Stop!" Charlie Joe, along with Muley, had already comprehended what had happened. The Longleys, Cantrell, and Avino were spellbound, numb to both the shooting and Muley's irrational action to halt any adversarial response.

A small-framed, sloppy, half-dressed man with long unruly hair jumped from the tree branches, rifle in hand. He raced behind the lodge. "Damn!" Muley yelled, "That crazy bastard, Fritz! He shot Buzz."

"Are ya going after him, Tatum?" Charlie Joe shouted, "Ya ain't gonna let him get away with this, are ya?" He stood tall in front of Muley, a confrontational challenge.

A wide grin developed on Muley's face. "What goes around comes around!" He answered Charlie Joe's demand, looked hard at Charlie with metal in his eyes and a grin set in his lips. "He shouldn't have kept kickin' the dumb ass when he already had him bested last time they was here at Uncle Pug's. You remember that don't you, Charlie?"

Bo Cantrell started, hand on his revolver, toward where Fritz rounded the corner of the lodge. He'd heard the exchange between Charlie Joe and Muley, but couldn't comprehend the full meaning behind it. As he neared the lodge steps, Uncle Pug threw down on him with a double barrel shotgun, "Stop right there, mister. Ain't no need to get another man killed here today, and likely it'd be you. Back off!"

"Don't shoot him, Pug. He's got no idea." Muley yelled.

"I'll not shoot if he backs down; otherwise I got no choice."

"Let's everbody simmer down". Muley took charge. His voice held a new authority that surprised Pete and Jess. The Mexican, Miguel, moved his black eyes from man to man anxiously. He'd not said more than a dozen words, all in broken English, since he'd arrived. Jesse had doubted that the man understood all that had been spoken, and as so, *'this ordeal must be more confusing to him than to anyone else.'* Miguel looked to Charlie Joe, ready to follow whatever his lead would be.

It didn't take long. Muley pulled everyone together. His strong reaction held store.

He told of coming to the lodge two years ago, he, Charlie Joe and Buzz Lathrop. They'd been up to Great Bend and needed a few days out of the sight of law people. Fritz had started trouble; went to the barn when no one was around, saddled Buzz Lathrop's horse and rode out. When Buzz caught him, he whipped him good; first with a quirt and then kicked the simple minded man for a period of time, broke his nose, and a couple ribs. Before Fitz healed, the three men rode off. And finally Muley told that the woman in the sod house, Fritz's mother, was Aunt Magdalena's sister, which made Fritz Muley's cousin. He couldn't let anyone kill him. And never again would he let anyone beat him as Buzz did.

"So there, the story's out, I've got a family member who's as loco as a bear eatin' soured persimmons." Muley grinned and added, "I guess every family has someone who has a dead squirrel in the attic . . . lucky for the Tatum family, they also got me to balance out." He laughed.

CHAPTER TEN

The next morning five men idly sat their saddles out front of the Tatum lodge. They awaited Muley. Pug watched from the porch, seated in the wicker rocking chair, his cane across his lap and pipe busied. He flicked the pipe stem at Jess who was rolling a cigarette, "Jess, next time I see you, I want to see a pipe, 'stead of them papers." His head bobbed.

"Guess we'll have to see, Uncle Pug, maybe I'll get myself a cane too." He grinned. Pug flexed the whiskers all about his mouth, an old man's refusal to grin back.

Charlie Joe pushed against his stirrups and leaned forward, "Today, Muley? We goin' today or you got some nurse-maidin' to do?" He turned to Miguel and twice threw a thumb to the Mexican and then back to himself. "You stay with me." Miguel nodded in response.

The lodge door swung open. "Thank you again, Muley." Magdalena was holding his hand between both of hers, her cheeks rounded, lips thinned and her eyes slowly blinked in a swell of affection she held for the man. "I am sorry for the man who was shot. I could not like the man, but for you I am sorry because he was your friend."

"It's okay Aunt Mag, he shouldn't have done what he did to Fritz; he just paid for it, that's all." Muley stepped away, looked over his shoulder to the door, "They're waiting for me, I've got to go, got to get Charlie out of here, he's still thinkin' about Buzz. He might do something really stupid, and if he did we'd have another grave to dig."

Muley stepped up into the silver trimmed saddle. He swung the black mare around and twisted, "So long, Pug. Thanks again for everything." He heeled the black and the six riders rode from the Tatum lands in a temperate gallop, heading for the North Canadian in Oklahoma Territory. Always ready with a cutting remark, Muley sung out, "Hold onto that hat, Cantrell, we may get somewhere where you can play a piano before the sun goes down tonight." He laughed.

Bo Cantrell's forehead bunched into lines and his brows hovered low over puzzled eyes. He yanked the cigar stub from his mouth and threw it to the ground angrily, yelled to Charlie and Miguel, "What the hell did he mean by that?" The Mexican shrugged his shoulders and pulled his chin strap tight. Pete and Jesse had become accustom to Muley's nonsense. They knew, and realized Cantrell was baffled. Muley made the remark to please himself. He cared not if Cantrell comprehended.

* * *

Rad Carson's Dodge City office was in the town center, a few short blocks from Satterfield's. He unlocked the door and stepped inside. It was a considerable improvement over the minimal resources of the Spickard jail house. A large oak desk sat centered in the room atop an ample square of pleasant maroon and sea green carpet. Behind it was a tufted brown leather chair affronting well stocked book shelves which, along with other handsomely bound editions, displayed more than a few law books. Some were identified as "*Laws of Kansas*", all of which were more current than those he'd purchased three years previous when he took the town marshal job in Spickard. Others were *Ordinances And Guidelines For United States Marshals.* Still others were specific legal renderings in Kansas and also listed the names of all judges in the state. Another set of two books dealt with laws, rules, and most every possible topic dealing with livestock, including buying, selling, branding, etc. There were also literary classics having nothing to do with law: *Moby Dick, Gulliver's Travels, Joan of Arc, The Oregon Trail, Rip Van Winkle, Lorna Doone, The Deer Slayer,* and the book that captured his attention, he searched no further once he held *Kit Carson,* by John S. C. Abbott.

A shining new coffee pot set atop the black pot-bellied stove trimmed in the same metal as the coffee pot. Under it was a note, '*Congratulations, U. S. Marshal, Rad Carson, please enjoy the coffee. It may be the most enjoyable part of your new job!'* It was signed, Judge Nathaniel Wilkinson. The note brought a smile as Rad looked about for a water supply.

His search was pleasantly interrupted. The office door swung open with an irritable squeak. A delightfully jovial, warm and very feminine voice rang out, "Hello, Marshal, welcome to Dodge City". Her eyes were bright, every bit as blue as the powder-fresh dress she wore so smartly. "I'm Fanny Cartwright, owner of the café across the street, *Fanny's Fancy Food*." She swayed her body and tilted her head.

"Well, thank you Ms Fanny." He was taken-back by the pristine, overtly attractive lady. The pause in his response, along with a slight blush of a man who'd just been enthralled by a lovely young woman, revealed such. He drew his hat from his head, "I appreciate that." He instinctively looked past her, wishing to monitor the eagerness that came over him. He glanced through the front window and made note of her business establishment. Pushing for a distinct voice, he said, "I feel sure I'll be seeing a good deal of you since I plan to be taking my meals out." He lifted a thumb indicating the direction of the boarding house, "I've got a room over at the Satterfield's." He caught himself . . . he was about to say he'd heard they had the best food in Dodge City, "But I'm sure I'll be taking food at your café often."

Fanny smiled; her lips drew one's attention when she spoke. They were perfect. "I'd be pleased to be the provider of food for any prisoners also, when you have some." She knew the only lock-up was a pair of holding cells, nothing meant for long term detention. A light chuckle exposed rosy cheeks and eyes replicating the sky on a bright spring day. "Well, you haven't told me your name, Marshal. Or do you want me to address you in such a manner, Marshal?" She said it in teasing, a chastising tone soft, and fresh as morning dew on a clover meadow.

"Oh!" Rad shifted, knowing his face must have reddened, "I'm sorry, pardon my bad manners, my name is Carson, Rad Carson. Please just call me Rad, since we're neighbors." He'd not felt this awkward since attending a dance in Spickard when a young lady asked him to dance.

"Thank you, Rad," she drew his name out with a pleasing smile. "I'll look for you over to my place . . . for coffee, perhaps?" She raised her brow very delightfully, a banter criticism of the fact he awkwardly held the coffee pot in his hand.

He was bested. "I'm sorry. I just got here and have to get things lined out . . . don't know where anything is." He lifted the coffee pot a few inches higher, "Including the water supply and stove wood. I think I'd better stay here and find myself, but thanks anyway, maybe later."

Fanny waltzed to the door, smiled, said a spirited good-by and shuffled away. However, her exit left a pleasing fragrance in the room, one that enticed Rad to watch as she tottered across the street. His lips twitched upward in a simple sustaining smile.

Carson held the fresh-brewed cup of coffee when George T. Hinkle, the Ford County sheriff, stepped through the door. He squeezed the brim of his neat tan Stetson and began his introduction by asking, "Rad Carson?"

"That'd be me."

"I'm Sheriff Hinkle." He pulled the vest back to expose a polished brass shield with the words *'Ford County Sheriff'* heavily embossed over an image outline of Ford County. "Glad to have you in town, Marshal." The smile under a heavy mustache was tepid. His face showed a presence common to the sun, and eyes that were darker blue than cavalry uniforms. He wore his gun belt high at his side and his choice of weapon was a Remington, scrolled-silver plated and a walnut grip. "Judge Wilkinson has told me some admirable things about you. According to him you've got more nerve than a man walking through a bed of diamondback rattlers with his boots off." His lips curled to push the mustache into a different configuration, near a smirk.

Rad stepped to shake hands with Hinkle, "Well, the Judge is a highly principled man, we both know, but he's also a man ready to give credits maybe a little heftier than what's been earned." He thought Hinkle to be around twenty years older than he, a bit shorter, but shoulders that threatened a door's width. He also noted the man had hands nearly big enough to grip a water bucket by the side.

"Wilkinson says Kit Carson was your grandpa, that right?"

"Yes sir. Now that's something I'm right proud of, also gives me something to live up to." Rather than talk more about the pride he had in holding the family name, he changed the subject, "How about some coffee, Sheriff? I just made some fresh." He held the pot aloft in offering.

Carson poured dark, steaming coffee into a white mug that was almost lost in the hand that held it, "You're walking on some pretty sacred lawman-grounds around here, Sheriff; do the cow hands drifting in and out of Dodge, looking to build a reputation, ever try to call you out?"

Hinkle poured sugar into his cup and stirred, "Fact is, I get the feeling they carry respect for my badge. Respect built by the men who wore it before me; makes my job easier sometimes."

Carson's mind drifted to the exploits characterized by the gang of men that wore badges in Dodge City and rammed their hard-line vigilante systems down the throats of most anyone they chose to be classified as outlaw or troublemaker. About the only difference between the lawmen and the law-breakers was who had a badge and controlled the keys to the jail.

Sheriff Hinkle lifted his chin and twisted his head slightly, giving thought to the statement he'd made, "But ya know this area has matured a mite, become more domesticated." Hinkle seemed to have something on his mind, not full at ease as he as he kept the conversation going. "Of course the town swelled with Texas cows when the quarantine was put in place up in Ellsworth and Great Bend. We still get hard case wranglers but the number of raw-boned gun slingers is fewer than used to be. We get some but they don't come in droves no more." He looked down at the coffee cup tentatively. "That don't mean this job is easy, never will be. We have the gamblers, thieves and whores that are magnets for more of their kind to size up and rub elbows, if ya know what I mean." He took a measured sip from the cup, looked up again and said, "That brings us to this, Carson, we're going to be working some of the same territory, and I'll respect your authority . . . and ask that you do the same. There ain't no fence between us so's it'll be up to you and me."

Rad didn't know just how to take that remark. He nodded, giving consideration before he'd answer. "Well, I'm not here to . . . ," he hesitated, "don't think the Judge or the Governor had in mind for me to disregard you, no sir, not for a minute. I'm thinking you and me can get along fine. My job is going to take me beyond the town and county jurisdiction more likely than not in many cases, but when I'm available I'll be of help, no hindrance, I assure you."

Hinkle's dark eyes looked deep into Carson's. He liked what he saw, his face relaxed and he drank, took three long swallows and finished the coffee. "I like you Rad Carson. Glad to have you in Dodge City."

Carson watched as the sheriff crossed the street and went into Fanny's café. His thoughts worked through a brief hesitation, *'Strange sort of introduction . . . hope the man knows his limits and don't come barkin' up my tree at the wrong time.'*

Rad left the office and began his walk toward Satterfield's. There was sign of dust low in the southern horizon; a cattle herd was a few miles in the distance. They'd be close tomorrow. Wranglers would be riding into town tomorrow night, anxious to see something more pleasing than a cow's backside. They'd have money when the trail boss would meet with his prearranged buyer and cash would change hands. Rad figured to have dinner at Fanny's tomorrow evening, to be near where trouble was to be.

CHAPTER ELEVEN

It started raining well before dawn. Heavy drops thudded against the building, pushed by a strong wind from the southwest that rattled the branches on the two large trees outside of Carson's bedroom. He rolled to a comfortable position and watched the shadows sway and twitch on the wall opposite the double window. Lightning flooded the room and erased the dark, sporadic figures from their wall-dance, giving depth to the fixtures inside the room. He listened, counting the seconds before the boom of thunder, setting distance from the lightning strike.

A rapid knock on the door was accompanied by a guarded, but fretful, baritone voice, "Marshal Carson, someone's at the front door asking for you." Mr. Satterfield beckoned.

"Okay, okay, I'll be right there." Carson jumped to his feet tugging at the shirt and canvas pants he'd laid over a chair near the bed last evening. His pants were snapped into place and one hand pushed the shirt tail in when he opened the door.

"There's a man in the front foyer that says a couple of cowpunchers have been shot down at the King's Folly Saloon." Satterfield carefully held his tone, not to awaken other guests.

Rad Carson, turned back to his room, slipped on a leather vest and stepped into his boots. He slapped his gun belt in place and lifted his hat from the dresser top; all in one continuous motion. He spun the cylinder on the Peacemaker and smoothly dropped it back into the holster atop his thigh as he came to the foyer where he gave the gray haired gentleman a once-over. The man tugged at his hat in his hands and tensely related, "I think one man was killed . . . the other's gut-shot!"

"Friends of yours?" Rad asked. He then thought about the herd of cattle distant to Dodge. It could be cowboys had ridden in from that outfit; might be some of them.

"Nope, they's just kids what drank more than they could handle, and it got 'em shot to hell for most no reason a'tall."

"What about the shooters, they still in the saloon?"

"Just one man, but he looks like a gol'dang killer what's set out to build a reputation." The gangly middle aged man was uneasily calm in his recollection. Carson gave credence to the man's words.

"Let's get over there." He pushed open the door for the man to lead the way. The two of them pulled coat collars tight and ducked their heads into the wind.

King's Folly was one of three salons on Beeson Street with light. Rad fingered the Colt as he looked over the batwings. A dozen men mingled on the boards outside, close to the building, guarding against the elements. The bartender, his arms folded, stood erect behind the bar. A trace of fear pasted in deep set eyes and face frozen around a dark handlebar mustache and three or four days of unattended chin whiskers. "That's him." Tom Flournoy, the man who'd summoned Rad Carson, focused his eyes on a young man dressed in black, except the white silk shirt, a slick vest, trousers, boots and hat, all to match. And two guns tucked loosely in black, tied down holsters.

"I see what you mean, the man's a gun-slick-signboard," Carson spoke quietly as he removed the coat and dropped it to the boardwalk. The *signboard* was very young; Carson figured him to be eighteen or nineteen. And the clothes hadn't been out of store wrappings more than a few days.

Rad pushed through the doors, his eyes dark and his face as solid as granite as he walked toward the gun-slick. "You shoot these kids?" Rad asked with a slight flick of his head indicating the two lying in sawdust.

The shooter saw the law badge. He glanced at the cowpunchers. Rad could see questions build in his expression. He turned back toward Carson, attempting a fearless sneer, "They asked for it, I'd say it was self defense."

"They was drunker than a by-God, wasn't they?" Carson rebuked.

The young shooter hesitated slightly, "I don't know about that!"

Rad's upper lip curled and nostrils widened, "I damn sure do, you oughta be ashamed. Neither of them emptied a holster."

The gunny's shoulders rolled and his eyes flicked toward the men outside looking over the pair of low-hung doors. "They asked fo . . . ," He didn't finish. Carson's revolver crushed the new black hat and the *signboard* melted like hot mush poured from a pan.

"My God, Almighty," the bartender blinked and slumped his shoulders; his lower lip dropped to his chin. "Thanks, mister . . . errr, Marshal"

"Somebody get the doctor," Rad instructed. He pointed, "That boy there is still alive." He asked the barkeep, "You got any rope or wire, behind your bar? I didn't bring my wrist chains."

The following morning Sheriff Hinkle found Rad at Fanny's Fancy Food, sitting over a stack of hotcakes and black coffee. "I guess I have to say thanks again, Carson. I didn't think much about that Duffy boy you put in the city jail last night, not until this morning, when Flournoy and a couple of the others that were at King's told me the full story. I guess maybe Judge Wilkinson's description of you and them rattlesnakes is pretty much right." Hinkle grinned and offered a big hand.

Rad accepted the apologetic handshake, "You say the boy's name is Duffy?"

"Yep, Alonzo Duffy. Far's we can tell he came to Dodge just four days ago. Seems he's been reading stories in them back-east papers; started workin' on a fast draw and figured on makin' a name. I suppose now he'll have plenty time to rethink his future while he leans and looks through jail bars."

"Can't say as I blame him for wanting to make a name, the one he's got ain't much." Rad sipped his coffee, "Too bad these kids get big ideas from those papers. The people that write those stories make gun-slick idiots look like big-time heroes and celebrities. I hope that sort of journalism gets straight before this country gets too far out of kilter."

"Oh, and by the way, Carson, that boy that was shot, he's doin' okay. Doc Hink says he'll pull through; course the other one, he's done gone to be with the Maker. We'll put him up on Boot Hill later today or maybe tomorrow."

Marshal Carson finished the hotcakes and lingered over an extra cup of hot coffee. He looked up to see Fanny coming toward him. He had to smile as he remembered their first meeting at his office, but he also felt a soothing as he caught another fragrant scent of the toilet water she wore so pleasingly. "Good morning Miss Fanny, won't you join me for a minute," he glanced about the room, "looks like things have slowed a bit."

"Good morning to you, Rad." She spoke his name with extra emphasis as she slipped into the chair across the table and placed her hands in her lap and said very femininely, "I heard about your display of bravery last night—I'm impressed."

"Please, don't be, I just did my job."

"It sounded as if you did it very well, but it could be your job isn't finished."

"Oh, and what does that mean?"

"You haven't yet met J. P. McMichaels. He's the slippery-tongued lawyer here in town that somehow finds a way to get his clients off. No doubt he'll take that Duffy boy as a client, he loves a challenge. The tougher it is the more he relishes the opportunity. And it sounds like this is just the type of case he'll dig into."

"Guess everyone has to earn a living." Rad looked over the top of his cup, "Mr. McMichaels will have his hands full on this one from what I understand of the witnesses, including Tom Flournoy."

"You couldn't know this yet, Marshal, but Mr. Flournoy has been a witness to this type of shooting before, and it didn't turn out so good. He just might be one reason that McMichaels will want the case!" She rose and rubbed her hands on the gingham apron before she gracefully rested them on her hips.

"Well, that adds a rock to a stew-pot." Rad's demeanor faltered, he set the cup down and fingered at some crumbs on the table top. "Thanks, Fanny, I'll try to remember that. I appreciate your help, and your hotcakes." Rad watched as she walked toward the kitchen. He stood, put a quarter on the table, smiled, and under his breath said, "*Thanks again.*" He contemplatively walked across the street and unlocked the door with a concerned thought, *'Some cock-a-mamie lawyers ain't no better than the trash they represent . . . hope she's wrong.'*

* * *

"Look there, Muley, I bet they got a bottle or two down there." Bo Cantrell pointed to a slipshod, low-slung sod-roofed log cabin set in a hillside. A rib-shine Indian pony, head drooped, munching hay and tail twitching at flies, was tied out front and being watched over by a squaw who sat the shade, leaning against the structure. Her face was dirty, feet bare and dusty. She had a dingy brown cloth draped over her shoulder and wrapped across her body. The crow-bait horse stopped chomping and looked up at Muley's troupe.

"Trading post." Charlie Joe spoke up. "Close to Indian Territory; likely trades in fire-water for the self-sacrificing bastards." Charlie raised a hand to shield the sun, "Don't look too prosperous does it?"

"You been here before looking lookin' for a drink, have ya Charlie Joe?" Bo chided, making reference that Charlie was maybe part Indian.

Charlie gave him a smirk and flipped the long braid over a shoulder.

A big Muley grin set in, "I sure could use some whiskey . . . got me a spirits toothache and it won't get any better until it marries up with a measure of sour mash blood thinner." The outlaw leader gently heeled the flanks of the black mare.

Pete and Jesse lagged back as the other four doggedly made way down the modest hillside. "What'cha think, Pete? We gonna stay with this outfit?"

The older Longley brother chewed at his lip, and with a deep breath he tolerantly responded, "For now . . . don't know for how long, but for now." They sat ponderously for another half minute before quietly falling in behind.

The four men reached the cabin but remained sitting loose in their saddles as Miguel spoke to the Indian woman in a configuration of Spanish, seemingly mixed with words in Navajo tongue. Her sad, empty eyes told more than the shaking of her head. There was no common verbal understanding between them but the message of adversity, hardship and suffering was apparent.

The four roustabouts slid from the saddles, seemingly refusing to show eagerness as they shuffled forward. Muley stood passively at the entry door before he went inside; he fingered a slim cigar held loosely near his lips, eyes fixed jadedly at the ill-fated squaw. Once inside he shouted, "Whiskey," and broke a wide smile to the disheveled, bearded man standing behind a dull board spread across a pair of wood barrels. Muley pulled black gloves from his fingers, one at a time, not saying anything more, but his grin had grown into a wicked, sarcastic sneer.

The post owner's mouth hung open over scraggy teeth etched with lines of dark stain, "Welcome, gentlemen . . . sure we got whiskey," he declared and reached low behind him, extracted two bottles and presented them admiringly on the makeshift bar. His smile grew as he ran his grimy fingers through unruly sprigs of salt and pepper hair, heavy at each side of his head. He pulled a cork and spouted, "Don't see many white men here, mostly Indians up from the nation." He stretched an arm straight and grasped the bar board with a hand, standing erect as if he'd discovered personal pride for the first time in several days. "Glad to have some white men come along."

Charlie Joe stepped forward, taking a place next to Muley, "Six glasses, if ya got 'em."

The encrusted bar man squinted as he looked behind the four men who'd made way into the obscurity of the cabin, the question was in his expression.

"Yep, two more outside, they'll be comin'." Muley took a bottle for himself, a disgruntled glare parked on his face, replacing the imminent grin. He stared at the unkempt man, contempt becoming more obvious, "That your woman out there?"

The answer came with a thin-lipped sneer and a tetchy bobbing of his chin.

Bo Cantrell pushed Miguel to one side and reached for the other bottle, but Charlie Joe snatched it away and glared at Cantrell, "Like always, I beat ya again."

"Just pour the damn stuff, ya over-growed cockroach," Bo Snapped back.

Muley Tatum leaned toward the bar man, lifting his eyes, letting him know he had a question. "What's yer name?"

An uncertain glimmer lifted the oddly whiskered face to respond. "My name?"

"Yea, what's yer name?"

"It's Lukins, Jediah Lukins, but friends in these parts call me Bull." A contrived swell of pride came over him.

"All right Jediah it is, since your friends ain't here." A short pause ensued before Muley cupped a hand to the side of his mouth, adding to the ambiguity, "About the woman outside," he questioned, "she belong to you?"

"Huuummm, you want some?" His attention rose with a sly smile. His voice was supple as he peered at Muley with sly ambition, "I usually charge a half-a-dollar for each man," he glanced about, "but for the six, I make it just two dollars for the lot of ya." He placed a hand, palm up, on the bar top awaiting payment.

"Well," Muley's inexplicable smile outstripped the expression fused on Jediah's face, he twitched his jaw in a mode of affirmation, "You sure?"

"Let's just call it a friendly arrangement between two gentlemen." Jediah's teeth showed through whisker covered lips.

Muley nodded, his eyes fixed on Jediah's, but Muley's hand swung over the butt of the Colt, to his back; deep shadows of the room sustained the secret for the moment.

"Aahhee!" The whiskered man screeched in pain as Muley's knife stabbed through the back of his hand, sealing it to the board. "You dirty no account son-of- . . ." his words ended as Muley struck him up the side of the head with the barrel of the Colt. Jediah's body sagged and his chest sunk to challenge the integrity of the makeshift bar. His eyes and nose gathered wrinkles, saliva oozed from his lips and he lay motionless with the side of his head flat on the board, not knowing if the worse was over or yet to come.

Tatum chuckled softly as he turned to read the astonished expressions of the others. He felt the authority they reflected, bent over, placed his face close to the ear of the man he'd knifed in the hand and said calmly, "Jediah Lukins that ain't no way to treat the squaw . . . you shouldn't lay a contemptible hand on her. I saw the slash marks where you whip her.

Her face is bruised too, that ain't right, by damn." His words were snarled slow and deliberate. "Now you go out there and put her on that pony and send her on her way; okay?"

"Yea, okay, okay," he cried out in anger and pain, "just get that blade outtta' my hand."

Muley upended the bottle, splashed whiskey on the hand, yanked the knife and wiped the blade clean on the man's shirt sleeve. "Ya won't use that hand again to beat the woman." Muley fumed, "Now get yer ass out there and send that squaw ta packin'."

Bo Cantrell, watched the event take place, laggardly removed the soggy cigar from between his teeth, knuckled at his chin whiskers, wiped his mouth with the back of his wrist and took a pair of long pulls from the bottle of sour mash before handing it to Miguel. The two of them followed the wounded man and Muley outside where Pete and Jess Longley had just swung down from leather and stood watching, not knowing all that had happened inside.

The bleeding, irksome man, with one hand, helped the woman mount her pony, all the while keeping an uncertain eye on his aggressor. The incessant quiet added to the anomaly as the woman pulled together the braided horsehair reins, gathered the nebulous length of cloth about her forsaken body and broke the silence only when she cheeked a start into the animal. She'd gone less than twenty paces when she turned, forced a smile through the uncertainty set in her expression and urged the pinto pony to move off.

"Good." Muley slapped the fretful man on the back as they traipsed back inside. "Let's get that whiskey, my toothache needs attention," he laughed.

CHAPTER TWELVE

Charlie, Bo and Miguel found chairs at a rickety table in a corner. A measure of light shone through where a board was pulled off the log wall, not by accident. It gave probability to a few minutes of man-pleasure with a worn deck of cardboards. Bo's hat recklessly bumped the oil lantern hanging over the table as he adjusted to land his backside in a chair, took a fresh cigar from a vest pouch, removed his derby, looked it over, sat heavily and scratched at strings of scrappy hair before clumsily shuffling the paperbacks. He sniffed, looked at the others and asked, "How 'bout five card, for say, a dollar?"

"I'm in for a few hands." Charlie Joe stepped over a chair back, reached into a front pant pocket and drew out a roll of bills.

Miguel, the Mexican, watched attentively. In short order he pulled a fold of money from inside his shirt, and said *"Cinco, Si."* He looked to Charlie for approval.

Muley stood at the bar's edge, watching, his attention divided. Trust in Jediah Lukins wasn't within him. Muley's judgment of Lukins type of person was adept. He knew reprisal was hovering in the man's mind. If given half a chance he would kill in defiance of the humiliation he'd suffered. The loss of use of the hand and the pain he'd endured would be something else, also a reason. He'd seen Lukens' short barreled scattergun under the bar, knowing he was making the consideration, but Tatum savored the situation of having control over a man that held hate for him. He fed on the opportunity, and keeping him close enough that the obnoxious odor of the man's skin lifted the pleasure. Thought of skinning Jediah's fat, repulsive body while it was hanging from a tree branch rolled through Muley's mind.

"Hey, Muley, see if the fat man's got another bottle of snake oil underfoot back there."

Charlie Joe yelled, "This one's a dead soldier." He threw the bottle against the wall where it clunked without shattering. Miguel rattled off a rapid dissertation of Spanish. Everyone looked at him, understanding not one bit, but it brought a barrage of throaty, disjointed laughter to the otherwise dismal room.

Jediah eyed the scattergun as he took up a bottle and pulled the cork with his teeth. The injured hand was towel wrapped, the arm drawn across his chest and the aberrant bandage tucked into the armpit. Muley grabbed the whiskey away from the man before he could tend it toward the three card players. "Thanks, just add that to our bill, won't ya'?" The guile remark initiated another round of chuckles.

The Longleys went outside. "That dark, clammy air in the cabin gives me the chills." Jesse lifted his head and took in a deep breath, the bright light and warm, dry air pleased him. He welcomed an opportunity to smoke.

"Roll me one of them," Pete Longley chided at Jesse, as the young man lifted a tobacco bag from a vest pocket. Pete twisted his head to study his younger brother from the corner of his eye, "That Muley's one mean sumbitch, ain't he?"

Jesse's answer was in his expression, a collection of contempt and disgust.

Pete went on. "I thought he might kill the man."

"It wouldn't have surprised me if he had." Jesse handed Pete the cigarette, "Ya want me to smoke it for ya too?" Jesse pulled a match across his thigh, lit both his and Pete's, and blew smoke from the side of his mouth, "I figure the man's got a granny knot in his brain somewhere. That squaw woman meant nothin' to him; seemed it was only a chance to put some hurt on the post fella, if ya' ask me."

"May be that you're right, but I don't fall in with that altogether. I'm thinkin' back about those women in the stagecoach; he had a chance to take everything from them, but he same as gave 'em a kiss on the cheek—no harm done to a purse or hair on their heads; I think he's got more of a penchant for women than most men."

Jesse gave Pete's remarks some consideration, "Could be that Muley's got superstition. Ya' know some people believe if they hurt a woman, they'll lose any luck that might 'oughta come their way. And we both heard Pa and the trail boss, Slatery, say that any man that would hit a woman is lower than a snake's belly. Could be that Muley had that kinda' upbringin'."

"Maybe so," Pete studied the smoldering end of his cigarette, his thoughts deepening, "but his upbringin' must have been real confusing, 'cause he sure don't hold back when it comes to wickedness toward a man, he kills easier than a lot of men spit."

Jesse casted his gaze to the distance and squinted into the sun, "Why don't we just climb in the saddle and head for Colorado?"

"Keep your shirt on, brother," Pete dropped the butt and heeled it, "we'll be headin' there before long." He ginned at Jesse, "You to the diggings, and me to the frilly little ladies."

"You keep sayin' that, Pete, but you don't make any move to back it up."

At Muley's order, Jediah stumbled out the door. Muley followed close behind with the man's scattergun and a rope hanging in the crook of his arm.

"What's goin' on, Muley? You ain't plannin' on killing him, are ya?" Pete questioned Tatum as he walked past. Jediah looked over a shoulder with sad eyes, having heard Pete. Muley leaned in close, covered his mouth with a hand to conceal the answer, "Naw, I ain't gonna kill him, just scare the hell outta him . . . but he don't know it."

Jesse and Pete watched. Muley marched Jediah to a tree several feet away. He bellowed, "Stop," and looked up, "this'll do."

"Please mister, don't hang me, I'd rather ya just shoot me so's I don't agonize for long." A tear came as he stood stoop shouldered and offered, "That squaw woman came to me, wanted me to protect her from others of her kind. She's feeble of the mind. I just whipped 'er once, gived her a lesson cause she stole from me that's all," he pleaded.

"Sit there." Muley pointed the shotgun at the base of the tree. "She stole from ya, did she? What'd she steal, food?" Jediah didn't answer, just sat awkwardly with his back against the tree, looking up at Tatum, fear thoroughly beseeched him.

"This here is where you're gonna spend the night, I ain't killin' ya, not yet." Muley tied Jediah Lukins to the tree truck, the final loop drawn tight under the man's chin. He stood back to admire his work, but also to give a final instruction, "Don't try to get outta that, cause if ya do, I'll hunt ya down and use the rope vertical, know what I mean?"

Tatum walked back to where the Longleys watched and waited, "We're sleeping here tonight; I don't want him in the cabin. We'll get ourselves a good night's sleep with a roof overhead and tomorrow morning we'll get on down to the Indian Nation."

The next morning, near a quarter hour after first light, Charlie Joe held a steaming tin cup of strong coffee, pushed back the dusty gunnysack curtain and howled, "He's gone, the ornery old bastard slipped off, Muley."

Cantrell walked up behind Charlie and looked over his shoulder. He turned to Muley, "I bet the man won't stop runnin' till he crosses the state line. You had him scared as a chicken riddin' a log over a waterfall."

Jesse stood in the doorway, coffee in hand, "Look comin' here, we got us some Indian company, looks like four of them, all ridin' ponies, and hey, look, there's the squaw with 'em, she's walkin."

"You think they's gonna be trouble?" Cantrell asked. "Two of 'ems got rifles."

Muley made a quick appraisal of the situation, pushed Cantrell and Charlie Joe aside, walked outside and took a firm footing six feet in front of the door. He looked things over, especially noting the woman he'd set free. She was wearing a long rawhide dress, beads strung around her neck, held in one hand a deerskin stretched across a circle of willow twig decorated with wildflowers and feathers. The long cloth that covered her before was in the other hand. He half turned and spoke over a shoulder, "They ain't no trouble. Don't nobody start nothing; keep your guns quiet, handy but quiet."

Two of the Indians wore Government issue cavalry pants and dirty white shirts, open neck to waist, sleeves cut off above the elbows. They carried the rifles. The other two wore breech clothes; one carried half of a red blanket over his shoulder. The other was wearing the shirt Jediah Lukins wore yesterday. He also had a man's ear strung on a rawhide strap draped around his neck. It was fresh.

The four Indian men said nothing, were unhurried, appeared untroubled, even dawdling in their actions. They flaccidly looped horsehair bridle reins onto the hitch-rail and gave drawn out stares at the whites, showed no fear, or any particular appreciation as they gradually made way into the cabin. The squaw remained standing outside, a wide smile set on her face.

It was indeed a strange gathering, everyone looking at one another as if *they* were out of place.

"They came for whiskey." Muley's voice was calm and resolved.

"Ummm, whiskey," one of the men in ragged cavalry drawers muttered.

Muley made his way back inside and edged behind the bar top. With arms folded and a staunch face, he bellowed, "Money," as he extended and worked his hand, rubbing his thumb across fingers.

The Indian appearing to be their leader said once again, "Whiskey."

Muley yanked the Colt, cocked it and shoved it into the man's face, an ugly sneer flashed into Muley's expression, "Stay ready, boys," he said loud and clear, "these fellas are playin' *'who's got the guts',* an old Indian game, jostlin' to be top dog. We need to show 'em we're in charge."

Miguel jumped into the fray; he put the tip of his revolver's barrel into the gut of the Indian toting the ear. His message was clear, words weren't needed. He'd been around Indians, knew their ways.

A cunning grin billowed on the face of the Indian leader. He reached fingers into a pouch and drew out a dollar gold piece and slapped it on the counter. The game ended. "Whiskey," he said again as the threatening air of trepidation within the room readily melted into subtle calm, and soon thereafter, gaiety, in a near irrational epidemic of laughter and back-slapping. The Indians sucked rot-gut sour mash for the next two hours.

"Never did figure 'em out." Muley mused after the four Indians had stumbled out of the cabin, clumsily mounted, and rode up the slope carrying two more bottles of Jediah's snake oil. "Wonder why the squaw came with them?"

"All I can guess is they were making sure there weren't more than one Jediah Lukins," Charlie slurred. "If there was, I suppose they was gonna trade her for whiskey rather than pay. There just ain't no way to understand them strange creatures. My uncle Rosco used to say 'If you put one of them magnifying glasses up to their ear you'd see light coming from the other side."

"Might be so, but them red men know twice as much about nature as any white man that ever walked this earth," Pete speculated.

"Do you think they killed the Lukins fella?" Jesse questioned, his voice subdued and opinioned, thinking it was so. "One of them was wearing his shirt."

"Maybe he traded the shirt for a horse . . . or another squaw," Muley offered in jest as he glared up the hill where the dizzy-headed band of redskins disappeared in the distance.

"Now what, Tatum?" Bo Cantrell said, speaking around the cigar clichéd between his teeth, "We gonna just leave this place with nobody to tend it?"

"Thought maybe we'd burn it, unless you want to stay? If you do, you can trade for the squaw. That what ya want?" Muley badgered, and snickered at his remark.

"Don't make no never-mind to me. This shack ain't my idea of a good life." Cantrell said back, "I got no hankerin' to stay here and I don't want no crazy-headed Indian . . . maybe I'd take an ugly white woman, but no idiot squaw."

Muley put a match to the coal-oil lantern and slung it into the stack of wooden crates behind the bar top.

CHAPTER THIRTEEN

Rad Carson walked the three blocks to the *DODGE CITY HERALD,* the newspaper owned and operated by Richard Barnett, a transplanted Richmond, Virginia native with a flair for making any event into a lightly investigated, but over-dramatized, front page news story. He was particular about his appearance, always in a suit of matched trousers and wide lapelled coat, white shirt, and smartly knotted silk tie. A blue, never dusty, derby hat normally sat on a nicely combed head of thick, light brown hair. Some of the locals continued to refer to him as the 'word-jockey-dude', even though he'd been in Dodge City for more than four years.

The bell over the door gave its' tinkling announcement as Carson entered. Barnett was busy turning the wheel with his one hand as he fed paper into the press and worked the treadle with a foot. Without glancing up he remarked, "Help yourself, today's edition is on the counter, leave your nickel in the jar."

"If you don't mind, I'll wait."

Barnett looked up. A pert smile came to his lips, "Give me minute if you don't mind, I'll be right with you."

Carson turned a newspaper around and began reading. To his surprise, his name topped the second column in large print. The next line stated, "Spickard Marshal To Dodge City," the next line, "Appointed U. S. Marshal."

"You'll need to put a nickel in the jar if you intend to read the paper," Barnett wiped his hands on a rag and removed the green cuffs from his lower arms as he pushed through the low rail separating the foyer from the work area. "Oh," Barnett caught sight of the badge on Rad Carson's leather vest. He extended his hand, "Glad to meet you, Marshal Carson, my name is Barnett, Richard Barnett, I'm the proprietor here at the *HERALD*."

"My pleasure, Mr. Barnett."

"May I ask what brings you to my establishment?"

"Let me start by saying Judge Wilkinson speaks highly of you, sir;" which was less than a sizeable stretch of the assessment made by the judge, "and he suggested I stop in and make your acquaintance."

"Well, that's nice to hear. I must say I hold the judge in high esteem as well."

Carson continued, "Secondly, as you know, and according to your paper here," Rad turned and pointed a thumb to the stack of the present edition setting near the nickel jar, "I'm new in Dodge, and would like to have access to past editions of the *DODGE CITY HERALD* in order to learn more, to catch up, if you will, on recent events as well as the past, some of the stories you consider most pertinent over the past couple of years. Can you arrange that for me?"

"I believe so, Marshal. I retain copies of all editions and have them cataloged in the room upstairs. And it may surprise you, but I set aside what I consider the special issues, if for no other reason than for my personal references. That's a characteristic I learned from my mentor, a Mr. Niles Zinsmaster, back in Richmond. He found past issues excellent information sources. As you evidently realize, and we in the newspaper trade know also, some events resurface over time and having appropriate reference materials makes it equitable in meeting deadlines."

"That sounds good, maybe better than I'd expected."

"You're welcome to use my materials, but I'll be very disapproving of any of those leaving my premises."

"I understand, and I thank you for offering." Rad removed his tan Stetson, turned it around in his fingers, "If you don't mind, Mr. Barnett, can you tell me offhand if you recall any news articles where attorney, J.P. McMichaels tried any cases where Tom Flourney was a witness?"

Barnett's thumb and forefinger cradled his chin momentarily as his lips wrinkled, but in short order his eyes gleamed and he answered, "Matter of fact, I do recall an instance about a year ago, maybe a little more than a year, where a killing was supposedly witnessed by Flourney. But in the end it seems the entire town was set back, couldn't believe the young killer was acquitted." Barnett wiped his hands on a towel draped over the leather tie of his printer apron, "Tell you what, I'm very busy right now, perhaps if you could come back in the morning, say around eight o'clock, I'll show you around upstairs and we'll see if we can put our hands on the story."

"I'll be here." The marshal nodded in appreciation, "Thanks in advance for your assistance." Carson started to turn and leave, but hesitated, "And if you would, I wish you'd keep this just between you and me."

"I can do that . . . be glad to." However, the thought left Barnett with a look of question.

The following morning Carson entered the newspaper office, where Richard Barnett greeted him, "I've located the article and additionally have some surprises for you Marshal Carson. I took the opportunity last evening to extract an issue pertinent to one of the most famous, long serving lawmen held office here in Dodge City. I think you'll find this relevant to the inquisitive statement you spoke of . . . about past lawmen of Dodge City."

"Humm, that sounds interesting."

"Here it is, Barnett replied, "November 9, 1877, the day William Barclay Masterson was elected sheriff of Ford County." He handed the paper to Carson. "He took over from Charlie Bassett. You may recall that Bassett petitioned the state, to set aside the statute in the constitution that denied him the opportunity to run for re-election, as he'd be exceeding the number of terms allowed. His plea was rejected."

"I was of the understanding that the Masterson brothers and the Earps all held law offices in Dodge City about that same time."

Barnett's reply was light-hearted, "That's true, they did. The last two years we had so many lawmen here they arrested one another in order to get the city and county to provide meals for the lot of them." He laughed, "I'll dig up more news articles for you."

The newspaper man wrapped fingers into the edges of the leather printer's apron and offhandedly offered, "Dodge City is a rawboned frontier town in need of better law enforcement. Managing the brunt of cattle drives and the inhospitable elements they create, such as rugged, untamed cowboys with a little money in their pockets and thirst for liquor and women when they land here makes it what it is." He blinked the thought away, "And here, Marshal Carson, is the paper you requested," Barnett glanced at the newspaper and continued, "the one where J.P. McMichaels represented a young man by the name of Bick Nielsen in the shooting death of one Kendrick Anderson. McMichaels got the jury to acquit Bick Nielsen . . . well, I'll just let you read it." He handed the paper to Carson and pointed, "Take that desk and chair over there if you'd like."

Rad Carson got comfortable and began to read just before the bell atop the door jingled. A spry-spirited, middle-aged lady with her hair pulled and tucked into a bun on the back of her head entered the newspaper office, "Good morning, Mr. Barnett, I'll just pick up my paper before school gets underway." She plunked a nickel into the jar. "Is there any excitement I should share with my students," she asked, and coincidently noted Carson pouring over the newspaper at the desk.

"Nothing is in the edition having to do directly with your favorite topic of history, Miss Grassley." He noted her studying the marshal. "Oh, let me introduce you, he motioned with a hand extended toward each of them, "Miss Edith Grassley this here is U. S. Marshal, Rad Carson. Mr. Carson . . . Miss Grassley."

Her eyes lit up, she looked over the dainty wire-rim glasses and asked, "Would you by chance be related to Christopher Kit Carson? It seems I remember that he had a grandson living near here?"

"Why, yes, as a matter of fact," Carson nodded, "I'm that grandson, I'm pleased to say."

"Oh my goodness, that's wonderful, Mr. Carson." Eyes blinking, her mind working, she fidgeted, and raised her small, compact body, "Mr. Carson, I'm the teacher over at the elementary school, east of here on Cedar Street, my students and I would love to have you come some day and speak to us about your grandfather, if you'd be so kind. He was such a marvelous and well rounded man, very creditable to the history of our young country."

Carson tipped his hat and responded with a tinge of humiliation showing, "I believe we can arrange for such a visit, but you'll have to give me a few days, I'm new here in Dodge City, and getting settled in my new occupation, and learning my way around town." Within, Rad thought there was a good chance the woman already knew more about Kit Carson, than he did. He'd only been around the man twice, once when he was six years old and the other when the elderly man passed through Kansas on his way to Washington D.C. for a meeting in the late 1860's. Other than that, he'd read some of the materials available to anyone interested in delving into the frontier man's life. He thought he might now need to learn more.

"Oh, that'll be fine." She gave him her brightest and most cheerful smile; looked him over vigilantly, much like a young girl might examine a potential suitor, gathered her long skirt in hand and made the door bell jingle.

When Rad rose from the chair and folded the newspaper, he handed it to Barnett. "What about the Earps? I haven't read anything of them, but I've heard of their reputation being ruffians, that hold true?"

"They mostly spent time on the south side, the other side of Front Street, where all the filth, gamblers and whores gather. They say the Earp brother named Wyatt ran a faro game down there, moved from saloon to saloon with it. I'm sure you know about that end of town!" Barnett bunched his lips, giving thought before he went on, "Wyatt had a strong hand and what I'd deem nefarious law efforts." Barnett pressed his lips into a thin line, choosing his words before he continued, "He was a hooligan on his own right, not a man to tangle with, law or no law."

Having met Rad Carson, Barnett decided he'd run another story about him; not just him, but all of the lawmen in the area. This one would investigate the governor's reason for the multilayer of law in Dodge City. He'd twist his reader's minds; get them to thinking whether Governor St. John put them all in place to police the lawless elements to boost his political worth, or if the lawmen were positioned to police one another. The story would generate conversation on the streets—that sells newspapers and solidifies the power of his establishment, both factors he considered to be sound justifications for the article.

The history of Kansas, preceding the civil war was violent. Kansas wouldn't enjoy statehood until the "Wyandotte Constitution" of January, 1861. Those facts weighed heavy in the decision of Richard Barnett when he was a printer's apprentice in Richmond. His love for journalism was weighted toward violence; it was primary in highly sought-after newspaper reading by the public. Ordinary citizens seemed to be drawn to reading about aggression and bloodshed. His research, coupled with his exploration of the frontier, led him to Dodge City, Kansas to set up his first business enterprise, *THE DODGE CITY HERALD.*

Permanent residents in Dodge City numbered over twelve hundred. Many more regularly passed through, due in large part to the Santa Fe Trail, which sat at the top of the hill overlooking Dodge. And once the train rails brought the cow-town into prominence in 1863, it grew rapidly. The void of highly sought-after minerals, which was the cornerstone of speedy growth for most of the West, failed to slow the boom of Dodge. Cattle. That was the mineral of the grassland. First it was the original wild cattle, the buffalo. Later the hunger for beef on behalf of the rapid population growth in the East proved to be the principal economic factor that established abundant commerce in the prairie lands.

Richard Barnett was inwardly a man of brutal personality, but outwardly, he resorted to an appearance of placid character, which allowed him to gain access to prominent, influential people, an important attribute toward his chosen profession. But with a demand he placed on himself, a self driven passion, he wrote news articles to arouse discord, a journalistic talent quite common to successful newspaper people. He was not a brave man, not in the least, which conflicted with the aggressive trait he put forth. His superb use of dialog was his savior. When challenged aggressively by a person who took issue with statements Barnett printed, he had an amazing ability to reconstitute the issue, making it appear to be misunderstood or contrary to their interpretation. He considered the day would come when he'd pursue a political career—maybe governor of Kansas, or a U. S. Senate seat.

CHAPTER FOURTEEN

Carson looked up straight away as the door swung open and a clutter of sounds assaulted his office. Boot heels clunked the walkway, muddled voices cropped up and the growl of a freight wagon trudging up the street cropped into the medley. The full assortment was suddenly overridden by a wagon-master's shrill whistle that stung the air as two men stepped across the threshold of the newly furnished office. Both twisted and looked over their shoulders. One promptly turned back, squinted, and faced Carson. He removed his high crown, felt hat and spoke as he coiled the hat around his fingers. "Would you be Marshal Rad Carson?" A scowl on the man's face gave a hint of somber intentions, "That'd be me alright, come on in." Rad looked the men over copiously, realizing they weren't of the local community.

The two of them stepped forward, the one richly outfitted spoke, "My name's Wade Weidenauer." He unbuttoned the swanky western styled coat and nodded toward his associate. "And this here is Hap Gieberg. Sheriff Hinkle sent us here to see you, Marshal Carson." His stern, sun-bronzed face, underscored by heavy, well trimmed brows, indicated their visit was other than simple or friendly. He went on, "Hinkle said you have authority beyond Ford County," his head jerked symbolically, "and my complaint would be in your realm of the law, not his."

The man was slightly larger than average build, the upper side of fifty. Rad couldn't keep from studying the man as he walked forward. His clothes were extravagant, reminding Rad of a carnival man he'd once seen, but more fancy than gaudy. The boots were tan ostrich hide and crafted by a remarkably gifted boot maker. No doubt he was of considerable means, with holdings much greater than a startup cattle ranch. He also smelled clean with barber shop fragrance, and his ornately stitched shirt couldn't be bought anywhere near Dodge, maybe Denver or Kansas City.

Carson put down the law book he was reading, rose from his desk chair and offered a hand for introduction, "Glad to meet you, Mr. Weidenauer, and you, Gieberg. Sheriff Hinkle's suggestion was proper. Have a seat there," Rad motioned to the pair of tucked-leather chairs affronting his desk, "and tell me what brings you."

Weidenauer bobbled his head and took the chair. He attempted to revive the creases in his expensive trousers by running them between the thumb and forefinger of each hand; cleared his throat and settled into the cushioned seat. "My trail outfit, bossed by Hap here, was driving two thousand head to Kansas railheads—they come up the Chisholm. They drove through Injun Territory and thought to drive 'em to Abilene, but Hap found out the market here in Dodge City was about a dollar a head better so he shook the Chisholm and headed on over this way."

"Let me interrupt you there, Mr. Weidenauer' could you start by telling me where your ranch is and where you put this herd to the trail."

The cattleman inhaled and gave Rad a remote, near indignant, cold stare, "I'm from near Weatherford, 'bout thirty miles west of Fort Worth." The Texas drawl propped up the claim.

Carson blinked a couple of times and grimaced as he spoke, "Isn't that where that Parker girl was stolen by the Comanche back in . . . was it back in fifty-five or fifty-six? . . . and, the story goes, some years later on she gave birth to a Comanche chief?"

"That's right; she became the mother of chief, Quanah Parker." His voice lowered an octave and his expression became dark, "That's not something we're proud of back home! Can we just leave at that?" He dismissed Rad's remark, undoubtedly a little irritated. "Let's just get back to my business for coming here to see you, Carson."

"You're right. Forgive me for bringing the matter up. I didn't mean to step on someone's toes, I was just recalling." His expression rejoined, "But it got a lot of attention at the time it happened, so I was told. You just go right ahead, Mr. Weidenauer."

The rancher's drawn brow gradually thawed and he started again, "Hap here is one of my ranch foremen, and he's also trail boss for my outfit, the Double W Ranch. Well, a couple of miles after the herd crossed the state line this side of Oklahoma Territory, a group of six men sittin' horseback blocked the trail, caught my man here, threw a damn rope around his neck and started making demands."

"Demands? Like what?" Rad looked to Gieberg, the trail boss, for the answer, but it was Wade Weidenauer that responded.

"They said they was agents for the Cherokee, and the land we'd crossed was under their control, said they had the right to charge a toll on behalf of the Indians." He rocked forward, "I've heard of that sort, but never had come across the problem with my outfit." He leaned back again, his expression holding a question, and continued, "They wanted a dime for each and ever head we had." His shoulders braced and his eyes flared a mite, "When Hap refused, the man pulled his revolver and put it up against my man's temple, like this." He put a forefinger to the side of Gieberg's head and pushed the thumb up, "and said he'd either shoot him or hang him if we didn't pay—said he had the law on his side. Would that be right, Carson?"

Rad shook his head and blinked in a motion of disparagement before he spoke. "The Indians have been known to collect tolls, but they don't send ruffians and outlaws as their agents, if that's your question." Carson's face clinched and his head tilted, eyes fixed on Weidenauer's, "The Indians negotiate peacefully, they usually do it with a showing of force and always well within the Territory," Rad explained.

"Damn right." Gieberg lurched forward and spoke up for the first time, "But a cocked six-gun pushed against my head put me out of position to negotiate. I paid him." He settled back in his chair with a hard scowl. "I wasn't expecting no hold up, rustlers maybe, but no outright thievin' of our cash money."

Carson responded, "Those men weren't agents looking out for the Indians, they weren't nothing other than simple outlaws that robbed you."

Gieberg again jumped in, "Damn right, they wasn't no more Indian agents than they was angels sent down from the heavens, just plain thieves, like you said."

Carson asserted, "If they'd been legitimate they'd had papers to show. It's questionable if Washington gave Indians the right to charge for temporary use of the land for driving cattle across, but some have done it, and cattlemen have paid to keep from the spoils of a fight, maybe loose more beeves," he scratched at his temple, "or maybe some men."

Wade Weidenauer's expression was empty of concern for Carson's statement as he took up the conversation, "I want my money back, Marshal, and I want those outlaws put to justice."

Rad opened a drawer and withdrew a pencil and paper, he could see the cattleman had a lack of patience for reason and cared nothing about trouble other drovers had experienced. "Tell me what the hooligans that took your money looked like." He focused on the trail ramrod, Geiberg, "And we'll get a start to see what we can do." Pencil in hand, he turned the paper, centered on the trail boss, and looked away from the auspiciously dressed Texan rancher.

"Well, the leader of the group, that's the one I remember best, he was a big man, dressed in all black duds." Geiberg's eyes casted toward the ceiling and his face contorted, he hesitated, "But there was a ornery Mexican with leather chaps, and this fella with a big gut on him wearing a wrinkled derby hat and sheep's wool vest; he was chewin' a cigar," he hesitated again, "and a couple of wranglers . . . they didn't do nothin', just looked odd, out of place, if you know what I mean." He squinted and wrinkled a lip, like he was trying to give reason to them being with the others, his mind taken back with thought.

Carson persuaded him, "Okay, so let's get more on the man that held a gun to your head."

"He was a nasty sort, had this God-forsaken wild grin, made me think of a wild man that might laugh at a man drowning rather than throw him a rope. He was big, like I said, had long black hair, dark eyes that set back, rode a black horse and," the man stopped, in momentary thought, "not much else about him except for that cruel, nasty laugh he kept going most all the time, and oh yea, the others called him Muey, or Muley, somethin' like that."

That being said, Carson leaned back and blew a soft whistle into the air. "I'd say they were outlaws alright. Muley!" Carson wobbled his head side to side, "He must be the same man that's played hob with me more than once in the past—even killed a good citizen in a town up the road a piece," he threw a thumb, "for most no reason a few weeks back."

"So you know this man?" Weidenauer questioned.

"I know who he is, and know him to be a mean one. Muley Tatum has been a thorn in the side of a lot of folks in this part of Kansas. He's liable to show up anywhere within a hundred miles in any direction of where we sit." Carson cut his eyes to Weidenauer's and focused sternly, "I'd say the spot your herd ran into him is about seventy to eighty miles from here." He rubbed his hands together as he hesitated. "Your incident must have been five or six days ago if you've gotten here with your cattle since then." He pointed an index finger at Hap Gieberg, "You're lucky to be sitting here and telling about it. Lucky too that you paid him, he'd have killed you alright."

Wiedenauer leaned in, lower lip extended, "Think you can catch him, Marshal?"

"Maybe so, but not easy. He's as slick as axel grease and meaner than a she-wolf protecting pups. I doubt he'd stay around down there for long. He's not the kind to take to the open spaces so much, he's more likely to settle somewhere where there's plenty of liquor and easy marks."

"So you're not going after them, that what you're telling us, Carson?"

"My chances of catching up with Muley Tatum down there in them hills, and whoever those fellas are with him, wouldn't be worth a speck of dust in a pig's eye. Believe me, gentlemen, if I thought it'd do any good, I'd be on the trail within short order, I got no likin' for that man at all." He sat back, an expression of thought moved across his face before he spoke, "I offer you this, I was figuring on putting out a dodger on the man." He looked first at his desk and the papers there before cutting the glance back at the two men, "I'll locate an artist here in town and get it done. I'll also work to get a reward set up from the state of Kansas to post up on the dodger; maybe we'll get some action when I get a distribution on the flyers through this part of the country." Carson gave a quick flick of his chin, an affirmative motion toward what he'd just said. "Someday I will arrest Muley and his sidekicks, and when I do I'll get your money back, but don't count on it in the next week or so."

"That's not much," the fancy dressed man answered. "Tell ya what Carson," he dug into a pocket inside his stylish coat, "I'll start your reward with two hundred dollars, losing money to that scoundrel is one thing but having him near kill my man here," his head tilted, "ain't to be tolerated."

Gieberg lifted an index finger, pointed at Rad, and with a huffy voice said, "I'll remember that man, the one called Muley Tatum, and if I ever see him again, I'll be ready, I'll put a bullet in his damn face and wipe that smile off."

The three of them stood simultaneously, everyone realizing more conversation wouldn't change a thing, and Carson responded, "Can't say that I'd blame you, mister, but if you do that, don't let me know about it or I'll have to lock you up—just keep it to yourself." Carson dryly reminded him.

The two cattlemen looked at each other; Weidenauer tapped his trail boss on the shoulder and indicated the door. They rose and turned back toward Carson, "We'll remember that, Marshal." He waved over a shoulder and they stepped out onto the hardboards.

CHAPTER FIFTEEN

Activity in Dodge City was heavy and the rail yards packed with raucous, bawling longhorns that had never before been inhibited with fences. They hated the confines of the stockyard corrals and showed it by bumping and wailing worse than a cantankerous teenage boy that thought he'd outgrown his britches and his parents' directives. Cowboys that lived on the trail for weeks with little rest and minimal sleep showed tempers and resentment toward the stubborn animals, blaming them for the torment. That hostility carried over once they left the trail. They'd endured pain from scrapes and cuts, broken bones, insects, snakes and impaired body functions. When darkness fell and the herds quieted, a long soaking bath removed the grime from the wrangler's bodies but grating attitudes couldn't be washed clean with soap and water. They took to the town's saloon row to mollycoddle themselves with beer and whiskey, female companionship or games of chance, most anything to settle the stored up spitefulness.

Bitterness from the cattle drive welled up inside the young minds and they released it on one another, or an authority figure, feeling they'd been unduly controlled with their hard work and the discipline required keeping the cattle orderly. This night in Dodge City was to be more despicable than most.

Sundown brought a warm stench to town. Carson pulled his hat down and walked in the direction of the gamey breeze blowing up from the cattle pens. This time of year cattle odors never vanished from Dodge for more than a few hours. Those few hours were when harsh winds from the west announced rain. Rain was a blessing as long as the wind was evident, but like many good things, once it halted, the lingering results intensified the conditions that prevailed earlier. Rad recalled in the readings of his grandpa, Kit Carson, where the frontier mountain man expounded on his explorations, *"A man that takes to the wild must be willing to accept the bad with the good."* This particular evening lacked even the possibility of good, and the air stunk to high heaven!

Tobacco smoke dulled the unwilling light of the oil lamps in the saloons, but it somehow swelled the noise. Rad knew it couldn't, totally ridiculous, but he felt the determination to weigh the possibility as he made his way around the town, known far and wide as the toughest cow town on the Kansas prairie.

Carson's presence went unnoticed in the first saloon he visited; just what he had hoped. But in the second, The Spotted Cat, he stood with a shoulder propped against a support post and watched the women of easy virtue work the crowd. A luridly attired lady with stylish hair, dangling gold earrings and an over-painted face, scuttled up to his side and warbled a throaty, "Good evening Marshal Carson."

He looked at her with school-boy eyes; the unknowing apparent in his awkward response. The thought that she must be near the age of his mother flashed through his mind, "I'm sorry, Miss, I don't believe I've had the pleasure." His hand went automatically to the Stetson as his head tilted.

"I'm sure you haven't . . . or I would have remembered . . . and you would too!" Her grin as submissive as the words.

He felt the color jump into his face and looked around the room as if wanting to become invisible, to hide the awkwardness, a feeling very foreign to him. Strange as it could be, the next thing to blaze through his mind was Fanny, the attractive restaurant owner. He quickly managed to recapture the mainstay of his person, the stalwart toughness that led to him being a resolute lawman, "You have the advantage, Mammn, but I'm sure we've never met."

She smiled wickedly, knowing she'd unsettled him, "You're right, Marshal, a mutual acquaintance pointed you out to me." She raised her eyebrows, "Mr. Richard Barnett, owner of the Dodge City newspaper, he's a regular here. I'm sure you know Richard."

Carson grinned, "Oh, I see. Yes I know Mr. Barnett, maybe not as well as I might have imagined, but you're right, I know him."

"So if you will Marshal Carson, let me introduce myself . . . my name is Estella . . . Estella Marks." She drew back a step and fingered the green, jeweled combs in her dishwater-blond hair intermingled with less than occasional strands of gray. It was as if she were seeking approval of her appearance, and her bodice adjusted appreciatively. "I'm half owner of this place." She pushed her lips together and blinked faded blue eyes that guarded the adjacent spider lines, "Many of the lawmen, some past, and some not so past, have found *comforts* in my place, and I hope that you will also."

Thinking of Barnett, Rad smirked inside, but kept it there. "I see, Miss Marks!" He gave her a guarded smile, "I'm still learning about Dodge City and am appreciative of any information you offer." Rad relinquished another grin, thinking more about Barnett than the lady before he went on, "My research of the lawmen of Dodge City didn't include that fine bit of information, but I don't for a minute doubt your statement." His grin pleased her. He continued, "Please don't think I'm ungrateful, but I keep a busy schedule, kind of a loner you might say; fact is it's said by folks who've known me for some time that I'm over dedicated to the law badge." He laid his thumb under the coat's lapel and exposed the bright silver and brass shield. Changing the tone of conversation, he gazed about the boisterous establishment, which was more than a little sinister in appearance, but animated and spirited otherwise, "This is quite a place you have here Miss Marks, I . . ."

She shut him off, "Please . . . call me Stell, my friends do and I hope we'll become friends."

"Okay, Stell it is." He pinched his hat brim and continued to make conversation, drawing back once again, "Sounds like you're a long time resident of Dodge."

"Absolutely, came here at the end of The States War. Fact is my husband was assigned to Fort Dodge when it opened in 1865. He was a major, in charge of sorties and the guard house."

"I see, and is he still wearing the cavalry blue?"

"As a matter of fact he was killed back in sixty-seven."

"Sorry to hear that."

"He was *dedicated* to the cavalry," she pointed to Carson's coat lapel, where he'd displayed the peace officer badge, "hardly took time for anything else," she offered a dreary grin. "All it got him was a Kiowa lance stuck through his back . . . and made me a widow." The soft, feminine voice diminished.

They made small talk as she attempted to advance a friendship. Rad tried to keep the conversation tied more to the business aspects when he remarked about the mahogany bar, which was extravagant compared to others in town.

She turned to face it and welcomed the opportunity, "I found that remarkable piece in San Francisco. The carving was done in China, some city there that I couldn't even pronounce the name, but I loved it—expensive too!"

"It looks expensive, and unusual for this part of the country."

Her eyes glistened and the smile was genuinely warm. "Barnett tells me," she shuffled a few inches closer and draped her fingers on his forearm, "you came here from Spickard," and coyly added, "and you're not a married man."

"That's right, Spickard's been my home for quite a spell; I really didn't want to leave." Rad backed up a step, his comfort being crowded.

Abruptly, from the congested bar, the explosion of a shattered bottle, simultaneous with belligerent shouts, took command over the buzz and howling laughter that favored the place. A cowboy stumbled and reeled backward from a fist that smashed his nose. His body twisted and rattled a cluster of wooden chairs as beer and sour mash whiskey splashed into faces and readied several cowboys to join the melee.

The entire room suddenly was awash with scuffling confusion. Cursing, grunts and slapping sounds resonated with rasping of boot heels and chair legs. The turmoil was emphatic, but brief, when as unexpectedly as it began, the cloud of smoke hanging overhead swirled as a shotgun blast roared through. The fighting slowed; exuberance fell aside quickly. It closed down with the exception of the bloodied-faced cowhand on the floor. He had a fist filled with a .45 revolver. It spouted flame and the shot slashed into the thigh of the man who'd plastered his nose flat.

Rad Carson landed on the shooter; one fist mashed his jaw and the other snatched the smoking gun. The drunken cowboy fell limp. Carson's lawman-diligence reflexed and his gun was out, pointed at the sidekick of the wounded man who was readying his draw. The man halted in an awkward transformation at the sight of the bored-barrel of Carson's Colt.

"Stop it! Stop it now!" The barkeep spat the words and raised another shotgun, both hammers cocked back.

Estella darted to Carson's side where she stood defiantly, her features hardened and she waved a .41 Spanish Rimfire. "Everyone out!" She screamed, "The place is closed!" She set a hand to her hip, the other propped high, holding the short-barreled pistol in front of her quenched face. She transgressed from a soft flower blossom to a thorny rose in the blink of an eye. Carson didn't know if he felt admiration for the woman, or sorrow for the life style she'd chosen after the passing of her husband. It mattered little right now, but it would revisit his mind later when the hub-bub had been put to rest for the night.

"You three," Carson threw a command at three drovers he quickly assessed with lawman eyes, "Stay. I'll need your help." As he bent to one knee he ordered one of them, "You," he pointed to a young cowboy standing open mouthed, "go get one of the town deputies. You other two, help that wounded man, and if he's bleeding bad, one of you go after Doc Hink."

Estella Marks rubbed at her forehead and watched Carson. His worth, respect, and the attraction she felt for him, notched upward. *'This was a lawman with real sand . . . not the foul, uppity badge totters that held the reins in Dodge City over the past half dozen years'.*

"Jake," she yelled at the barman still holding the scattergun and hustling men out the swinging doors, "get them girls to straightnin' this place up. When we clear the scum out of here, we'll reopen—the night's still got hours to make up for the losses."

CHAPTER SIXTEEN

Governor St. John and Judge Nathaniel Wilkinson had made good on their word to issue written instructions to Sheriff Hinkle and the two Dodge City marshals which Carson selected to be left in place. As U.S. Marshal, Rad Carson was to be the priority lawman in Dodge City and Ford County. And they were warned that the reputation of law enforcement in Dodge City as performed by the Earps and Mastersons was to change. The governor and the judge opted that *crack-over-the-head* punishment when fights broke out and no weapons were fired would be left to good judgment. But the lock-up-and-steal from the culprits, referring to it as fines, as Earps and Masterson practiced, was to be put to rest.

Barnett's DODGE CITY HERALD newspaper headline proclaimed and questioned, "NEW LAW—SAME TACTICS?" It went on to inquire if the citizens noted any *real change* with the exception of U.S. Marshal Rad Carson's appointment and his apparent fondness of the food at Fanny's restaurant. Barnett's article belittled the role of the two town marshals, referring to them as "Watch Dogs Chained To Doghouse". Carson felt a flicker of hostility when he read the byline, but overcame it, knowing the initiative driven by the journalist was a desire to sell newspapers by creating disharmony.

Later the same day, town marshals J. R. Landry and Chalk Dinsmore, were sitting in front of their office when Carson walked toward them. Upon seeing Carson, still some twenty yards distant, Dinsmore dropped the newspaper to the plank walkway, cupped his hands at either side of his face and made sounds like a barking dog. All three men shook in muffled laughter as Carson continued toward the other two. It was obvious the town lawmen knew the traits of Richard Barnett.

Both were big men, mid-thirties, and more moxie than almost any man Ford County that wasn't of outlaw sort. Landry was a long-time ranch hand with one of the best managed ranches in all of Kansas. Dinsmore had been a horse soldier and from a good stock of second generation immigrants from Scotland. "You got a new chain for us?" Dinsmore quipped with a spacious grin as he stood with an outreached hand to welcome Carson.

"I'm glad you found the humor in that rubbish Barnett spouted," Carson said, shaking the hands of both men, "Maybe if he rattles on about us he'll leave some other poor folks alone."

"Maybe so," Landry said. "For the first time in a long time he's takin' jabs at the law. The Earps wrecked his shop when he poked at them. They made their point; what else they might have done I don't know, but after the run in with them he wouldn't print the truth, that I'm sure of. No sir, they had that man's hide ready to stretch to the side of a barn if he'd belittle them a second time, and he never did."

Dinsmore added to Landry's remarks, "Barnett's okay . . . not much backbone, just tryin' to make a livin' the best way he knows how I reckon. Most folks in town know he's got less snap than a green bean. We just put up with him." Dinsmore flipped his chin to the side and added, "We need that rag he calls a newspaper to print legal notices, or we might just hitch his fancy britches to a cattle train, and send him packin' back East," he chuckled lightly.

"I see you gentlemen carry the considerations about Barnett that I'd come to." Carson reassured himself as he accommodated the marshals. "We've got quite a job in front of us in takin' the town's reputation from the miserable lot where its' been, to well, whatever we can do."

"This jail," Landry threw a thumb toward the door, "won't hold too many more waitin' for Judge Wilkinson." He lifted his hat and scratched through thick brown hair, "Moren' half of them in there keep offering us money, up to ten dollars to set 'em back out on the street. They'd heard that's how a man gets outta jail in Dodge, and they're findin' it hard to believe they've to wait for the judge. He'll be here in two days, and that ain't none too soon"

"How about the man what did the shooting over at Estella Mark's place, you got him in there don't you?"

"Yep," Landry drawled, name's Alonzo Duffy. We got him and another that stabbed a man last night. We also got three or four thieves. That Duffy character had a notion to become a gun-slick several days back, over at the King's Folly."

Carson's mind reverted to the story Fanny told him, the one where Tom Flournoy was the witness that J. P. McMichaels turned into a pile of mush and got a client off. "Has McMichaels been in to visit Duffy?"

"Not only has he been in the jail to see Duffy, I understand he's been telegraphing Duffy's mother back East, in Cincinnati I believe it was. The key-punch fella says Duffy's family is made of money, made it in the beer business back there in Ohio."

Rad Carson pushed the Stetson back on his head, "Seems Fanny was right, thinking Flournoy might back-up on his testimony, and if he does I might get an investigation under way to look into McMichaels' and Flourney's arrangement." Carson's expression hardened and a spark set to his eye. "I don't take to money-bent lawyers trifling with the law and twisting basically honest men into deceit. We'll let the charges on Duffy simmer; we just might be wedging for an extension for that court date ourselves."

Chalk Dinsmore spoke up, "Carson, I like that. Getting the trash off the streets is one thing but shootin' the fox that's suppose to be guardin' the chicken house puts real metal in the law badges we wear." After a short pause he continued, "The judge told us the last time he was here that he'd likely fine the drunks and fighters close to a month's wages. He said he figures it'll take that to convince them to behave or stay out of Dodge."

"That's a considerable fine," Carson reflected, "the type that'll turn things, but it'll take time, at least a year, maybe more."

Landry took on a troubled look, his face wrinkled, he asked, "I wonder what the judge has in mind for them that don't have that kind of money, or have a friend to stand for it."

Carson gave the answer, "He's bringing a law-clerk, a man that's assigned to him by Governor St. John, that will see to it they sign a promise note payable to the county and the state; and if they don't have it paid within ninety days, they'll go work the rock pile over to jail in Wichita for the next ninety days." His expression was steadfast, "I suppose some won't ever pay; they'll be on the run and stay clear of Dodge City."

"That's pretty strong for a man drinking too much pop-skull, or something as simple as fighting." Landry whistled as he frowned slant-eyed at Dinsmore.

"It shows Kansas is dead-set serious about making changes here," Rad put in.

"With that kind of reprimand for drinkin' and fightin', what's gonna happen to those two that did the shootin' and stabbin'?" Dinsmore glanced back toward the jail.

"My guess is they'll be looking through bars six to seven years if the verdict ends with them guilty of assault with intent to kill." Rad Carson's face was hard. "Word will get around that breaking the law in Dodge City carries a stiff penalty." He looked over his shoulder to the direction of Barnett's newspaper office, "It'll be interesting to see what Barnett writes about the governor and Judge Wilkinson when he hears the kind of jail time they're handing down."

"He's written plenty bad things about the town." Landry answered back, "Referring to Dodge as the place where the prairie drops into hell and Satan's family walks the boardwalks when the sun goes down. I doubt he'll have anything good to say about the new law in Dodge City being upright or respectable, it just ain't in the man to tell things straight."

As the three men stood talking, a twin-seat carriage rumbled close, avoiding the heavy wagon traffic of mid-morning. It was Fanny. She was smiling a bright smile, appearing to enjoy a remark by the match-suited man in the bowler hat driving the rig. Her jovial eyes never caught the implausible stare of Rad Carson. As they went past, Carson's gaze lingered, a fact fully noticed by Dinsmore and Landry. "Who was that?" Carson asked of the two men, his gawk remaining fixed on the backside of the carriage now some distance up the dusty street.

"That was Fanny Cartwright . . . from the restaurant."

"No! I mean who was the ham-fisted gentleman in the fancy suit of clothes and hat driving the team?"

"Not sure." Dinsmore proclaimed, answering as if he held little concern. As he studied Carson a few seconds longer he added, having an inkling Carson had a ting of jealousy, "Was he someone you think you might know?"

"Well, I just thought . . ." Rad caught himself realizing he didn't like the idea of Fanny enjoying the company of a strange man, one he'd never seen in town before. He faltered, struggled for words, and settled with saying, "The face was familiar, just didn't go with the kitschy clothes he was wearin' that's all." His face took on a shade of red as he awkwardly tried to let the event dissolve. He responded, "Let's see, where were we?" But with another glance to the speedy spring wagon, he came to terms that maybe he held more than simple fondness for Fanny.

The next morning Rad sat over a warm breakfast plate at a table nearest the front window in Fanny's café. Fanny caught his eye but he quickly looked away in an attempt to disallow the hazy blush that set to his face. To avert awkward humility he glanced out the window in a weak attempt to scrutinize the street view. Something did indeed draw his attention. Four rugged, unshaven, rough looking hardcases wearing new fangled coats and trousers coated with trail dust, reined in at The Spotted Cat Saloon across the street three doors down. They stepped from the saddle easy-like, totting as much iron as a small army. Rad figured them to irrefutably be outlaws. They made no attempt to conceal it, just the opposite. They wore the title with arrogance. Rad lifted the cup of coffee, keeping his eyes busied over the oval of the cup as he sipped lightly. They stood in a loose knot after looping leather over the rail. Words were exchanged lazily as they broke apart and took to the steps. Their manner was easy and their focus steady toward the batwings.

"Good morning Rad Carson." The pert voice of Fanny broke the lawman's concentration on the new arrivals in town. She rubbed her hands on the apron, her smile inviting the question as she eyed the idle plate of food and dipped her head, "Don't care for the blue-plate special breakfast?"

"Oh no, it's not that. Something drew my attention up the street." He looked down at the plate of food, "There won't be a crumb left when I get into it." He grinned. His eyes caught hers and locked there momentarily. They simultaneously blushed. "Well . . . . I . . . I," he stammered as his eyes searched, "I could use some grape jam."

Her lips half puckered, "Is that all? She teased.

Cason's attention was divided but he swept away the ungainly clumsiness, making a mental note to investigate the new arrivals. He made a final glance at the foursome, turned his full attention to Fanny, feeling obliged to do so, but also giving in to his momentary lack of full responsibility of putting law work ahead of everything else in his life, a rarity for him.

CHAPTER SEVENTEEN

Dodge City Marshal, Chalk Dinsmore, stood talking with Gus Matthews, owner of Pride Saddle and Tack when Carson spotted him in the late morning. "Chalk," Carson called out as he approached.

Chalk and Matthews stepped apart, Gus Matthews going into his store. Dinsmore took a couple of steps toward Carson in response, "Morning, Carson, what brings you out this way, aren't going to check the livery for a new horse, are ya?" He joked.

"Don't need one, but I got a question about an outlaw bunch I saw this morning, was wondering if you'd seen 'em."

"Outlaws?" Dinsmore half smirked, half scoffed, I'd have to guess which ones. You got some of the regular locals in mind?"

"Well they was new to me. Four of 'em," he drew a breath, "just come in from the trail, horses lathered some, they kicked down and went into The Spotted Cat like they had an appointment."

"Is that it?" Dinsmore was yet to think the situation held merit.

"Truth is I'm sniffing out a suspicious feeling." Rad squeezed his chin between his thumb and forefinger. "I thought if you'd seen the four of them maybe you'd feel the same." He looked back over a shoulder, "Could be I'm wrong, but I'm going to make another walk around and see if I can find out where they landed, if they're still in town."

"Big day tomorrow," Dinsmore threw in, "Judge Wilkinson will be holding court. We can use your help handling some of the prisoners, moving from the cells to the court room and all."

"I'll be there. I'm planning to see Wilkinson, having supper with him tonight, and the two of us plan to go over the court docket in the morning before he sits for the formality. I'll be to your place about an hour before court convenes in the morning, say nine o'clock—that be okay?"

"That oughta do fine. Me and Landry plan to bunk in the jail tonight so's we can get the lazy, no-account assholes up and around, try to make them presentable, ya know."

As they said their good-bys Carson abruptly studied something Dinsmore had said, *'check the livery'*. And as it was close he decided to look in on it. The broad doors were wide open, allowing the easy morning breeze to work through and nullify a portion of the usual odor.

"Howdy, Marshal Carson," the hostler's boy, Adam, waved as Rad drew close. The boy, chewing a stalk of straw, pulled it down to his side as he spoke again, "You still puttin' your horse up over at the Satterfield's barn?"

"Shore am, Adam. But if ever I change, I'll send for you." Carson placed a hand on the youngster's shoulder, bent and peered into the bleak light of the enormous barn. "You didn't by chance stable four horses, pretty well spent and lathered, this morning did you?"

"Yes sir, I did. Them men musta come from a ways, their mounts were wore plum out, thirsty, and hungry too." Adam answered as if reporting to a lawman's investigation.

"Did they say where they come from?"

"No, sir, and I asked 'em that." The ten year old boy said. "Fact is, they said I didn't need to know, said for me to not ask questions, and the way they said it, I wasn't about to." The boy's eyes saucered when he spoke.

"Rough actin' lot, huh?" Carson tried to down play Adam's description. "You put their horses away for the night, did ya?"

The boy bent forward, his voice quieted, "The man with the hand that was wrinkled like this," Adam attempted to fashion a claw with his left hand, "said for me to rub 'em down, water and feed 'em some oats, but not too much cause they'd be back around later to get their horses and leave town." He grinned wide, stuck a hand in a back pocket and withdrew a five dollar gold piece, "Lookee here."

"A dollar?"

"Sure 'nuff, and this here is mine, he gave me a couple others for my dad." He leaned forward again and near whispered, "The man said this one," he opened his hand again, "is for me."

"You're a good man, Adam. I know your father's proud of you." Rad thumbed his Stetson back, "And if I feel the need to change care for my horse, you'll be my man."

"Thank you, sir."

Carson once again weighed the suspicion he held. *If the four questionable men were going to be leaving town, why are they here in the first place, evidently rode hard to get to Dodge, and leaving again the same day didn't make sense. They weren't the type to be in town for business, not honest business anyhow.* He began to put more sand in his suspicion about the four loathsome looking men. With the horses boarded they could have gone anywhere, leaving no outside evidence of their whereabouts. The job just got tougher, but he was bent on finding them and trying to put some reason to their sudden presence, and perhaps their equally sudden disappearance, if the boy's information was to stand up. But Rad had a problem, not much time!

The Spotted Cat Saloon was a good place to start. He now wished that he'd gone there after breakfast, maybe before. He could have left Fanny's place, even leave the food on the table. '*Too late to think that now.*'

Rad Carson pushed the double doors back and stepped into the saloon. He looked the place over hoping Stell Marks would be there and handy. He thought she'd probably accommodate any questions he'd ask with straight answers. Rad had seen her wear either a soft or tough front equally well, but he was confident she was straightforward when it came to the law. Her place wasn't known as one that ordinarily catered to the ruffians, the outlaw type, which those four men absolutely depicted in Carson's assessment when he looked through the window and saw them while he was sitting at Fanny's. He sauntered over to the bar where Jake, the barkeep on duty the night the fight broke out, Rad stopped the shooting, and the saloon was shut down. "Jake." Rad spoke softly and with a twitch of his head motioned for the man to come his way. The barman acknowledged and shuffled over. He stood rigid in front of Rad, hands pushed against the back of the polished, dark mahogany bar top and Carson asked, "This morning four unruly looking men I characterized as outlaw-type, came in here together, you recall them?"

The shaved-head, thickset man with arms like stacked hams, raised his heavy eyebrows, making his solemn eyes appear to fade over swelled, rose-colored cheeks. He slanted those dark eyes at Carson, making Rad wonder of he'd hear the truth. But before he spoke, a blinking-eyed man with a messy curled mustache and front teeth missing whistled to Jake and lofted an empty beer mug. "Be right back, Marshal," Jake bemoaned, "I'll tell you about them boys in a minute." And he shuffled off to serve the dour-faced bar-fly, allowing for time to determine what message he'd convey to the lawman upon his return.

He ambled back to stand before Rad, hands wrap-dried on the white apron, looked Rad in the eye and said, "They was here," he nodded to a table several feet distant and pointed a thumb, "sat over there."

"You ever seen them in here before?" Carson asked, glaring into the round face with a hard look demanding a forth-rite answer.

"Nope," he lied.

"Did you hear anything, hear what they talked about?"

"Couldn't hear nothin' they said." He rolled his eyes toward the batwing doors, "Didn't stay long—drank near a full bottle of sour-mash whiskey though." He looked back at Carson and decided he'd best offer a bit more information if the lie was to be discovered later, "The man with the withered hand seemed to be in charge." Jake braced a stare at Carson, "Hardcases; bad-ass men, all of 'em. My guess would be, judging from the likes of men I've seen here in Dodge over the years, they intend to rob something or somebody, anyhow, they shore did look the part." He waffled his head up and down, "I was glad to see 'em leave!" He nodded and threw a thumb at the lower back side of the bar, "I had my hand on my scattergun when they was walking out"

"Thanks, Jake. My feelings about them fellas was the same as yours." Carson turned and took a step toward the door with a thought smoldering in his mind like a fresh branded steer, *'I hope I find them snakes before any damage gets done.'*

Three hours and a dozen light conversations later Carson had to give it up. The two banks in town tightened security and armed themselves when Rad gave them the information about the men he saw. Other than the banks, he'd been in The Harrington House, Elephant Head Saloon, Long Branch Saloon, Big Ed's, etc. More than once he felt he'd been given erroneous information, but had no way of proving the sources wrong. He couldn't determine if the informants, or *un-informants*, were unaware of the culprits he sought, or if they simply denied knowledge. He couldn't lay blame on the people he questioned for not coming across with information. The business owners and citizens of Dodge City had been held in contempt for several years by lawless elements, and in almost as many instances as not, by law officers that were as corrupt and evil as the depraved men they proposed to thwart. He could see the uncertainty in their faces, which strangely made him think of Wi Chong, the Chinese baker, and him studying on whether or not to bake pies using a peck basket of apples that had set in the cellar well past their prime. Bad men, like corrupted apples, can't always be recognized if there's enough care taken to hide their corruption.

It was late. He could do no more today except continue hoping his intuition was wrong, but deep down he couldn't accept that conclusion. He would have to wait. Maybe the judge would have some knowledge of a gang lead by a man with a distorted left hand. He'd make it a point to inform the judge of the men he'd observed.

Carson was early. He arrived several minutes ahead of the scheduled time he was to meet Judge Wilkinson at The Drover's Palace. This was where the finest steak in town was served on dinnerware imported from Scotland and eaten with real silver utensils from Spain. The wine the judge always insisted to be served with his meal was also from Spain, made from the tempranillo grapes of the Upper Rioja.

Rad waited, he'd decided to hold his question concerning the visitors he'd spotted early in the morning. He was anxious but he knew Wilkerson always insisted on dinner first—legal talk was to come after dinner, not to interfere with the delicacy of the meal and the wonderful wine afterward.

The judge swirled the imported Spanish red wine in the tall stem glass and with his hand lightly waved the aroma toward his flared-for-the-occasion nostrils. The ordeal struck Carson as being far-fetched, perhaps the most untypical action he'd ever seen in Ford County, Kansas, or anywhere else he could muster to his thoughts.

"As usual," Wilkinson proclaimed as he folded his dinner napkin and placed it next to his desert plate before lighting a cigar, "the dinner was excellent." He smiled largely, "I always look forward to court sessions in Dodge, because of dinner here the night before."

Wilkinson was a proud man. The scheme he and Governor St. John put together in an effort to restore proper law and order added to his pride. "Tomorrow, Rad, this town will take note; they'll see real penalties levied in my courtroom, penalties that will be the start of breaking the hold the lawless have had for years." He looked down, tapped ashes from his cigar and jerked his head back up, "Ten days ago the local newspaper editor, Barnett, called on me. He said he was aware there were major changes coming to the way the law was to be handled in Dodge and wanted an article for his newspaper. I gave him one; told him the penalties and fines were being increased substantially and we were going to take Dodge City away from the worthless, irrational outlaw elements and turn it over to good citizens that will make it grow, make it prosper." His smile was authentic, but fell away when he noted the stern, somewhat anxious face, of Rad Carson sitting across the table, "You don't look as satisfied as I thought you might be, Rad, something bothering you?" He tilted his head back and expelled a plume of gray smoke, awaiting an answer, knowing the marshal had something up a sleeve.

Rad puzzled for a few seconds, not wanting to distinguish the gaiety the judge held. In preparing to answer, he laced his fingers together and rested his hands on the sleek white table cloth, "Since you've ask, your honor . . . I saw a man in town, matter of fact, it was four men, I'd swear a couple of them was a step above the most ornery thugs I've seen in town in the time I've been here. But two were well dressed, looked like new clothes that'd come off the counter not more than yesterday or today." He hesitated, giving thought to his memory before going on, "One of them had a withered, malformed left hand; he seemed to be the leader. I was wondering if you'd come across such a man in this part of the country?"

Wilkinson's mouth dropped, allowing the cigar to sag. But he quickly recomposed, the cigar came erect, his eyes shot a lurid, freighted expression, one Rad had never imagined the judge had in his legal-minded arsenal. The aged, court room authority-figure leaned forward, his mustache minced, and he asked, "Here, here in Dodge you saw this man—today?"

Rad felt like he'd just handed the judge a stick of dynamite with a sizzling fuse. He lowered his head a mite and cautioned as he answered, "Sure enough." His gaze moved uneasily to analyze Wilkinson's face. "That surprises you? I . . . I mean that the man would be here in Dodge City?"

"It surprises me that the man would be anywhere except the state prison in Wichita," He flexed his shoulders and braced his back against the chair that shrieked in response, "Maybe it's not the same man . . . couldn't hardly be." He bounced his head up and down slowly and minced his cigar between his teeth before he asked, "You say there were three other men with the fellow what had the bad hand?"

"That's right, Judge, saw them myself. They had been riding hard and all had a callous look, wasn't a doubt in my mind they were a dangerous lot, but I had nothing on them, couldn't take 'em in for just riding into town and looking mean." Carson saw concern remained in the judge's face, "What's the story on the man, the man with the bad hand?" Carson asked.

"If it's one and the same," Wilkinson held the cigar between his thumb and forefinger, studied it momentarily and scratched at the bridge of his broad nose, "That'd be Milt, The Possum, Tucker. I sent him to prison last year. He's to do twenty years for bank robbery and murder, a man was killed, gunned down inside the bank. That McMichaels fella, was his attorney." He saw Carson's quick glance. "Seems that man's name comes up a lot when trouble's in the air—didn't do Tucker much good, made him madder'n hell at McMichaels though." Wilkinson's eyes rolled, "I'll check in the morning to see if Tucker's broke out? Damn, I hate to see that man on the outside, especially here in Dodge!"

Rad Carson went to bed at Satterfield's boarding house feeling anxious. He had the stableman saddle his horse, Caesar, and tie him just inside the barn door. This was only the second time in two weeks that he took that precaution, but he had '*that feeling*'. He fell asleep *thinking 'If the bad-handed hombre was indeed PossumTucker, what was it that brought him to Dodge City?'*

CHAPTER EIGHTEEN

It was three o'clock, commonly the peaceful portion of the night, when the explosion rattled windows. Rad jumped to his feet and fretfully peered into the bleak, obscure night. Sparkling embers punched holes in the darkness above the center of town. They gave depth to the cloud of black smoke which billowed high and wide, momentarily crippling the glow of the three-quarter moon. Rad pulled at his clothes and stomped into boots as he pushed the door back with an elbow, both hands busy with the gun belt.

The front yard of Satterfield's boarding house began to fill with partially dressed people. Their attention was drifting from the sky above building tops and to one another as Rad leaped into the saddle and galloped up Elm Street.

The few blocks he rode toward town's center were hastily coming to life. He darted past people that began to apprehensively gather in the streets; some of fear, others out of curiosity. Men were running, but not toward where the explosion centered, they were going the other way! It was the jail. Someone had blown the jail to smithereens! Splintered boards, once the walls, were scattered, the roof was gone, blown off the building and into the vacant lot next to what was the jail.

Rad jumped from his horse and ran to the jumbled smoking debris that had been the front half of the building, the office portion. Smoke continued to clear and papers fluttered softly to the ground. Chalk Dinsmore and J. R. Landry's bodies were rope tied to remnants of chairs. The cells were empty, doors swung open; no doubt they'd been unlocked, not blown open by the blast. That explained the numerous men running.

Fury flashed throughout his body. Rad was filled with hate, hate for whoever did this! Lanterns in the hands of onlookers provided minimal but sufficient light, but also rendered an eerie, peculiar, almost sinister atmosphere as shadows leaped from object to object through the smoke and debris when the lanterns shifted. The acidic odor of gunpowder was intense.

The four men he'd seen yesterday—it had to be them. If the man with the misshapen hand was indeed Possum Tucker, it must have been, but why? Nothing else to do now but cut the town marshals, Landry and Dinsmore, from their bindings in respect for them. But as Rad stood over Dinsmore the man jerked meekly, his body wrenched. He was alive! "You," Rad screamed to a man who'd approached, "get Doc Hink—now!"

The livery! Rad mounted his horse with a leap. He had to see if the four horses Adam had cared for at the livery were gone. He swung Caesar in a circle and yelled to others that had gathered, curious of the mayhem, "Take care of those lawmen. Make sure the doctor gets to Dinsmore quick. I'll be right back."

Rad left the curiosity seekers to themselves, to reach their own conclusions. Most were infuriated with the circumstances. They had begun to hold confidence honest citizens would be able to cope, live peaceful lives free of rowdy cowboys, outlaws, and raucous law men. This was a setback, maybe a signal that their hopes were not to become reality. But a few young troublemakers grinned and exchanged snide remarks, finding absurdity in the possibility of honorable law enforcement in Dodge.

The hostler, Gentry Ralston, stood just outside the livery barn with Adam at his side; both stood in their britches, no shirt or boots. Carson rode to the open door, leaned precariously and looked inside, "Those four horses—are they gone?"

Ralston spoke loud, his hands cupped around his mouth. "They took 'em out about an hour ago, woke me up when they did."

"Did you see where they went?"

"Just rode that-a-way." He pointed toward the main part of town.

Carson quickly rode back to the jail. Several people had gathered. Doc Hink's carriage pulled up and the wiry, white haired man stepped down with his black bag in hand. "My God," he bellowed, blinking over his glasses. "Which one is alive?" He was directed to Chalk Dinsmore. Picking through the rubble he saw Deputy Landry. He quickly focused on the man's body but realized he couldn't be breathing, two sizeable shafts of splintered wood protruded from his chest and one from the man's neck. He picked his way through to where Dinsmore had been laid, head propped up on a rolled blanket, having been untied, and a man was attempting to give him a sip of water from a canteen.

Judge Wilkinson arrived and quickly settled in beside Carson as Rad leaped down from his ride from the livery. "This isn't coincidental," the judge quipped, "jails don't get blown up just to get a prisoner or two out, no sir, there's more to it than that."

"You're right, Judge, that's the way I see it too." Carson pushed his hat back with his knuckles and scratched at his hairline with an index finger, "I'm thinking this is a message meant for you and me, and Governor St. John." Carson's voice was low and drawn. "Makes our job harder, don't make us stop, just going to take longer than we might have thought."

Wilkinson piped up quickly, "I'll get a wire off to the prison in Wichita first thing in the morning. My guess is that Milt Tucker somehow escaped and is behind this. The man is a crafty son-of-a-bitch, and just about as nasty-mean as they come." The judge raised his eyes to meet Carson's, "When he was drug out of the jail and chained to the wagon that was to take him to prison he was cussing and screaming, said he'd have his day, the law in Dodge City would regret putting him in the lock up. Looks to me like this here incident is the retort he had in mind."

"I'll get a posse together," Carson said back. He watched the doctor a few seconds as he tended to Dinsmore before turning to the Judge, "Will you cover this with Hinkle? He's gonna have a big job on his hands for a few days." He slowly cast his eyes through the gathering crowd, thinking about men for the posse. The time he'd been in Dodge was too short to become familiar with men that he knew to be tough, good saddle men and law-worthy. Most he'd become to know were store owners and clerks, not the type for posse work. His abrupt stares stopped; there was the newsman, Richard Barnett. He was standing well back, analyzing the crowd, evaluating their response to the violence imposed on the reorganized law of Dodge City. '*Good*', thought Carson, '*I don't want him in my hair right now.*' He undoubtedly was not a man to take to the trail after fugitives.

Rad walked over to where Doc was examining the injured marshal, "How's he doing, Doc?"

Doc Hink peered at the lawman over the top of his glasses and answered halfheartedly, "He'll pull through. Looks like the desk there saved his life," Hink nodded in that direction, "it sealed his body somewhat from the blast. He's got cuts and bruises, and a busted eardrum, maybe both. He'll heal in time, but it'll be a good spell before he can hear much of anything other than the sound of a ringing bell." He looked up at Rad with narrowed eyes and spoke with a bleak tone, "He won't be able to answer questions unless they're in writing."

Carson noted the condition of the room, the placement of the oak desk, and the location of Dinsmore. He agreed with Hink's assessment, that the desk had diluted the impact for Chalk Dinsmore, and Rad experienced a greater confidence in the doctor, "I'd say you're right." Carson's analogy of the blast went on, "Evidently they placed a considerable amount of dynamite in the room, over there," he pointed. "After they tied up the marshals and released the prisoners those bastards planted the dynamite with a twofold purpose, to destroy the building and kill these two men. I'd guess Dinsmore was able to flip his chair onto its side and below the desk to avoid the direct blast." Rad then directed a question to the doctor, "Did either of these men have gunshot wounds?"

"Can't say as I found any—not for sure because of the many injuries from the explosion, but right now, I'd say neither was shot."

Doctor Fredrick Hink had been in Dodge City for almost four years, having come from Missouri, near Kansas City. A certificate to practice medicine from the neighboring state, which hung in his office, indicated he'd completed studies of internal medicine. Kansas had no requirements for a physician to be a general practitioner of the healing arts: anyone could hang their shingle over a door, and after he'd treated a gunshot wound, delivered a baby, and had a black bag to carry a few doctor's appliances, if he looked like a doctor, he could be one.

Several men and a few blanket-wrapped saloon girls with smudged rouge and curls dangling over their foreheads stood nearby. The solemn expressions denoted sorrow and concern for the wrath unleashed against the new law in Dodge City. They leaned, heads together, hands clasped and held under their chins, they spoke to one another softly. Expressions conveyed personal grief for the injured men.

George Hinkle, Ford County Sheriff, arrived. He'd shuffled his way methodically from the room he took as sleeping quarters in the rear of his office three blocks away. He stood slumped over, inhaling deeply, next to the judge when Carson stepped over debris, onto the plank walk and back into the street. Carson heard Hinkle arduously question Judge Wilkinson about who was thought to have been responsible for the ruination of the city marshal's office.

"Not real sure just who's behind this." Wilkinson studied the damage thoughtfully, considering the lack of adequate facilities for prisoners in town and remarked almost inconsequently, "But other than not having a roof over them," he grinned wistfully, "the cells don't look much damaged, I suppose we could still lock somebody up, maybe put a tent over the cages; that is if we had anybody to man it."

The sheriff gave the judge a despairing look, but then realized the judge was making mockery of his own failed handiwork in bringing new law and order to the town. "The town council will have to get their heads together right quick," Hinkle reacted, "they can't sit on their butts and pat their big bellies like they usually do."

"That's pretty strong language, George," the lightheartedness of seconds before vanished quickly and the judge reprimanded him, "I think you might want to reconsider your opinion, at least your *public* opinion. Open animosity by civic officials carries over quick like, gets the citizens riled and tends to take the community down a wayward trail. We don't need any more of that in Dodge," his dressing-down continued.

Carson moved to affront Sheriff Hinkle, to tell him he was going to go after the men that blew up the law office, but the message he intended was interrupted. Adam Ralston, the livery barn boy came running, yelling, "Marshal Carson . . . Marshal Carson." The boy ran to Carson, reached out and touched him, but bent and breathing heavily, rasped, "They came back!"

"What?"

Adam glared at the demolished jail building for three or four seconds, he shuffled his bare feet in the dirt and looked up, first into Carson's face, but then searched the expression of the other two, Judge Wilkinson, and Hinkle. Uncertainty gripped him, his demeanor faltered momentarily, not knowing if he should tell what he knew in their presence. But he went on, "Two of 'em came back to the livery."

Carson leaned and grasped the boy's shoulders; he spoke heedfully, "You mean the four men I was looking for that rode out just a short time ago?"

"That's right." He related excitedly, "Two of 'em rode in just a minute ago—they didn't see me, I was hiding behind feed barrels. They left the saddles on their horses and climbed up into the loft like they was hidin' from someone."

"Just two? You never saw anything of the other two?"

"No sir. I didn't wait around either. I slipped around through the tack room and went out the back door real quiet and come runnin' to tell you." The boy's face was as tense as his voice.

"You did good, Adam. You'll make a fine lawman someday."

Rad reached out and grabbed Hinkle by the elbow. His focus bore down on the ponderous sheriff, "Did you hear that? We can get 'em. There's a pair of them up to the livery."

"Get who?" Hinkle's brow wrinkled, a complex expression set into his face. He looked the boy over head to toe, "What's he squawking' about?"

Judge Wilkinson's head never stop turning, looking back and forth between Rad and Sheriff Hinkle, he questioned Rad, "Is he talking about the four men you described to me last evening Carson?"

"That's right, Judge." Carson's attention turned, going to Hinkle again as he gripped the sheriff's arm tighter and raised his voice, "The men that did this," he flashed a glance at the destruction, "and killed a marshal—they're hiding out at the livery right here in town—two of 'em anyway." Rad released Hinkle's arm, slipped his Colt out of leather and flipped the cylinder open; a habit when he knew he was going to be firing the sidearm. "You goin' with me?" Rad bluntly asked of the sheriff, and following a very brief hesitation, started toward his horse.

Hinkle looked around, saw Doc Hink's carriage, scampered toward it as readily as his bulkiness would allow and put a foot on the stepper, "I'm coming," he yelled as Rad swung up, sat the saddle and restlessly looked back to allow an answer.

"Don't take my carriage!" Hink yelled, "I've got to get this man over to my office, you can't have my rig."

A man unknown by the lawmen hurriedly stepped forward with bridle reins in hand, "Here, Sheriff, take my horse."

It took a few seconds for the sheriff to get his bulky body astride the horse. His hulking size kept him from being a regular on horseback. He was, by the nature of his bulk, a buckboard and cart man. Carson didn't wait; his horse's hooves dug into the ground and shoved forward, churning toward the livery. His mind busied with a plan, recounting the configuration of the livery barn and its surroundings.

CHAPTER NINETEEN

Carson leaped from his horse several feet from the big barn, newfound bitterness welled up inside. The thought of town marshal, J. R. Landry's punctured body and stone cold eyes urged him on. He darted, almost stumbling, into the darkness through the livery doors, bent low and took transitory cover at the edge of the first empty stall. Pungent odors of hay and horse droppings were magnified by the summer heat. Fully black, unidentifiable images blotted against inky backgrounds. With his right hand gripped on the Colt at his side, he cupped the left hand to the side of his mouth, "I'm Federal Marshal Rad Carson, you two, up in the loft, come down now."

The first response to Carson's demand was nothing other than an uneasy nicker from the horse he could reach out and touch and the fretful cooing of pigeons that had settled on a rafter near the roof. Carson waited. His eyes readily adjusted to the near total darkness and his ears strained to hear sounds of their movements overhead. He had no idea who these men were. They weren't acting as crazed gunslingers; if they had been they would have already stepped forward and thrown down on him. If Tucker was the sly devil Judge Wilkinson said he was, he wouldn't be one of the men in the loft. Rad's assumption was the men he had treed were lesser men than Tucker, likely recruited by Milt Tucker on short order for the specific job they'd just completed, blowing up the jail. "I know you're up there." Carson yelled and thumbed back the hammer.

"There ain't no law that says a man can't sleep in the livery."

"No." Carson hollered back, "But there's laws that makes blowing up a building and killing men plenty illegal enough to get ya hung."

A moment of hush spread through the murky, rancid air, a quiet that would make a dead man's eyes blink. But it was radically blunted by a stabbing flame that stung the darkness, throwing a shaft of angry sparks. The bellow of the .45 sent simultaneously sent splinters twisting over Carson's head. Horses whinnied and bumped the enclosures, setting off a bevy of additional confusion. Overhead sounds of shuffling feet, muffled a mite in the layers of supple hay, became evident. They scooted toward the back of the loft. Carson kept his shoulders hunkered down and felt his way along the stalls keeping with the direction of sounds from above. He was careful not to worsen the startle of the animals.

Firing back at the men above, shooting through the wooden floor of the loft, would offer little hope for wounding the culprits and only further alarm the horses, perhaps creating a melee among the animals for the outlaws to escape in the darkness and turmoil.

Rad heard Hinkle yell out as he arrived at the front entrance. With him in place Rad could cover the back side of the barn and keep the killers at bay. He yelled to Hinkle, "Stay out there and guard the front, Sheriff . . . they're in the loft. Don't let anyone slip out your way," Carson then added emphatically, "and I'll cut them down if they try to escape back here."

Hinkle shrieked back, "I've got my scattergun ready, aimed at the door. If they come this way I'll put big damn holes in their hides."

Another shot boomed from above and ripped through the wood some six to seven feet from Carson. He knew they were becoming fretful, realizing they'd trapped themselves in a foolish effort to hide out rather than skedaddle out of town. Perhaps that was a scheme thought through by Possum Tucker to keep the law from his trail. He probably suckered these two simple-minded hooligans and he was likely kicking spurs to his horse miles away and grinnin' like the possum name he was tapped to carry.

"You got no chance boys. You can live to stand trial or you can kiss the undertaker's . . ." Rad's remark was cut short with a series of bullets crashing through the floor from the upper level, missing Carson and somehow missing all of the animals. But the horses had all they could take. The combination of being restrained in close dark quarters and gun shots stung their nerves worse than a swarm of bees. They struggled, reared and kicked, letting go a barrage of unrestrained ferocity. The sounds of boards splintering intensified as the thrashing of heavy animal bodies shook the barn. In short order several horses swarmed out the doors, including the two fully saddled mounts of the culprits hiding out above.

Hinkle fired the scattergun, adding to the dilemma. The combination of noises broke the night open like the roar of a rain-swollen, flash flood through canyon walls. Carson took a blow to his chest when a tempered stallion smashed into him before he could side-step. His knee buckled and he went down, landing full weight on his right hand. Another horse lunged toward him. He yanked his body to the left and felt the wet nostrils of the animal brush his cheek as it thrust wildly, seeking the opening that bequeathed freedom. His wrist, the gun hand wrist, screeched in pain. The Colt Peacemaker was gone, dropped onto the obscure livery floor.

"You okay, Carson?" Hinkle yelled, and followed with, "Weren't nobody on them horses."

"I'm okay, just mad as hell, ready to shoot a couple of assholes that caused all the trouble in here," Rad roared back. He continued the mockery, not letting his injury and loss of the revolver hinder his posture as predator in the minds of his prey. He kneeled and calmly moved his hand across the dark, uneven floor in search of the Colt. The hand tingled, partially numbed. He flexed the fingers to determine the severity. A throb took the place of the original sharp pain. *'It'll be fine in another minute or two, maybe a sprain, but nothing broken'.*

Bent and searching for the fallen Colt in a slow, deliberate motion, the side of his boot thumped. The solid feel of heavy metal shifting slightly brought an inner satisfaction. His fingers confirmed the thought; the Colt was found. He shifted it into his right hand—*'No, it's better in the other hand'. But that's fine, I could always shoot almost as well left handed as right'.* Rad pushed his back firmly against the support post in the center of the big barn and listened. The clatter gave way and near silence bolstered his temperament.

Hinkle bellowed from outside, "Should I come in and spray the loft with heavy buckshot? That will get them bastards down outta there one way or the other, either peaceable like or full of holes."

All got quiet once again, a slow minute, seemingly like the stillness preempting the fury of a tornado. The outlaws had to be thinking about taking lead, and within the next few seconds Hinkle howled, "I've got four more armed men out here, Carson, all friends of the marshals them hombres killed back at the jail. They're ready to set into the livery if we give the word. We can flush them varmints and cut 'em down in no time."

Carson shouted back, "We'll give 'em another minute before we'll set all the hounds loose for the kill." Carson flexed the fingers of the injured hand and at the same time tweaked his ears for a response from above.

A large shadow dropped from overhead, hitting the floor with a thud fifteen feet from Rad. A groan was followed instantaneously by the multicolored blast from the barrel of a six-gun. A slug whistled through the air over Rad Carson's head and he reeled. His six-gun belched twice and the dark figure jerked backward. The first of the outlaws made a bad decision and paid for it with his life. Five seconds, seeming like an eternity, followed before Carson reported to Sheriff Hinkle, "Stay put, Hinkle. I just killed one—we'll see if the other one is as eager to meet up with the Devil as this idiot." The two remaining horses in the murky darkness whinnied and pranced within their stalls before another short lapse of silence ensued.

"Don't shoot, lawman, I'm coming down."

"Throw your gun-belt down first, with guns in it."

"Just got one gun."

"Don't be lyin' to me, ya skunk. Toss 'em out, everything you've got, and wait until I tell you before you come down the ladder." When the belt and holstered gun thumped the floor, he retrieved it cautiously and confirmed the culprit's claim, a single gun. "Okay, come down slow and keep your hands high. I wouldn't want to make a mistake in this dim light and shoot you because you kept a hand where I couldn't see it good and plain."

"I tell ya I only carry one hand gun, my rifle's left in the saddle boot with my horse. Don't go ta shootin' like a crazy man; I ain't the one behind all the trouble at the jail." The man's voice was uneasy, steeped with fear.

"I won't shoot if you're straight with me, but if another gun comes near your hand, you'll be a dead man before your boots set down." Carson inched away from the loft ladder. His head kept moving in an effort to put as much light behind the decent of the rascal as possible. He didn't want to kill the man; he'd fire to wing him if he had to shoot. Rad wanted him alive so he could question him, to learn more about the two that had evidently left Dodge and didn't run for cover back at the livery.

"Carson?" Outside the sheriff's nerves were raw. "Carson, what's going on in there? Everything okay?"

"Got things in control, Sheriff." Carson yelled and turned his face slightly toward the door without taking his eyes off of the deep-shadowy figure descending from above. You can come on in but do it easy like, and bring a set of shackles. We're taking a prisoner—that is unless this man tries something funny and I have the pleasure of layin' him out with the first one."

* * *

With the first hint of light, dim purple clouds with a milky top layer vaguely shone on the east horizon. In the distance an ambitious rooster aggressively yapped an approval. A new day arrived in Dodge City, but the inauguration of new law enforcement suffered a setback.

As he promised, the judge was at the barber shop that doubled as the telegraph office when Dolan, the key-punch operator and barbershop owner, fished the door key from his pocket. The latch clicked and they went inside without a word between them; it wasn't necessary. Dolan had been present at the jail along with dozens of others during the night. He walked around the barber chair and stepped behind the counter, removed his hat, snapped the green visor snug to his forehead and slid a yellow pad in front of the judge. "You sending to the governor again, Judge Wilkinson?"

"He's next. This one's going over to the Wichita prison." There were no secrets; the key punch man knew everyone's business. He kept well informed in his dual capacity, perhaps more so than Richard Barnett, editor of the Dodge City newspaper. Wilkinson put the pencil down and lifted the pad to study the message he'd prepared. "Okay, send this one, Dolan, and I'll get another ready for Governor St. John while you're doing it."

The man kept his finger busy while he talked. "So you think ol' Possum Tucker broke out over there do ya?" The ticker halted and Dolan remarked, "Makes sense, the man was crazier'n a bed bug and meaner than a foamin'-mouthed coyote when they hauled him out of here." Fred Dolan gave the judge a smug look and continued his banter, "He's just the type of sneaky cuss that could break outta jail and there ain't no doubt he'd want to kill some lawmen here in Dodge." He finished the message and took up the next one. His fingers rested over the button as he read the words on the pad and prepared to send, "You and that Carson gent sure got your hands full this time."

Wilkinson didn't answer. His blank expression was sufficient. He'd been displeased with the man's analogy of his messages before, he didn't need his questioning. But he did need the man's talent and diligence to duty so he accepted the comments as he'd always done before, without words of dissatisfaction, and the offer of a simple smile. "You'll get right back to me when those replies come in won't you? I'll be over to the Drover's Palace or they'll know where you can find me."

Rad Carson sat with an elbow on the red and white checkered tablecloth. The front window of Fanny's Fancy Foods provided a street view where he could see the judge coming from the telegraph office. He'd not had a chance to get more sleep. He and Hinkle put the cuffed man in the holding cell in Hinkle's office. It wasn't much more than a boarded closet with a reinforced door and a hole in it the size of a man's head. The prisoner refused to talk about the other two outlaws that were a part of the jail blasting, just saying he didn't know who they were or where they'd gone.

Carson stayed on to stand guard. Hinkle was a sturdy man, strong, but on short order. His size drained him of energy quickly. Rad thought it best not to leave the man alone with the prisoner for the balance of the night. They agreed the likelihood some of the prisoners the man helped escape just might make an effort to concoct an idiotic plan and reverse the roles. They knew outlaws helping others of their kind wasn't normal'; the blasting of the jail wasn't intended as help, it was of direct intention to spoil the law efforts to bring legal process to Dodge City, nothing else. By the time morning rolled around, if none of the escaped prisoners were discovered in town Rad surmised they would all have made way to nearby farms for horses. Catching all, or a considerable number of them, was impossible, and even if they were caught there was no place to hold them.

"I got the messages off," Wilkinson said as he slid the chair back and sat down. The judge tolerated the lack of sleep well. He seemed fresh, no noticeable wear for the ordeal. He was, Rad thought, a more sturdy man for his age than was Sheriff Hinkle. "Being as early in the day as it is, I doubt we'll hear anything for at least four hours, most likely be longer, maybe noon." He twisted around and spoke from the side of mouth, looking for Fanny, "I sure could use some strong, hot coffee."

Fanny moved toward them with the striking smile encased in both innocence and charm. The combination of her shapeliness, full rosy lips and soft blue eyes, as usual, captured Rad's awareness like the jaws of a steel trap on the leg of grizzly, or maybe more on the order of a honeybee's flight back to the hive with nectar gathered from a flower garden. He was beginning to realize he was smitten. The sight of this woman, from the curl that adorned her delightful forehead to the light touch of her foot to the floor brought rise to his inner-self he'd never previously experienced.

"Good morning, gentlemen," she cooed around perfect white teeth, "you're out early. I suppose the ruckus last night must have taken away your ability to rest."

Judge Wilkinson, responded with a "Hummph. I guess you could say that, Miss Fanny." He cut his eyes to Rad and arched his bushy salt and pepper brow, fully knowing the answer beforehand, "Did it keep you awake, Carson?"

"Some." He responded with a slight shake of his head and a partial smile, looking up at Fanny, "But the ruckus, as you named it, Fanny, didn't hinder my morning appetite . . . I'd like one of your blue plate specials, and about a gallon of that fresh brewed coffee I smell."

"Want to know what the special is?" She tilted her head to the side and puckered her lips ever so slightly back at Rad.

"Don't care." His eyes met hers and they both froze for a second or two, "If you recommend it, I'll have it." Her grin indicated she realized Rad was pleased with her.

Wilkinson could see the allure between them. He leaned back in his chair and laced his fingers across his middle. "Hummm," he started, "I'll have the blue plate special also." Fanny didn't respond or look his way. His voice raised a mite, "And black coffee," he added, drumming his fingers on the table, a grin finding his lips and his mind.

CHAPTER TWENTY

The cluster of tall elm trees stood out on the prairie flatland and beckoned to Colonel Green, so he told folks when asked about selecting his location for the stage line. It also sat west of Wichita near midway between Pratt and Dodge City, a route rapidly gaining popularity. He called his new endeavor The Cannonball, a nickname he wore proudly during the States War. There were already six families settled nearby when he staked out the ground.

Not too many years before, the Kiowa gathered here, a place that offered shade and seepage of water from the ground, forming a pool which the Indians lined with stone. The buffalo scuffed the ground in forage of the moisture for many decades before the Kiowa made such use of the place, and of course it was the buffalo the Indians sought. Passing of time brought the white man, first in intangible numbers, only a few trappers, and then traders, buffalo hunters, and eventually the settlers.

Within a year following Colonel Green's initial startup of the ambitious plan, Greensburg boasted a dozen structures, principally sod and adobe. In due time the Colonel built the first wood structures, a post office, and soon thereafter, a small building that offered overnight rooms. Both were accommodations that well served Cannonball Green's stagecoach line.

Milt Possum Tucker and a fellow prisoner escapee by the name of Luther Combs, had stopped in Greensburg three days ago. They quietly drank their whiskey at the trading post saloon and made acquaintance with a pair of empty-pocket-ruffians that were heading for Dodge City, having come from Kansas City by way of Medicine Lodge. Tucker quickly assumed the leadership role; plans were put in place in a matter of an hour over the sour mash liquor and the four of them took advantage of Cannonball's enterprise. They robbed the stage office and the rest-house guests, taking personal valuables and everyone's money before leaving town. There was no law in Greensburg, no one to step forward and offer resistance as would Colonel Donald Green, had he been there. But his business interest had taken him to Wichita the previous day.

This afternoon another roughshod group rode into the little Kansas settlement where tall elm trees stood as affable visual guardians. Understandably the citizens became alarmed well before the six newcomers stepped down from leather. Muley Tatum led the way into the post saloon. On his heel were the men that had ridden with him for the past four weeks, Charlie Joe, Bo Cantrell, and Miguel Avino, along with the Longleys. Tatum picked up a gathering of newspapers lying on the bar top, handed them to Bo and instructed Bo, "Hold onto these, we'll take them along when we leave, I like to know what's going on."

Cantrell gave him a quizzical stare but knew better than to question, just answered, "I'll do that, kind of like to read a mite myself." It wasn't true, but Bo thought it was likely to please Muley.

The longley brothers, Pete and Jesse, remained outside, finding solace in the shade of a big tree with two chairs placed there for such purpose. The brothers each had rolled a smoke and looked over the quaint little settlement from their peaceful vantage point, having no idea they were being cautiously scrutinized by a half dozen locals.

Jesse tilted his head back and blew a plume of gray smoke toward outstretched branches of the tree, "I'm for going on to Colorado. This heat is playing hob with me; I'm thinkin' it's hotter here than it is in Texas." He hesitated, looking up and down the town's one street, "The mountains of Colorado have gotta be cooler, don't ya think, Pete."

Pete removed his hat and wiped his brow with the back of his wrist, "You sure it ain't the gold that's got you all primed and half-cocked?"

"That too," Jesse acknowledged. After a brief pause, he continued, "We still got a sizeable poke from that stagecoach holdup, and a bit from ol' Muley brow-beatin' that trail boss outta money down by Indian Territory. It's a dang more than we could make pushin' cows."

Pete dropped the cigarette butt and squashed it with a toe, "Hell of-a-choice ain't it, brother, drive cattle or outlawin'." The older brother used words like they were rationed, not the type to explain his thoughts even to Jesse, and never to lesser known folks.

Jesse put back, "It don't have to be that way, we can set ourselves up with whatever we need, file a claim in Colorado and put to minin'." He twisted a look over to Pete, "With a little luck we could buy a whole herd of cows and put some other suckers to workin' for us." He grinned wide, but Pete showed no expression.

Pete put his hat back on, adjusted his gun-belt and turned toward the open door leading inside the small adobe and rock structure, "Let's go inside and get a beer." Jesse snuffed out his smoke disgustedly. He was having a difficult time reading his older brother's thoughts. Pete wasn't the kind of man to take things from other people for his own benefit, but for some reason he wouldn't break away from the sordid likes of Muley Tatum. It didn't add up.

"Well . . ." Tatum bellowed and brought a chill to the room. He followed with a smirk as he waved a welcome to the Longleys coming through the door. "The sons of Texas have chosen to bless us with their presence!" He hoisted his glass in a mockery salute, "Give them boys a beer, Mr. Barman, and put it on my bill." He slammed a twenty dollar gold coin to the board serving as a bar top, "As matter of fact, give them anything they want," he leaned across the board and laced his fingers around the barrels of the shotgun he'd spotted when they came in, "including this here scattergun." He swung the double barrel twelve gauge in front of his body and shoved it, barrel pointed skyward, toward Pete. Bo Cantrell and Charlie Joe exchanged disparaging looks, feeling trouble was brewing in the nefarious mind of Muley Tatum. They'd seen it start with this type of twisted beginnings before.

"Don't want no shotgun—don't plan on shootin' anything." Pete remarked without emotion as he calmly sauntered toward where Muley stood at the bar. With his thumbs hooked over his cartridge belt, Pete shook his head inconspicuously and refused it. He knew his actions, be they anything other than docile, could bring about a bizarre riposte from the loud, eccentric man who stood holding the gun, but Pete was betting otherwise.

Tatum backed off, laid the gun on the bar and slapped Pete on the back, "Now here's a man with sand—got more brains and guts than most any other man I've ever called friend." He leaned back and focused his attention on Pete, "Jesse, you're lucky to have this man for a brother." Everyone in the room was quiet. Waiting! But nothing happened. Surprisingly Muley wasn't in for some cockamamie, delayed reaction. His words were evidently genuine. Not many men would stand up to Muley Tatum. The torrid outlaw dressed in black had a way about him that made men uneasy, so uneasy that they couldn't be true to themselves. His vile mannerisms and charismatic leadership turned them into string-dancing-puppets.

Not so with Pete Longely, he stood quiet but confidently.

The dimly lit room absorbed the event without recourse. Conversations started again and the *look-at-Muley* charade passed. The barman, who had stood rigid and quiet so far, started talking. His eyes low and indirect, he spoke subserviently, but feely of the small settlement. "Not much of nothin' here, just poor, simple folks trying to scratch out a meager living." His eyes remained downcast as he talked in a hushed tone.

The newcomers listened and sipped whiskey, their eyes moving slowly, one to another.

After a brief spell of quiet, the barman twisted an off-colored towel in a glass and began telling of the holdup of three days past. He told of the four hooligans, one with a gaunt left hand, that robbed the stage passengers of all their valuables, took a mail bag, all the money and a case of dynamite from the stage depot. "Caught everybody by surprise, they did," the white mustached barman that walked with the help of a cane related. As he talked, his gaze halted briefly at each of the men riding with Tatum. "Cleaned us all out—this whole town couldn't raise two dollars between the lot of us by the time they rode away." His motive, recognized by every man present, was intended to dissuade. Did it work? Probably not, but the Tatum gang rode out of Greensburg with no more than they had when they rode in. The only difference was the twenty dollar gold coin Muley left with the heavily mustached, aging gentleman behind the bar. The man reminded him of his Uncle Pug.

* * *

"You were right Judge." Dolan handed the telegraph to Judge Wilkinson and stood with his arms folded as the judge accepted the paper, preparing to read. "Tucker and another man by the name of Luther Combs broke out together five days ago."

"And killed a young prison guard in the process." Wilkinson responded and nodded as if reminding the barber as he looked over his glasses. "Their escape wasn't discovered until the next morning," the judge continued, "that gave them a few hours head start."

Dolan pinched at the bill of his green visor, "Your assumption was correct. It had to be Possum Tucker, him and that Combs fellow that blasted the jail to pieces."

"Anything from the governor?" Wilkinson urged.

"Nope."

"You'll let me know right away?"

"Yes sir."

The telegraph man turned on his heel, starting away. "Wait." The judge called him back, "I want you to take this telegram to Marshal Carson." Wilkinson refolded the paper, handing it to Dolan. "Tell him to come over to Drover's Palace and meet me in the dining room." He indicted the dining room with a slight toss of his head. "And," the judge gave a minute to thought, "if you don't locate him right away, you come back here and let me know. You got that?"

"You can be sure of it, your honor." The judge turned to go but Dolan caught his arm. "Judge, there's something you ought to know, in my capacity, I'm not suppose to divulge information, it's all to be kept private between the parties." He blinked, clinched his lips, and went on, "Our newspaperman, Barnett . . . well he sent a telegram to Tucker over at the prison ten days ago. I don't know if it means much of anything, but he informed Tucker of the new law enforcement here in town. Seems to me he was either trying to get him riled up, or maybe just pouring salt in the man's wound, if you know what I mean."

Wilkinson removed the cigar from between his lips slowly, squared his eyes on Dolan's, a look intended to chastise the man for not disclosing this information sooner; but at the same time he approved, understanding the responsibility of his position. "Thanks." The judge gazed to the distance and gave the side of his nose a light scratch before lending submissive approval, "That newspaper man gives as much effort to creating the news as he does reporting it." He went on after flicking ashes from his cigar, "I'll never understand journalists. I wish they'd keep to their business of informing the public instead of loading slop troughs for the pigs."

"Huh, what's that suppose to mean?" Dolan scratched back.

"Never mind." Wilkinson figured he'd said more than maybe he should have. "When you hear from the governor let me know."

"Wantin' to get started rebuilding the jail building, huh"?

"Yes, just as soon as we can." He knew the man was referring to the telegram sent to the governor about obtaining brick from over in Coffeyville where soil offered up the unique clay required for production of amber building brick. Wilkinson was shrewd enough to know the Dodge City town council would make a lengthy deliberation of funding the project, perhaps delaying it for months. If such procrastination were to take place, the progress of law enforcement in the area wouldn't advance as Wilkinson planned. The judge's request for funds from the state would put smiles on the faces of the town council and prompt timely action.

* * *

Rad Carson handed his prisoner two biscuits and skillet fried bacon wrapped with a cloth. He pushed it through the access notch in the otherwise solid wood door. The prisoner swiftly accepted the food but scornfully blurted his contempt, "Don't I get hot coffee?"

Rad took it to be an opportunity, "Maybe," he drawled, eyeing the man contemptuously, "Could be I'd get you coffee if you tell me who the other two men were that was with you, and where they went."

The frazzled man rolled his bleary eyes, giving consideration to Carson's answer. Rad could tell he wasn't a man that held strong conviction to honor, and likely sufficient time had passed to appease his token self-worth. He rasped back, "I'll tell ya what I know, but ya also gotta take this honey-pot outta here, I can't eat with it in this hell hole."

"Okay." Carson retorted, but not allowing the prisoner even a slight opportunity, he drug a wood, ladder-back chair with him, to the holding-cell door, "You stick your hands out, both of them, through the hole and hold 'em there."

"What? What good will that do?"

"Just do as I said."

The man's hands extended and Carson lifted and thrust the chair back over his hands and quickly cuffed them so the chair created a barrier. "What the hell!" He barked, shaking the chair and commenced to understand.

Carson took his time; he stood with hands on his hips and glared at the prisoner, "When I unlock the door, you push the pot out with your foot. And don't kick it over or you'll get no coffee and can't eat either. You'll be locked in there with the chair hanging over your hands all day and more flies for company than you'd care to swat after."

The man cursed and did as instructed. Using his foot, he cautiously slid the clay vessel through the wedge opening. Rad slid the pot away, rebolted the door and stood back. The man waited for Carson to remove the chair . . . but he didn't."

"Well!" He waited, cursing under his breath.

"I'll be needing a couple of answers first."

"But you said . . ."

"I didn't say. Now let's get on with it before that chair gets heavy." Rad grinned within, thumbed back his hat and glared, "What's your name and the names of the others?"

The prisoner closed his eyes and gripped the chair, anger swelling.

"Don't do anything stupid," Carson warned. "I'll take the cuffs and the chair off when you tell me your name and the names of the two men that rode with you bombing the jail, and then I'll get you some good, strong coffee to go with the biscuits and bacon."

The man stared maliciously through the hole, around the chair, like a wolf inclined to chew a man's leg off.

Following a deep breath, he blew in a dismal tone, "My name's Logan, Logan Saffley."

Following a pause, Rad questioned, "And the two men?"

The answer came discernibly, "Milt Tucker was one; the other man, that rode with him, called him Possum." The man gave names like he'd been wanting to do it but thought giving up information unproblematic would make him appear less formidable, not tough. Carson kept at him, "How about that other man, what's his name?"

"Luther Combs, I believe's what he said."

"Okay, so now we're getting somewhere." Rad took a step closer, raised his hand with the keys, moving them close to the cuffs, "So where was Tucker and Combs off to when they sent you two simpletons back to the livery barn?" He scowled at Saffley, waiting for the answer before an attempt to remove the wrist chains.

Soon Logan Saffley regained his disapproving attitude and snarled over a rolled bottom lip, "They kept talking about Pueblo, Colorado. Tucker said he knew a man that owned a mine on Fountain Creek just south of town there. The man had struck it big, made a fortune. He and Combs were going there, going to kill both the man and his wife; seems he'd stolen the woman away from Tucker near on to two or three years ago." His hooded eyes glared, "Now take these damn shackles off."

"Did he say what that man's name was?"

"I ain't here to give history lessons—just take them things off my arms; I don't know no other names damn it!"

"Okay, you've earned it." Rad unlocked the cuffs and stepped to the other room to get the coffee he'd promised.

* * *

"It's going well, wouldn't you say, Carson?" Judge Wilkinson stood under the shade of the overhang in front of Kennedy's Cigar Store, watching the workers lay bricks around a barred window. "Governor St. John did more than he'd said; the state kicked in half the costs, seeing as much as we now have a U. S. Marshal's office here in Dodge."

Rad half-smiled, "Don't want to sound ungrateful, but we sure need to get that jail roof on so we can get back to making the law meaningful. We've got idiots on the near verge of becoming too far out of hand, running around here half the nights. And if I don't get that Logan Saffley out of that cramped closet of a cell soon I'm afraid his legs won't ever straighten up. We need to lock him up in a real jail or hang him."

The judge nodded and puffed longingly on the stub of cigar before he ventured out with some news about the town marshal injured in the explosion of the jail, "Doc Hink says Chalk Dinsmore can likely be witness after next week; his hearing is good enough in one ear to understand, so he can be ready to testify." Staring at his cigar, before he went on, he added, "We'll get that man in front of a jury and settle his starch with a necktie party."

"So you've already proven him guilty, have you?" Richard Barnett spoke from behind the two men.

"Not exactly," the startled judge said as he turned. Blowing a sizeable cloud of smoke toward the newspaper man, he blipped, "Oopps, sorry." Wilkinson grimaced. He disliked the newsman and it could be seen by even those who wouldn't have known otherwise.

Barnett stepped backward, eyes growing. He was aware most law enforcement people had little use for him but it didn't stop his prying for news articles. He decided to drop the subject of Wilkinson's comment to Rad, he'd heard all he needed to hear on that matter. Instead he offered up a reflection about the construction under way, "Looks like you're expanding the capacity for the jail, planning on more prisoners, are you?"

"The town's growing," Rad countered, his words spoken with slight insolence.

"I suppose the brick is to be a more secure fortress, one that perhaps can withstand an ordeal such as the one we had three weeks back." Barnett commented in a snippet manner as he made a note on a pad of white paper.

"Well, if we can keep your friend, Possum Tucker, on the run and away from here, I figure it'll do the trick," Wilkinson remarked.

Barnett withdrew, "Who did you say?"

"Milt Possum Tucker—the man we'd sent up to Wichita Prison several months back. You do remember him don't you, Barnett?" The judge asked the question in a manner that Barnett had no doubt he'd gathered information about the telegram he'd sent to Tucker.

But Barnett wasn't about to let on. "Oh, I guess I do recall Tucker. He was the lunatic that made a fool out himself when he was lead away and tied in the wagon, going to prison for killing a man in the bank holdup." Barnett nodded a few times, "I remember."

The conversation between the three was uneasy; words came with notable abrasiveness. Rad's mind wandered, comparing the struggle between the lawmen and the reprehensible journalist to the wickedness of the frontier and the expansion by folks coming west from the conservative large cities of the east.

Only when Barnett was a few doors up the street did Carson and the judge take up their conversation. "Wonder what the man will write about the two of us this time!" Wilkinson said in a flat, worrisome tone as he tapped away cigar ashes. "I'll bet a dollar against a knot hole he'll have something in that paper of his that gives upholding the law a heartless shadow."

"He's a hard man to figure alright." Carson cocked his jaw to a near frown, "Every town needs a newspaper; we just happen to have a man running ours that's bent on throwing kerosene on every little fire he comes across."

CHAPTER TWENTY-ONE

Given the time table for completion of the new jail and the trial for Saffley a week off, Carson decided to leave the prisoner to Sheriff Hinkle and make the trip to Bucklin he'd been putting off. From Bucklin he'd to go on over to Greensburg. He'd never been to Greensburg, but had met Colonel Donald Green once when Green had driven one of The Cannonball stages to Dodge City five weeks back. The man seemed quite proud of the little settlement that'd been named after him and he'd asked Carson to come there, hoping the two of them could select a town marshal, he'd suggested such to Carson.

And there was also a man that rode into Dodge two days ago. He told a pair of stories that had been related to him several days back when he passed through Greensburg. One was about two men that robbed practically every person in town as well as the post office and stage depot. Another Greensburg event the man related took place two or three days after the big robbery. That situation concerned a group of a disreputable sort that stopped in at the trading post saloon. They appeared to be on a rant led by a large boisterous man those with him called Mukey or Muley, something like that, so the man told. That information motivated Carson like putting a match to a fuse of DuPont dynamite . . . another sighting it seemed, of Muley Tatum!

* * *

"Much obliged, Mr. Satterfield, for your saddling Caesar and bringing him out. Your Misses wrapped me some trail food, maybe you'll thank her once again for me." Carson stepped into the stirrup and swung a leg over the trail pack tied behind the saddle. He reached back and tapped a hand on the saddle bag, "Got my fryin' pan and coffee pot all shined up last evening. I reckon I'm gonna miss the fried chicken and beef steak from here, but a man has gotta put up with the bad sometimes in order to appreciate the good." He chuckled and reined his big stallion toward the gate. "I'll see you in a week, or if I'm not back, you might send somebody out to find what's left of me." Carson laughed again and put heels to his horse. He waved as he passed the trees that bordered Satterfield's yard, kicking Caesar into a cantor.

The prairie was warm. Tall grass swayed constantly with gentle balmy breezes. Occasional tumble weeds danced unevenly when persuaded by stout wind gusts. The land held few surprises. A man could see miles ahead if he sat a knoll. The low rolling hills were to give way to an even flatter landscape once the trail stretched east of Bucklin. Carson could imagine the Kiowa sitting proudly on their ponies and watching for signs of buffalo. Their strong bodies, which were husky, compared to most Indians, were brown and well muscled. They'd carried bows carved from buffalo ribs when hunting from horseback. The bow had to be strong but short and maneuverable. They were kept flexible with sinew backing attached with hide glue and rubbed with oils from glands behind the hoof of the bulky animals. Dogwood, ash, chokeberry and black locust were preferable woods for straight, strong arrows. Those could be found near water sources which were spread considerably by the level plains. The buffalo provided most everything the Indians needed; food, clothing, a part of their housing needs, hunting bows, bow strings, strips of hide for several applications; even tools and trinkets carved from horns, bones and the animal's hooves. Whites who had lived with the Indians were astonished with the variety of resources the beasts imparted to the livelihood of the primitives.

An occasional coyote loped across the lands, principally in the waning of the day or when a loathsome jackrabbit happened near the shade of rock or beneath brush where the predator waited for such an event. The prairie flourished with life, life that was little seen, but always functioning, above and below the sandy soils.

The trail ran southeast toward Bucklin, almost parallel to the Arkansas River, usually within two to three miles of the waterway. Rad could regularly see signs of the shallow river in the distance, sighted easily by the greenery near its banks. This was the route utilized by The Cannonball Stage Line as well. Marks in the soil left by the iron-rimmed wheels were clearly perceptible. Those marks symbolized the movement of the country's population westward by Rad's consideration. Many of the people coming west wanted to live free of big city roughshod violence, the growth of the country depended on it. His job as a lawman was to see to it that those folks were not exploited by outlaws and thieves. He was dedicated to it. Living through the hardships and elements of the land was trouble enough.

Rad reined Caesar toward a grove of spindly willows and a spattering of large cottonwoods. A generous sized shallow pool lay in the shade. Wind-shucked cottonwood limbs were protruding from the water in mysterious configurations. Growths of cattails and willow sprigs laced with vivid green leaves that flexed with a slight breeze bordered the pond. Lilly pads with sullied white blooms sporadically decorated the far side of the busy shallow water surface. He urged Caesar forward, scanning the area for an equitable clearing where he'd build a fire, boil coffee and partake of the hardtack, salt pork and can of pears Mrs. Satterfield had packed for him.

He gathered stones, nudged them into a circle and placed small sticks of dried wood in a loose stack with dry grass mingled throughout. He put a match to it and soon added larger pieces of kindling. Satisfied with his fire, he fetched the coffee pot, filled it with water from the pool, poured a handful of dark bits of coffee beans in the pot and sat it on the flat stones he'd neatly aligned in the center. Once it was boiling freely he'd drop in a cup of cool water to sink the grounds.

After frying the salt pork he placed it amid the fold of hardtack and bit into it. A sip of hot coffee made the chewing comfortable. "Tasty." He said to himself, "Been a long spell since I'd been on the trail." He rested on his backside, propped up on elbows with his legs extended, watching insects make small circles atop the water. Caesar raised his head, still chomping on the coarse green grass, eyes flinching, he nickered and perked his ears. The breeze lifted again and a gust brought a slight ripple on the pool. The horse perked, stomped and nickered again. "What is it, boy?" Rad knew his horse to be the best watchdog a man could have. There was something the animal didn't like—something out of the ordinary.

Rad sat the tin cup beside the fire and stood, casting his eyes in the direction that garnered Caesar's awareness. He squinted and was able to make out a partially submerged black hat. He edged to his right a few feet and cautiously peered through a sizeable opening allowed by willow branches. There was a man, his torso partially stretched into the water face down, his shoulders beyond the water's edge as were both arms. He held a mud-crusted six gun in his right hand.

Carson walked to where Caesar stood uneasily, snapped the reins around a tree limb, drew his .45 and began slowly working his way around the willow-laden edge of the pool. There was no odor of gun smoke, no sounds beyond those of nature, and the body gave off no odor of death that blowflies could detect. Rad could tell the man was positively lifeless, but evidently hadn't been dead for long. The water kept the body from festering. He cautiously moved closer, keeping his eyes peeled and his ears set for any sound beyond the rustle of the large leaves of the tall cottonwoods. There was nothing.

It was a young man, dressed in black, except for the white silk shirt. Rad pulled the body clear of the water and turned him face up. It was Alonzo Duffy, the boy working to be the fast gun, the one he'd arrested for killing one of two young wranglers at The King's Folly saloon three weeks back. "Looks like that McMichaels lawyer fellow lost a client when this boy was blasted out of jail by Milt Tucker with the others." He shook his head in disgust, "And he's lost for good. I'd guess from that bullet hole in his forehead he already found somebody faster on the draw than him." Rad looked to the distance, "Well, I know where at least one of them prisoners Tucker released got to". Fresh tracks of three horses leading away were evident. One of them probably the horse Duffy had been riding. Carson kneeled on one knee, an arm rested across the other, he thumbed back his hat and fixed his gaze to the distance, "There must be at least two more of them somewhere up ahead."

Carson used his skillet to dig. The coarse, sandy soil was challenging, would have been grueling with a shovel, and demanded a full hour to reach a depth Carson deemed reasonable. Satisfied with his work, he rolled the Duffy boy into the shallow hole, placed the boy's hat over his face, raked the dirt in and gathered what stones he could to finish the burial. Rad wiped sweat from his brow with the back of his wrist and before retrieving his hat from a bush top, stuck the handle of the ravaged skillet in the soil at the grave's top, crossed his hands before him and said, "May You bless his soul, Lord. And may his mother find peace."

The lawman poured the murky remnants of his coffee pot on the smoking vestiges of what was his first camp fire in months. He then dipped the pot in the pool to wash it—the thought struck him . . . he'd made coffee from the water where a dead man had lain. The thought provoked him; a deep frown and a grimace was all he could do about it

But he then became irritated anew about the destruction of the jail, the loss of the law breakers and Milt Tucker. Tending to the law wasn't going well.

The sun had moved low in the sky, creating a haze parlayed into scattered strings of white clouds similar to tattered window curtains. It was well afternoon when Carson topped the rise and gazed down on Bucklin. It was the closest town to Dodge, closer than Spickard, but in the opposite direction. Rad had been to Bucklin two years ago, as he recalled, but the town had grown a few new roof tops since then. He walked the horse to the water trough sitting in front of the mercantile store, stood down and let Caesar muzzle the water. A pair of turtle doves cooed their disapproval, and four brown, streaked sparrows fluttered and chirped noisy condemnation, forced to give up their roost on the shady side of the water trough.

"That you, Rad Carson?" Town marshal, Wiley Fitzsimmons, stood on the boardwalk in front of the barbershop next door to the mercantile. He pushed back the coat front and continued buckling the gun belt around his skinny waist as he spoke.

"Yep, it's me, Wiley." Carson offered up a grin.

"Well, you're just in time to congratulate me on my barber-hair-cut." He laughed. Rad recalled that Wiley chuckled about most anything—'*but a haircut?*'

"Okay, congratulations!" Carson wagged his head slightly and laughed back.

"Come on, Rad," Wiley waved a hand, "let me buy you an early supper."

"I might like that. My lunch was ruined." He stopped short of telling the marshal about finding Duffy's body, deciding Wiley couldn't do a thing about the Duffy boy and it might be best not to relate the incident here and now. Supper seemed a better idea. It might just allow the dead-man-water he'd made coffee from drift out of his mind.

The café was small, comprised of only six tables. The food tasted good; Carson was hungry and ready to listen. He let Wiley do the talking, which he liked to do. Wiley Fitzsimmons was tall and thin but tough as leather. His sunken cheeks peeked from behind a curled mustache and together they made him appear older than his years. "Glad to hear they made you a U. S. Marshal, Carson. We're getting lot'sa settlers and more commerce out here. We're needing a deeper kind of law enforcement. Oh, and by the way," he added quickly, "I heard about you losing your jail, kind of a parody ain't it?" His shoulders shook, head bobbed, and he went on, "You becoming a federal law officer but losing your jail!" The snicker was discernable.

"Thanks for reminding me." Carson smiled a gentle, belligerent smile. "But we'll have a new one, bigger and stronger than ever in a couple more weeks."

"Yea, I heard that too. The loads of bricks coming over from Coffeyville passed through here; said they were making for Dodge and a new jail." He laughed again, "I told them they could drop them bricks off right here, I'd like to have a fancy-built lock-up too!"

Rad Carson said little during supper, mostly nodding agreement. His mind kept turning to Dodge City; Wilkinson, Barnett, Fanny, and the Duffy boy. He decided he needed to talk with Fitzsimmons about that. But he'd wait until after supper. Meanwhile he'd let Wiley carry the conversation. He wondered if that was the primary reason Wiley had invited him to visit in the first place, just wanting a different face to talk to about the law business.

The two of them sipped coffee after pushing back empty plates. Wiley kept up the chatter, and Rad kept listening. "Getting late, be dark in another hour," The Bucklin marshal looked through the wavy front window glass. He yelled a happy '*thank you*' to the owner, Marvella Hays, as she pushed aside a curtain, heading for the kitchen. He stood, folded his napkin and dug a pair if two-bits from his coat pocket. "This one is going to be on town council," he chuckled again.

They found their way out the door and started for the law office. "Would you have happened to see a couple of men ride into your town," Carson asked, "two men, with an extra horse in tow?"

Wiley stopped mid-step and turned toward Carson, a seriousness look formed on his face. "Matter-of-fact, I did, saw that just before noon today." He blinked a thought into words, "Only one horse was saddled. The man that rode it had another tethered behind, and the other young fella with him was riding bare-back. Why do ya ask?"

Carson explained finding Duffy and three sets of prints. Wiley's description brought more thoughts, *'Stolen horses—only one saddle'*. It made sense. "Did you see them go in anywhere, or did they just ride on through?"

Wiley, who found humor in most anything, gave a throaty, buoyant serious response, "They went in Faraday's Saddle Shop." He moved his head side to side slowly as if the notion of the two men needing a saddle seemed reasonable at the time. "And they rode out not long afterward—didn't have the extra horse with 'em, but both had saddles."

"Let's go visit that shop," Carson injected. "You reckon he's still open this time of day?"

"Makes no difference," Wiley answered, "he lives in back of the place. We won't have no trouble finding him."

The day was settling into evening; large flocks of Starlings clattered in the trees, having come to roost from the fields, by the time Carson and Fitzsimmons, with Mr. Faraday alongside, walked to the corral behind Faraday's shop. The two lawmen hadn't told the man about Duffy, or what they suspected about the two men.

"Them damn birds, they always pester the dickens outta' us this time a'day." He shook a fist conservatively as he looked from the trees before nodding toward the corral, "That's the horse they traded for the saddle,"

Faraday said, "that one right there." He pointed to a dark gelding with a white marking between his eyes. "Fine horse, good lines, looks to be about four years old."

"I can't argue that," Carson agreed, "good piece of horse flesh alright."

"Seems you fells got a special interest in either this horse or them wranglers," Ivan Faraday lamented. "You thinking maybe the horse was stolen, that what's going on?"

"We're not rightly sure, Ivan," Wiley answered, "but Carson found a man that'd been shot—killed like a mongrel dog, up the trail there about fifteen miles, close to Little Cotton Creek where the freshwater pool is. We're thinking maybe the men you traded a saddle for this horse," he threw a thumb at the gelding, "had something to do with it."

The shop owner lifted his eyebrows and immediately collapsed his face into a hard frown. "They sure didn't seem that kind." He pushed his lips together, "If I had any idea . . . ," and the anger dissolved. "Like I said, they told me they'd been with an outfit driving a herd of cows up from north Texas and the trail boss gave them this fine animal as bonus. They said their other saddle was stolen from them over in Dodge City." Faraday shook his head, "That town is rougher than a fresh plowed field. You sure got your hands full Marshal Carson!" He hesitated, waiting for a response, which he didn't get. He scratched at his cheek and started again, "They told me they'd planned for sharing the bare-back riding," he threw a hand in the air, "clear on back to Texas, but by the time they got here, they'd decided against that." Faraday fixed a look on Wiley Fitzsimmons, "These young folk ain't as all-mighty tough, and maybe not as upright, as they sometimes like to act."

"It doesn't sound like you did anything wrong, Mr. Faraday," Rad assured the man. "We didn't come here to point a finger at you, and we can't be sure those men you dealt with are guilty of anything. But," he paused, "the pieces of the puzzle fit real snug with them plugged in as a part of it." Rad turned his face downward and peered from beneath his hat brim looking toward the fast fading sun as he spoke. "Looks like we'll have to let it simmer overnight." He turned to Wiley, "I'm staying the night here in Bucklin." He lightly tilted his head to the east, toward Greensburg, "Maybe I'll pick up a trail in the morning."

The two lawmen thanked Faraday and again reassured him he'd done no wrong before they found their way back to the street. "You're welcome to come over to my place, I've moved in back of the office, makes for an easy walk to work," Fitzsimmons cackled.

"You're not planning on me sleeping on a jail bunk are ya?" Carson scoffed in mock reply.

"If ya did that, I might have to take breakfast to ya," Wiley chuckled, "and I shore as dickens don't like that idea even a little bit." His big grin was reassuring.

CHAPTER TWENTY-TWO

Morning broke with no assistance from the sun. Dark clouds gathered in layers and moved precariously at low levels, deep grays with rounded tops stacked over the low dark ones. The horizon beneath was the color of a wool blanket. Carson pulled the rain slicker from the bedroll before he mounted. He set a look at the Bucklin law man, "When them dodgers come on that Tatum outlaw I told you about I guess you'll post some around town, won't you, Wiley?"

"I'll be looking for 'em, Rad. You sure you don't want me to ride with you for a spell? I've done a good bit of tracking in my time." Wiley Fitzsimmons held his high-ridge hat in his hand and waved it toward the trail Carson would take out of Bucklin.

"No need, Wiley." Rad looked up and gauged the sky from west to east, "Looks like it'll be raining within minutes, fact is, I can smell it in the air. Tracks left by those young fellas won't be anything but mud by the time we could separate them out of the mess left over the past few days." Carson stepped in the stirrup and threw a leg over, turned and pushed the bottom of the brown slicker down behind the cantle. "I'm hoping I can get lucky and catch up with them. I'm of the mind they may be hunkering down somewhere not too far up the way."

"My authority ends at the town limits, but I'd sure be glad to go along anyhow." The tall, skinny man put in as a final effort to assist. His inner thoughts were that Rad Carson wasn't going to be able to overtake the two varmints; they'd be hightailing, not to let anybody get close on their back trail. Over coffee, in the wane of last evening, the lawmen concluded that the Duffy boy must surely have met his demise at the hands of the two men Faraday had traded a saddle for a horse.

"You might oughtta' wait until this storm blows through." Wiley shouted into the wind, knowing his plea would go unattended.

Carson pushed his tan Stetson down tight, pulled the slicker to his chest and gently pushed heels into the stallion's flanks. "I'll see ya when I come back through, maybe bring those two back here and put 'em in your lock-up." He waved an abbreviated final good-by and set to the trail.

Thunder rolled across the plains, giving depth to the otherwise silent, desperate landscape. The wind, which blew in brutal gusts in advance of the rain, calmed once the storm front moved through and drug heavy drops behind that pelted the land. The moisture made the foliage take on a sheen that caused it to appear to grow with a newborn aggressiveness. Tall prairie grass bent with the added weight, but the resilient stems refused to yield, drawing strength from the moisture. Rocks, once invisible without the dampness, improved their numbers, bringing realization that the earth was heavy with stone and the light layer of multicolored soil was merely a dressing to cover a root system that gouged deep into the cracks and crevices of the hard, underlying mantle of earth.

Rhythmic large raindrops flopped against Rad's slicker; the sound easily distinguishable from the splashing on the felt brim of his Stetson. Rad squinted as he looked over the rhythmic bobbing of Caesar's head, ears twitching against the slight sting of heavy drops. The burden of loneliness confounded Rad's mind; his sight limited by silver lines of raindrops, coupled with misty fog, he gazed from under the brim of his hat, his collar turned up, close to his ears.

The storm limited sight to a hundred yards through the streaked gray light of morning. Horseshoe prints had dissolved but blurred crevices of wagon wheels marked the road. Rad allowed direction at the will of his horse. The Kansas prairie became pock marked. Rivulets gathered into small tarnished pools and the rain fed them with eagerness. Flashes of lightning crackled and boomed with hushed echoes on the horizon all around.

The storm eventually set into a slow, stolid, unforgiving pattern. "Looks like this forsaken rain will last the day out ol' partner," Rad spoke aimlessly as if Caesar had asked. "Least wise the sun's given us a reprieve," he said, looking into the sky through the drips arranged by his hat.

Having covered eight to nine miles, Rad decided to rein Caesar away from the road, believing the two men he sought might have come the distance yesterday. And if he was lucky, they might have slept late and stayed put when the early morning storm set in, if they had shelter. He didn't want to happen on them unprepared. Chances were they'd see him first. They'd be watching the road, he figured, if they had any smarts about them at all. He wandered north roughly a half mile and settled back to the direction needed, but off the road.

Before he'd ridden another mile, rain soaked and squinting, the remnant of a structure a couple hundred yards south of his position came into view, closer to the road than he sat. A pair of trees set between him and the walls of the vacated, dilapidated sod house. "Looks like the Kiowa ran a settler off; I'd guess somewhere around twenty years ago." Again, Caesar's ears twitched at Rad's voice and a slight shake of his head appeared to acknowledge the comment. He reached under the slicker and withdrew binoculars, unwrapped the strap and careful to keep them as dry as possible, he raised the glasses.

"My, my, look there partner," Rad spoke with a hush, as if to his horse or maybe to himself, without lowering the glasses, "we just might have found the fellas we're looking for." Two horses stood alongside an adobe mud wall where a ravaged portion of roof angled downward protected them. The horses, one a pinto, the other a buckskin with a dark mane and tail, matched the descriptions the saddle shop owner gave Carson. Saddles had been removed. Rad lowered the binoculars and flared his nostrils, "And I believe they've got a fire going." He carefully raised a flap on the left saddlebag and slid his spyglasses inside. The lawman twisted his head and carefully searched the immediate area, "Right there, boy, that's where you'll have to wait." Rad edged Caesar fifty feet away where a swale surrounded with tall, thick grass would conceal the horse. He stepped from the saddle easy like, pulled the Henry rifle from the boot and slipped the reins around a bucket-sized rock. "Now you behave, partner, and I'll be back here to collect you in a few minutes." He looked to the sky, "Let's hope the rain stops right soon."

Hasty, catlike steps carried him, the rifle held snug to his slicker-covered body. He'd removed his gloves, the bulk of soaked leather wouldn't fair well if he needed to work the rifle's action hurriedly. Growing closer, he went to his toes, not allowing boot heels to make the sucking sound pulling from the oozing top soil. The smell of frying bacon fetched his senses and gave him confidence he was catching them at ease and unaware. *'They sure don't seem to be in no hurry to get back to Texas'*, Rad thought. He also knew it wasn't uncommon for young cow wranglers to avoid a quick trip back home once they'd come so far and had money in their jeans, money like they'd never had before.

Rad pushed a shoulder against one of the trees ten yards from the crumbled wall and ducked his head around. The horses watched but gave no reaction. He decided to wait, give the animals time to get used to his presence so's not to spook and give warning to his quarry. The soddy's roof had given way from the decayed far wall intermittently, leaving the poles and some measure of thatch-sticks arranged as a lean-to structure.

Carson inched forward. The relic of a window opening was there. It allowed a view inside. He hunkered down, removed his hat and slowly lifted his head to peek. The two wranglers were nestled under the shabby protection. They sat on their bedrolls. The area they occupied was protected from the rain but minimal. One of them reached to fiddle with the skillet that sizzled with hog-back, a coffee tin in his hand. The other man pulled a tobacco bag from under his saddle and was separating a paper from the tiny envelope. *'Now is a good time'*, Carson thought. He hurried to the corner.

But they'd heard!

The bacon-frying-man dumped the skillet. The fire leaped to engulf the grease as Carson leveled the Henry and shouted for them to *freeze.* The other man wrenched his body and rolled, jerked back and had a shiny Remington revolver pushed up in front of his face, pointed in Rad Carson's direction. Without hesitation to allow question about who the visitor might be, the cowboy wildly fired off a pair of rounds. Carson pulled away, his back held solid against the adobe wall and with the rifle held vertical, he screamed, "I'm the law, put your guns down."

Another two rounds shucked in his direction, both thudding into the adobe wall.

"Last chance, throw 'em down or get yourself killed." Carson shouted through the rain, his back still braced against the aged mud-brick wall.

"Don't care who ya are mister, you better git 'ta hell outta here while ya can."

From his position Rad could see a boot, not much else, but the boot scuffed against the dirt, giving reason that the man was scratching to get loose from something. Amid the firing and the scrambling by the pair of men inside there came a boisterous rattle of poles and roof debris. A sizeable section of the rickety roof collapsed. The man with the extended boot yelled out, his body becoming well covered by the heavy rubble. Rad lifted the barrel of the Henry, cocked, and methodically fired a bullet into the man's foot.

Another scream and a pound of curse words jumped from the tangle under the tattered roof. The other man slipped out of the meager confines. Carson figured him to be scooting to land on the back of one of the horses. Rad quickly retraced his steps to the corner where he could see the animals but not expose himself. Sure enough, a man snapped the bridle rein, pulled it loose and scurried to jump up. "Stop!" Carson yelled.

The man's Remington wildly stabbed a flame toward Rad; lead whistled past his ear. The lawman slung the rifle around and answered with a bullet of his own. The man's head jerked violently and a spout of blood leaped from his neck. His horse quick-stepped and the wrangler was tossed into a heap, his flaccid body writhing in the mud, reminding Rad of the Duffy boy who was left to wither in the cottonwood pool yesterday.

The wrangler remaining inside screamed, "Don't leave me, Rusty—don't leave me!"

Carson shook his head in dismay, eyes squashed down for a moment before he looked up into the inconsiderate sky above the old decaying sod house. He then bent and retrieved his Stetson, shook it and put it on his head and pinched the brim in place. He lightly shook his head side to side peering at the youngster's body through the heavy drizzle and lamented sadly, "Boy, you didn't have to die."

"Rusty, you there, Rusty?" came from beyond the wall.

Carson again rounded the corner of the settler's ruin, rifle in hand. The man he'd shot in the foot looked up at him from under dark hair plastered to his forehead, "Who the hell are you, mister?"

"Like I said, I'm the law, name's Carson—out of Dodge City." For a moment Carson allowed that he found his job distasteful, killing young men, no matter what they'd done, was a part of law work that conjured up a sour bitterness in his stomach and throat, something he knew he'd never get used to.

The foot-shot young wrangler lay on his stomach, elbows propping him up and a pile of roof trash crashed across his lower body. He blinked rain from his shallow brown eyes, "What about Rusty . . . you kill him?"

"Yep, I did. Didn't want to, but I did." The sour-acid feeling inside was still heavy.

"You gonna kill me?"

"Not unless you give me good reason. I plan on taking you in, but the way you get there, either with yer backside in the saddle or belly-side down, it's up to you."

The man blinked several times more, mopped his brow with his forearm and asked, "For what, I ain't done nothin'."

"I'm arresting you for killing a man," Rad lifted a thumb toward his back trail, "several miles back, before you traded a horse for one of them saddles there." He pointed.

The brown-eyed youngster glanced at the saddle teary-eyed, then back to Carson. He said nothing.

Carson pulled the saddles from the debris and put them on the two horses. The young cowboy listened, trying to comprehend what was going on the other side of the wall as Rad placed Rusty's body on one of the horses and tied it securely. Carson mounted the other and tethered the mount with the dead wrangler's body behind, rode to the edge of the wall where he could bend and see the foot-wounded cowboy he'd left entangled inside. Rad called out to him, "I'm going after my horse," he nodded to the distance, "where I left him just down the way a piece." He then shook a finger at the trapped man, "Don't you go making more trouble for yourself—I'll be back in five minutes and we'll head to Bucklin." Rad knew the man couldn't get far, even if he was fool enough to try, not with a bullet through his foot and no horse, and on top of that, he was trapped with a pile of wet, half-rotten lumber on top of him.

Rad was reasonably confident he recognized the two men as being among the prisoners that were being held in the jail back in Dodge along with the Duffy boy. Evidently they'd teamed up with Duffy during the breakout and got themselves some stolen horses. He'd get to that in proper time.

Once Rad returned to where he'd left Caesar he slid from the one saddle, stepped into the stirrup and swung onto the big gray stallion. "Looks like we got us a parcel of trouble to deal with 'ole boy." He spoke to Caesar and looked at the sky which still hung heavy. "I recall Grandpa Carson saying there wasn't anything like a heavy rain to bring snakes and skunks out of their holes. I reckon today has just about proven him right."

"What's your name, boy?" Rad asked as he helped the young wrangler mount the pinto, his hands tied and crippled foot dragging outside the stirrup.

"Blaine."

"That your given name?"

"Yep."

Carson stared at him, waiting for more.

"Blaine Dalton," he said with a sneer.

"Okay, Blaine Dalton, you just ride peaceful like and we'll get along fine. Otherwise, I'll make the ride more miserable for you than that foot is already." Carson sat astride Caesar with the lead rope tied to his saddle horn tethering the pinto. The buckskin, hauling the dead wrangler lashed to the saddle, brought up the rear. They rode in docile quiet for five miles, Rad watching over his shoulder at any squeak of saddle leather beyond the tempo set by the horses.

The unsympathetic, wearisome rain ultimately gave out. Dreary light drizzle, which signaled the storm's final efforts, eventually faded away and the sun made variable, successful attempts to push the clouds aside and take command of the prairie sky by the time the three of them achieved a good distance up the road. The horses' hooves plunged through the muck steadily, creating a squishing, rhythmic sound that made a man feel lonely and his eyelids heavy. The warmth of the rain slicker clinging to Carson's body added to the mystical, near semi-consciousness that found its way to shadow the tall lawman. Rad shook his head to erase the cobwebs when he heard, "It weren't no murder."

Rad reflectively half turned in the saddle to face the cowboy, "What'd you say?"

They came to a full stop, the wounded wrangler's face drooped, and his lips pinched slightly, "That gun-slick, the one named Duffy, back at the pool, he was with us when them men busted us out and the jail got blowed up." He glared at Carson with his brow drawn tight and dark eyes narrowed.

The marshal stared back. His gaze paused and meandered toward the horizon with his thoughts. A few seconds passed. "That's what I figured."

"He stole a horse, same as me and Rusty. But Rusty's was the only one with a saddle on." He bit his bottom lip before he continued, "That Duffy fella, he tried to steal Rusty's horse. Rusty caught him . . . it was pretty much that simple. It turned into a shoot-out, it weren't no murder."

"Damn shame," Carson shook his head, "two men died for a saddle." He turned back toward the road, nudged the big gray, and started up again.

* * *

"Well glory be!" Wiley Fitzsimmons lifted his tall hat and scratched behind an ear, "Ya done caught up with 'em, didn't' ya? Made it all in less than a day too." He laughed, "Guess that one there gave ya some trouble, huh?" He pointed at the body draped over the saddle.

"He made a bad mistake." Carson gave Fitzsimmons a sad look, the corners of his mouth tailed downward. "He'll meet with your undertaker." Carson stepped down.

"I'd like for you to process this one into your jail, Wiley." Rad handed the town marshal the reins to the horse ridden by his prisoner. He pointed to the mounted cowboy "He'll be needin' a doctor to look after him. "Charge him with breakin' out of jail; seems the two of them, along with the man I buried out at the cottonwood pool had all escaped from the Dodge City jail when it was blown up by Milt Tucker. We may add a murder charge later."

"Ya don't say?" Wiley had to offer up a throaty giggle as he awkwardly stepped off the plank walk and reached for the tie-lines Carson pulled loose from his saddle horn.

"I'd appreciate it if you'd see to 'em, Wiley" Carson tugged at his collar, "I'm wanting to get myself a bath and a change of clothes, that rain pretty much soaked me . . . made me feel more like a frog than a human."

"Sure. Use my place. You know where everthing is." The wide grin popped up, "You still planning on making it over to Greensburg, Marshal Carson?" Wiley asked, tow lines in hand, as he stood gazing at Marshal Carson, his respect for the man had moved up a notch or two.

"Yes I do. I'll be heading out," he looked up, "first thing in the morning, if the weather stays generous." He lifted his Stetson, inspected it mindfully, shook it twice with a flip from the wrist and spoke again, "When I left Dodge, I had a plan and I'm figuring to keep to it."

CHAPTER TWENTY-THREE

Carson rose before dawn, looked out the window and pulled his clothes on. He left a note for Wiley, who was snoring voraciously when he slipped out with his possibles pack and the skillet Wiley had given him. It was tucked away in the saddlebags. He stepped through the slick corral poles, grasped the gear and went about saddling Caesar. In short order he looked back to the door he'd exited, nodded a silent good-by, and stepped up.

The weather was good and the road friendly, so much different than the previous day that it seemed new, unlike he remembered. Within minutes the little town was out of sight. He put the stallion to a brisk lope, having no intent to linger near the gloomy events of yesterday.

The quiet, open prairie had a way with a man's mind if he let it. Thoughts of the early people, the plains Indians, the buffalo, Spaniard explorers deSoto, Coronado and Cortez, and mountain men, Jedediah Smith, Porvost, Pike, Bridger, Fremont and Rad's grandpa, Kit Carson. Later came the wagon trains led by Joseph Meek, Elijah Elliott, Majors and Russell and many others. The history was elaborate, but also filled with despair and desperation; there were Indian massacres, disease, and people lost, never to be determined what happened to them. Many were buried and their graves misplaced to nature. The prairie land, the history and anguish, blended into the law man's very being, every bit a part of him, and he knew it would always be that way.

The sky was bluer than any ocean and the land seemed virtually as vast and empty—but it was changing! Settlers from all points east were coming, quick to occupy the land; many of them recent immigrants from western European countries, but also from far eastern Europe and even Asia. They flocked to America, which was known throughout the world as the land of opportunity, and the land of the free. America had riches to be discovered. There was gold, silver, copper, and lands that offered opulent food crops, superb grazing for livestock, abundant timber and stone for building materials. A man could have land for the taking and provide for his family if he was strong in mind and body. But men who were weak in character or seeking an easy life, easy that is, to steal from those who earned their way, came also. They gave cause and need for people like Rad Carson; strong, righteous men to uphold the law and allow honorable citizens to live in peace. The frontier was short on such men.

Greensburg was on the horizon, and soon within a few hundred yards came into view. Carson was immediately impressed with the trees. He understood how Donald Green so quickly became enthralled with the area and set his roots here. It was indeed a grand location, calling out for people to stay once they'd set eyes on the abundant growths of trees and the easy rolling terrain. The plentiful source of exceptional good water was here too, free from odor and a taste comparable to that found in mountain springs.

There were few structures making up the settlement. Some stood out from the others, the straight, white painted clapboard buildings that belonged to Colonel Cannonball Green. One new building was under way; walls complete and three men were placing cross members atop the sturdy frame in advance of the laying of the wood shingles to complete the roof.

Rad found the office of The Cannonball Stagecoach Line. He looped the reins over the stone-posted hitch rail and looked up to see Colonel

Green pull the door shut and offer up a recognizing welcome grin. Green gestured and spoke, "I was about to walk over to the café and get coffee; I'd be right proud to have you join me, Marshal."

"I'm not one to turn down coffee," Carson said as he stepped up to greet and shake the hand of the man he'd met once before. "Glad to see you again, Colonel." Rad looked up and down the street of the small settlement, "I see you've got another building going up."

"Sure do. This one's to be a shop for farm supplies and sorts of leather goods. A couple of brothers from Topeka, the Sherwines, are making their start in business here. It took me a little talking to convince them, but they come out two months ago and liked what they saw." Colonel Green beamed as he admired the process of the new structure.

The Colonel was a man of medium build, a mite on the side of short, and with the whitest, well trimmed beard and mustache of any man Carson had ever seen. He wore a tall, deep-valley off-white hat, a finely tailored buckskin coat with long leather fringe dangling across the back from the shoulders and down the arms to the wrists. Shiny brass buttons decorated the front. The combination of the man's facial hair, his coat and the royal blue shirt made a presentation that looked like something out of a colored eastern billboard promoting Buffalo Bill. The man drew attention everywhere he went.

The two men carried on a light conversation as they ambled up the street and found their way to the front door of the Crystal Café and Millinery Shop. As they sat, Martha, the wife of the owner, Hoot Collins, delivered coffee. "Afternoon, Mr. Green." She then turned to assess Rad with a wide, very genuine smile, "Welcome to Greensburg, mister."

Green said as he placed a hand on Rad's shoulder, "Martha, this here is Rad Carson, the new United States Marshal from over Dodge City way."

Her eyes widened and brows arched. "Well, I'll give another welcome to that." The warmth in her expression was genuine as she nodded and bequeathed a smile.

"It's a pleasure to meet you, Mammn," Carson tipped his hat and smiled.

She turned, surveying the rear of the establishment, "Hooty was here a few minutes ago, he must'a gone out back." She then hurriedly faced the two men again and pointed, "Take that table over there if you will, and I'll go get Hooty. I know he'd like to meet the marshal." She scurried away, tugging at the apron with one hand and smoothing her hair with the other. At the same time, she yelled to her daughter who was placing napkins and utensils on another table, "Willetta, would you get these men some coffee, please . . . and you should outta' put on a fresh pot, they'll be wanting it to go with the apple pie I'm gonna bring 'em." She grinned back at Carson and Green.

Green started the conversation, "You'll like Hooty, he's a fine man, lots of energy and got a right smart head on his shoulders."

"You think maybe he'd make a good town marshal?"

Green answered back without hesitation, "He'd make a good mayor—not tough enough to marshal though; not a man to handle a gun. Back in the war he was a paper man; did strategic planning with maps and kept records of all the regiments, did that for those of us that rallied the troops and set the front lines. He's as honest and loyal as a man could ever want to be around too."

"Do you have a man in mind to carry a badge?"

"Yes, sir, I do. I'm planning to take a walk down the way and have you meet him. Hooty and I have discussed the situation. We figure he'd make a good man for the job. He has experience working with some unruly types, even found himself on the wrong side of the law once back up in Colorado. That's one of the things I wanted to discuss with you, Carson, before we got too far, before we put our feet to the fire ya might say."

Rad pushed his lips together as his eyes widened, "You got my attention with that, Colonel."

Just then Hooty Collins pushed aside the long curtain from the kitchen and stepped into the dining area. "Morning, Cannonball," he said with a perky voice, "Martha tells me this man here with you is Marshal Rad Carson." He continued forward with a hand extended. "I've heard some good things about you Marshal . . . and I'm familiar with your grandpa, Christopher Kit Carson, having read of him even back in the war years."

Carson grasped his hand, "I don't know that I'll ever be of the caliber he was, I am somewhat taller and weigh about forty pounds more than he did in his prime, but I'd not say that makes me a bigger man." Carson smiled as they shook hands.

The three men sat, taking a minute to become familiar. Willetta, Hooty's teenage daughter, set three cups of steaming coffee on the table, her eyes shifting rapidly in a shy manner and a cautious, fluctuating smile inhabited her face. Hooty twisted his head around and glanced up at her, "Thanks, honey . . . Willy, this here is Rad Carson, he's the grandson of the famous mountain man, Kit Carson, that I've told you about."

Willetta made an abbreviated curtsy, blinked several times, and replied, "Very happy to meet you, Mr. Carson. Father has indeed told me quite a lot about your grandfather."

Hooty went on, "Yes, sir, a mountain man and maybe the finest scout the cavalry ever had, and a genuine leader of men, Kit Carson was." Hooty Collins calmly exclaimed, sounding as if he was readying to pin a metal on the man's chest. He lifted his coffee cup, in a toasting manner, "I'm proud to have you in our establishment, Mr. Carson." He nodded a salute.

"Why thank you, Mr. Collins, on behalf of my grandfather, I accept your kind homage."

From across the way, in the millinery portion of the building, where Mrs. Collins was assisting a lady customer, she raised an open hand to the side of her mouth and called out, “Willetta, get those guests some of that fresh apple pie from the window sill, it should be cooled just about right.”

Green looked at Carson, with a questionable expression.

Rad raised his hands, palms upward, “I’d not turn down apple pie. We got time, Colonel?”

The Colonel rose, removed his hat and held it to his chest, “I’ll not suggest we leave here without giving you a chance at Martha Collin’s apple pie, Mr. Carson, that’d be like closing the gates to heaven.” Green chuckled aloud.

Everyone, even the lady customer in the millinery shop, laughed openly.

The three men, having finished the pie and second cup of coffee, talked about Emmitt Shay, the man Colonel Donald Green suggested to become Greensburg’s town marshal. “He’s a stout built man, I’d say six feet tall and strong as an ox. He’d been a Pinkerton man back in St. Louis where his primary function was security for a group of four banks, all owned by the Slumann family. The story goes that he hated the job, and didn’t like the folks he worked for, seems they demanded too much out of their employees and paid them considerable less than what they earned.” Green hesitated, a vague grin came across his face, “It didn’t take long for him to realize he’d made a mistake going to work for the Slumanns. He quit, told them he wanted to be an out-of-doors man, left the big city and headed for the mountain country.”

“Not too much unusual about that, a lot of good men tell of back grounds of that sort,” Carson said, “leaving the hub-bub of city life for the open spaces.”

Green went on, “The first job he landed was back-breaking work as a wood cutter, supplying wood for the stamping mills around Black Hawk and Central City, west of Denver. Three or four months after he settled in the mountains, a big outfit he was supplying wood to was needing a man to take over the position of security chief. That was the Carter Hill Holdings Company, biggest mining conglomerate in the area." The colonel stroked his white beard as he continued, "They found out about Shay's background and hired him on for the job." Colonel Green smiled, "It payed a lot more than cutting wood, and made for fewer blisters."

Hoot Collins chimed in, "He's no stranger to hard work and knows his way around with a shotgun and .45 revolver sidearm as well."

"You said he once got sideways of the law out there, what was that about?" Carson asked with a dry voice.

"As I understand it, and Hooty here will back me up on this," Green lamented, "I checked with the local law out there in Central City when I hired Shay because I needed a man to handle the work he does here," Green waved a hand toward the stage barn, "and also figured on using him to ride extra shotgun when we carry valuables on the Cannonball Line such as payrolls and bank funds going to holding companies back east. I have to be cautious you know."

Carson nodded, understanding the foundation the two men were putting in place; listening and keeping an open mind.

"I saw the letters the sheriff sent from Colorado," Hooty put in.

"Hill, the principal owner and boss man for the Carter Hill Holdings, filed charges against Emmitt Shay for robbery . . . contending Emmitt stole money from his office in Black Hawk. And I guess on the surface that did; well, it sorta happened." The look on Green's face as he spoke was both emotionless and confident. "But like a lot of times in life, the upfront appearance doesn't necessarily offer a real picture and the genuineness has to get squeezed to the top in order to set things straight."

"We've all seen it happen," Carson responded.

"Here's how the problem got started;" Green continued, "One pay day Hill's company gave all of his mine workers bank drafts, payment for a week's wages instead of the usual cash-on-the-barrel-head. The next day, when the men went to the bank on which the drafts were written, the bank said there wasn't money in Hill's account to pay from. Well as you can imagine, the men raised wild-billy-hell and clamored up the mountainside to the company's office, making demand for cash."

Marshal Carson reacted, "A man expects to be paid for his work. Not many have extra money to live on, and honest wages having been earned, they deserved to be paid."

The Colonel held out both hands, palms extended, "Most of the rest of the story I got from the court transcript the sheriff sent along with his letters, so I know its fact—fact according to the records anyhow, and that's good enough for me." Colonel Green carried on, "Now here's the sticky part; Emmitt and the company book-keeper were the only men in the office when the miners showed up demanding their pay. Once Emmitt got them miners settled down, they showed him the bank drafts, and the book-keeper knew about it—he just did what Hill had instructed him, he'd prepared the drafts. But he went running out the back door . . . didn't want to face up to the men!"

Carson shook his head, understanding, but apprehensive about where the story was going.

Hooty then exclaimed, "Some of the men started after him, said they were going to string him up. But Emmitt put a stop to that—drew a gun to stop 'em."

"Now for the law trouble part," the Colonel picked up again, "Emmitt knew where the book-keeper kept cash," Green's eyes widened, "and he lined the men up and paid 'em what the drafts called for."

"He took quite a load on his shoulders when he did that," Rad Carson retorted.

"The situation with the Hill Company wasn't much different than the bank people he worked for in St. Louis," Hoot Collins said. "They expected a lot from the people working for them but didn't like giving proper pay for their services."

"So I guess the Hill Company filed charges against Shay, did they?"

"Yea, they did, and the case went to court. And now for the good part," Green's face brightened up, "Hill wasn't liked much by local folks, seems the company short-suited a number of locals in the past, so the jury hearing the case was like having special fiddle players show up for the barn dance! Not only did Emmitt walk free, the judge gave Carter Hill's people the dickens for paying their employees with improper pay vouchers."

"Sounds to me like that judge was a reasonable man," Carson said with a skewed jaw, looking both men in the eye.

Hoot added quickly, "The jury also praised Emmitt, saying he was proper in paying the men as he was a responsible employee of The Hill Company." Hooty chuckled, "Of course Shay lost his job, and in the process he put a few knots on the heads of two of Hill's straw bosses that'd been sent to fire him in an unfriendly manner. He whopped them boys and sent 'em scramblin'."

"Sounds like he can handle himself on the unrefined end of trouble too," Carson said. "If the two of you agree on offering the marshal job to Emmitt Shay, I'd like to meet the man."

"Well let's go on down to the shop," Green said. He rose and led the way to the door.

Martha Collins shouted from the millinery as the three men made way to exit, "Glad to meet you, Marshal Carson, come back soon."

"And thanks for the pie;" Carson shouted back, "it was as good as the Colonel said it'd be."

Emmitt Shay had worked for Colonel Green the better part of a full year. He served as general maintenance man for The Cannonball Stage Line and also occasional shot-gun rider. When Carson and the others arrived he was reshaping a wheel rim with an eight pound sledge against a huge anvil. "Hold up there Emmitt," Green barked as he ducked under the edge of the tin roof, "there's a man here I'd like to have you meet."

The big man with bulging biceps, laid the hammer aside, wiped his brow with the back of his hand and took a couple steps toward Green. "Sure enough," he said as he untied the heavy black leather apron to lay it aside.

"This here's U. S. Marshal Rad Carson from over Dodge City." Green announced Rad with a sweep of his hand.

"Hope you don't mind a hand with a little grime," Emmitt said, wiping it against the thigh portion of his Levi's before offering the howdy-hand.

"And I'm pleased to meet you Shay." Their hands clasped.

"What brings you over this way, Marshal?" Shay asked, "Would it happen to be those fellows that paid us a visit a few days back?, I understand a couple of them were involved in blowing up the jail over in Dodge, and killed a man, I was told—sorry to hear it, Marshal."

"That's a part of it," Carson said, "but there's other business these gentlemen have on their minds."

Emmitt threw a thumb in the air, "I was over east a ways, had to take a carriage out and pick up some stage passengers that was stranded 'cause of a broken axle. I wish I'd had been here, maybe I could have broke up the robbery pulled against Cannonball's holdings."

"Well, that brings us right to the business these men have in mind."

Shay looked at Green and Collins with a questionable expression. "That got something to do with me?"

Carson grasped Hoot by the shoulder and urged him forward, "I'll let these two gentlemen answer that."

"It's this simple, Emmitt," Hoot said, "Cannonball and me, we thought you had the makings to be the Greensburg town marshal. We wanted Carson here to be in on it, so we asked him over for a visit to add a mite of legal law and order to our doin's you might say."

"I'll be . . ." Shay took a step back, "town marshal?" He glanced full face at each of the three men who'd come to see him. "You know what? I think I'd like that . . . you aren't kidding with me are you?"

Carson spoke up, "They told me about the situation back in the Colorado mining district, and I agree with the judge, you were wrong, but you were far more right than you were wrong. That convinced me, and now that I've met you, and with all that these men tell me, I'm convinced you'd make this town a fine lawman."

"Sounds good to me." Shay put up a wide grin and rubbed his chin, "Is that all there is to it?"

"Since you don't have a legal, state recognized mayor," Rad looked at Donald Green and then Hoot with a vacant expression, "or a town council, I believe maybe we'd need for Judge Nathaniel Wilkinson to swear you in. He'll be up this way making rounds before long, I'll leave that to him, but I'll put the bug to his ear when I get back to Dodge City."

"Congratulations, Emmitt," Colonel Green smiled and shook the man's hand. "This town has taken another step, makes me right proud!"

"Well Mr. Emmitt Shay, as your first appointed duty," Carson quipped with a gleam, "I'll be sending over some dodgers—posters on an outlaw by the name of Muley Tatum. He's wanted for murder over in Spickard, and he stole some money from a cow outfit near the Indian Territory three or four weeks back. I'd be obliged if you'd post some of the dodgers around town when they come. He's been riding all over this part of the state and he just might show up around here." Rad hooked his thumbs in his cartridge belt as he went on, "He's a mean sort, not the kind you'd handle without a gun in your hand, just to warn you in advance. Not much I'd like more than having him as a prisoner in my new jail for a few days, until it can be arranged for a rope to stretch his neck."

"I'll help if I can, Carson. I'll be looking for those dodgers."

Carson gave the men a description of Muley, emphasizing the boisterous manners of the man and his odd sense of humor, and said he figured to be ridding with four or five others.

Shay scratched at his chin, "Sounds a good amount like a man that set fire to the trading post off that-a-way," he snapped his head to the south. The story came by way of a drummer name of Styles, who'd met the man down by the nation . . . had his ear cut off by some Injuns, the ol' boy said."

"You don't say?" Carson's eyes lit up.

"The big fella, according to Styles, got mighty pushy, set up a situation with a shotgun that could'a got out of hand except for another man riding with him, that got it set aside. Styles said they raised hell, burned the man's trading shake and rode out heading that-a-way." He pointed northwest.

CHAPTER TWENTY-FOUR

A fair distance northwest from Greensburg, a segment of the Kansas landscape buckled from the earth's crust thousands of years ago. At far less than a snail's pace over time, the earth's wrinkle continued being pushed from both east and west. The result was a jagged, snarled land mass that jolted skyward more than fifty feet in some places. The land is hostile, primarily comprised of shale, gray rock, laced with veins of white alkaline, not suited for neither man or animal habitat, other than horned creatures, snakes and the like that seek out the hot sun. A few slight, twisted trees that grow to six, maybe seven, are there. Otherwise only minimal, scattered pads of thick-bladed short grass survive in the harsh soil. Over the eons, heavy rains eroded the surface with gashes that cut deep, uneven patterns in the already ruthless ground thereabouts.

Rad knew of the area by references from locals. It was known by Santa Fe Trail guides as *Hell's Acres*. The trail near there, *the dry route*, which ran north of the Arkansas River *wet route*, passed within a few hundred feet of *Hell's Acres*. It was considered dangerous, and as such, most folks steered clear. Some said it was haunted ground. Locals told of the Indians' indifferences toward the perilous land; they wouldn't travel within a mile or two of it for fear of evil spirits.

The nature of the desolate land, lending isolation and secrecy, attracted outlaws. There were only two passages through the unrelenting terrain accessible by horseback. Those could be easily guarded if a small passel of men chose to do so. Otherwise a man would have to be afoot, climbing slanting shreds of jagged loose alkali shale. A man on the hunt could be an easy target for the hunted.

Rad figured he had a full day before he'd need to hit the trail back toward Dodge City and the *Hell's Acres* wasn't far off the path he'd follow; maybe he'd give the place a look. He'd travel Sanat Fe Trail's dry route rather than the stage line road that skirted the grass lands and the Arkansas River as it neared Dodge.

Carson crested a small rise which was marked with wagon wheel ruts within two hundred yards of Hell's Acres. He turned Caesar, lowered his head, eyes shaded by the hat brim from the bright yellow mass that dominated the sky. He squinted, focused down, to be sure, thinking he'd seen a light wisp of smoke rising from the low horizon a mile distant. "Its smoke alright, Caesar," he spoke in a hushed tone. He sat quietly, beads of sweat trickled down his temples and the warmth of the sun burned at the thigh of his leg through the brown trousers. "Could be trouble, boy." He nudged heels into the stallion, "We'd best have a look."

The sight was dismal. The gray smoke had faded, leaving only a light curl rose from the rear of a wagon. The billow cover was gone; burned, and a woman sat in a wooden rocking chair under a windblown, flapping piece of canvas held aloft by wooden poles, her face buried in her hands. As Carson drew closer he could see a man's body lying nearby.

Carson thought first of Indians, but none had been reported in the area for more than five years, and those were of the friendly sort; remnants of the Kiowa that had converted to the ways of the white man. Their settlement was north and represented by not more than a dozen who'd become sheep herders. But the bitter devastation of a Kansas prairie tornado, and three year drought, they were driven off, never to return and take up the fight for survival. They felt the final swirling wind was reprisal by the earthen Gods.

Rad drove his heels into Caesar's flanks and bolted toward the scene of obvious disaster.

He swung from the saddle, gun in hand, and cautiously made his way to where the woman sat sobbing in gasping antagonism. His eyes flitting in rapid focus as he searched the nearby terrain. Another dead man was nearby; a Mexican with chaps over ragged, aged-out denims and a faded green shirt that had a large, dark stain of plastered blood extending from his collar to his waist. The Mexican's arms and legs were oddly contorted and his crushed sombrero, the chin strap stretched over his shoulder, partially covered a dark handled, long barreled revolver near the outstretched fingers of one hand.

Carson holstered the Colt and removed his gloves as he knelt at the feet of the woman. His face was drawn, lower lip curled between his teeth. His knees settled into the heat of the coarse soil as the canvas flapped noisily overhead. The early-thirties aged woman lifted her head and peered between fingers. Her auburn hair, beyond what was matted with tears, floated in the breeze. Her long, flower-print, puffed shouldered dress, wafted easily with the light wind. Rad looked about, trying to give reason to what had taken place. No doubt the man at her feet was her husband. *But what about the Mexican?* Had he been traveling with the couple—or could he have been killed by the husband? And the canvas?; Surely she hadn't erected it as protection from the glaring hot sun and then decided simply to mourn his death from beneath in the shade it provided! Nothing made much sense.

"Mammn . . . ," the word came reluctantly, "what's your name?" Rad felt awkward. He knew he was inept, he had never felt comfortable when it came to women. "Is this man your husband, mammn?" He nodded, indicating the man lying next to the squeaking wooden chair that supported her troubled body.

"Yes," she cried softly, her voice laced with grief, "he's my husband." She somehow knew Rad meant her no harm, even before she was able to see the star pinned to the leather vest. "They killed him!" Her voice shrilled softly amid sobs.

"Who did this, mammn?" Rad's voice was limp as he knelt, his hat pushed back and his eyes searching her face between her fingers.

Suddenly she stood. Crying out defiantly, she pointed to the dead Mexican with her arm fully extended, "He did . . . he killed James." She drew in a big breath and screamed angrily as she exhaled, "We gave them the money, every dime we had, they didn't have to kill him."

Carson rose and stepped back, her violent reaction caught him off-guard. The rigid sobs continued, her hands busy flailing but all words had ceased. It was as though she was reliving the exasperating events that had demoralized her.

"Did your husband kill him?" Rad offered hesitantly as he motioned to the Mexican.

Her eyes widened, the sobbing eroded, and she spoke, her broken voice overflowing with anguish and hate. "No! The big man dressed in black did." She began describing the events in brief sentences, each filled with sniffing, gasping breath. "He," again she pointed to the Mexican, "kept looking at me . . . he smiled at me with those black teeth showing." She inhaled with a pair of short, choking breaths, "He touched my hair with his dirty hand and said something, I don't know what it was . . . my husband slapped his hand away, protecting me, that's all he was doing, protecting me." Her hand went to her eyes and the bawling erupted anew as she dropped back into the chair. "The man in black killed him with a knife," she sobbed.

While she sat in profound mourning Rad shifted over toward the wagon. He didn't know what he might find. The fear of a child injured or killed plagued him. But after a brief investigation he discarded the thought; nothing indicated the couple traveled with any youngsters. And even though he was confident the woman would have displayed some normal motherly panic had there been a child, he couldn't discount her unsound mental anguish until he satisfied himself that none was present. Pieces of dark ash cluttered the contents; mostly furniture, but there was also a wash tub, wooden crates, a single blade plow, shovel, an axe, bag of flour and a large tin of sugar and some bottles Rad thought must be vinegar or sorghum and the like. Undoubtedly the couple was intending to become homesteaders, another family to settle the frontier. The bag of flour had small black holes burned into it but otherwise only slight damage had been inflicted on the items, primarily scorched furniture, Carson could see signs that there had been several people in the camp, boot prints were numerous and variable. Horse hoof prints from the edge of the area were distinguishable. The homesteader's four tall draft mules remained in harness but loose from singletrees and the wagon tongue; the traces firmly tied to a chain that was looped around a rock that jutted upward more than three feet. It would have held three teams of like kind. It appeared the couple was relocating from a farm, probably from Missouri and with mules they already owned before setting out. They were supplied up more than most folks from points further east.

Rad returned to where the woman remained, tears still flowing but quietly. She had gathered some wits about her. He had many questions but he also made some confident assumptions. The water barrel's lid was intact and half full. He picked the tin cup from its thong tie, dipped it and took water to the lady. "Here."

Her tear-drenched, sad eyes studied him sluggishly; she reached for the cup wearily and whimpered, "Thank you, mister."

Minutes passed; few words passed between them. Rad knew the lady needed some time, he didn't press her. He figured that wouldn't do any good and even though he held very little confidence in his understanding of women's ways, he had a thorough comprehension of grief when someone lost a loved one. There wasn't much he could do regarding apprehension of the men who'd caused the devastation, and the man, according to the lady's word, who killed her man, was lying dead himself. The whole thing could be sorted out, but it would have to be done later; neither he nor she was going anywhere. And there were things that needed to be done, stock to be cared for and two dead men to be buried.

Rad rekindled the fire. Coffee was a good pacifier; he and the lady could use it as a centerpiece to become acquainted. Once the pot boiled he dropped cold water in to stay the grounds. He then poured strong, black coffee, handed her a cup and settled where she'd face away from the dead bodies to talk with him.

He was right, the couple was from Missouri. Their farm was in Platte County, thirty miles north of Kansas City. There'd been a flood of the Platte River three months back; it destroyed their newly planted crop lands, their barn, and worst of all, their two children were drowned; a boy aged nine and a girl of seven. The children waded into the muddy waters to retrieve their pony and were swept away. Once the bodies were found and buried, their homestead heavily damaged, within days James and Elizabeth Porter decided they had to leave. They couldn't bear to return to the sad, empty house where the family had enjoyed time together. They'd grieved, feeling their lives had no purpose, nothing more in Missouri to live for. Elizabeth read from a Kansas City newspaper, accounts of settlers relocating, moving to opportunistic, but sparsely populated lands throughout the West. The paper told of prosperity gained from resources the land offered and of lives fulfilled. James and Elizabeth Porter packed up all they had left and struck out to start anew, to begin a new life, as the newspaper depicted.

Rad Carson was a good listener. His heart ached for the poor woman. Now her husband was gone too. She began to weep heavily again, "I hadn't told James yet but I'm sure I'm with child now. I was going to wait until we got to Santa Fe. It would have served as a beacon to renew faith for him. I did so look forward to that moment." Tears gushed once again.

Three cups of coffee and an hour later, Elizabeth was able to convey a descriptive account of the ordeal that brought the outlaw gang into their camp and the tormenting they brought. She started, "The group of men—there were six of them, rode into our camp peacefully, appearing to be of a friendly nature. The man that was the leader was a good natured man, extremely courteous to me—not so much with James though." She paused and an empty expression formed on her face before she continued, "He smiled almost constantly, like a friendly gesture." She hesitated again, as though she was reconsidering.

"You said they took your money."

"Yes, after we'd eaten, two of the men started rummaging in the sides of the wagon. James asked them in a forthcoming manner to not bother in our belongings . . . , well that was kinda the start. The man wearing a derby hat pulled a gun on James and pushed him back. The other man put a match to our wagon—you can see what happened!" She flipped her wrist to the direction. "James tried to cut the canvas bonnet loose and partially yanked it away before the fire could burn our valuables."

Rad shook his head, envisioning the turmoil, understanding the damage to the furniture and the smoke he'd seen from the distance. Carson put a hand to the canvas covering over the chair where Mrs. Porter had sat, "What's this all about?"

"Well, that was later—after they'd robbed us and killed James. And after he, the leader man, stabbed the Mexican man in the neck and killed him, he made the other men put this tent up. He said I'd need shelter from the sun." She shook her head side to side very slowly, "He was a strange sort, meaner than a starved coyote one minute, and then as nice and gentle toward me as a man could ever be." Elizabeth Porter glared at Rad, her eyes heavy with wonderment, "You suppose the man could have been crazy—out of his mind?"

Carson said nothing to the Porter woman but he was convinced it was Muley Tatum who was the man in black she described. And the men with him were likely the same as when the Texan, Wade Weidemier's, trail boss, Gieberg, paid toll money for their crossing the Indian Territory, a few weeks back. This incident with the Porters tipped the scale for him on Muley Tatum, it was now a burning hate. Carson knew he'd have difficulty arresting the man instead of killing him on the spot once he was close enough to make the shot. But for now he had to control his anger, there were chores he had to attend to.

The afternoon sun was unrelenting and the air heavy. The breeze fell, no longer enough to move the flame of a candle. There wasn't any way he could get the Porter woman with her belongings and the pair of corpses into town soon enough, the heat wouldn't allow it. He'd have to do the burying. He hefted the shovel and started to lift James.

"Over there, in those trees, if you will Marshal Carson." Mrs. Porter motioned toward a small group of cedars that crowned a slight rise thirty paces away. "In the past several days," the tears began anew as she nodded her head slightly to the east, "we passed graves lying along the trail; some were desolate. In acknowledgement James remarked about the emptiness and void of green vegetation. He quietly expressed sorrow, nodding, "The poor people buried there, with nothing about, and only the dust to gather over their graves."

The grief-stricken look she offered was all it took. Rad answered, "That looks like a good spot alright." He lifted the man gingerly and started toward the cedars.

By the time he'd put James Porter in the ground proper the first early evening stars dotted the dark eastern sky. Elizabeth Porter stood at the grave for several minutes. Carson filled the opening and completed the elliptical ring of stones around the fresh turned earth. He wiped his brow and neck with the kerchief and stood in silence for a moment before returning to the campsite. There was still the Mexican to tend to. That would be by moonlight.

Morning broke bright. The air smelled of hot, dusty grass and a hint of alkali. It was stuffy and close, another hot day was in store. Rad raised his head from the bedroll set against his saddle. In the supple gray light he could see Elizabeth Porter. She stood amid the cedar grove where her husband was to spend eternity, the palms of her hands pressed together below her chin. He knew he didn't have the right words should he go stand beside her. He'd stir the coals and start coffee. In time she'd come back and they'd take a bite of breakfast. Afterward, he'd hitch up the mules and prepare for departure. Caesar would follow along behind. Dodge City was two, maybe three days away, considering the pace of the mules.

Mrs. Porter was reluctant when the time came. But after awhile she allowed that Rad could help her up to the wagon seat. She sat quietly, staring at the cedar grove through moist eyes. He gave her another minute, the only sound being the soft, warm breeze.

Rad whistled the mules and snapped at the traces. His final glance toward *Hell's Acres,* less than three to four mile distant, served as a reminder of Muley Tatum. The place, he figured, was properly named.

CHAPTER TWENTY-FIVE

Carson looked over the long ears of the slow paced mules. The wagon creaked and groaned across the easy-rolling Kansas land. Emptiness of the prairie that settled softly against the distant horizon made him wonder what the future held for this part of the country. A maverick tumbleweed, pushed by a searing breeze, bumped along on the harsh ground. It halted abruptly. A stand of sage interrupted its path at the edge of the trail. *'That oval piece of brush just might hold the answer,'* Carson thought. The migration of people heading for more distant lands, not stopping long in the area other than by an impediment being forced in front of them, as had happened to the Porters. Their goal was commonly Colorado or California gold.

Riches inspire some men more than a commitment to a family on a plot of ground. Of course there'd be carving out a living, but a man unwilling to work wouldn't make it either way. But the domesticated life style held much greater probability of success than the ten thousand-to-one odds of a gold strike. But still they seek the improbable glitter of rich ore. Perhaps the fixation that drove men more than anything else was the unknown, something other than what he'd already obtained, something a man's imagination conjured up, more akin to a dream than a hard and fast object touched or hand held. Rad puzzled over it.

That reminded him, he'd need to find Elizabeth Porter a place to stay, someone to take her in. He thought first of Miss Grassley, the schoolmarm, she lived alone and was a friendly sort. Maybe she'd like a boarder. And there was Fanny . . . a faint smile came to his face as he remembered the last conversation they had. He'd thought about her more than a few times since he'd been away. He pictured her shapely frame and that pretty smile of hers as she tilted her head to look at him from the corner of her eye. She'd somehow taken over a piece of his mind . . . he wondered of that was how real affection, maybe love, started! The thought was comfortable and warm but somehow also seemed distant and unreal, something like the dream of gold to a lot of men.

"Are we close to town?" Elizabeth questioned.

"To the best of my reckoning we'll get to Dodge City late tomorrow." Rad searched the woman's face, hoping for a hint of satisfaction. "I'm thinking on just where you'd be made to feel at home. We've got a lot of good folks there, friendly and accommodating folks, I know you'll like it."

A lurch of Elizabeth's body got his attention. She threw an arm out in front of him, "I'll not go on, I'll stay here." Her head bobbed with a jerk in affirmation of her remark. She turned to look straight on at Red, raised her hand to shade the sun and sniffed back the need to cry. "I can't leave James." Her lips trembled and tears welled from her eyes as she gazed at Rad with a long, forlorn expression, the top of both cheeks beginning to shine with moisture.

Carson tugged back on the reins. "Whoa . . . whoa, mules."

He gave the woman a hard look and searched the surroundings, all the while knowing he'd not allow her to step down. But it gave him time to gather a reply. "There's no water for at least five miles, and what's in your barrel won't last more than two days." He took in a deep breath and went on, "This area is known to be infested with rattlers, some near big around as a man's arm." He saw her eyes investigate the layers of rock and inhospitable, parched undergrowth that covered most everything lying beyond the trail. He took measure of her thoughts and in his best *'please-the-ladies'* voice, he offered, "Mrs. Porter, your husband would hold me over to the devil himself if I was to let you set here."

She closed her eyes, pressing tightly, and through clinched teeth remarked, "I'm sorry, Mr. Carson, I just can't stand it; I know I'm not thinking straight. You'll have to excuse me." Her hands fluttered to her face and blotted her transgressions from the world for the moment. She drew a lengthy breath through her nostrils and a soft, throaty whimper escaped from beneath the protection of her hands. Again she uttered, "I'm sorry."

"Things will be better when we get to Dodge, you'll see." He looked her over offhandedly; notioned that she was okay, snapped the reins and whistled, "Get up mules." When the traces were brought rigid, he turned back to Mrs. Porter, "You just sit tight, the sun will let up soon and we'll be able to draw reasonable breath." Between the sluggish mules, Mrs. Porter's disapproving manner, and the blasting heat, Carson had his hands full. He thought about his grandpa once again. *'The man's constitution must have been remarkable to have overcome the obstacles he faced repeatedly; the Injuns, weather, hunger, insects, all with the lonesome, desolate country constantly trying to kill him, and he was able to overcome it all. I hope I've got enough of his patience inheritance in me to fulfill my obligations.'* The final thought he reluctantly tolerated was *'it must be the heartsick-woman what rubbed my salty-side most'*. He didn't allow that he'd ever understand womenfolk.

The second day wound down, the sun hazed low. Soon thereafter, the dingy, cotton-gray streaked clouds obligated the air to stay hot and the first stars of twilight dotted the deep velvet sky. Dodge was less than eight miles beyond the low, strung-out hills. Carson figured to be pulling into Dodge two hours or so after solid darkness.

Whistling the mules on grew harder. "Yeeeaaa," he yelled and snapped the whip to the lead teams' backside. They were accustomed to rest before sundown and as such, were indifferent, challenging the demands. "Stubborn." Rad commented. He grinned to Mrs. Porter, whistled again and snapped the traces, "It'll be a fight, but we're going to get these critters to Dodge City before the whole town shuts down for the night." Her response was a side-glance followed with a wrinkled brow. He wondered if she'd even heard the remark.

The trail swung south down a long meandering incline where it met with the wet route trail, crossed the Arkansas River, the rail line, and led straight into town. The odors and sounds of bawling cattle were obvious and the gay tinkle of piano music playing a hasty, dance number struggled into the air as Carson urged the mules onto the long plank-board bridge. Dodge City's evening sounds and depraved carrying-ons came to Carson's mind. In his personal gratification for being home, he'd failed to comprehend the negative impressions the town could have on the woman, especially this time of night. The better side of the community was much more apparent in mornings, even mid-day. Ladies could rarely be seen on the boardwalks after the sun went down, at least the ladies that considered themselves good homemakers and churchgoers, they stayed to home at night mending and seeing to family needs. Vague doubts, backed by questionable regression, jumped into his mind.

The clunk of their own hooves on the planking of the bridge invigorated the pace of the mules. They drew on fresh energy, seeming to appreciate the civilization. Carson tugged back at the reins with a smile, the feeling of a bit of satisfaction mingled with lax expectations. He was pleased to be back; but he was yet to get Elizabeth Porter settled, even for the one night. He'd deal with finding her a home, a temporary home, sometime tomorrow.

"Almost there, Mrs. Porter." He glanced over to her, vision being poor due to the darkness. But he could see downturned lips and the sheen of moisture on her cheek. “We’ll put you up in the hotel for tonight—get you a nice soft bed and fresh cool water to wash up with.” His voice tone was supple, maybe too soft he thought after he spoke, to override other sounds that found their way to the wagon, sounds of the abrasive side of Dodge City.

“I’ve never been one to take to the bustle of city life.” Elizabeth Porter replied with an uneasy voice. And then referring to Tatum and his gang, she said sensitively, as if equating them to the fear Rad could see on her face, “Those men back there . . . they were so vicious and dirty mouthed.”

There were seventeen saloons in town, counting the ones away from the primary streets, those that placed the joys of men visiting with loose women above the sale of spirit drinks. Rad could tell the cattle yards were busied, the air smelled of it. That meant raw, young cow hands would be on the frisky side; there’d be a long count of drunkards, fights and robberies. “I sure hope Sheriff Hinkle’s got things under control,” Carson said under his breath. He made quick glances along the streets as the wagon made way toward the hotel where he’d place the Porter woman. He spoke in a manner not intended to be heard by the lady at his side, but the words came a mite louder than intended, “I’m dog tired and shy on temper tonight—don’t need no foul words or orneriness to put me into a flap.”

“Fine, Marshal Carson,” Elizabeth Porter puffed, her eyes blinking like a horse fretting about flies, “I’ll be of no more trouble to you . . . there’s the hotel, just halt the mules and I’ll be out of your hair right now!”

Carson flushed, realizing she thought he was thrashing at her. “No, no, Mrs. Porter, I wasn’t addressing you—I was voicing some irritation about the dang-blasted men . . .” Again, he knew he’d said the wrong thing. His brows arched and in a half grin, said, “Mammn, I apologize for my bad talk and thinking out loud, I suppose I’m back to being a lawman since I’m back in Dodge. I’m sorry.”

Her head dropped, chin on chest, her tender, forgiving feminine side took over. "I'm the one that's sorry, Marshal. After all that you've done for me, I'm ashamed, please forgive me."

"We both are plum tuckered, Mammn, let's just be thankful we're here. You're safe and I'm back to where I belong. Let's leave it set at that." The smile on his face was genuine. He lashed the reins to the long brake handle and stepped down, walked past Caesar and around to Mrs. Porter's side of the open-bowed wagon. He offered up a hand. "Easy now, watch your step."

When Rad Carson first opened his eyes the next morning, the scene confused him; it'd been quite a spell since he'd slept so deeply and his Satterfield room was comprised of nicely crafted furniture, far different from the hard ground and open prairie he'd grown accustomed to. There was also the smell of bacon and biscuits. That brought a glinting thought of Fanny, but it faded by the time he threw back the cover and came to grips with the new day lying ahead.

He rubbed his forehead, squeezed sensitively at his eyes with a thumb and forefinger, blinked and rolled his feet to the floor. He recalled checking Elizabeth Porter into the hotel, remembering he'd anticipated The Drovers' Palace to be filled with men of strong language so he'd taken her to The Empire. He put her wagon in the hands of Gentry and Adam Ralston, the livery man and his sharp-as-a-tack son. He told them to hold the wagon inside; shelter the mules after providing a straw-rub, grain and water, but they would be better natured under the corral lean-to, not the barn.

Carson dressed hurriedly, having slept a few minutes later than usual. He quietly stalked into the kitchen. "Mrs. Satterfield . . . ,"

She cut him off, "We're glad to see you're back, Mr. Carson. I knew when you came in last evening, her warm smile lacked any sign of recourse, "Would've welcomed you then, but it was late."

"Yes it was; if you'd be so kind, mammn, I'd like to take breakfast here in the kitchen rather than with the others in the dining room. I'm a bit late for a meeting and as such, lack time for extra visiting." That slight bend of the truth seemed to be in order.

The elderly woman again smiled widely, "That'll be fine. I understand. I'm sure there'd be questions about your travel." She took a plate from the cupboard and began filling it. "You just take a seat right there, Mr. Carson." She poured steaming hot coffee and put it and the plate of food on the table. She bent and said in a hush, "I'll not let them know you're here."

Rad quickly ate, pushed out the back door and hastily started his walk for the town center. Once again he considered where he'd attempt to find a home for the Porter woman. His thoughts were that she'd require at least a semi-permanent residence, needing another woman to help her through the hardships of losing her husband in such a violent manner and learn the ways of her new-found frontier home, a rough and tumble town to say the least. But Dodge was on the grow, and soon, if his plan worked out proper, it would become a solid, law abiding place to raise a family, better for women and children, where they could be on the streets without need of their men-folks being alongside for protection.

Elizabeth had talked little during the long ride to Dodge. But she did speak of teaching the children some book learnings. That gave Rad a consideration about taking her to Edith Grassley's place. Edith Grassley was a small frame woman filled with moxie. She wore her hair pulled straight back over her ears and tied in a bun on the back of her head. The gold-framed glasses lent an air of knowledge and self-assuredness. She was a straight-talking woman, never one to withhold an opinion. But she never gave an opinion in a harsh tone, she always spoke with an open expression, making it difficult to determine whether she was angered or simply quietly reprimanding because it was the proper thing to do, considering the issue. And she didn't smile much to give light to her temperament. Rad figured it was her subjectivity that had kept her from marrying; she held high expectations and precise, orderly mannerisms, not an easy disposition that most men could accommodate.

Rad Carson told Elizabeth Porter when he left her at The Empire the previous night he'd be back today, a Saturday. He'd take the Porter woman to Edith Grassley's home. No school today and they'd be a pretty good fit.

Fortunately the schoolmarm was home, as Rad thought she would be.

Miss Grassley welcomed the Porter woman jubilantly. She'd softened more than Carson figured possible once she'd heard of the happenings out by Hell's Acres and Mr. Porter being murdered, leaving two little children with no father.

In less than an hour he'd made the introductions, carried Elisabeth Porter's things inside and left the two womenfolk sipping tea in the parlor.

Rad was quite uncomfortable in these surroundings. His awkward presence didn't go unnoticed; it was more than evident to the ladies. "I suppose you'll be needing to tend to your marshaling business, Mr. Carson," Miss Grassley offered over the tip of her tea cup. Her manner of speech was the only invitation Carson needed—and she knew it!

The good-bys were brief.

And now he'd gotten that matter put aside, he'd have to view what progress had been on the new jail and he'd need to check on things at his office. There was plenty to do, but such was more to his taste.

"Good morning, Hinkle," Rad shouted and waved across the street traffic. He waited as a pair of freight wagons and a cowboy leading a string of four horses made their way and the worst of the dust cleared before he stepped out to accompany the Ford County sheriff.

Hinkle raised a hand to the side of his mouth, "Glad to see you're back, Carson." He then hefted the wide belt cartridge belt, patted the dark handled Remington holstered at his side and tugged the lapels of his tweed coat to cover his expansive middle as Carson gained the space between them.

"Been trouble has there?" Rad questioned as he stepped up onto the boardwalk.

"Not more than the usual . . . matter-of-fact it's been quieter than I'd expected." He rubbed his chin whiskers, scratched at the base of his neck, and continued, "But there was a herd of beeves come in yesterday, they'll likely be loading up today, so you know what that means."

Carson looked toward the cattle yards, "Young wrangler . . . they'll be in town tonight, got money to spend and be needin' to see if they can run some of the saloons low on whiskey, I reckon."

The two lawmen gave a glimpse up and down the street, the passage of people and vehicles being notable. "I suppose the local folks all know to get their city chores put aside early, need to avoid the trouble later on," Hinkle quipped, his eyes moving back to Rad.

Rad nodded in silence, a long minute passed before saying, "I'm heading over to see the progress on the jail. You want to come along?"

The walk gave Rad the opportunity to inform Hinkle of his finding the three jail-breakers on the trail between Bucklin and Greenburg. He related the killing of The Duffy boy and his shooting the young cowboy who'd killed Duffy. "Wiley Simmons over in Bucklin is holding the other young man. I'll let Judge Wilkinson know about that."

Hinkle absentmindedly twisted one end of his abundant moustache and continued an indifferent visual assessment of town-folk, "Well, that accounts for three, but we ain't seen any of them around here. I suppose they all skedaddled, didn't want any more to do with Dodge."

Carson then advised Hinkle of Greenburg selecting a town marshal. And finally he told of the Porters and how she'd described the men who had killed her husband. “I think we’ve had another couple of incidents of Muley Tatum.” Carson gave details of the events he’d experienced, completing the happenings of the past few days as they affronted the new jail structure. “Someday soon I hope we can put that Tatum bastard in this jail—if I don’t kill him first,” he added passively.

“Looks good.” Carson offered as his gaze took in the full structure.”

“They’ll be finishing up with the iron work before the week’s end,” the sheriff pointed out, “using a mesh of three inch strap-iron for the holding cells—even putting a ceiling on each cell of the same.” He paused before pointing, “Them bricks make for a formidable looking building, don’t ya think, marshal?”

Once the lawmen made their lengthy inspection of the interior of the building, they made their way back outside, into the heavy sun. “Plenty of windows,” Carson commented. “Makes for a breeze through inside from most any direction.”

“Yep, if them bars allow for it,” Hinkle jibed back with a chuckle. He turned, pulled at the watch chain and lifted the timepiece from a low vest pocket, “You ready for an early lunch over to Fanny’s place?”

CHAPTER TWENTY-SIX

Bo chanced a question, "When we gonna get the hell outta this God-forsaken snake pit, Muley? This damn filthy white dust clings to us like fuzz on a peach . . . burns my eyes day and night. It's getting to where I'd sooner face a lop-eared lawman, me without a gun, than spend another day here."

Muley gave Bo Cantrell a fleeting, hard look from the corner of his eye. He laid the newspapers aside and fixed a sideway stare until Bo looked away. He didn't like anyone assuming a position with him. "You got a bug up your big ass, Bo?"

Bo threw a glance over to Charlie Joe, wanting a word, or at least a sign, from him in agreement to move on. He didn't get it. Instead he lifted a cigar from his shirt pocket, trying to negate his remark as he bit off the end. "Ah, I guess I'm just tired and need a soft woman to take my mind off my restlessness. I'll get over it, Boss." His grin was awkward.

Pete Longley stood, allowing Bo a break. He gave up the rock with his saddle blanket folded over it. "We still got hot coffee," he stated and dusted his hands, took the few steps toward the fire, stooped and picked up the coffee pot with a folded glove. "Anybody else want for coffee?"

Jess measured Pete's manner, knowing he saw a need to squash a problem. "I'll take you up on that, got an extra cup over there?"

Muley Tatum rose, walked a dozen or more steps apart from the others, jerked his hat off and slapped it against the dust covering his shirt front and arms. The sun was hotter than blazes and the air still as death itself. He rolled his head, eyes moving at all angles, and stopped as if a trance assumed him. He then slowly, very slowly, shuffled in a circle, taking in the bleak, dismal surroundings. They all watched uneasily as he took in the ugliness of the jagged terrain surrounding their limply shaded campsite.

"Anybody else want coffee? There another cup or two in here." Again Pete broke the silence.

Muley turned to face the group, "You're right, Bo, we been here long enough. The horses are needin' some graze." He pushed his black hat back on his head, "And I'm needin' whiskey. Let's move on, this place ain't all they make it out to be."

Everyone moved cautiously, awaiting signs from Tatum. There was no doubt in the mind of any man, Muley Tatum was to set any event in motion for the pack of them. In short order he instructed Charlie and Bo to gather the horses from the tie-line and ready the gear. He gave the Longleys a lasting consideration, knowing they weren't cut from the same swath as the hard-cases. Pete was of his own mind; Jess would do whatever Pete's actions inclined.

Movements were hasty, but guarded, no one wanting to appear anxious. But any man with an inkling of savvy could see it, almost as plain as a new life pecking from the shell, clumsily ready to explore the new world, everyone wanted out.

Bridles were looped over perked ears, the squeak of saddle leather and buckling of belly straps brought life to the strange group of men. "I'm thinking we'll go west," Tatum announced and lazy-eye-gazed that direction as he tied off slack from the cinch and dropped the fender. "I've got me some unfinished business." Signs of the cruel grin once again etched his whisked face. "There's a man up there there that owes me."

The newspapers Tatum gathered at Greenburg had articles about Milt Possum Tucker's jail break. And the articles he read from the *DODGE CITY HERALD* informed him of Rad Carson's appointment to his position as a United States marshal and burning of the jail. He said no more about either event but busied his mind and he stuffed the papers in saddlebags.

The Longleys rode behind the other three, as was usual. Pete peered over his shoulder, a final farewell from the decrepit landscape that'd held them captive for three days. He took note that Jess kept glancing over, wanting his attention. He kneed his horse closer. The younger brother had something to say—he slowed and allowed Jess to come along side.

"What do you think Muley's got in mind?" Jess mouthed uneasy like.

Pete opened his hands in response, the reins resting in his palms, but said nothing.

"It ain't good, Pete, I can tell." His eyes moving toward the others and back again, "That man ain't like you and me, and he's taking us on some kind of tomfoolery, you know that just as well as I do."

"And the next thing you're going to tell me is you think we should take leave and go off to Colorado, ain't you?"

The dire look on Jess's face was answer enough. Annoyance was plain, but he said it anyway, "Why not?"

"Maybe . . . let's talk about it tonight when we set camp." Pete kicked his horse to move up and Jesse slowed, shaking his head and lips pursed tight.

Six hours riding time split between a trail eating gallop and slow, drudging walking of their mounts brought them to a wide plain of stirrup high prairie grass. The horses, with necks stretched occasionally to snap a mouthful of tall-stemmed grass were weary, needing water and no doubt they longed for the tenderness of moist sod. Muley halted, half-turned, stood in the stirrups and flipped a finger toward a strung out pattern of tree tops visible beyond a rock-pocked rise in the distance, welcome signs of good water. They'd be there in minutes.

"Looks homey, wouldn't you say, Charlie Joe?" Muley slid down, dropped the reins and allowed the big black horse to muzzle water. "Be a nice place for a man to set with his woman and look about a youngen or two." All of the others stood down likewise, pretending not to hear Muley's comments.

The water pool, fifteen feet in width, was still, other than the plops initiated by a pair of frogs that leaped into the nominal nature-built pond. The hushed, smooth stream showed ringlets, signs of insects atop the pool and small dark shadows wiggling away from where the men and horses stood. Signs of deer and antelope dotted the area.

"I'm a wonder that no sodbusters have settled here," Charlie answered back. He looked to the hill a few hundred yards distant. His gaze froze, he saw it, at the same time Pete and Jess did, a single short-horned cow silhouetted by the blue-gray, stretched-cotton cloud backdrop of the Kansas sky. Her tail flipped placidly as she returned the stare of the five men watching.

"Will ya look at that?" Jesse mused, "You reckon she belongs to someone?"

"Could be just a maverick that straggled," Charlie's answer was anxious. His hand flew to his hat. He jerked it from his head and made three long strides to his horse, "Don't know who she belongs to but she looks like steak agittin' ready to be fried up for supper from where I am." He clapped the hat back atop his slicked-back hair, locked hands tight to the saddle horn and forked his bronc is a single smooth motion. "Get some fire wood readied, I'll be back," he yelled over his shoulder, heels kicking into the flanks of the dark roan.

The lonely cow flinched, turned with a sudden jerk and kicked up dust as she disappeared out of sight. Charlie screamed like a Comanche and spread a dirt cloud of his own as his image dropped from view over the horizon. A few seconds later the hollow bursts of a six-gun broke the silence. Tatum grinned and bobbed his head, taking the measure of the others before he slapped at his upper leg and gee-walled, "Ole Charlie is bringing supper boys, let's get a fire going'."

Several minutes passed, horses unsaddled, hobbled for grazing and a cook fire put underway. But Charlie Joe was yet to be seen.

Muley rose from the fire where the coffee pot was readied, hands on hips, his eyes locked on the site where Charlie Joe rode out of sight. He studied the spot intently for a long spell, and then spoke disconcertedly, "Jesse, why don't you go up there and give Charlie a hand, he must be figuring to butcher the whole damn thing before he comes back."

Jesse looked to Pete.

Pete nodded to Jess and twitched his head toward the hillside.

Before Jesse was able to retrieve his horse to be saddled, Charlie came into sight. He whistled a high-pitched whistle and waved. As he moved closer it was clear, a rear quarter of beef, hide still on, was tied on behind and he had a look plastered on his face that any school boy could interpret. "That ole cow did belong to somebody, had a brand on her." He pointed a bloodied glove hand to an old, washed out mark on the stiff hair. "Didn't see no buildings though—no way anybody heard my shots. I rode a circle mor'n a mile to see what else was around, maybe a cabin, a barn, or the like—wasn't nothin'." He jumped down, pulled the grizzly looking full quarter from its tie, dumped the bulky meat onto the ground and dug into his saddle bag, "Cut the tongue out too, best damn eatin' a man can have," he exclaimed with a big smile as he pushed the limp slab of rough-topped meat toward Bo.

Bo flinched, not wanting anything to do with it, "Maybe for you half-Indian sons of Satan, but I'm more of a mind to roast a chunk from that hind quarter." He squinted and backed up.

Charlie Joe let the Indian reference roll off, he was used to it; never squawked back, just shook his head, leaving the long braid of hair to mystify those who challenged his heritage. He was long legged and lean, had a line to his jaw and dark green eyes that denied a red man's blood to be in his veins. He liked the confusion though and let be known, "You go ahead and feed on that ole cow's rump, white boy," he harassed, "I'll have me some meat from the critter's better parts."

Tin plates in hand, Jesse took his brother aside and gave the pathetic threesome a pitiful glance, "Look at them," Jesse curled his lip, "they're a sorry sight, wouldn't you say, Pete?"

"They're men without a purpose. I've been studying on it." Pete's solemn response was a surprise to Jesse. "They don't want for anything like normal people do," Pete continued, talking slow and soft, "they don't have direction, seems they try to escape from life its self." He stared a whole through Jesse—no blinking, empty of emotion, less expression than a sand toad basking in full sun; he said it again, "Men without a purpose."

"What do 'ya mean by that?"

Pete let his eyes switch side to side in anticipation of what he wanted to say before he said it, "They're dead men, just ain't died yet. They don't want for anything, no wife and kids, no family, don't try to learn, and want nothing tomorrow but to do nothing." He rubbed at his jaw like he was trying to force words out, feeling lax toward making his point.

"Even Muley?"

"No . . . not Muley." Pete's dry lips parted a little, the hint of a smile surfaced. "He's not like them, he wants for a woman, maybe a wife." Pete set his plate on the ground between his feet and appeared to ease into relaxation. "But he's afraid."

"Afraid of what?"

"Maybe afraid he'll let his meanness out at the wrong time, maybe kill when he don't want to, I'm thinkin'."

Jesse sneered, tucked his chin to his chest and retorted, "You kiddin'? The man's a killer through and through, always 'cause he wants to."

"Nope. But the man's mean, got a string of the Devil in his bones." Pete twisted his neck without movement of his shoulders, and halted his visual appraisal with his glare posted on Muley Tatum. "He's confused; likes women, hates weak men." Pete licked his lips first then curled the bottom lip under and bit down on it lightly with his lower front teeth before he went on, "Problem is, he don't know why."

"So he kills?" Jesse looked up at Pete, his brow raised in uncertainty. "Don't make sense, brother."

"It's God's truth." Pete jerked his head full toward Jesse, smiled and said, "You and me, we ain't going to change it either." Hands on hips, he looked toward the west, "We ain't going back, Jess. Once we get as far west with them as they're goin, we're not goin' back."

"Does that mean we're going on to Colorado?" Jesse's expression perked.

"Yep, we're going to Colorado." Pete gave Jesse a trustworthy smile. "I figure three, maybe four days." Pete stood close, leaned and whispered, "Don't say nothin'."

There were times Pete feared for Jess's life; troubled that Muley might lose patience and find some off-handed reason to kill him. And Pete had resigned himself to kill Muley if he was to see it about to happen. The days they'd spent with the demented man taught Pete some lessons in life, and in death. The time, although it was generally dreadful, gave Pete insight far beyond what life in Texas could ever do. He learned it well, knowing from these days going forward, life would be more precious, have more meaning than the days he'd spent herding cows and never before expecting to have enough money to have his own outfit, complete with a ranch, cattle and a woman to share it. But he was going to do it honest. He'd have no part in outlawin'. He'd tasted the bitterness of lawless life and made up his mind it wasn't going to take him in as it had others—men with no purpose.

CHAPTER TWENTY-SEVEN

The bright morning sun cascaded through the café window. Fanny's light golden hair coiled gently over her shoulders atop the pale blue, finely pressed blouse. "I heard you'd been gone out of town," Fanny said as she set the breakfast plate on the checked oilcloth in front of Rad. She drew back slightly, "Sheriff Hinkle was in, he told me." What she didn't tell him was that she'd asked about him. Hinkle also told her about Rad bringing the Porter woman into town. He voided giving details, and as such, Fanny's curiosity had worked to a height that kept her mind from her usual lofty attention to detail in the café.

Carson's voice was subtle, near a whisper as he leaned forward. "Can we talk?"

His question surprised her. She glanced around the room, taking a fleeting inventory of the customers. She didn't want to appear anxious, "I need to refill some coffee cups first . . . , but I'll be back." Fanny couldn't fully brush away the smile of satisfaction that slipped into her face as she dropped her chin and turned toward the kitchen.

Rad kept his eyes fixed on her as best he could. She soon reappeared out of the back and moved about the room in lackadaisical fashion. To Rad it seemed as though she made efforts to remain distant. Eventually, she found her way back to his table, coffee pot in hand. Her lips parted with a nimble smile.

"Please," he offered with a confident grin of his own, "won't you sit for a minute?" He reached the chair-back at the end of the table to his left and turned it a quarter turn for her to sit. She did. He leaned toward her, "I've missed seeing you."

Fanny's brows responded over her blue eyes as a hand rose and a finger found a curl draped over her shoulder, "Oh?" Her lips retained the shape after the word was out.

"Can I call on you this evening?" His face flushed just enough to highlight the rounded cheek-top below the eyes.

"I'd like that."

"Can we say seven o'clock?"

"I don't usually get away from here until . . ." her eyes perked up, "but I'll leave things with Bonnie earlier than usual. Seven will be fine."

Each of them shared a pleasant feeling of gratification, like an obstacle that held them apart had been set aside. Rad started with his plate of food, not fully realizing what he was eating.

The tiny bell over the café door tinkled sharply. Sheriff Hinkle appeared, his abrupt entrance catching the attention of everyone in the room. His quick glances, filled with anxiety, caught Rad's lawman intrigue. He lifted a hand and waved ineptly, not really wanting it to be true, but he felt his presence could be the sheriff's intended quest. Sure enough, Hinkle scuttled his large frame toward Carson. He leaned with a hand on the table, "You may not believe this, but I got word that Possum Tucker was back in town."

Fanny read the discernment between the two men and rose from her chair giving sign the two of them could talk without her involvement; she moved aside, looked down at Rad and nodded questionably, "Tonight?"

"At seven," he responded unaccountably.

Hinkle covered the chair vacated by Fanny and looked up at her, inciting time for privacy between him and the marshal. The big man's eyes cast about the room and he scratched at his jaw before dropping the hand and staring bluntly into Carson's face, "One of my old friends here in town said he saw Barnett, the newspaper man, talking with a man that he was sure was Possum Tucker; said he saw them together at The Spotted Cat Saloon, Stell Marks place."

"Tucker would have to have got some guts, coming back here. I'd have thought he'd figure he was too well known in these parts to let his face be seen anywhere close to Dodge City." Carson wasn't convinced.

"My friend says the 'ole Possum grew a moustache and is all decked out in fancy duds, nothin' like he was wearing before. And he's also got himself a pair of gold-framed glasses he looks over, like a successful business man, or maybe a drummer from back East, gives him a dandy disguise." Hinkle's eyes enlarged as he said it. "But that bad hand of his is a dead giveaway, something my cagey friend would spot and he says it's Tucker alright."

"Interesting that Richard Barnett would be talking with Tucker, but then Barnett has never seemed to be much on the side of lawmen. Wonder what Barnett figures to gain—he's a newspaper man, a slant-sided journalist who has created as much news as he'd ever reported otherwise." Carson continued to explore his thoughts about the word-jockey. He then searched Hinkle's demeanor, questions racked his brain, "Sounds like we'd best check it out." His jaws muscles stiffened, "There ain't nobody I'd rather lock up in that new jail than Milt Tucker, if indeed that was him over to *The Spotted Cat.*"

Sheriff Hinkle twisted a fresh cigar between his lips, lifted it free between a thumb and forefinger and responded to Carson's elaboration on Barnett, "You gotta remember, the newsman makes his money, and his reputation, by searching out things other people overlook. I'd be willing to wager my man's not just blowin' in the wind." Hinkle bit the tip from the cigar, looked about for a place to spit it, but elected to consign it to a side pocket when he saw Fanny watching. He turned back to Rad, "I'm going over to Stell's place to look into the possibility for myself." He lightly tossed his head in that direction. "I thought you'd like to come along."

"Barnett's a case to figure . . ." Carson thoughtfully followed up, "Reminds me of the telegram he sent to Tucker over to the prison in Wichita. The man's hell-bent on crafting a news story. Seems he'll go to any length," Carson paused, "we might have a case against him for aiding and abetting a crime." He paused again, looked at Hinkle inquisitively and added, "Something we could think about!"

Hinkle didn't answer other than with a side-twitch of his head; he rose languidly, flexed the cigar to the other side of his mouth and sluggishly started for the door. Rad waited a second, placed a quarter on the table and began to follow.

Fanny, barely lifting a hand, gave a fragile four-fingered good-by wave as Rad looked her way and fell in behind Sheriff Hinkle. He read her thoughts. The expression questioned the time table set between them for later in the evening.

The walk to Stell Marks establishment would take four to five minutes. Street activity was light. Lengthy morning shadows stretched well beyond the center of the hard-pack separating the rows of buildings as they trudged north up *A* Street, past Spruce and Cedar, and then bent into the sun on Elm Street. The Spotted Cat Saloon came into view. Carson hadn't yet decided on talking with Stell. He knew she was an adamant business-type, not one to give over information damaging to her customers, or clients, as she referred to some. It could harm her reputation, making her appear too obliging when it came to law enforcement. A saloon in a town with a well-earned anti-law reputation could stand out like a cougar at a calf-branding. But she was also a woman that held respect for the law; that had sand to Rad's way of thinking. It could be that she wasn't even aware that Tucker had been in her place.

Rad's mind was busied putting together an approach that would prove out. If Milt Tucker was in Dodge and visited *The Spotted Cat,* it wouldn't do much good just to confirm it. And if Tucker was to catch wind of his having been recognized, and the law was on his backside, he could either slip out again or change his disguise. Probably he'd go, at least for some time, but that would depend on why he was in town in the first place.

Rad shuffled his feet and stepped in front of Sheriff Hinkle, held both hands chest high and spoke his mind, "Let's hold back." He spotted a stack of freight under a wood overhang, still eighty or so feet from the entrance to Stell's saloon. "Over there, he pointed placidly; let's take a minute to think this through." He hastened his cohort to the darkened area, behind the pile of freight boxes and out of view of saloon's swinging doors.

"What the hell's this about, Carson? Why'd 'ya push me over here?"

Glaring back, Rad made his point, "If we go busting in Stell's place like hounds on a hot trail we'd likely come out with nothing more than a day old sniff of Possum Tucker. And he'd sure enough find out we'd been there. We'd lose the advantage, giving it over to him." Rad drew back, waiting for Hinkle to absorb the logic he spouted. A short span of silence proved effective for the both of them. "Our best bet is to take Tucker by surprise," Carson deplored sensitively. "Otherwise we're likely not to take him at all."

Hinkle sat on a wooden shipping crate, resting uneasily. The unbuttoned coat fronts moved somewhat over his broad chest with his deep breathing. His moustache flexed and his eyes constantly casting from behind the stack of goods to the saloon and back to Carson, he panted, "I'm listening, what else you got in mind?"

"I can't quit wondering what Barnett's doing talking with Tucker." Carson lifted a boot, set the sole to rest next to Hinkle's wide backside. He dropped an elbow across his knee, "Maybe we should have a light-hearted talk with Barnett, ask him a few questions. If he's in cahoots with Tucker, maybe we need to find out what they're up to." Sheriff Hinkle was ready to listen and Marshal Carson went on. "It won't do us much good to talk to Stell, I'm thinkin'." Carson turned and looked the other way, "Rather than tip our hand here, I'm going over to Barnett's print shop and see what I can learn."

"You're in charge, Marshal," Hinkle put forward. "You want I should go with you?"

'No, I want to do this on my own." Rad stared to the distance as a sudden breeze dusted the street. When it settled Rad continued, "If I tie Barnett into Tucker burning the jail . . ." He never finished the half-restrained, subtle statement.

Barnett was working alone in the office. He stood when Carson entered, "Good morning, Marshal." Barnett grinned and pushed up at his green-cuffed forearms, "Good to see you; I was hoping to get by your office, wanted to get some details on your travels, which I heard about last evening." His voice was melodious. "As you know, I'm always looking for stories to print that arouse the interest of my readers, keeps me in business."

Carson gave the man a dark look, his temper perked and fractionally exposed. In a near-unrestrained voice, he exclaimed with bitterness in his tone, "Only after you answer some questions for me, Barnett."

"You sound angry!" The newsman backed up a step, his eyes rambling semi-focused, he surveyed the room, stopping at the door. Determining that not to be a solution, he responded to Carson's glare, sniffed and lifted his shoulders, "What's this about?"

"I won't beat about the bush." Carson's eyes narrowed, "I want to know about the connection between you and Milt Tucker."

Barnett flexed the lines in his forehead, trying to appear in denial. He spouted back with a sour voice, "You're barkin' up a wrong tree,

Carson. I don't even know the man—never had a thing to do with him and wouldn't, he's an outlaw." He snarled the word 'outlaw' like it was an incurable disease.

"I'm going to ask nice just once more." Carson's demeanor evoked rigidness that was unconditional, "If I don't get a forthright answer you're not going to like what I'll do next!"

The newspaper man tightened his face and sulked an unmerited appearance of denial. Seeing not a speck of invalidation in the lawman, his shoulders drooped and the resentment he tendered subsided. His eyelids closed, shuttered, and with a half turn, he sought temporary refuge; found a chair and professed, "I need to sit down."

"Look, Barnett, "Carson snapped, "don't peel off some bullshit. I want the truth, anything else and I'll take you and your outfit apart." Tucker's disappearance the night of the jail's burning knifed into his mind; that, along with the image of the town marshal, Dinsmore, his body punctured with chunks of splintered wood played through his memory. "You best start talking while I still hold my temper." Both of them knew it was near too late for that.

"You damn lawmen," Barnett whimpered, eyes reddened and moist. Mastersons . . . then the Earps, and now you, you all defy my newspaper telling what you all are."

"If you're using them as your reason for chicanery with me, you're gonna spend time looking through those jail bars from inside." The huff Carson blew reddened his face; he pulled back, gathering himself, "Now, I'm going to say it once again, you'd best tell me what the connection is between you and Possum Tucker."

Barnett's despising expression came to the front, he blurted out, "There is none."

The wrist shackles flew into Rad Carson's hands, he stepped forward with them, ready to cuff the man. "Wait," screamed the newsman, his demeanor dissipated momentarily as he glared at the floor before the next words came. "He's my cousin." A five second silence ensued. He spoke again, "His mother and mine were step-sisters. My mother always insisted that I look out for him when we were kids 'cause he had that bad hand, he was born with it. I was five years older than him, smarter, and could talk the both of us out of trouble—that was back East." Barnett rubbed at his eyes, "He looks me up time to time. Yea, I know he turned wicked and mean, but he always respected and liked me, for what I did for him as youngsters." The belittled man looked up at Carson with calf-eyes, "I never did anything illegal, nothing that was in violation of the law, just treated him like a friend, that's all."

The marshal scratched at his forehead, ran his hand across his mouth, glared at the man and then spoke, "That's all, huh?" He slipped the wrist irons under his belt, "What did the two of you talk about last night?"

Barnett melted, "So someone recognized him did they? It wasn't Stell was it?"

"Not Stell." He said it with conviction and Barnett acknowledged with a nod and facial gestures. "Doesn't matter who, but it wasn't Stell, that's all I can say." Carson finished.

Barnett's face became rigid as he tried to summon up strength of character he felt he'd lost with his previous response. "Just . . . small talk, mostly . . . family . . ." he stammered in desperation.

"Damn it, Barnett, I told you no bullshit. The man was responsible for the death of one man the night he blew up the jail, and rightly should be held accountable for at least two more—don't lather me down with *'small talk'* crap!" Carson grabbed the front of the man's shirt over the top of the leather apron, "I'll shut your newspaper down and arrest you for harboring a fugitive—a killer; you'll do at least a year or two in jail . . . you like those outlaws, you can live with them in the hell hole behind bars!" Barnett's head flew back, his hands flipped up to obstruct his face. He wasn't a physical sort of man; hostility with bare fists wasn't within him. He was fear-struck with the thought and it showed.

Carson held him, his fist clinching the man's collar under his chin, "Why's Tucker in town?" The hold he had on the news man tightened, "It's plain that he has cause to be here, and the disguise, that's a dead giveaway that he's up to no-good. You're going to jail, or are you ready to talk? This is your last chance."

Fright and distress etched heavily into the man's face. "Okay." His eyes rolled upward as he spoke in a delicate tone, "Mother forgive me!" Carson released the hold and the unstable man bartered in a feeble voice, "I need to sit down again."

The marshal stared at him, solid anger remaining apparent. With hands on hips at the top of the cartridge belt, the fingers of his right hand flexing down to the dark walnut grip of the Colt, he waited impatiently.

"Those papers there, editions of the past two weeks, I put an ad in some that Milt asked me to publish." Carson turned to see the papers he referred to. Barnett went on, "It's in a code, a code special to Milt and a man he knows by the name of Tatum—Muley Tatum." Carson's eyes popped, then blinked and focused resolutely on the newspaper man. The confession caught him off-guard; it was more than he'd anticipated. "Even I," the tentative, belittled man continued, "don't know what it means for sure, but it's intended for Milt and the Tatum man to meet up." His eyes searched Carson's, inquisitively searching for a sign of satisfaction.

"Show me the ad." Carson ordered.

Barnett ruffled through the pages and handed three of them to Marshal Carson, pointing out the ad Tucker had him run in *The Herald.*

New wooden barrels for sale reasonable.
8 gallon and 20 gallon for wagon travel.
Leave your name and order at news office.

M.T.

Having read the advertisement over three times, Carson put the papers on the desk. He turned to Barnett, "Seems to me the message isn't difficult to figure. They both have the same initials, M. T. so the notice is easy to identify." He gave Barnett a sorrowful look, realizing the newspaper man must have figured that also. "And since Tucker placed the ad, he's putting Muley Tatum on notice to meet up him August twentieth—that's right simple." Carson glanced at the calendar hanging on the wall next to the desk, "Just two days from now. And it seems this office is going to be their meeting place."

Carson studied on the situation for a minute, debating with himself in silence before demanding, "Where's Tucker?"

"God's truth, Carson, I don't know." He read the repulsion on the marshal's face. "Honest, I don't know."

"Here in town?" The marshal didn't let up.

Richard Barnett hunched his shoulders. "Likely, but I don't know where, he wouldn't tell me. I suppose he figured to keep it secret. He's been that way ever since he served his term in prison the first time, a few years back." The man was depleted, all squabble and argument capital out of him, "And Marshal, I'm glad I don't know, because this way I can't tell you." The sneer on the man's face fortified his statement.

"Barnett, I'm going to give you the privilege of being the first man I lock up in my new jail."

"But I told you . . . !"

"That's right, you told me. Not because you wanted to! You deliberately opposed the law, lied, and now, I'm going to keep you from telling Possum Tucker or anyone else." Carson drew the wrist irons from behind his belt.

"We don't need that, Marshal. I'm no common outlaw you have to forcefully restrain; I'm a practical man, not some callous villain!"

"I'll trust you won't tell, as long as Tucker can't find you, and that ain't gonna happen." Carson once again put the shackles away, shook his finger in Barnett's face and warned, "We'll go without the irons, but if you make any trouble, any at all, I'll not only put 'em on you, I'll put the barrel of this Colt, across your head and drag you to the lock-up." He half-lifted the revolver from the holster with three fingers under the grip.

The marshal marched the newspaper man to the jail with little hoopla. It appeared as though they were having a cordial conversation, exchanging words quietly, neither of them desirous of a spectacle to draw attention from the regular citizens. That could desecrate the silence, the secret each wanted, but for different reasons. Getting Milt Tucker in his grasp, even though he was confident without a smidgen of doubt the cussed outlaw was in town, wasn't going to be simple run-of-the-mill act of justice. Tucker was waiting in Dodge for the man Rad Carson wanted in his custody perhaps as much as Tucker—Muley Tatum. The thought of building a single gallows for the both of them to swing from brought a smile of satisfaction to Marshal Rad Carson's face.

CHAPTER TWENTY-EIGHT

The lock cylinder clicked with a raucous metallic snap once the key was turned, "At least it's clean," Barnett quipped and drew the blue derby from his head and dropped it alongside his body as he ambled into the cell. He made his way to the bunk and flopped like a hound that'd lost the scent of the fox he'd chased and given up, not a move exemplar to the style Carson had witnessed in the man.

Carson looked around for Chalk Dinsmore, the local deputy almost killed in the explosion some weeks back. He sat a new chair behind the desk. Dinsmore nodded to Carson, the look on his face conveyed a 'thank you' but he said nothing. A new deputy that was hired and put in place by Sheriff Hinkle examined both the prisoner and Rad Carson with curiosity, "He the newspaper man?"

"That's right."

Rad nodded toward three men in a distant cell; "They locals?"

The deputy spun a glance at them, "All cow wranglers from Texas."

"Minor-offense prisoners?"

"Two for drunkenness, the other for robbery."

Rad thought about the situation. Satisfied, he told the deputy, "I'm holding this man for his protection." That wasn't fact, but it would do, rather than fill in all of the gaps needed for explanation of the truth. "Nobody, and I mean absolutely nobody but you two, he indicated the fresh deputy and Chalk Dinsmore, me, and Sheriff Hinkle are to know he's here." Carson's fixed stare demonstrated the strength of his statement.

"Yes, sir; I understand, Marshal. Noboby!"

"And that means nobody even looks in." Rad studied the other prisoners sketchily, "Don't let none of them out of here until I say so. Understand?"

"I'll make sure of that, Marshall Carson." Dinsmore spoke up.

The fresh, new deputy nodded his head several times as Carson looked him over. Satisfied with the circumstances, Carson turned and left, leaving the deputies in charge.

Milt Tucker stood before the mirror in his hotel room at The Empire, tapped the false moustache in place with the index finger of his good hand and accepted the appearance in the looking glass with an extended lower lip and a head-bob. A copy of the Dodge City Herald lay on the bed along with The Police Gazette and a Wichita paper he'd taken from the stage depot. He was preparing to go out for a few hours in the evening, the cover of darkness becoming an ally. He wisely spent the daylight hours holding up in the room for the past three days. "Two more days and this circus act will be over," he spoke to his mirror image.

Tucker slipped his arm into the shoulder holster and checked the pocket gun loads. He hooked the spectacle's temple pieces over his ears and approved the mirror image a final time. *'If Muley got his hands on a newspaper, he'll be here, but if he didn't, I reckon I'll take care of that fat, idiot sheriff my-own-self,'* the loathsome man thought inwardly.

The hate Tucker held for Hinkle dug deeper than the conviction that sent him to prison in Wichita. The Ford County Sheriff had put a bullet in Tucker almost a full year previous to the bank robbery killing that put Tucker away. Hinkle had no idea who the two men were when he threw down on them with his Remington .44 outside the Prairie Flower Saloon. That was the night Tatum and Tucker first met. Each of the two hard-case outlaws had watched high stake poker played by a pair of well-heeled cattle brokers for over three hours that night. They'd each stood alone on opposite sides of the room. By the time poker ended both Possum Tucker and Muley Tatum had contrived a plan to become the eventual holder of the four thousand dollars the prevailing stockman left with.

Sheriff Hinkle was making his final round of what had been a calm Dodge City evening; calm until Milt and Muley left the Prairie Flower; the trail, smelling of four thousand dollars, was locked in each man's nostrils.

The big-winner at poker stepped into the street. Tatum closed quickly, knife in hand. Before he could strike, ole' Possum shot the cattle broker point blank. The two thieves stood over the man like a pair of snarling coyotes, both infected with surprise and contemplation. Tucker, gun in his good hand, blocked Muley's thrust toward him with the knife. The dead man's bankroll spilled onto the street and each demented coyote dove to claim control. As the two of them wrestled, Hinkle fired. Four shots stung the air, one found its mark. Milt Possum Tucker caught the slug in his side. Muley grabbed Tucker, who had gathered the bulk of loose cash, and hustled him to the horses as he fired at Hinkle over his shoulder in the darkness.

The loutish, thick-skinned twosome slapped leather to horse flesh out of Dodge City together. A friendship built on a nefarious stunt was oddly initiated. Two days later they rode into the yard of a big barn-looking building, Pug and Magdelana's buffalo lodge. Muley, a man that held admiration for strong, independent people, especially if they had a lawman's bullet in them, had taken to Milt Tucker like a rat takes to a sack of shelled corn.

The outlaw twosome stayed on at Uncle Pug's for a month as Possum Tucker healed. The pair digested most every bit of reading material in the place and Tucker told Muley about his cousin, Barnett, owning

The Dodge City Herald. *One* of the *Herald* newspapers happened to be among the materials they read during the process of healing. The two garnered respect for one another as they shared life's happenings and bonded. The newspaper owned by Tucker's family member became a focal point for meeting up again someday in the future. That tidy little agreement was formed on the day they rode away from Pug and Magdalena's, each in different directions.

Possum Tucker knew very little about U. S. Marshal Rad Carson, the two of them had never seen one another face to face. He couldn't recognize Carson, just as Carson couldn't identify Possum Tucker, other than the flaccid hand, without the descriptions afforded him by others. Tucker's knowledge of Carson was dependent on his cousin, Richard Barnett, what he had written in The Herald, and in their personal conversation. In-as-much as Barnett held a cynical viewpoint for all officers of the law, Tucker embraced a dislike for Marshal Rad Carson. His lack of respect, however, would leave him at disadvantage if a personal confrontation was to come.

"*Tatum and Tucker . . . that's a pair,*" Carson mumbled to himself as he began the stroll over to check on Hinkle's watch of Stell's saloon. "*Just as well leave Hinkle in place,*" Carson told himself, "*could be that Tucker will drift back in*".

Hinkle had located a chair on the boardwalk fronting a drug store not far from the crates where he and Carson stood earlier to view Sell's place. Hinkle sat with the hardwood chair's rear legs strained, leaning back against the storefront, his hat tilted low on his forehead.

Rad stood silent a few seconds gazing at the hefty man's cozy posture with his fingers laced at rest on his protruding midsection. Carson gently kicked a chair leg. Hinkle snapped his body awake, the front chair legs thumped the walkway, he pushed his hat back and the cumbersome lawman blinked Carson into focus as his lips squished, "Damn, I musta dozed off."

"Yep, reckon you did." Disgust showed in Carson's expression briefly before his center of attention moved to *The Spotted Cat's* batwing doors, "I don't suppose you caught sight of Tucker?"

Hinkle waggled his head and scrubbed at his eyes, "Not a thing."

A stint of silence ensued before Carson informed his lawman friend of the happenings he initiated at Barnett's newspaper shop.

"You've got Barnett locked up?" Hinkle's eyes grew into saucers.

"Yep, in the new jail."

Carson then informed the sheriff about Milt Tucker being Richard Barnett's cousin. "Damn," Hinkle coughed, threw his hands up, dislodged his hat and was just lucky enough to catch it before it completely fell away. Again, a short silence ensued, Hinkle's hand sat to his brow, his thumb and fingers in a pinching pattern, as though messaging the information into his brain. "Now that's a piece of news the people of this town would like to see printed in that fancy scoundrel's paper."

"Tucker's about as cagey as they come," Carson asserted as he surveyed the street once again, "not the type to wander around town without sniffing the air first. We'd best keep to the shadows—don't want him laying eyes on us before we see him."

Hinkle cleared his throat, and scoffed, "From what you said Carson, maybe we should outta stake out the newspaper office, keeping to distance, and wait for him and Muley Tatum to meet up there—it could be that'd be the only chance we'd have to catch the both of 'em."

* * *

Flames of the campfire fashioned orange and yellow fluctuating streaks on the faces of the five men who stood encircling the hissing, voluminous burning stack of dry wood. Sparks sporadically stung the air in nondescript intervals, as if in celebration of the expansiveness the fire attained in the brief time span it lived. Tatum threw two more chunks onto the fire. "You plan to burn the whole damn world, Muley?" Bo Cantrell laughed, holding his hand to shield heat from his face.

Muley rolled his head slightly in response, gaining an intense view of Bo. "You musta gained some smart in the time we been together, Bo." He grinned, teeth showing, "Maybe not burn the whole world, just a little spurt town the other side of Dodge, a town called Spickard—ya ever heard of it?"

Bob Cantrell's eyes inflated, the fire reflected in them like a message from hell. "Yea, I know the town." He narrowed his gaze and swung the intensity to the others who stood in silence; a speculation of wonderment absorbed into each man's face. He turned back to Muley, "Really?" He probed with hesitant curiosity, "We burnin' a whole town?"

"Really." Muley answered. "A friend of mine has the know-how to burn damn near anything." Tatum stared into the fire with a empty expression and spoke, "We're gonna meet up with him real soon . . . we got a chore or two to tend to, some kind of work he wants done in Dodge, and when we get that tended to we're going on to Spickard." The vicious Muley Tatum smile encased his face, "And turn that little cow town into a stack of ashes. You might say we got scores to settle."

Bo hunched his shoulders lightly, turned to Charlie Joe next to him and said, "Sounds like some fun's gonna come our way, Injun."

"'Bout time! I'm tired of saddle-sittin' and bein' short on whiskey." He offered up a nasty grin, "Maybe I'll be lucky enough to get a couple of scalps to add to my collection." He tapped the flap of the saddle bag hanging over his forearm. He kept no scalps but he determined to keep the Injun game going.

Young Jess Longley's rigid stance couldn't have been a more beseeching message if he'd handed Pete a schoolroom slate with the word

'Help' scripted in capital letters. He'd assessed Muley Tatum as a brutish barbarian several days past. The big man dressed in black had once again, with the words and actions he displayed, proven Jess's analogy. Jess turned from the erratic dancing flames to a lost-spirit in search of his bedroll and saddle, knowing he'd not be able to sleep. But he needed the reticent quiet it represented. He wanted an escape from the hellacious incident he'd just heard about and couldn't imagine being a part of it.

Pete studied the three men, Muley, Bo, and Charlie, examining the detachment from sensibility they harbored, the emptiness imbedded within, and he swore to himself, he and Jesse were different—different enough they might have to stop Muley. He'd wondered what the something big Muley planned in Dodge City could be. And then there'd be Spickard, a name he'd never heard of before, the town the crazed butcher wanted to burn. His mind was full of possibilities as he laid out his bedroll.

In the cover of darkness some distance from the fire, Jesse edged toward his older brother as he spread his blankets, "We ain't doin' it are we, Pete?" Jesse whispered.

"Shuush . . . no, we ain't doin it—go to sleep." Pete lay on his back, pulled a blanket across his mid-section and swung an arm to his forehead, watching the skimpy layer of clouds move over the moon. "*Somehow, Jess', we ain't doin it*", he said inwardly.

CHAPTER TWENTY-NINE

Possum Tucker had lain awake for two hours waiting for the daylight to cancel darkness. He threw the sheet aside and dropped his feet to the rough wood floor. His patience running thin, he stepped to the window and drew the flimsy curtain aside with his weak hand. "Muley should be here today if he's coming," he muttered, looking toward the bleak skyline.

Three wranglers walked the boards across the street, rubbing their eyes; one yawned. They had skipped sleep for the better part of the hours of darkness, but their ruffled clothes showed signs of activity that was confirmed when two young, partially dressed girls, stood waving good-by to them from the door the youthful fellas had exited. "*Nothin' like being young*", Tucker hitched his brow and one side of his mouth flexed upward.

After a brief rinsing, he toweled off and dressed. The disguise had grown troublesome, the glasses caused a headache and the costume mustache was starting to droop on occasion. City-gentleman clothes made him weary. Today he'd not use the fake clothes and glasses. He let lay the shoulder holster and strapped the cartridge belt around his middle and approved the weight of the iron held in the holster that had hung from his side for most of his years. He took up a small bundle and his Henry rifle, unlatched the door and stepped into the sparse hallway to gain access to the stairs. A whiff of fresh brewed coffee welcomed the fifty-two year old outlaw to the harsh, dim-lighted barroom below.

The desk clerk, his eyelids heavy and the strands of dark, oily hair draped over them, gave Milt Tucker thoughts of jailed pigeon eggs. They two men meagerly nodded, as was the usual greeting over the past four mornings, but the simple man behind the counter blinked, he wasn't sure who the man was who'd just come down from upstairs

Tucker had laid out plans previously and re-established them in the predawn hours as he rested, sleep not able to come. This was the prescribed day for meeting up with cousin, Muley Tatum.

Milt Tucker, always a precautious sort, a trait which was instrumental in earning him the nickname, 'Possum', stood atop the roof and behind the wall that stretched high over the storefront of the McHenry Stoves and Hardware Store, almost two hundred feet distant from the building housing Barnett's newspaper office. He had foregone the disguise, feeling his presence for the day was to be guarded and knowing he wouldn't be readily recognized by Muley with it in place. His vantage point offered him a good view of his cousin's work place, The Dodge City Herald. He knew Muley was a brazen-nature kind of man, not the type to plan an inconspicuous appearance, if indeed he had gotten the coded advertisement in The Herald that he had Richard run several times during the past three weeks. Tucker had with him a small leather case that held an expandable telescope and a mirror the size of a playing card. He'd also brought along his .44 Winchester rifle.

Tucker's plan wasn't complex, but neither was it simplistic enough to allow him to be captured if Tatum was too careless. Once he laid eyes on Muley, he'd use the mirror to flash a sun-aided signal to him. Tatum wasn't necessarily a careful man, but neither was he totally imprudent, he'd comprehend the signal and abandon the prescribed meeting place, and then wait for Possum Tucker to make contact. Or at least that's the way Tucker planned it.

It was nine-thirty, *'Richard's late for arrival at his office'*, Tucker thought. He lifted the telescope from the case, extended it and began to scrutinize the news office. Nothing. The curtains stood partially closed, contrary to usually being pulled back to allow for more light inside. He shifted a few feet to his left, providing a better view of the street scene. His curiosity was beginning to heighten but he remained self-assured cousin Richard wouldn't have squealed.

Sheriff Hinkle was stationed inside The Herald. Carson placed him there well before sunrise. The big man being slow of foot and plainly distinguishable due to his robust build, he could be easily spotted by Tucker if anywhere visible on the street. The dull interior of the news office provided respectable cover. Possum Tucker had sworn the bulky sheriff to be his mortal enemy when he was pulled, screaming and cursing, from the jail when taken to the train in route to the Wichita prison. Knowing that threat to have taken place, Rad figured Hinkle to be one reason for Tucker coming back to Dodge anyhow. Hinkle's role in capture of Tatum and Tucker would be better served in support, to be called on if, or when, needed. The big man did, however, have a reputation in Dodge for being good with a side arm.

Rad Carson also had an eye on Richard Barnett's place of business. His vantage point was from inside an empty storefront next to Ralph Showalter's leather-goods shop. The marshal sat a chair inside, near the window. A wall separated him from shop activity. From there he could view the front of the news office and see maybe a hundred feet south. He'd made it clear to Showalter, who owned the building and was a man of constant conversation, he was to ask no questions and make no reference to customers about the law man's presence. So far the man had obliged those instructions.

* * *

Muley pulled back on the reins and jerked his horse in a circle ahead of the four men following behind. A craftily painted sign, the sign's post extending above a two foot high square base of adobe brick, announced: DODGE CITY 2 MILES. "Hey, look what we gone and found," Muley laughed.

"Dog-gone if we didn't." Charlie Joe chimed in, "Get me to the whiskey, my belly's been mad at my throat for ni-on-ta two days, just waitin' for some of that sour-mash snake oil."

Muley left the others, he told them to wait until dark before riding into Dodge. He wanted to go on alone. His instruction wasn't questioned. He looked each man in the eye, testing their metal. He gave Jess Longley a double look laced with question. Pete stared at the crazed outlaw almost daring him to say more to his brother. Pete's mind was made up!

Each man was left to draw his own conclusion as to Muley's purpose in stating the directive. The longleys had witnessed this kind of action from Muley when they'd first tied in with the man. That was when he'd returned to Dodge to retrieve his big black horse and he also learned from a couple of teamsters about a bank-money transfer which brought on the plan to rob the Cimmaron stage, an event the Longleys despised, but couldn't be undone; they'd have to live with it, including Pete's shooting of the shotgun rider in order to save Jesse's life.

* * *

Tucker leaned on one foot and then the other, standing atop McHenry's building. He'd found temporary comfort in the shade of a large oak tree growing alongside the structure, but even that was becoming uncomfortable in the noontime August heat. His thirst had grown considerable, a small matter he'd overlooked in setting his plan.

He determined to take another extended gaze at the news office and the surrounding area through the looking glass. Nothing had changed, no sign of either Muley Tatum or the law. He grew fidgety and decided he'd take a few minutes away from his post to wet his whistle, maybe take a cautious walk to Fanny's café. There he'd be less likely to be recognized than if he'd visit a saloon where a good deal of his time was spent in months gone past, before the stint in the Wichita prison. He was aware of the café, just a couple of short blocks away. He grinned, remembering the extra pretty young lady, Fanny, who owned the place. She never paid him any attention before, and if he'd put the fake mustache in place and keep the withered hand in a pocket, the odds of him being recognized by Fanny now, or anyone else for that matter, was doubtful

The distraught outlaw dropped from the roofline onto the next level where he took the stairway to the ground behind the building. He ran a forearm across his brow to void the sweat as he edged along the dingy whitewashed structure toward the street. No sooner had he stepped to the boardwalk out front than Muley reined back on his big black horse and readied to dismount in front of The Dodge City Herald almost sixty yards away. This wasn't in Tucker's plan at all—he'd brought his rifle but left his spyglass and mirror on the roof. His plan to signal Muley was out-the-window. He thought quickly as Muley swung down and was about to snug the reins to the hitch and start toward the newspaper office door. "Damn, the man throws caution to the wind. Leaving things to his way would likely get us both killed," Tucker said under his breath; his mind racing. He drew back but knew he'd have to step out and get Tatum's attention soon.

Up the street, the opposite direction, Rad Carson jumped from the building where he'd been secluded. Things were coming to a head quickly. He had to get there before Hinckle got the idea to try to take the Muley Tatum by himself. Hand on the Colt six-gun, Rad started a brisk but cautious pace toward the news office. Rad Carson whispered under his breath, "Stand pat, Hinkle, don't do nothing stupid."

Possum Tucker braced his lips and whistled, he'd not seen Carson, but wanted Muley to get away from the newspaper office. Tucker was still apprehensive about the darkness inside. He'd felt uneasy about its strange appearance from the first time he laid eyes on it from his vantage point atop the McHenry building.

At the sound of Tucker's whistle, Muley turned, spotted Tucker almost immediately and waved, still completely unaware of the trap set in place by the lawmen, Carson up the street and Hinckle inside Barnett's office.

Then it happened, just the thing Carson feared most, Hinckle burst from the door, his revolver leveled at Muley, hammer clicked back, he shouted, "Hold it right there, Tatum!"

Tucker jacked a shell into the carbine's spittin' chamber, threw the Winchester to his shoulder and snapped off a shot at Sheriff Hinckle. It struck the big man in the meaty part of his upper arm—he twisted and his gun discharged harmlessly into the boards beneath him. The enormity of his arm saved him from a deadly bullet driving into the side of his chest, but he was down, and an easy target. Possum, still several yards away, lowered the long gun and hastily stepped forward, ready to finish off Hinckle with another shot. Muley Tatum cut a big grin Tucker's way, knowing the man with the fledging hand wanted Sheriff Hinckle dead and he was going to watch! *'It'd be a pleasure to see the big man with a badge buy himself a plot in the Boot Hill Cemetery.'*

Carson, still at a distance, witnessed the shot the outlaw had placed in Sheriff Hinckle. And he could see the robust sheriff was about to be shot again. Rad yelled and on the dead run fired at Tucker with little consideration of accuracy—there wasn't time. The shot missed as Tucker drew back around the corner.

Not willing to oppose Rad Carson again, Muley Tatum flew into the saddle, bent low, and in his typical fashion when lawmen fired at him, he skedaddled, kicking, and arms flailing astride his horse, straining for all he was worth. Possum Tucker stood straight up behind the corner of the building, his rifle held in front of him. He watched, his head turned to the side and pressed against the boards at his back. His eyes widened as his villainous friend, Muley Tatum, galloped past. Looking over his shoulder, Muley shouted to Tucker, "North of town!" Friend or no friend, Muley Tatum, a cold blooded killer, was not the type to put his life on the line against Rad Carson when open spaces came available.

Carson ran to where Hinckle lay sprawled on the boardwalk and knelt beside him. He put a hand on the sheriff's shoulder, "You alright?"

Hinkle squashed his face together in pain and spat back, "I'm okay . . . go get them assholes!"

Milt Tucker peeked around the corner. He saw Marshal Carson kneeled beside the sheriff. '*Now's the time to kill that sumbitch,*' he thought as he stepped out from cover. Anxious to kill, he jerked the trigger. The shot was wild, shattering a lower window pane in Barnett's office building. But it brought a tempered reflex from Marshal Carson.

Rad twisted as he methodically lifted his six-gun, and allowing for the distance, it flashed with a boom and flung a Colt .45 slug in Possum Tucker's chest before the man with the crippled hand could jack another cartridge into the rifle. The middle-aged, hard-case outlaw thrust backward, his head lurched and knees buckled, the rifle clattered to the ground. He rolled face down in the dust. His body trembled, scratching, refusing to let go . . . but it failed, he soon went limp and lifeless. The grandiose plan he'd carefully concocted to meet up with an old friend, Muley Tatum, and kill Sheriff George Hinkle was dead, and so was Milt Possum Tucker.

Knowing Hinckle to be okay, Carson hurried cautiously to where Tucker lay in the dirt, his body oddly contorted, his six-gun secure in the holster of the cartridge belt. Carson saw the man's feeble hand as he bent and picked up the rifle. He poked the barrel in Tucker's kidney, checking for response. Nothing. He guardedly rolled the man's body onto its side exposing a pool of blood. He then jostled Tucker onto his back. No life. The eyes were fixed and blood oozed from the corner of his mouth, dirt caked to the side of his face and his chest. Carson's gaze lifted to the direction Muley Tatum rode from Dodge City, and with lips barely moving he softly said resolutely, "You're next, Tatum."

Within minutes Doc Hink was there. They loaded the wounded sheriff in Doc's carriage. His arm had been placed in a sling. "We'll get that slug out of you, George, and the arm will heal right quick like." Doc Hink had taken a chunk of lead out of the bountiful man he called friend before, just over a year ago. "Maybe if you wasn't such a big target!" Doc Hink laughed lightheartedly, knowing the man's pride hurt most, the injury only superficial.

U. S. Marshal Carson returned to the jail where Tucker's cousin, Richard Barnett, was held. The lawman informed Barnett of Muley's arrival and the subsequent death of Milt Tucker, following Tucker's wounding of Sheriff Hinckle. Marshal Carson took his time, drawing out the details little by little and watching Barnett's response. Carson took a piece of pleasure out of seeing the journalist having to accept a portion of responsibility for the death of his cousin by printing the coded message Tucker had him insert in his paper.

"Oh, my God," Barnett cried out, when Rad's final words were spoken, his fingers gripping the bars, "right in front of my office! How am I going to explain this in my paper?" Carson found it dumbfounding that the man was stung most by his newspaper's disposition over the death of his cousin; he knew Barnett was an odd sort, but this was icing on the cake.

Chalk Dinsmore, the deputy town marshal almost killed in the explosion of the old jail, stood, and with a limp, walked over to affront the cell holding the newspaper man, "Why don'cha just tell the truth for a change—would it be because you figure the town-folks wouldn't know what the truth is, 'cause ya always told lies?"

Barnett blinked as if he was trying to see the words. He backed up, his eyes still in a flutter, "How dare you!" That was all. He pushed loose locks of hair back from his forehead and sat on the bunk, his hands clasped over his eyes and he fell into a void of anguish and apprehension, a condition he'd not experienced since becoming a newspaper editor years ago. For Rad Carson, there would be no hurry to put the newspaper man back on the street. He'd stand in front of Judge Nathaniel Wilkinson someday soon and the feeling he was experiencing now would become secondary to what he'd fall into at that time.

Carson headed for Satterfield's. He'd have to put together a few things for trailing Tatum. The lawman recalled the last incident where Tatum was reported being seen. It was the killing of Elizabeth Porter's husband, James, and the Mexican, who was one of Muley's gang. According to the Porter woman, when Muley left her he did so with four other men trailing along. Whatever it would take, he'd handle it. Carson's hate for the man grew by the hour. He couldn't recall feeling such exasperation and anger for a man in his life as he was feeling for Tatum. His respect for legal justice was strong, but he didn't know . . . it might be he'd kill him outright.

CHAPTER THIRTY

By the time Muley gave his order for everyone to stay put and he disappeared from sight, Jess Longley stood down from the saddle and built a cigarette. He crushed the tobacco bag in his hand, "That's it, no more smokes."

"Maybe we should ride into Dodge and supply up," Pete grinned at Jess and saw a mixture of both question and skepticism in his brother's expression. "As I recall, the last time Muley left us to go to Dodge City, we didn't see him for three hours. I figure we can get to town and back in about a half hour, it's only two miles according to that sign."

Jesse's eyes lit up, "Ya mean it, or ya just funnin' me?"

Bo Cantrell and Charlie Joe stared in disbelief. Bo spoke up, "I don't reckon ya better do that, boy." Bo rolled the cigar stub in his lips before removing it with a thumb and forefinger; with a snarl he grumbled, "You know Muley's got a hell of a temper—he don't take to nobody crossin' his orders, could be he might shoot ya or use that pig-sticker of his on ya."

Charlie had a different take on the Longley's exchange of words. He was all smiles, "Ahh, he wouldn't do nothin' of the sort." He pointed a finger at Jesse and warbled with a toothy smile, "Get me a couple bottles of whiskey . . . if yuh go, I'll pay yuh's when ya get back, even give yuh a five dollar bonus!"

Bo cautioned once again, "If yuh go, boy, I'd suggest you don't come back." Bo was dead serious, his brow wrinkled, his eyes set firm and harsh, "Muley's as liable to shoot yuh as not; he ain't gonna allow that yuh violate his orders." He shook his head in imagination of a gruesome sight he wanted to convey to the younger Longley boy.

Charlie Joe snapped a laugh back at Cantrell, "He ain't gonna shoot nobody, the boy's got a right to smoke, don't he?"

Jesse's head spun from one to the other as Bo and Charlie swapped thoughts. Meanwhile, Pete took hold of the cantle and horn, put a boot toe in the stirrup and stepped into the saddle, "Com'on, brother, I'm wantin' for a smoke myself." He quickly turned the sorrel in a circle, "We can be to Dodge City and back by the time the two of them decide on anything."

Jesse ginned, readily followed the lead of his older brother and swung up into his saddle.

With his hands cupped at the sides of his mouth, Charlie Joe yelled as the Longelys rode out, "Rye whiskey, if they got it."

* * *

Muley high-tailed it out of town. The last look he had at Dodge City over his shoulder burned into his mind rock-hard. He saw Possum Tucker take a hit. He saw him fall. And the way he fell signaled he was hit bad, likely fatal. The sight kept coming to him. He wasn't able to shake it out of his mind. He was sure that Tucker put a slug in Sheriff Hinckle, and Rad Carson had done the same to his pal, Possum Tucker. *'Why was Hinkle waiting inside The newspaper office. It wasn't likely that Carson was in the area by luck, the two lawmen were waiting for him and Tucker. Why? Did Barnett spill the beans?'*

Muley had become aware of the appointment of Rad Carson as U. S. Marshal and his assignment to Ford County. He read about it in the

Herald newspaper, the same as when he'd gotten the coded message from Tucker. His anger leapt out of control! *'He'd kill them—Hinkle and Carson'.* Muley's horse was paying a price; he gouged and beat the animal mercilessly with his spurs. Using a short, braided-handle whip he never let up, the poor beast was the recipient of the callous man's unrelenting rage.

The Longleys spotted a rider coming toward them like the Devil was on his tail. He was swinging a whip and kicking hard into the flanks of his horse like he was to get him to fly. "It's Muley." Pete blurted, "He must be in trouble to be riding like that." Pete gave the roadway a quick surveillance, "Over there," he yelled, pointing a fist wrapped with leather reins. The Texas brothers quickly fell in behind a cluster of scrub cedars and thick brush.

The malicious man in black flew past without seeing them, like he was on fire, his mind entrenched in the shootings he'd witnessed. His eyes watered with the wind and the hate built like wildfire, it consumed him.

"The man looked possessed." Pete said as he and Jesse kept their eyes on Muley's backside as he rode past them and into the distance. "Whatever it is, we're through with him."

"Thank God," Jesse wheezed. He thumbed his hat back on his head and squinted, hopefully taking his last look at Muley Tatum. They turned their horses back to the road; Dodge City was less than a mile, likely just far enough to melt the knot in Jesse's stomach.

The brothers rode in silence for a ways before Jesse wafted, "I'm glad that's over. If we'd been back there," he motioned over a shoulder, "he might kill somebody, maybe everybody."

Pete nodded in agreement, then rose in the saddle as buildings came into view, "I reckon it won't take long for us to learn what ran Muley out of Dodge City, given the way he was ridin'." The brothers exchanged guarded smiles and clicked their mounts forward.

A gathering of Dodge City town-folk walked alongside a tall, thin man in a white shirt with sleeves rolled up and a black stovepipe hat on his head, he was pushing a two-wheel cart. A pair of legs hung off the back of the wood-crafted handcart. The brothers from Dumas, Texas rode leisure like, all the while watching people scurry about and whisper to one another. "Looks like somebody cashed in their chips," Pete drawled. Thoughts of Muley and what he might have done bounced around in his mind.

"By the crowd, I'd say the man was important." Jesse responded. He twisted his head around, trying to get a better look. He leaned closer to Pete, "You think it could be that Muley killed him?"

"Won't take long to find out, all we gotta do is listen." Pete pointed to The Spotted Cat Saloon, "That's a busy place; I bet we can find out what's been goin' on. Let's tie up there and get a beer."

Things were abuzz. Corner-of-the-eye stares, which allowed for more than a couple of customers to catch a breath, were leveled at the Longleys. An elbow resting on the bar, Pete waited patiently; Jesse stood calm, offering a slight grin in return if a glace from a bar patron lingered on him.

The barkeep shuffled over. "Two beers," Pete directed.

The barkeep slid to the side, filled the mugs and slapped them on the bar. "What's goin' on?" Pete winched out a smile, his eyes claiming total obscurity.

The bartender leaned in, "You don't know?"

Pete turned a thumb toward Jess, "We just this minute rode into town." He handed a mug to Jess and raised his to drink, his face slightly turned down but his eyes up to look the question back to the burly man behind the bar. "It looked like maybe someone was killed!"

"Sure as byGod, someone was killed . . . shot by United States Marshal, Rad Carson."

"Someone important?"

"Damn . . . you did just in town didn't ya? I ain't got time, you just stand and listen, it's the only thing anybody's talkin' about." The barkeep slipped back to join the men where he stood before drawing beer for the Longleys.

Within an hour Pete and Jesse had heard the story three or four times over, but there was already more than one rendition. The basis was the same, however; a man named Milt or Possum, Tucker, who'd blown up the jail sometime in the past had shot the Ford County Sheriff, and Marshal Carson had shot and killed the Tucker fella. Another outlaw, Muley Tatum, was in on it, nobody knew how for sure, but he got away. The Longleys could vouch for that—but it was best that they didn't. They were satisfied to just listen, and feel sure that Muley Tatum wasn't going to be in Dodge City looking for them, not right away anyhow.

By late afternoon the brothers had walked their horses over a good portion of Dodge City to appease their curiosity. The last time they were in Dodge, over a month ago, they'd tied-in with Tatum out on the range the previous day and stopped in the mercantile for supplies. They had briefly met up with Sheriff Hinckle, who'd questioned them in conjunction with the killing of a gambler who'd come from St. Louis. Pete recalled thinking they'd been lucky to avoid trouble.

"Some kind of town, huh, Pete?" Jesse remarked. "Dodge City must be three, maybe four times the size of Dumas and wild as a loco-juiced longhorn."

"The cattle, that's what put it on the map," Pete responded. "When the States War ended folks back east wanted beef. And being as how the railroads put track down this way, people like us pushed cows up the trails for shippin' beef to sell back in Kansas City, Chicago and even New York. There's lots of money back that-a-way and those city people want the meat of our cattle more than we do. Folks say there'll be trains that run clear down in Texas someday," he hitched his brows, "that'll be the ruin of Dodge City."

"I don't know, Pete, seems there's plenty of graze land around and the ground looks to be good for plantin', I suppose more settlers will come here to stay, cattle trains or no cattle trains."

They stopped at a drug and tobacco store where Jesse bought smoking materials and Pete treated himself to a couple of three cent cigars. The store sat directly across from the finest hotel in town, Drover's Palace. The Palace was a two-story, white clapboard building, a much finer appearing building than anything else in town; almost shined when the sun was right. "Let's go over there, looks top notch for sleeping quarters," Pete smiled. "And since we ain't slept with a roof over us for quite a spell, let's do it up right."

They walked their horses to the hitch, tied up, sidled into the hotel, determined to register for a room. They'd never seen such a glamorously appointed place in their lives. Plush carpets adorned the floor and enormous paintings of cattle herds, cowboys and mountains, some with snow-capped tops, hung on the walls. Brass chandeliers were overhead and enormous stuffed chairs lined the sizeable lobby.

After signing, Pete jerked his chin toward the adjoining dining room which was complete with ironed cloth table tops and padded chairs. "I see you've got fancy eatin' in there," he said to the desk clerk. There were men servers dressed in fresh-pressed white shirts, and customers wearing catalog-type suits, some smoking long cigars. Pete and Jess eyed them suspiciously with Texas cow-puncher curiosity.

"Looks mighty swanky," Jesse said, soaking up the full glamour of the place, "I think I'd rather find a place to eat supper where it's not so uppity." He shuffled a step closer to the registration desk and leaned, "Anywhere near 'round that a fella in wrangler duds that's a mite dusty could eat without looking outta place?"

The middle aged man behind the desk, his pure gray hair parted in the middle of his head and slicked back, sharply dressed, complete with a brass buttoned coat and thin black bowtie, smiled, "Sure enough is, mister; there's Fanny's Fancy Food, a place up a block and around the corner to the left." He cupped a hand to the side of his mouth, "It's named '*fancy*', but it isn't—just good home cooking. I'm sure you'll find it to fit your taste." He took a plentiful look at the two, "You can leave your horses to the barn out back with our hostler. He'll look after them in whatever manner you instruct, do it right good too." The man smiled and handed them a room key, "You two can re-enter the hotel through a door in the rear . . . number eighteen, down that hallway there." He nodded and shifted his eyes hard to the left, a big smile indicating the location of the room he assigned them, convenient to the back door.

"There's the eatin' place," Jesse pointed. He brushed at his clothes with his hat. "I wish we'd gone ahead and cleaned up a mite when we was at the hotel, I feel a little scruffy."

"Don't worry about it, Jess," Pete didn't miss a step, "this place likely serves cow-punchers regular, it don't look to have that expensive glow that was back there." He tossed his head over a shoulder toward Drover's Palace.

Fanny was standing near a table where two men were seated drinking coffee, having finished dinner. The shooting of Sheriff Hinckle and death of the man named Tucker remained the topic of conversation at their table and another right beside where the Longleys took chairs.

The Texas brothers sat, feeling uneasy but righteous in their decision to have supper at Fanny's as they surveyed the other customers. "Ain't that the man that filled our order at the mercantile a few weeks back?" Jesse cut his eyes that direction and indicated the gentleman with a slight head-tilt.

The man glanced up as Pete was giving him a brief study. He smiled first, but then wrinkled his face in thought, trying to bring his mind to recollect the young men before turning back to conversation with the man across the table.

The Longleys were into their plates when the mercantile owner came and stood next to them. "Hello again", he said, "I'm Elmer Farnsworth, owner of the general store," he pointed with his index finger. "I believe I recall you fellas being in my store, maybe about three or four weeks back!" He paused, waiting for confirmation. "Didn't go on to Colorado, huh?"

Pete rolled his head and looked up, a chunk of potato readied on the fork, his elbow rested on the table top. He continued chewing thoughtfully as he studied Farnsworth's face. "Yes, sir, I believe I do remember that—decided against Colorado though."

The store owner's attention suddenly turned to a tall man coming through the door. It was Rad Carson. Rad walked to where Fanny was standing. She brushed back a long curl at her temple before her hands became busied with the white apron she wore, and a quiet, close conversation between them ensued. Farnsworth bent and said softly, "That there's the United States Marshal, name's Carson; looks like he's getting' ready to set out after that outlaw, Tatum."

The Longleys large-eyed one another; Jess leaned in, "Maybe we should tell him." The words came out, part fact, and part question. They had talked earlier and agreed it was time for them to cut clear of the outlaw ways, it was against the grain of their upbringing. And having experienced it briefly, they figured to set things straight by helping the law catch up with Muley Tatum.

"You boys know the marshal, do you?" Farnsworth asked, noticing their attention toward Carson. His expression held doubt.

Pete his fork put down and ran the checkered napkin across his mouth, looked coldly at the man standing over them as he scooted back his chair, and said sardonically, "I need to talk with him." Pete stood tall and deliberately placed his rolled-brimmed hat atop his head as he took the first step toward Carson. Jess looked Farnsworth away, his eyes and forehead firmed when he rose from the chair. He fell in behind his older brother.

Pete, with Jess on his heel, walked to where Marshal Carson stood, "Beggin' your pardon, Marshal, I've got some information I'm sure you'd like to know."

Carson looked the Texas wranglers up and down as they stood there in denim shirts and dusty, brown canvas pants; holstered six-guns at their sides. Pete's face was somber, his eyes steadfast. Rad felt the unexpected confrontation to be meaningful. He'd had more than enough hollow conversation in the past hour after the shootings, this would be different. His lawman experience readied him to believe what the cowboy had to say was laudable. "Over there," Carson said, indicating a table near the back where privacy could be had. The Longleys started that way as he'd intended and Rad's raised-brow-look to Fanny was sufficient. She knew he was to be involved with law work.

CHAPTER THIRTY-ONE

Introductions were brief, names exchanged, not much else until the Longleys had provided a few details, including Tatun's ranting claim. It didn't take long. Carson drew back and blurted, "Tatum burn Spickard?" He was bowled over. "The man's crazy as a mange-eaten coyote with rabies." His eyes darted from one Longley to the other. Nervousness gripped him; he started to stand, but settled back, he had to hear more from the young wranglers.

"So there is a town named Spickard?" Pete squinted, seeing he'd struck a nerve in the marshal. "I thought the man might have just gone outta his mind," Pete's empty gaze took in the red and white blocks of the table top in dismay. Promptly his eyes began to slowly move about. He twisted his head and glared at Carson, "We gotta stop him! Can you send a telegraph?"

"Spickard's too small a town and off line of the railroad; telegraph wires won't be run over there until this time next year. I'll have to send a carrier or get over there myself." Rad chewed at his lower lip a few seconds before stating his decision, "I best go, the young Spickard marshal will have his hands full if that no-account devil tries to go through with the threat."

Carson gave thought to throwing the two young men in jail for safe keeping and force more information out of them. But he realized they'd come to him without prompting or demands, maybe they were just as they said, ready to help put a senseless outlaw behind bars or at least put a stop to his fanatical ways. "Tell me, Pete," Rad crossed his arms and narrowed his eyes, "how is it the two of you know Muley Tatum; you been riding with him?" Carson's face drew tight and his eyes flashed from one to the other as he studied the Longleys.

Pete built a gaze on Jesse, answering the marshal's question straight up could bring on a passel of trouble. They'd considered as much when they'd made the decision to swing their weight with the law. Pete laced his fingers atop the table, "Marshal, all we're going to tell you is, we thought we had a friend in Tatum, but we found out different, we ain't cut from the same configuration he is and as youngsters we was taught right from wrong, taught with some bible readings along with school books. We rode with him for a short spell, but found out we didn't belong." Pete looked deep into Rad Carson's eyes, "I'd like to leave it at that."

Rad scratched at an eyebrow, his mind surveying the underpinnings of the young wranglers. He thought about Elizabeth Porter and the murder of her husband, James. Her account of the ordeal with the Tatum outfit made mention of two young men. A few long, quiet seconds later, he responded, "Okay, we'll leave it there." He figured his acceptance of the young men's petition wasn't a full reprieve; an accounting of their exploits with Tatum could come up later. Under the circumstances, considering they'd sought him out, Carson was willing to move on without pressing the issue.

Pete and Jesse informed the lawman of the other hooligans riding with Tatum, Charlie Joe and Bo Cantrell. Telling Carson those two culprits were simple, minimal tag-a-long followers ready to fall in with most anyone who pushed direction so long as they were kept in whiskey and cash. Pete hypothesized Cantrell and Injun Charlie Joe couldn't muster up enough brains between them to plan a hog-wash unless someone else pointed out the mud and water; they weren't much other than a symbol to Tatum, a symbol that put him in charge, nothing more.

With hesitation on the part of the Longleys, Carson prodded information from them as to where Tatum and his men might go other than directly to Spickard and they related particulars about Uncle Pug and Magdelana's buffalo lodge. The Texas brothers had kind thoughts for Pug and Mag, they were good people who happened to have a pitiable nephew that used them on occasion. They were no threat, just different than most settlers because of the big old building they made their home and the half-crazed, relative boy living near them. After hard-pressed thinking, Carson recalled mention of such buffalo lodge, but had never heard names associated with it.

A full half hour was spent with the three men sitting with their heads in a knot and arms on the table top, conversation had been deep. Carson became aware the Longleys spent a good deal of time with Tatum, knew the man well enough and had troublesome feelings for him, feelings that overcame an earlier approbation they'd gingerly built before spending much time with the bizarre outlaw. Rad scuffed his chair back, worked his mouth for a few seconds in thought without speaking, and then said, "You boys ready to ride with me to take in after Muley Tatun and those other two?"

Pete and Jesse's eyes met, both nodded and Pete said flat out, "We're ready, Marshal."

"It's late, be total dark in a quarter hour," Rad responded. "Knowing Tatum, he'll either be sitting in ambush, ready to kill anybody that comes up the trail that he can lay eyes on or . . ." he hesitated, "he'll be kicking wind into his horse to get as far up the road as possible 'til the horse gives out. He's not the type of man to be caught in a fair shootout. And I'm bettin' he's runnin, bein' the skunk he is."

Pete answered, "That'd be my bet too."

"We'll not go tonight. We'll set out at first light, that'll give him false confidence no one's on his trail." Carson snapped, "Gives us a slight edge."

* * *

"What the hell you mean they rode to Dodge?" Muley's voice reverberated hate. His eyes smoldered as he kicked wildly and flung his hands. Charlie Joe and Bo stood back, realizing anything they might say could call Muley's gun into play. "I'll kill 'em, you can count on it," he barked amidst several pounds of curse words.

Injun Charlie took the reins of the tall, blaze-face black stallion from the wild man. Its mouth and neck lathered heavily as he blew through weighty, flexing lips, fighting the bit. Muley was hard on the animal, never a man to appreciate his mount; much the same as he never showed reverence or respect to a fellow man. Cantrell and Charlie stood quiet, accepting the thrashing for the Longleys being gone. Tatum filled his gut with torment; spittle flew from the man like wind-lashed rain.

Muley, Charlie Joe, and Bo rode in near silence for six hours until darkness overtook them. They rode north for the better part of two hours before turning toward Spickard, leaving a false impression as to their destination. The moon was a mere sickle and clouds were gathering by the time they came upon a rock layered ravine A few scrub bushes grew through the crumbling rock seams, a half dozen scant cedars and two crooked-limb sycamore trees stood atop the rise. "We'll camp here—no fire." Muley grunted, "We don't want no hair-brained lawman sniffin' us out in the dark."

"Ain't nobody ridin' behind us," Charlie Joe ventured off-handedly. "I been watchin' and there ain't been no dust other than our own."

Tatum's glare berated Injun, "I said no fire." He reached into a saddle bag, withdrew a bronze colored bottle and tossed it toward Charlie Joe. "Put some of this in ya."

"Where did you . . . ?" Charlie Joe didn't finish the question; Muley was in no mood.

Morning broke with a deep, drab sky; no sign of the sun through the ugliness that stretched overhead, horizon to horizon; except far to the east a faint glow tried to escape from behind a thinning layer of gray. The air was still, the only sound being a low nickering of the horses wanting tending.

Muley was motionless, sitting on his blanket, his knees up and wrists resting there, a thin cheroot in his lips and eyes fixed. This was a different Muley. One could clearly tell he was in a deep, provoked thought. Bo had gathered enough wood to build a small fire and stood questionably, his arms filled, looked to Muley. Inasmuch as the sky lacked color and the air was heavy, Muley unconcernedly nodded approval for coffee.

Within easy reach Charlie Joe remained asleep; a mild, repetitious rasping came from beneath the skimpy blanket pulled over his head. Muley raised his eyes as if returning from a dream and looked around. He blinked and kicked Charlie in the back with the heel of his boot, "Git the hell up, Injun," he shouted. "Ya ain't sleeping off no drunk—we got a lot to do." Tatum figured to carry out the plan he developed three nights ago when he stood over a roaring campfire—he was going to burn the town of Spickard. '*That would teach Rad Carson a lesson—he'd be sorry he ever set after Muley Tatum . . . from the day in Spickard when Carson killed Luckas and put Patch Gillis in jail.* Hate for Rad Carson had stuck in the nefarious man's craw ever since. And now, Carson having shot Possum Tucker, it'd inflated decisively.

The sky lighted with exception of a low, obscurity directly overhead. Soft, sporadic drops of rain fell as the outlaw trio set to the trail, heading toward Spickard.

Within an hour the body of the storm pushed northward, away from Ford County, and what was a negligible spatter of drizzle ended in a matter of minutes. The three of them remained set to the saddle, indifferent to the spell of rain. Drabness of early morning faded, giving way as the impulsive sun spread scattered patches of color over a portion of the prairie and gave sparkle to twisted blades of grass. “Good.” Muley scanned the skies, looked over a shoulder and barked to his sidekicks, “There won’t be no rain to save them; that chicken-scratch of a town will light up like Lawrence did back when Quantrill sent it to hell.”

Charlie Joe pushed his pinto forward, the Injun’s heavy braided strand of hair bouncing across his boney shoulders. He sidled up next to the big man in black, “What we gonna do, Muley? We just gonna ride in and start shootin’?” Cantrell kicked his horse forward to be in step, having heard Injun’s question. He chewed the stubby cigar and was anxious to do just that—to ride in shootin’. He was of the same irrational make-up as was Muley, brutal, but quieter of nature, not a man to over-think the simplest of situations. He’d held a smoking gun over bloodied corpses a dozen or so times in his life; he liked the rush of superiority, and never a tinge of remorse.

Tatum eyed the two of them, shaking his head imperceptibly at their thoughtless attitudes. “We’ll shoot, but after we’ve got flames lickin’ them dry, ugly buildings, ‘specially the marshal’s office and the Yellow Moon Saloon.” A shallow laugh lifted from his throat. As they rode easy, Charlie and Bo kept their eyes on Muley, wanting to hear more.

“We’re buying coal-oil; I figure a couple gallons,” Muley pacified his followers, “build a half dozen torches,” he glared at them. “And I’ll tell ya’s where the two of you are gonna plant ’em.” The three of them shared snarl-lipped smiles. Muley eyed their gun belts copiously, "Ya got plenty cartridges?"

* * *

As planned the previous night, Pete and Jesse quietly pulled shut their hotel room door, and with everything they owned in hand, they strode through the back hall of Drover's Palace, made their way to the livery, located their gear and began saddling their horses. The old hostler stood watching a bit before he spoke. "Pullin' out mighty early ain't ya? The weather looks a bit unfriendly, could be you'll be getting' yourselves soaked, if you're heading west?" He searched for an answer.

"Maybe so." Pete bent his neck, looking to the harsh, gray predawn sky from under the open double door of the livery barn. He shook the saddle in place, "Been wet before," he grinned, "kinda' liked it."

"Speak for yourself, brother." Jesse spat back with a grin equal to Pete's. "Can't say I'm of the same mind." He jerked the cinch tight and dropped the fender in place. Pete could see it in his younger brother's demeanor; being free from Tatum had set his mind at ease.

The hostler handed Jesse his possibles-pack and bedroll, keeping the rain slicker apart, "You might want to put this on before you mount up young fella," the white whiskered man offered.

"Don't think so," Jesse said, "I'll roll it behind the cantle for now, can reach it if need be." Pete had done the same in his preparation to meet Marshal Carson at the marshal's office; planning to be there within a quarter hour of sun up.

"Going west, are ya's?" The elderly man tried again. The old gentleman was of easy-nature, liking folks of ordinary convictions and he took pride in judging people by the manner in which they selected and cared for the horse flesh that served them. The Longley brothers impressed the old man and as such, he offered fatherly advice, "If ya go west be mighty careful, a number of good people like yourselves have found some powerful big trouble out that-a-way."

"We'll be riding with Marshal Carson." Pete responded, "He'll set our direction. I believe you're right, likely we're heading west." Both young wranglers swung into saddles that squeaked in appreciation of the weight, and they slowly kneed their mounts to exit the livery. With a finger snap to hat brims they left the hostler tugging at his long chin whiskers in thought as they rode out to meet Carson at his office.

"Step inside." Carson stood in the doorway, holding it open, allowing Pete and Jesse time to swing down. He raised his chin and drew his head back as they stepped up onto the boardwalk, "We've got a couple chores to take care of."

Jesse turned to Pete as he studied Carson's words, "What's this about?"

Pete hitched his shoulders, "Guess we'll see!" They stepped inside. The thin smile arranged on the marshal's face was pleasing and relaxed.

Carson pulled open the desk drawer and withdrew two nickel-plated stars trimmed with shiny brass, "I'm making you men deputies." He stepped affront the two of them and pinned the badges to their leather vests. "We want to make this legal—raise your right hand," Rad lifted his right hand, palm out. The Longleys did likewise, their expressions similar to a not-so-eager bridegroom. "I now pronounce the two of you to be deputies, serving under me, Rad Carson, United States Marshal. He smiled negligibly, "Say, 'I so swear'." And it was that easy, Pete and Jesse Longley were official, working for the law.

"Well, I'll be, wouldn't the folks in Pampa be proud," Jesse glistened a pint-sized smile.

"Both of you got rifles and know how to use 'em?" Carson drawled, knowing before he said it they looked the part. Their holstered hand guns provided a hint of know-how and the dark leather coloration showed slick where the cartridge cylinder pushed against it when the six-gun barrel dropped in place.

They both nodded, "And plenty ammunition." Pete responded. His tone was firm, with a spark of pride, "We both learned to shoot hand guns and rifles when we were not much taller than the long gun. Our daddy always said if a man was to live very long in Texas there were two things he'd best know well how to do . . . they was find water and shoot."

Carson cut a glace from the corner of his eye, "Ever shoot a man?"

Pete's eyes, unblinking, remained fixed on Carson's but no words came out of his mouth.

"Each of us killed more than a couple of wild raiding Comanche back home in years gone by." Jess answered hurriedly, remembering the strange, forlorn reaction Pete suffered when he shot the scattergun rider during the stagecoach robbery Muley rigged up the third day after they'd fell in with him.

The truth was, Pete had shot and killed a Comanche, killed the thieving Indian with a rifle when the redskin thief cleared the lower rail of the corral holding a hand full of a Longley's horse's mane. Pete was fourteen and Jesse only ten years old at the time. The following day six more Comanche tried to storm the house. Pa Longley was gone; had ridden out looking for some stock, figuring the Indians had taken them. Pete and Jesse scared off the raiding party with rifle fire when they were still distant from the farm lot but none were killed.

"Killing is something no man should take lightly." Carson glowered at the brothers.

The marshal had made a commitment and trusted a feeling within; he was confident the Longleys, especially Pete, could hold their own in a squabble, no matter how tough it might be. He wasn't sure when it came to Jesse. The younger Longley, he thought, was trustworthy, but light on ruggedness.

"Okay," Carson quipped, "looks like I've got the right men."

The three of them rode slowly toward the edge of town, giving Rad opportunity to relate his personal closeness to the town of Spickard and his hatred for the outlaw. "It's likely Tatum made the threat about burning the town because of me. It was there in Spickard that I first had discord with the man. I ran him out of town. But he came back a few days later, got liquored up and killed a man." Carson took a deep breath through his nostrils, "That man was Miles Courtney, one of the men that helped to settle the area—a finer man never lived in the state of Kansas." Carson went on to relate the shootout with Muley and the fact that he'd killed one of Muley's cohorts and arrested the other. He finished with telling that Tatum had slipped out of town. But Rad left it there, not telling of the subsequent trial and other details. "I suppose I have a block of hate for Muley Tatum eating at my insides for him killing Courtney. It was downright vicious, no good reason at all." Carson was quiet for a moment, but went on, "I've never let any hombre get under my skin like he has." Carson shook his head in anguish, "He's a wicked son-of-a-bitch."

Rad studied the reaction as both of the Longleys nodded repetitively. Jesse wanted to draw out details, but Pete threw a guarded, disapproving frown at him before he could muster a response. "Nothin' we'd like more than to see the man locked away," Jesse said, holding back in comprehension of Pete's fixed stare.

CHAPTER THIRTY-TWO

"What in the world you fellas gonna do with coal-oil and gunny sacks?" Bert Coffeld, proprietor of the Spickard feed store, asked as he scuttled along at a snail's pace ahead of Muley, Bo, and Injun and mopped the back of his neck with a bandanna.

"We got a family of skunks livin' in holes under the barn," Muley told him. "We're gonna soak the gunnies in coal-oil and stuff 'em in the holes leadin' to their den. My uncle Pug told me it's the best way to rid 'em so's they'll never come back."

"Might be," Bert shrugged, "but I never heard of it." He stopped beside one of the barrels laying crossways in a rack at the back of the building.

"I take stock in what Pug says," Muley frowned at the man.

"You'd best be mighty carful," Bert warned as he shut off the spicket after filling the three canteens with coal-oil, "so's the soaked sacks don't catch fire . . . this stuff will burn with not much more'n a flash, you don't want to get yer barn afire!" He shook a finger at Muley, "And ya'all best throw them canteens away, you'll never get the taste outta 'em." The old whiskered gentleman hitched up his cord-striped pants and yanked the dirty red and blue suspenders taunt after thumbing the two dimes into a front pocket.

"Yep, we know that," Injun Charlie Joe cackled. "Reminds me of the time I mixed axle grease with tincture alcohol." A gargling laugh spewed from his lips, "Got drunker'n a' by-God and sicker'n a snake-bit dog . . . puked till my toes turned up and my eyes yellered like gold in a pool of lard."

"Shut up, Charlie, we all knowed ya was dumb, ya didn't have to prove it with your story tellin'." Bo Cantrell slapped at Injun with his dusty bowler hat.

"When ya got skunks to rid of, ya need to use the right stuff," Muley's big toothy grin sat on his face like a Halloween carved pumpkin. "And we got a parcel of 'em."

Coffeld braced his hands on his hips and stared at the three men as they rode away. "I'd lay a bet them fellers are gonna burn down that barn," he said to himself, lifted a hand and scratched at the side of his neck, "but ain't no skin off my behind." He shuffled his way to the corner of the building and rounded the corner.

* * *

Carson and the Longley brothers halted their fatigued horses. The mounts needed a break from the long gallop that was behind them, and the men too were deserving of a needed rest. They'd ridden hard before they pulled up in the shade of a pair of cottonwood trees near a growth of tangle weed and a broad stand of brush. Within the undergrowth was the sparse visible remains of a ramshackle, ill-constructed, small adobe cabin. It was nearly undetectable with the brushwood and weeds that had set about nature's reclamation. But Carson had been here before.

"Used to be a spring-fed, hand dug, cistern over there." The marshal said as he indicated an area behind the defunct structure; if it's still there we might be able to give these horses a little water."

All three men calmly dismounted in unison, being tired and saddle worn. "Hope so," Pete answered, "they've earned it." He pushed toward the area indicated by Rad.

Carson wiped sweat from the lining of his Stetson, nodded to the distance and said, "Spickard is within three to four miles thataway."

The sun had bleached away the earlier grayness of the sky and large portions of deep blue now separated only a few lazy clouds. "Looks to be close to noon," Carson declared as he squinted to the brilliant oval overhead.

The three of them worked attentively, brush was pulled away and eventually a small pool revealed. Jesse dipped a hand into it, lifted the bare, cupped hand and smelled the water. "It's okay," he reported with a smile.

The horses took turns at the water. As they did so, Carson and the newly appointed deputies uncorked canteens for their personal use. Pete stood back, poured water into his hat and held it under his horse's muzzle, "Didn't want him to have to wait," Pete cajoled, "I figure he's as thirsty as I am."

A pleasing spell of silence was broken as Carson shouted, "My God!"

The brothers yanked their heads around.

Carson glared at the sky in the direction of Spickard, "Looks like a lot of smoke," his face tightened, "that dirty, no-account Tatum might be keeping his promise." Carson wrenched Caesar's reins around, pulling him away from the undergrowth. He thrust a boot toe into the stirrup, "Mount up, men," he instructed; his voice brash and assiduous. The thick brush they'd manipulated their way through to gain access to the cistern crunched and crackled in the melee created to force their way out.

The Longleys were suddenly in their saddles and the three of them hauled out, slapping leather and kicking heels. "Sure as hell," Carson yelled, "that smoke's coming from town." The scorn he held for Tatum revisited him, swelling like a sponge drenched with a bucket of water, that along with the rasp of guilt he felt, he galloped toward Spickard, a man uninhibited.

Pete and Jesse pulled hat brims down tight, eyes fixed on Rad Carson's large frame racing ahead of them. They simultaneously notched into their minds images of Muley torching buildings as he'd described, which they'd never actually seen. But the dark, stacked billows of smoke were real enough. '*Was Injun Charlie and Bo Cantrell in on it?*' The Longleys figured it so. And they each considered, now deputized as lawmen, they might be called on to shoot the men they'd ridden with, camped with, and eaten with, just a few days ago.

Pete had considered taking Muley down a notch or two more than once before; he knew he could put the man away in a straight up gun fight. He was evil, unlike any other man Pete had ever come across. It was like Tatum wasn't genuine, not a person of flesh and bone, more of a spirit of Satan, similar to what Pete pictured when he was a boy as his mother read of the Devil and angels of Satan in the bible—that depicted Muley Taum, not bona fide flesh and blood! '*Could I shoot him, shoot to kill?*' He'd make that decision when the time came. He'd made a commitment, sworn to it by Carson. And a man was only as good as his sworn word.

Up front, Carson swung his hat into the flank of the big gray stallion. The bitterness stored up inside pushed him as much as his affinity for the little town he'd made his home for the past several years. He knew the buildings were dry and brittle. Fire could leap from structure to structure. But he knew also that the few streets were wide, it wouldn't be likely for flames to cross the streets, and the air was still, no wind to whip the fire. The piles of dark smoke boiled higher—there were four of them, all signifying heavy, crackling flames eating away at dried lumber, much of it Carson remembered as barren and unpainted.

Gunshots! Rapid fire of rifles and the pop of hand guns broke the air as the three lawmen drew closer. Evidently the citizens of Spickard were fighting back. Carson punched his hat tight on his head and the other hand flew to the Colt on his hip.

The fleet, demanding strides of their horses had become labored and unsteady. Thankfully they'd given the animals a rest and much needed watering. The past several minutes played hard on the creatures, they were driven to near exhaustion.

The first building at the edge of town, Arliss McKevitt's barn, stood like a sentry as they rushed past, the horses heaving for air, dirt flying from hooves; Carson and the Longley boy's legs and elbows flailed out rhythmically in their efforts to unfetter final energy from their horses.

Flames leapt from the hotel. Surging streaks of fire shot from the double door and flashed unmercifully through first floor windows, crawled upward in vicious crackling of brilliant red, orange and yellow jagged pillars and onto the front balcony like sheets of lightning. Ferocious, sinister clouds of smoke boiled, pushed upward by the raucous heat. Four men stood watching in trepidation, empty buckets at their feet, their bodies arched away from the heat, arms and hands raised to shield their faces from the waves of thermal blasts of air that'd forced them to retreat. Their efforts to thwart the ever-growing, unrelenting flames were useless.

Across the street, the Yellow Moon Saloon was ablaze; small explosions repeatedly pushed churning flames and acrid smoke from the structure's openings as if they were escaping the inferno of hell.

Muley and his men had done their work thoroughly. More buildings, including the marshal's office and jail and the mercantile store were well engulfed. There' be no saving any of the structures. Fires were placed to inflict damage in such manner that they were out of control in a matter of seconds. Torches had been positioned in multiple locations in each of the structures, making efforts to extinguish even one of the numerous fires impossible, and there were far too many for the few men, even if they'd had an adequate water supply.

The new town marshal that Carson scuttled into the job with his leaving Spickard, Travis Floyd, rushed to where Rad Carson and the Longleys had leapt from their horses and stood, guns in hand, looking for Muley and his fanatical sidekicks. As he did so Rad saw Jenny Courtney step through a doorway and take a bee-line for him, her face twisted with rage and her hands churning like she was ready to strangle someone. He knew her to be a handful, not a person to back away without a fight, but he was in already in a fight himself; he looked away

Fifty yards up the street from where the lawmen landed, two men hefted another man, their hold on him signifying he was likely dead. They grasped his underarms and raced to the boardwalk, toting him face down, allowing the toes of his boots to drag ragged furrows through the dirt. Rad stretched his neck in an effort to identify the men, but failed to do so.

"It's that Tatum outlaw," Travis screamed, making his voice heard over the thunderous commotion of the fires and men who'd quickly gathered. "Him and the other two rode through town throwing torches. One of 'em, a heavy man with a bowler hat, broke windows, kicked 'em in with his foot, and tossed torches inside."

Sizzling, boiling heat encased in swirls of wafting smoke and the stench of scorching fumes created whirling funnels that rushed skyward and lifted grimy street dust within. People were running from all possible escape routes, anxious to vacate not just buildings, but the town itself.

"After they torched ever thing, they rode all down through here shooting at anybody they saw." One of the townie's shouted, his arms flailing. "They killed Bob Overstreet and Kendall Martin." He yelled, his hat held aside his face to block the heat, "They plugged 'em, killed 'em when they rushed out to stop the bastards."

"They even shot at the women folks," another retorted, his voice quaking as he took note of the Courtney girl heading their way. "Miss

Courtney there," he nodded and pointed toward her, "nearly caught a bullet—she got into Millie Walker's dress shop just in time!"

"I think I got a chunk of lead in at least one of 'em," Travis shouted. "The one that looked Injun. He slumped over in the saddle when I shot." He jerked his head, "One of the others rode along side and helped him pull away."

"Who were those fools, Marshal Carson?" Jenny Courtney screamed, standing before Carson, her lips drawn and eyes swimming in tears that streaked down her cheeks. She pinched her lips tighter, sealed in anger, and with strings of hair clasped in perspiration about her face, she glared at Rad as if he shared in blame for their horrific actions.

"One was Muley Tatum, the man that murdered your father." Rad rasped at her, his expression steeped with anxiety, knowing his reply would make the explicitly agitated woman come close to bursting wide open like a melon dropped from a wagon back.

"Ooohh, how I hate that man!" She shrieked, throwing her shoulders back as she erupted from the spot and ran to the dress shop from which she'd exited. Everyone but Carson figured the Courtney woman hurried to seek shelter, but he knew her to be relentless when it came to revenge concerning her father's murder. Maybe she had intentions other than her personal safety! He added that possibility to his list of troubles.

The Longleys saw flashes of anxiety in Rad Carson's expression, his eyes following the lady's retreat. They could see he desperately wanted to help her, but better judgment required otherwise—there was a lot to do, her frustration would have to wait.

"Won't do any good to try to put these fires out, wouldn't be possible" Carson yelled, hands cupped to the side of his mouth, shouting over the fire's constant pops and loud crackling and sparking from all around. "The buildings are done for; all we can do is make sure everyone gets out."

The men awkwardly moved to avoid the inferno and choking smoke which darkened the sky over the little prairie town and spread beyond. Simultaneously the locals who'd gathered, tendered frowning, quizzical stares at the Longleys, not recognizing them, but realizing they'd ridden in with Carson.

Taking heed of the curious stares, Rad threw a thumb toward the Longleys and barked, "They're with me . . . . my deputies."

"Anybody see where Tatum ran off too?" Pete cried out as he casted responding glances from man to man. He shook off any misconceptions aligned toward him; his concerns were anchored to locating Tatum

One of the men shrieked back, "The three of 'em rode that way." He pointed to the south end of town, toward the feed store. "Looked like they ducked in behind Bert Coffeld's building when I saw 'em last."

Pete gave the man a sequential look, questioning the name, Bert Coffield.

"The feed store," The man bellowed in response, realizing Pete's uncertainty.

"Take these horses," Carson ordered the man, "we're gonna see." He gathered the reins of the three horses, his and each of the Longleys, and thrust them toward the man that'd made reference to the feed store.

Carson and the two Longley's started off in that direction, guns in hand. The density of the smoke restricted their vision, limiting them to cautious advancement, halting every few steps until they were near the street's end. When they reached the front wall of the feed store Carson signaled his deputies to hold while he peered around the corner.

"There they are!" Carson half-turned and spoke, half hushed, from the side of his mouth. Pete and Jesse sneaked a quick look over Rad's shoulder.

"Let's get 'em," Jesse whispered and stepped out. It was too late to stop him . . . Carson's bid to do so subsequently required the Marshal to quickly confront the trio of torching raiders ahead of an organized effort.

Bo Cantrell was bent over Injun Charlie as Charlie sat on an upturned bucket. Bo had fashioned a sling from the neck scarves from the two of them, had tied it at the back of the man's neck, under the long braid of hair, and helped Charlie fit it about his limp arm. Muley watched, still astride the black horse, his face snarled sadistically in a half grin, seemingly annoyed. He glanced up in reflex of the movement of the lawmen; readily sighted the Longleys and Marshal Carson, and yelled, "Look out!" He acknowledged Carson at once. His head snapped even higher in recognizing Jess and Pete as they stepped up alongside Carson. "I knew it, those sons-bitches has turned on us!" Muley kicked spurs into the big black, yanked the reins and instantly ducked out of sight, leaving his cohorts afoot and to fend for themselves.

Bo jerked his six-gun from leather and fired incoherently, even though he could tell the lawmen were beyond pistol range. Injun Charlie clumsily rolled to the ground and sought cover behind the barrels of coal-oil. In the same instant Carson turned on his heel and darted off, he bellowed, "I'm going after Tatum, you two handle these snakes."

Pete and Jesse found protection behind a freight wagon. "Cover me," Pete barked once he'd analyzed the situation. He sprang up and ran ahead, staying close to crates and barrels as he hunched his shoulders, bent low, and moved forward with awkward strides in near recklessness. He was driven with rectitude, discussed with his lack of adherence to his better judgment earlier.

Jesse fired off three rounds in the direction of the scoundrels with whom he'd been a sorrowful ally only a few days past. Ever shot fell considerably short, as he'd anticipated. He discovered, however, in that instant that he was ready to abide by the oath—the oath that required him to shoot to kill.

"What the hell you two doin?" Charlie belched out loudly; I thought you's with us."

Cantrell screamed at Injun Charlie, "Shoot 'em, Injun, they's trying to kill us, ya iggit."

Pete drew a bead, slowly, squeezed the trigger and put a .44 slug in the high upper right side of Injun's chest, the opposite side from the arm dangling from the crude sling. The shot intended to impair the man, not to kill.

Injun went down, jerking in pain and separated from his pistol. The fight was taken out of him. His injuries bolted him to semi-consciousness coughing and reflexive spasms.

Cantrell moved from behind the kerosene barrels, walking forward in a strut of confidence, a blunt cigar crunched between his teeth, his tattered buffalo vest swinging open and the bowler hat dropped to the top of his eyebrows; guns firing rhythmically from both hands. He'd figured to kill or be killed!

"Stop, Bo!" Pete screamed, "We don't want to kill you!"

"Go'ta hell, ya Texas school boys," Bo shrieked and continued pumping lead.

Jesse squinted, his teeth clinched; he fired the revolver, his gun bellowing before Pete's. As his father had instructed years before, he aimed high, allowing for the distance. The bullet whined through the smoke-drenched air, past the older brother, and thudded hard, burning a smoldering hole into the middle of Bo Cantrell's chest.

Bo's head dropped, anguish locked into his face, then his gaze slowly came upright again, disclosing squinting eyes that flared at Jesse under a crumpled brow. His knees shuddered momentarily, blood belched from his whiskered mouth; his guns slipped through limp fingers and fell silently to the dust. The cigar stub tumbled from his twisted lips and the fierce grimace from dark, empty eyes, signaled he knew he'd been killed . . . by the man he feared least.

CHAPTER THIRTY-THREE

Standing most anywhere in the town, a man could tell the fires were going to consume everything. Blazes stretched high above the aged wood structures, licking at the sky like tongues from hell, bent on devouring the community that had grown to respectable size over the past two decades. The only buildings likely to evade total obliteration would be the few that stood independent, distant and alone. They numbered less than ten, mostly houses, but also including McKevitt's on one end of town and Bert Cofeld's feed store at the far south edge of town. Flames leapt maliciously, building to building, eating viciously at dry walls like they were not much more than heavy paper.

A single pump stood near the mercantile store and three watering troughs were strung along the main street. But several times that amount of water would not be enough under the circumstances, the number and extent of blazes were simply too much.

Muley heaved with pride and jubilation. He rode swiftly from one location to the next lavishly admiring the annihilation he'd brought down on the settlement as he kept moving, looking over his shoulder for Carson. The villainous scoundrel couldn't leave town, there was a chore he had to tend to, something Bo Cantrell had done earlier that he had to rectify. He unmercifully kicked spurs into the big black horse. The animal whinnied in desperation, his mouth ripped from the senseless, exaggerated alterations of direction poured on him by the nonsensical tyrant berating the animal from his impulsive domination in the saddle.

Muley Tatum had spied Bo Cantrell's attempt to kill the young lady who'd sought shelter in the dress shop—that made his blood boil at the time. He couldn't accept seeing a man treating a woman ruthlessly. It was just something beyond reason for him, not acceptable under any set of circumstances. He'd always held to that conviction, and today, even though he was unerring in his efforts to purge the town of Spickard from the Kansas prairie, his vile mind could allow no tolerance for efforts to defile womenfolk. He brutally yanked his used up horse through the boiling smoke and raucous heat to the street close to the dress shop, one of the few buildings yet to become engulfed in the fires. His purpose was defined by his unique perspective favoring womenfolk. Once he attained the closest proximity he could muster he swung down, and holding his arms in protective measure from the blast of heat he hurried to the door of the little building. The two women, Jenny Courtney and Millie Walker, exited the door just as Muley Tatum got there, their heads sheltered in protection, they didn't see the notorious outlaw, not at first. They inadvertently bumped into Muley in their haste, and unassumingly scurried around him without consideration, other than the realization that a man appeared, a man they suspected that had come to their aid, to help them from sure death from the fires if they didn't flee the dress shop readily.

"I'm sorry," Muley expounded; his futile attempt to apologize for Cantrell's callous action caught up in the fury of the moment. He thumbed his hat, but was disregarded.

Not until the two women saw Marshal Carson racing toward them did they pay even passive notice toward the man dressed in black they'd skirted past aimlessly.

"Get away from them, Tatum!" Carson yelled, his hand filled with a Colt and voice gripped in rage. The women sensed that Carson feared for them as they turned to reassess the big man they'd submissively thought had come to protect them. Carson's threatening scream instilled an overwhelming realization in Jenny Courtney, she recalled the name, Tatum, and came to the comprehension that she'd just been affronted by the man who'd killed her beloved father.

Astoundingly, almost in theatrical fashion, Muley tipped his hat to the women, still not realizing who Jenny was, but intent on his purpose only, that he'd come to apologize for the earlier behavior of one of his men.

Carson shouted his name again, gaining the full attention of the villainous man. Both men came ready, holding guns leveled toward the other and straining for a clear view of their adversary.

It was then that Jenny Courtney reacted decisively!

Boom! A gun sounded behind Tatum. His knees buckled. He grimaced, his head flung back and hands upward. He pivoted slowly, an expression of amazement frozen into his hard-featured face. The big man turned and crumpled gradually, the realization that he'd been shot was forced into his mind as he awkwardly studied the woman standing with a smoking gun in her right hand and her open, lace-lined purse in her left, a deep smirk of satisfaction starkly carved into her soft face. Muley's eyes locked on Jenny's. The six-gun eased from the outlaw's fingers and plunked onto the plank walkway as a blood-oozing-grin formed, "Sorry," he gurgled, "I guess I had that comin', ma'am." Even in death the loathsome, despicable man held to his stalwart, inner connection of sensitivity toward womenfolk.

Carson rushed to where Jenny stood; he grasped her shoulders, holding her before him, he fleetingly searched her face. Her blue eyes fixed on his; the message between them was exchanged that simply. She had revenged the death of her father.

"Jenny?" Millie Walker puzzled, hands folded under her chin, she leaned from the waist, her eyes blinking from beneath a wrinkly brow,

"Why did you do that?" A striking segment of fear was captured in her remark together with overwhelming surprise.

Jenny didn't offer an answer. She stood in silent, seemingly self-reverence. It took a few seconds before Rad Carson provided the response, "That," he indicated Muley's body with a brief nod, hands still clasping Jenny Courtney's shoulders, "was the man that killed her father." He added, after a second glance at the big man dressed in black lying motionless on the plank boards, blood oozing from his body, "And she did the state of Kansas a favor by riddin' us of a filthy soul that brought nothing but grief."

Carson's mind flashed back to the day Muley had killed Miles Courtney, and then to the Porter woman, whose husband had been killed and she was left stranded on the prairie. He recounted also, the rancher, Wade Wiedenauer, from Texas, that was robbed by the no-account wild man.

The next morning the town lay quiet in devastation, rubble of buildings smoldered, sending tendrils of reminder-smoke rising from ashen remnants. The Kansas prairie town was left in a grouping heap of cinders and odd chunks of charred wood protruding from the ruins with small gasps of smoke lifting above. The few houses that went unscathed morbidly housed the remaining citizens during the hours of darkness as they gathered in meek groups awaiting the morning, a time they knew would be appalling. A meeting was planned, to be held at Coffeld's building, the single standing structure capable of such a meeting.

The people would have to decide. Would they rebuild or pull stakes and head out for Dodge, or elsewhere to begin anew. Prairie settlers lived harsh, abrasive lives. Nothing came easy. There were some that had suffered losses due to fire before, such devastation wasn't uncommon, it'd halted the growth of many a young town, not only in Kansas, but throughout the great Southwest. For some, this was another momentous impediment in their search for a peaceful life on the young country's frontier.

Daylight broke with a few local folks standing sorrowfully, surveying the devastation, sadness frozen in their drained, weary expressions as substantial and lasting as lava flow from a volcano. Words were few and came suppressed in sobs and absorbed in fervent tears by the ladies; whereas a knot of men-folk who'd gathered, grumbled, cursed and spoke in recollection of the labor undertaken to build the town over the years and now lost to the cruel shenanigans of three dimwitted outlaws in a matter of a few minutes.

Pete and Jesse gathered supplies, most of which they absconded from Injun Charlie's and Bo Cantrell's saddle bags which had been bought and paid for by the Longleys in prior days. They said their good-bys after having given considerable thought to going back to Dodge City and staying on with Marshal Carson, as he'd offered, but with a handshake and deep-felt *thanks*, they returned deputy badges and set on the trail west, headed for Colorado.

Later in the day, having stayed on for the Spickard town meeting, where Rad spoke resolutely in favor of rebuilding the town, U.S. Marshal Carson took his only surviving prisoner, Injun Charlie, and rode back toward Dodge City. There Charlie would stand trial in the courtroom of Judge Nathanial Wilkerson.

Rad Carson was confident his work in Kansas would keep him in the law business for a long spell. There was much that was yet to be done. Cattle drives would bring more restless, youthful seekers of adventure. Unruly, disruptive men would continue to invade the frontier in search of fast, easy money, searching out methods to get it by trickery or thieving. And they'd do so by waging injury or death to those who would defy their efforts. Also, young fanciers of gun-play, believing they'd earn a reputation as a man to respect or fear, similar to what they'd read about in dime-novels, would keep on coming.

There was plenty to be done for a man of the law.

And there was Fanny! His mind was made up, he'd call on Fanny. He'd do so in a mindset void of the unintended impulse that had previously denied him deep felt affection. He'd court her in a manner favored to marriage and a family.